CARPENTIER FALLS

T0165480

The Kurt Maxxon Series

Masonville
Kings Rapids

CARPENTIER FALLS

A Kurt Maxxon Mystery

JIM OVERTURF

iUniverse, Inc.

New York   Bloomington

Carpentier Falls
A Kurt Maxxon Mystery

Copyright © 2010 by Jim Overturf

All rights reserved. No part of this book may be used or reproduced by any means, graphic, electronic, or mechanical, including photocopying, recording, taping or by any information storage retrieval system without the written permission of the publisher except in the case of brief quotations embodied in critical articles and reviews.

iUniverse books may be ordered through booksellers or by contacting:

iUniverse
1663 Liberty Drive
Bloomington, IN 47403
www.iuniverse.com
1-800-Authors (1-800-288-4677)

Because of the dynamic nature of the Internet, any Web addresses or links contained in this book may have changed since publication and may no longer be valid. The views expressed in this work are solely those of the author and do not necessarily reflect the views of the publisher, and the publisher hereby disclaims any responsibility for them.

ISBN: 978-1-4502-3265-4 (pbk)
ISBN: 978-1-4502-3266-1 (ebk)
ISBN: 978-1-4502-3267-8 (hbk)

Printed in the United States of America
iUniverse rev. date: 5/25/10

Dedicated to:
Karen: My editor, wife, and friend,
With special thanks to
Laura Cavender & Margriet Stelling

PROLOGUE

Friday, September 8

<u>*Joshua and Jacob, 4:30 AM*</u>

"Jake?"

"Yeah."

"You asleep?"

"Yeah."

"No, ya ain't." Joshua rolled onto his stomach, staring warily at the darkened camper a few feet away. "Bring your shoes. Let's go."

"Whar?" Jacob asked.

"Keep your voice down," Joshua lectured. "We don't want Mr. Kurt to hear us." He grabbed his ratty tennis shoes and crawled on his hands and knees until he was out of sight of the camper, then slipped the shoes on. Jacob was slower, but he eventually joined Joshua.

Joshua led the way from the camper up the driveway to the side road. They climbed over the locked chain-link gate. The moon had set, and high, thin clouds dimmed the starlight.

Several hundred yards away from the camper, Jacob asked, "Where we going, Josh?"

"We gonna check out that dumpster behind the Trattoria. Hell, if they throw away good food what don't get ate, we can use it ourselves. Take some to Auntie Jean. She go hungry more'n not. Save the rest for us."

"How we gonna keep it from going bad?" Jacob asked.

"In grocery bags. Sink it in the river. There was a whole lot of food throwed out while we were there last night."

"I know," Jacob said as they walked along. "I like Mr. Carlos."

"Me, too," Joshua agreed. "He be cool, and he nice, too."

"You trust Mr. Kurt to help us?" Jacob asked.

"I kinda do, but we gotta be careful, Jake. If he turns us over to the social people, they just gonna send you one place an' me another. Me and you, we gotta promise. If they do that, we just run away, first chance we get. Go to the bridge over the river down by the airport. The one where we stayed at first. We wait for each other there, okay?"

"Okay," Jacob said. "We do that."

"Yeah. They ain't gonna keep us apart."

"That's good," Jacob said.

The two boys walked along in silence to the Trattoria. The building was quiet and dark, with night-lights at each corner bathing a small area and casting shadows everywhere else. In the far corner of the parking lot, a lone car sat under an inadequate streetlight.

"You really think Mr. Kurt will help us, Josh?" Jacob asked again. "I don't want to stay if he just wants to turn us in. Then we gotta run away."

"I think he's gonna help us, Jake. I really do."

They walked in shadows to the dumpster, where they stood ready to bolt, furtively glancing around them. After several minutes, Joshua said, "Okay, nobody 'round here. C'mon, I'll get you up on my shoulders, Jake, and you dig around to see if you can find anything."

Wobbling on Joshua's shoulders, Jacob fumbled with the lid, but finally whispered, "It be too heavy, Josh. I can't get it up." Joshua moved slightly. Jacob almost tumbled over. Then Jacob said, "Hey, Josh, the lid at the other end is already open." Jacob leaped to the ground and the boys peered around the corner of the dumpster. "That end be in the light from the building," Joshua pointed out.

"It ain't that bright," Jacob said. "And there ain't nobody around." The boys moved cautiously around the corner and crept toward the open end of the dumpster. When Jacob reached out to find Joshua, Joshua had vanished.

"What the hell?" Joshua yelled, and he sprawled out, scraping his knees.

"What happened?" Jacob asked.

"I just tripped over something," Joshua said as he sat up and looked at his knees in the dim light. "Just skint," he said, and then he scooted to the object. "It be a man," he yelled.

"A man?"

"Goddamn, Jake, it be Mr. Carlos."

"You sure? What he doing here, sleeping?"

"He look dead," Joshua said, clambering to his feet and running back toward the racetrack. "C'mon, let's get outta here, and get Mr. Kurt."

Jacob struggled to keep pace with his older brother. "Hey," he yelled, "wait, don't leave me."

CHAPTER ONE

Friday, September 8

Kurt Maxxon, Early Morning

I thought I'd left the TV on again. Occasionally, when I fall asleep in my recliner, I wake up to the TV news. Voices had brought me out of my deep sleep, and, nearing consciousness, I suddenly realized I was in my camper—and sat bolt upright. I listened until the pounding started again. I heard voices yelling, "Mr. Kurt, Mr. Kurt, wake up, wake up!"

I slid out of bed and opened the camper door to look down at the wide-eyed faces of Joshua and Jacob. "What's up, guys?" I asked.

"Ya gotta come look at Mr. Carlos," Joshua said between gasps for air.

"He look dead," Jacob chimed in.

"What? Where did you see Carlos?" I asked, hoping I was still dreaming.

"Behind his building," Jacob said.

"Behind the Trattoria?" I asked.

"Yeah," both boys said, in unison.

"Where's he at?" I asked, not grasping what was going on.

"By the dumpster," Jacob said.

"Laying on the ground. Ya gotta come look," Joshua said again. "Quick."

I shed my pajamas, slipped into my pants and shoes, shoved my cell phone into my jeans pocket, and backed down the camper steps. All three of us dashed to my truck. I clicked the remote to unlock the doors and opened my door. The two boys ran around to the passenger's side and scrambled into the passenger seat. Joshua fumbled with the seat belt. I reached to buckle the seat belt across them. "Can you dial 9-1-1?" I said as I dug my cell phone out and handed it to Joshua. He held the phone with both hands, deftly punched the buttons, and then handed the phone to me. I'd started the engine and was pulling the gear lever into position, when the buzzing ended, and I heard a female voice say "Nine, one, one, what is the nature of your emergency?"

"There's a man lying in the parking lot of the Trattoria Restaurant at the corner of County Road J and Speedway Road. It might be the owner, Carlos Guerrero." I clicked the gate opener on my sun visor and had to wait a short moment while the gate chugged open. I sped the short distance down the road.

"Do you know the condition of the man?" the voice asked.

"Not yet. I'm just now turning into the parking lot," I said. I parked with my headlights aimed at the person lying facedown near the dumpster. I swung out of my truck and stopped to observe the motionless body. All my instincts told me "dead." From the clothes, I was sure it was Carlos Guerrero. Holding the phone to my ear, I walked to Carlos's body, knelt down, and felt for a carotid pulse. Nothing. "It's Carlos Guerrero, the owner," I reported to the operator. "He's dead."

"A Pierre County sheriff is on the way," the female voice said. "What is your name, sir?"

"My name is Kurt Maxxon."

"The race driver?"

"Yes, ma'am."

"Will you please remain at the scene until the deputy gets there, and tell the deputy all you know about this situation?"

"Yes. I can do that," I said. "But I don't know a whole lot about what happened. I'll be here, though." I looked down the road and saw a pair of blue and red flashing lights coming toward us. I said, "They're nearly here."

"Thank you, Colonel Maxxon," the voice said.

I turned toward my truck and saw the boys peering around the corner of their open door. "He be dead?" Jacob asked.

"Yes. We got here too late," I replied.

"The cops are coming," Joshua said. He was almost hyperventilating, and I sensed his fear of dealing with law enforcement people.

"Yes, you two just get up in the truck and stay put. I'll handle this. What were you doing over here?"

"We be looking for food they throwed away," Joshua said. "We came to see about that."

"It wouldn't be in that dumpster," I said and pointed toward a dumpster inside a fenced area near the kitchen door. "The dumpster over there by the kitchen has the food, because of the health laws. Carlos is by the *trash* dumpster."

"We figger, if you rat us out, and they send us to different places, we just gonna run away an' meet up again," Jacob offered.

"An' if we do that," Joshua said, "we be needing places to get food. Besides, Auntie Jean, she always needing more food."

Remember to pursue this discussion later, I told myself, *and find out who Auntie Jean is.* A white, brown, and green sheriff's car pulled into the lot and stopped next to my truck, letting the headlights augment the lighting on the body. I walked to the car, as the deputy was getting out and adjusting his equipment belt. His jaw was square with a heavy shadow of beard that matched his coal black hair. He wore metal-rimmed glasses, set on a straight nose with a heavy line of black eyebrows above them. His uniform was the signature Western style adopted by many sheriff departments in the valley, greenish-brown with a Western-cut shirt and dark brown pocket covers and epaulets. I walked to meet him, and he stuck his hand out toward me. "Pleased to meet you, Colonel Maxxon."

I shook his hand, reading the name on his brass nametag above his right pocket, as he said, "Joe Bradley."

He scanned the area. "Anybody else around?" he asked.

"Just me and the two boys in my truck over there," I said, pointing with my chin toward my pickup. "They discovered the body."

"How old are the boys?"

"Twelve and ten."

"How'd they find the body?" the deputy asked.

"They apparently tripped over it," I said. "From the conversation I've had with them so far."

"How much did they mess up the evidence?"

"I don't know. I can talk to them and see," I said, hoping the impending interview of the boys by the cops could be short and direct. I worried that the normal procedures of questioning might make the boys nervous enough to run away. Maybe the cops would allow me to comfort them somehow.

"Are you responsible for them?"

"Yes, sir. They're staying with me."

"Okay," the deputy said. "We can talk to them later."

His use of the word *we* made me relax a little.

The deputy retrieved a four-cell flashlight from the dashboard and swung it around the area in front of the dumpster. "Did you walk up to the body?"

"Yes, sir."

"Did you touch the body?"

"Yes, sir."

"Do you remember how you walked up to the body?"

I moved slightly to the left, more in line with my truck door and the body, stopped, and swung my hand, palm vertical, up and down to show the approximate path I had walked.

"Good," Deputy Bradley said and walked toward the body in the same general corridor. He felt for a carotid pulse and shook his head. He carefully shone his flashlight over and around the body, stopping to study the gash at the base of the skull. "Looks like someone hit him pretty hard from behind," he said over his shoulder. He got down on his hands and knees and leaned in to get a view from ground level. "It's the owner, Carlos Guerrero," he said as he stood up and dusted his knees with his hands.

The deputy walked back toward me, carefully staying in the same path as his approach. He straightened his equipment belt again, clicked the microphone clipped to his left epaulet, and said, "Com … fifteen." I listened to the radio exchanges, as Deputy Bradley reported the details and requested the medical examiner and crime-scene technicians. I felt sweat trickle down my back and gather at the waistband of my skivvies about the same time a cold shiver rolled down my spine. *Here you are, Maxxon. Another dead body.* I went to stand by the passenger side of my truck.

Squad cars, crime-scene vehicles, and the medical examiner's hearse arrived, and the boys grew more apprehensive. The parking lot and the street were a sea of red and blue lights whirling around and around. We watched the busy activity in the parking lot, and I worried about how the boys were dealing with it all. I knew both boys would probably have some reaction to finding a dead body. I decided it would be best if they talked about it. "After you found Carlos, what did you do next?" I asked.

"We run like hell back to get you," Joshua said.

"You didn't walk around the body or touch anything?"

"No way," Joshua said.

"We don't like dead bodies," Jacob added.

"You came over here to look for food," I said, "and, as you moved to the other end of the trash dumpster, you tripped over Carlos lying on the ground."

Both boys bobbed their heads in unison.

"Did you see anyone else around here?"

"Nobody," Joshua said, shaking his head. "We waited a long time in the dark over there and looked the place over." He waved toward the trees behind the dumpster.

"It was still pretty dark," Jacob said. "We didn't see anyone else."

"Did you see any cars leave the parking lot?" I asked.

Both boys shook their heads.

"Okay, the cops will want to talk to you, just so they get your story. Don't worry about it, just tell them what you just told me," I said. Then I thought about the dumpster diving. "Maybe you shouldn't tell the cops you came over here dumpster diving."

"What be dumpster diving?" Jacob asked.

"Yeah?" Joshua chimed in.

"Looking for stuff in dumpsters," I said.

"Okay," Joshua said. "You told us there ain't any food in that dumpster anyway, right?"

"The food is in the dumpster behind the kitchen," I reminded them.

"The cops going to arrest us?" Jacob asked.

"No. They just want you to tell them what you did and saw. You did the right thing coming to get me. They'll like that. Both of you are good citizens; that's what any good citizen would do."

They both beamed and sat a little straighter.

Deputy Bradley and a crime-scene tech walked toward us. The deputy told me a sheriff's investigator was on his way. The crime-scene tech introduced himself and said, "I'm a big fan of yours, Colonel Maxxon. I like your Web site, too," he said, pointing to the red lettering along the bottom of the truck's doors: KurtMaxxonRacing.com.

I'm Kurt Maxxon. I drive stock cars in the Swift River Valley Stock Car Racing Association—the SRVSCRA to many people and the "Shrev-scraw" to those bold enough to try to pronounce it. I'm sixty-two years old, five eleven, and only a few pounds overweight. If you round up my height in centimeters, and round down my weight in kilograms, my BMI is just about right. What hair I have left is steely gray, far different from the lush mane of brown hair I once sported.

I've been racing stock cars for twenty years, especially hot and heavy since I joined the SRVSCRA after retiring from the U.S. Marine Corps with twenty-six years of service as a fighter pilot. Duke Ford sponsors Nikki, my number 27 red and white Ford Taurus, with a little help from my store, Maxxon Auto Parts. I've taken first place 31 times out of 151 races, which keeps me upbeat and optimistic, just like I felt flying my A-6E Intruder during the Gulf War. I've never crashed in an airplane, although I did forget to lower the landing gear once during my training. However, experiencing six crashes in the SRVSCRA has given me a great respect for speed and control of automobiles. I enjoy the constant strategic decisions required when driving a car at high speeds, just like those made while flying sorties over war zones. I'm always pleased to meet a fan, so I reached into the truck, grabbed one of my Maxxon Auto Parts keychain flashlights attached to a card I had signed, and handed it to the tech. He chortled with delight. "I'll go put this to use right away!"

Ernesto Vasquez, the Trattoria's maitre d', arrived and opened the doors for the sheriff's people to go in and check out the building. Eventually they cleared one corner of the dining area for us to use, and the boys and I had a place to sit. Ernesto's oldest son, Chico, arrived with boxes of doughnuts and breakfast pastries, and he quickly had carafes of hot, delicious coffee available for the dozens of people on the scene. He also made cups of hot cocoa for the boys.

Damon Hertz, a sheriff's department investigator, arrived soon after. He was a young man, mid-twenties, sun-bleached hair with a flattop cut, round face, blue eyes, my height but a lot thinner around the waist, and dressed in a sharply creased uniform. When he asked me to spell my name twice, I decided he was not a race fan.

As I stood talking to Damon, a weathered sergeant in a wrinkled uniform walked up to me and shook my hand, saying "How you doing, Colonel Maxxon? I'll be rooting for you Sunday."

"Thanks, Mort," I said. I'd known Mortimer Chrysler for the twelve years I'd been racing at the Carpentier Falls track. He was always somewhere around the track during race weekend.

Giving me a wary glance, Damon looked at Mort and asked, "You know Mr. Maxxon?"

"Everybody knows the colonel," Mort said, throwing his left hand into the air as he walked away.

Damon's forehead wrinkled into a puzzled frown. "What's the 'colonel' for?" he asked.

"I'm a retired light colonel from the United States Marine Corps," I said.

"Is that why 'everyone' knows you?" Damon asked, emphasizing the word *everyone*.

"No," I smiled. "I drive racecars in the SRVSCRA. I get my name and mug shot in the newspapers every once in a while. 'The Colonel' is my nickname around the circuit."

"The SRVS ... um, say those letters again? And what do they stand for?"

"The SRVSCRA is the Swift River Valley Stock Car Racing Association," I said. "Sunday is the race here in Carpentier Falls."

"Sorry I didn't know you," he said. "I'm more into tennis than car racing."

"That's okay," I said. "We all have our things. I collect Raggedy Ann and Andy dolls, Mercury dimes ... and I talk to my car."

"What's wrong with talking to your car?" Damon said, smiling.

"Freud probably wouldn't approve."

Damon chuckled and nodded agreement. "Getting back to the business at hand, I'm going to talk to you and then to each boy separately in one of those rooms over there." He pointed with his chin to the meeting rooms along the far wall. "As soon as they clear us to use them."

"Probably not a good idea for the boys," I said. "The boys will just clam up. You need to interview them together, and out here in the open, so they can see me. I won't try to coach them. I think you'll get more information that way."

Damon studied me for a long while, and I watched his eyes, as he analyzed the grandfatherly advice I'd just given him. He swung around to survey the table arrangement in the main dining room. "You may be right; I'll interview them over there." He pointed to a large, square table in the far corner. "Before that, I want your statement out of their earshot."

"Deal," I said.

I gave Damon all the information I could, telling him I'd known Carlos for many years, because of racing at the racetrack across the street and a shared love of Cuban food. I told him the boys and I had eaten supper at the Trattoria the night before.

"You and the boys ate supper here last night?" Damon repeated.

"Yes."

"Was Carlos here last night?"

"Yes. That's the last time I saw him alive." I told Damon how Carlos had taken to the boys like a doting grandfather, feeding them specially made *pappas rellenas* he had prepared himself, along with other Cuban dishes, and then *cuatro leches* cakes with dulce de leche topping. The boys had swooned over the cooking at the Trattoria and loved Mr. Carlos.

"Carlos told us he would prepare us his special recipe, *huevos habaneros* for breakfast," I said. "I am so fond of Carlos's huevos habaneros, if Carlos had a restaurant in Centralia; I'd eat them every morning."

"What time was he going to fix breakfast?" Damon asked.

"Carlos told the boys they could come help him open at five. That's why they were over here and found the body."

"They found the body and ran to get you."

"Right. I was still sleeping when they came back. You know how kids are when something comes up." I wondered if Damon knew anything about kids but decided to bluff my way through this.

"So Carlos had probably arrived to open and someone accosted him," Damon said.

"The clothes Carlos had on this morning when we found him were the same ones he had on last night," I said.

"You think the killing happened last night, rather than this morning?" Damon let a frown cloud his face.

I pursed my lips and shrugged, tilting my head in an I-don't-know gesture.

"Interesting," he said. He went to the boys and asked them if they would answer a few questions. Both boys eyed me warily. But I said, "Go ahead and tell Deputy Hertz what you saw and heard and did." They accompanied Damon to the corner table and climbed up onto the chairs.

I got a fresh cup of coffee and sat on the other side of the dining room sipping it. I overheard Joshua say, in a loud voice, "We were just cutting across the parking lot when we found Mr. Carlos. It scared the living daylights outta me. We run like hell to get Mr. Kurt."

I hoped Damon wouldn't make an issue out of Joshua's cursing.

I thought about calling Brad Langley but then decided to wait for him to hear about the killing through the normal channels. Brad is the chief of the Central Investigation Division (CID) of the state police's major crimes unit. I wasn't eager to let Brad know I'd stumbled onto another dead body. When I discovered a body the first time, four years ago at Masonville, and the second time, three years ago at Kings Rapids, I'd wound up getting involved in discovering who the killer was.

The first time Brad nearly disowned me. The second time he begrudgingly congratulated me. I was not eager to find out his reaction this time.

CHAPTER TWO

Friday, September 8

Kurt Maxxon, Morning

The boys apparently complemented each other's memories and told a convincing story that dovetailed with mine closely enough that Damon saw no difficulties. The sun was an hour above the horizon when the boys and I got clearance to leave. We decided to go to Grandma's Café for breakfast, because it was the nearest eatery offering breakfast, and I enjoy Grandma's special-recipe squash and blue cornmeal pancakes immensely.

The morning was warming up, with clear skies and light winds. Even with what we had been through, the world seemed at peace. We drove silently; the boys were unusually quiet. Grandma's Café is in a strip mall a couple of blocks south of Roosevelt, on Jackson Street, one of the major north-south arterial streets. The area is part of an older neighborhood that is now multicultural. It is thoroughly American, with linen tablecloths and napkins, large old silverware, and huge plates. White lacy curtains and sheers camouflage the windows. The entryway décor is antique furniture with needlepoint, and quilted items cover the walls. Each table has a doll on it. Grandma is an avid collector of Raggedy Ann and Andy dolls, which made the place irresistible to my late wife, Vicki.

The diner was nearly full, but we were able to find an empty booth midway along the west wall. Joshua helped Jacob climb into the booth, and I noticed Jacob had trouble reaching over the edge of the table, so I went to get him a booster seat.

"Man. That was something else," Joshua declared once we got comfortable in the relative privacy of the booth. The diner clock said 7:15.

I'd forgotten my wristwatch when the boys rousted me out of bed. I'd been keeping track of time the best I could, between the dashboard of my truck, the equipment readouts in Deputy Bradley's cruiser, and then the clocks inside the Trattoria. The time had dragged, as we waited for them to question us.

"Man, them cops, they ask a lot of questions," Jacob said.

I nodded my head. "Yes, they do. You boys did great; telling them everything you knew."

"They gonna forget about us now?" Joshua asked.

"For a while," I said. "But they may want to ask some more questions."

"About what?" Joshua asked.

"They always find new lines to follow, new questions," I said. "They sit and think about the answers you gave them, and that causes new questions to come up. They are always looking for clues in everything they hear and see."

"What be a clue?" Jacob asked.

"A clue is something that will help them figure out who killed Mr. Carlos," I said. "Fingerprints, footprints, clothes, little differences in people's stories, stuff like that. That's why that lady took your fingerprints and made prints of your shoes. They know you were at the scene, so they'll eliminate those clues from all the other fingerprints and shoe prints they find at the scene."

"Like on TV," Joshua told Jacob. "Remember them cop shows on TV?"

Jacob shook his head, and I realized it had been a while since the boys had lived with TV with any continuity. Jacob probably was the least indoctrinated to it.

"Mebbe they leave us alone," Joshua said. "I hope so."

I nodded my head again.

A waitress arrived to take our orders: coffee, milk, and orange juice. I went along with the boys and ordered oatmeal and fruit, since we'd had several doughnuts at the Trattoria, even though I might have been able to eat my normal order of the Hungry Man's Breakfast.

After we finished our food, I sipped on my coffee and listened to the boys' chatter. They quieted, as they finished their milk and orange juice. In the silence, I overheard two men in the booth behind me talking about Carlos's murder and the Trattoria. One voice said, "The action in the games was pretty good last night; I left with $125."

Another male voice, barely audible, replied, "Yeah. I left with a few bucks extra. But my girl didn't show up."

"She didn't?" the first voice said. "Hell that just means you saved yourself some money." I heard the chuckle distinctly.

When I noticed the boys had picked up on my eavesdropping, I said, "They were talking about Mr. Carlos being dead." The two men stood and walked past us toward the cashier near the door.

"I've got to go to a meeting this morning," I announced, quickly changing the subject. Both boys studied me for a minute. "It might last all day. I want you boys to stay close to my camper today. I'll take you over to the office to meet the lady in charge of the track. You can use the bathroom in the drivers' lounge, and there's a TV you can watch, too. Can you do that?"

"Sure," Joshua said, "we can do that." The worry lines between his eyes eased.

Jacob nodded agreement.

Leaving the boys to go to the meeting made me edgy, but their agreement made me feel better.

*   *   *

Chaundra Dunkin

The sun woke her, and she sat up in bed, startled at how refreshed she felt. Sleeping in her old bed had done wonders. She'd only turned one trick the night before, early in the evening. Just as she was about to meet a regular who normally paid her for all night, her mother had showed up and convinced her to leave and talk things over. They'd driven here to the house. She remembered most of the issues they had talked about until well past two in the morning, sipping on white wine. It felt good to have her mother's undivided attention, something she had sorely missed when her mother divorced her father and took up with the man who eventually became her stepfather. Her mother's indifference to Chaundra's problems over the last two years justified choosing the life of a prostitute.

She sat on the edge of her bed and looked over the trophy wall of her old room. It contained the memories of a popular teenager—trophies for the champion softball team sitting on a shelf, football cheerleading awards hung in a diagonal formation above the shelf and punctuated by pictures of herself as homecoming queen in her junior year, escorted by the captain of the football team. There were many science fair awards. There was the certificate for winning the school's spelling bee, which had been a major item to her, even though she had lost in the next round. And all the pictures … friends, teachers, coaches … were memories.

She never knew why her mother and father divorced but, for a long time, felt like it was her fault, as though it was something she did that made her parents want to go their separate ways. Over the last few months, as she dealt with the adult world, she had come to the realization that love, sex, and emotions are things best not thought about—not worried about. So she no longer felt responsible for her parents' breakup.

She realized some of her rationalizations came because of her mother's marriage to her stepfather, which had only widened the schism between her and her mother. She felt her mother didn't care about her problems—the difficulties of growing up in society—school, boys, sex, peer pressure, drugs, alcohol, and everything else she had to deal with. Her mother just wanted to channel all her love toward this new man in her life—and to hell with anyone else.

Chaundra remembered when the principal had called her into his office to discuss her grades dropping from As and a B to mostly Cs. The principal tried to counsel her but set off alarms and sirens when he told her he intended to talk to her mother about the matter. If the principal had said he was going to talk to her father, Chaundra might have reacted differently. With all the warnings blaring in her head, she had left the principal's office and gone out through the doors resolved never to return to school again. The rest was just a blur. She remembered the businesswoman with the fancy leather briefcase who asked if she would like to make more money in a day than most men make in a week. That was a no-brainer.

Now, this morning, part of her wanted to commit to the new life she and her mother had talked about last night. Her mother had made some sweeping promises. *Had it been the wine talking?* Her mother had committed her husband's wealth.

Her stepfather owned a moderately successful insurance agency that dealt exclusively with farmers in and around Pierre County. He'd impressed Chaundra as being stingy with his money, especially when it came to goodies for her. *Was he suddenly ready to open his wallet, as her mother had promised last night? Was he ready to help her get through college? Or was that just her mother's wishful thinking?*

Could she come back? Over the last year, she had become accustomed to her new lifestyle. Was she ready to give up the independence she had achieved? *The money? The luxury apartment? The prestige among the other girls?*

She hadn't committed to her mother last night. She had listened and promised to think about it. What had been new and different last night, however, was that her mother was not demanding, ordering her around, or trying to dominate her. It seemed as if, for the first time, her mother realized that she was an adult now. She was an adult woman with a body that men would pay to use for a few minutes—pay a lot of money for.

Life as a prostitute wasn't all that bad. She'd almost immediately become the favorite girl of several men, which let her charge more. She turned more tricks. She took taxis everywhere. And she loved her independence.

Can I give all that up? If I don't give it up, how long will it take to save enough money to get out of the business? How much have I saved so far? She replayed the latest deposit of a thousand dollars into her savings account. *What was the balance? Forty thousand dollars? Dammit, I should have put back more than that by now. But there were so many things I wanted for the condo. And I like the clothes I've been buying. I'll have to go to the condo and get them. Move out. If I do that early this morning, I might be able to avoid that damn Tammy.*

Chaundra had come to realize that as an independently wealthy woman she could live wherever she chose, come and go as she damn well pleased, and belong to the organizations she wanted to. If she kept her savings account secret and let her mother and stepfather pay for college, she would come out even further ahead than if she tried to save enough from being a prostitute. *Can I trust my mother? I learned that lesson well—people will pay a lot of money to get what they want. My mother and her husband will, too, if they're interested in getting me through college.*

She fluffed the pillow and then snuggled under the covers. Another hour of sleep would help her decide.

No matter what her decision, she knew the future was going to be much different from the past. The next major hurdle was going to be something Chaundra had recently decided, but her mother had never given a thought to. How was her mother going to deal with Chaundra's sexual preference?

*   *   *

<u>Kurt Maxxon</u>

Penelope Jaconowitz is the administrative assistant to the track manager, Abraham Marshall. She's a big woman, an inch taller than me, with a generous girth. She is good at her job, allowing Marshall to come and go without worrying about the track's business going astray. In fact, Abe had told me that he preferred to let her run the business, since she did it with consistency and objectivity.

I knew Penelope had at least six great-grandchildren. Her silver-gray hair framed a round face with soft blue eyes that always glowed with rosy happiness. I figured she would be just the person to watch over the boys while I attended the special meeting.

After I introduced her to the boys, I said, "Would you mind keeping tabs on them today while I go to this special meeting at the Speedway Hotel?"

"I'll be happy to watch them," she said with a wide smile. "There's TV in the lounge next door and games in the storage room. You boys like to play Monopoly or Clue?"

The boys looked at each other, then at me, and then at Penelope. "Is Clue like what the cops do?" Jacob asked.

"Kind of," Penelope said, laughing. "You have to solve the murder to win."

"We play Clue," Joshua declared. "Be like them cops this morning."

"You guys good at figuring things out?" I asked.

"We good," Joshua said.

Jacob nodded.

"They'll be just fine, Kurt," Penelope assured me as she shooed me out the office door, eager to start her babysitting role. "You go to your meeting, and don't worry about these two young'uns. I'll make sure they fly right."

*   *   *

This special meeting of the board of directors is to discuss a change in tax structure and rates for the Maplewood racetrack, set by the Cramer County Commission. The association schedules most meetings in the same town, and during the same week, as the next Sunday race. That makes it convenient for everyone involved, especially me, because I can fit it neatly into my schedule of arriving at the racetrack late Thursday night and running practice laps Friday, before or after the meeting. The notice for this special meeting mentioned it would last all day, so I wouldn't be able to practice as I usually did.

I had driven to Carpentier Falls on Thursday, arrived about noon, and then run practice laps most of the afternoon. Nikki, my three-year old Ford Taurus, had run wonderfully, and I'd reoriented myself to the racetrack's characteristics. After practicing, I'd leisurely rehydrated on Gatorade and potato chips, my theory being that salty stuff makes you thirsty, so you rehydrate faster.

Then I'd gone to the drivers' lounge to shower. I had almost finished dressing, when I heard a loud crash in the kitchen area. I investigated and found two boys. The older boy had struck his head when he fell off the kitchen counter. The younger boy had appeared frightened, as he clambered off the counter to check on his brother. When he'd spotted me coming toward them, he'd frozen and then started to run. He'd nearly slipped by me, but I was able to get a grip on his T-shirt and hold him in check, while I knelt down to examine the boy on the floor.

The older boy had eventually struggled into a sitting position, with his face resting on his knees. He had trouble focusing, but I gave him water and put a cold rag on his neck. I took the boys in tow, herded them to my camper, and offered them bologna sandwiches, potato chips, and Diet Coke, along with the promise of a good dinner later at the Trattoria Restaurant.

I had tried to find out where they lived and why they were in the drivers' lounge. They were naturally reticent, but, as they warmed to me, I learned their names. I also learned that their mother had disappeared several weeks earlier, leaving for work one morning, but not returning that evening. The boys had taken to foraging for themselves, living under a highway bridge in cardboard boxes, and visiting an Auntie Jean for a meal every once in a while. That revelation startled me. *What's happened to our society?*

The boys told me they had come to the lounge to rummage for food in the refrigerator and cabinets. I wanted to help them and decided not to call social services. I'd read lately in the newspapers about a lot of problems with the local programs—besides, I liked these kids. I took the boys to the bridge where they "lived" to collect their ragged sleeping bags and a small cache of personal belongings. I knew harboring the boys violated at least one law, of some kind, and decided I wouldn't do anything other than keep track of them until after I talked to Christina Zouhn and Marguerite Grossman. Between them, those two women have infinite qualifications to advise me on how to proceed.

Christina retired as the administrator of the Albertstown Consolidated School District a few years ago. In that capacity, she dealt with children of all types and problems. Marguerite is the chief of police in Kings Rapids and African-American like the boys. Talking with them would be no problem, because Christina, who had been Vicki's best friend and was now my closest female friend, would be arriving Saturday evening. Marguerite and her husband, Terry, would be arriving Sunday morning for the race.

Thinking about my quandary caused me to drive right past the Speedway Hotel. I realized my error about three blocks north of there and turned around. The parking lot was nearly full of vehicles, the only spaces being in the far back of the lot. But that's where I usually park, anyhow, so I backed into two spaces and went in to find the meeting room.

CHAPTER THREE

Friday, September 8

Kurt Maxxon, Midday

Alexander Andrews has been the board chairperson for the last three years. He's tall and lanky, and his unruly white hair frames an angular face with chiseled features. His skin has a permanent bronze cast from the many years he spent in the sun, managing the company he owned, Reliable Construction Corporation, in Centralia. Alexander retired twenty years ago, turning the company over to his two sons. He didn't quit showing up every day until he was seventy-one, when his boys gave him an ultimatum: "We can handle this company, Dad, so you take Mom on a vacation to Tahiti for the next six months."

I have yet to find a more efficient chairperson. I've been the president of the SRVSCRA for seven years now, voted in by write-ins to serve four two-year terms. Comprised of drivers, car owners, sponsors, and other backers, the association members elect a president and vote for six board members every odd-numbered year. Then the president asks one of the board members to act as chairperson to run the day-to-day business of the association.

Alexander and I arrived at the same time, so he and I arranged the tables and chairs for the conference. Other board members drifted in as we worked, and we chatted with one another to get up to speed with our lives since the last meeting.

Alexander called the meeting to order at ten sharp, guided by his no-nonsense approach to managing everything he undertakes. He never ceases to amaze me, especially with the meetings he chairs. He develops a schedule and an agenda and then follows those with few deviations. Board meetings always start on time and never last longer than the business requires. I hope I am as spry as he is when I'm eighty-three.

Alexander got my undivided attention when he said, "The first item on the agenda is to discuss betting on SRVSCRA races."

Shocked, I focused on the printed agenda.

Alexander said to the board attorney, "Ivan, would you present what you've learned about the betting on races happening at the Trattoria Restaurant?"

When I heard the name *Trattoria*, every one of my instincts went on high alert. The other members fidgeted in their seats.

Ivan Farley stood and read from a sheaf of papers he held in his left hand, lawyer-in-court style. "A few months ago, the Federal Bureau of Investigation advised the Pierre County sheriff about off-track-type betting on auto races at Pumpkin Hollow International Speedway, including the SRVSCRA race in September. Apparently, they identified a bookie working principally out of the Trattoria Restaurant. As soon as they received the information, the county attorney's office advised me of it. The feds have been digging into it to see if it's connected to similar operations around the country. Right now, it's an ongoing investigation, very early, so they don't have much to go on at this time." Farley looked around the room.

"Do they know if the owner, Carlos Guerrero, had any connections to it?" I asked.

"They suspect he did," Farley said, "but Carlos was good at covering his ass. My guess is that, since they found Carlos dead last night, the authorities will probably be moving more aggressively. So I suggested we add this item to today's agenda, even though we principally planned this meeting to discuss the Cramer County tax issue."

Alexander looked at me. "We'll assume you didn't know anything about people betting on the races."

"You're right, I didn't," I said. "If I had, I sure wouldn't have eaten most of my meals at the Trattoria."

"Damn good food," the recording secretary said, dipping her head with a smile.

"That was the only reason I ate there so often," I said, "plus, it's right across the street, so to speak. I could walk there." I noticed all their eyes focused on me. I grinned and decided to stop talking.

Illegal gambling—was that a possible motive for Carlos's murder?

For the main part of the meeting, Alexander introduced Lyle Hendricks. Lyle is a tall, thin man, with wire-rimmed glasses that perch on a hawk nose, and he's bald. While he shaved the wispy white doughnut above his ears, I wore mine with pride in still having some hair.

During the next five hours, my lack of sleep and my lack of interest in the meeting caused me to doze off and then shake myself awake, trying, as always, to be inconspicuous. Lyle Hendricks is a very intelligent person, a fountain of knowledge about taxes, and he speaks well.

I am really going to miss Carlos's huevos habaneros.

*   *   *

Fran Michaelson

"That's it," Fran said aloud through pursed lips. She scanned the numbers again and then bobbed her head in satisfaction. She moved the cursor to the ledger entry, deleted the incorrect $15.28 entry, and typed in the correct $15.82.

She let a smug twist cross her lips and said, "There's the damn fifty-four cent difference." After saving the file, she stood to get a coffee refill. While the partners, and even the accountants, advised her to round entries up or down to even dollars since it was merely the office slush fund, Fran had always reconciled the account to the penny. "Every penny counts," her mother's voice said in her mind, "and you should count every penny."

In the break room, she refilled her coffee cup and turned to leave, but she noticed that someone had left the carton of half-and-half on the counter. She returned it to the refrigerator and then walked back to her office, surveying the bullpen full of clerks and stenographers busily pounding on computer keyboards.

She stopped to look into the law library immediately to the left of her corner office. Fran surveyed the bullpen area reflected in the windows of the library. Most people watching her would think she was idly observing a law clerk in the library and sipping her coffee. She suspected that as soon as she disappeared into her office the hustle and bustle of the clerks and stenos would slow down.

Staring at the reflections in the window allowed her to view her own general appearance. She had gotten very little sleep last night and had worked with her makeup to cover up the damage. Her auburn hair was sprayed into perfect shape, her round face looked fresh and alive, and her brown eyes (her best feature) were keen and bright. Her forty-one-year-old body was still in good shape for her five foot five, one-hundred-and-forty-pound frame. The red and blue ensemble she had chosen for today looked very stylish.

Fran had come up through the ranks as clerk, secretary, and, eventually, had achieved the rank of legal secretary to Elton Williamson, the oldest partner in the firm. When the partnership had reorganized and moved into their present offices, they had selected Fran to be the office manager. Even though it meant giving up the thrill of being an aide-de-camp to a popular trial lawyer, she liked the idea of being in charge and making sure everything was done following strict rules of documentation.

Today, the firm was Williamson, Mayer, Henry, Petersen, and Anderson. Douglas Peterson and Timothy Anderson had become senior partners in the years since Fran had become the office manager.

The firm employed six paralegals, all of whom were administratively under Fran, even though their offices were on the sixth floor. Everyone on the fifth floor reported to Fran, except the training partner, whose office was down the hall from the law library.

As Fran entered her office, her phone rang, and she rushed to her chair to answer it. Senior partner Elton Williamson asked her to expedite the McMurry files, because the judge had denied the DA's request for a continuance, and the trial was going to begin on Monday morning. "Everything will be ready this afternoon," she told him, knowing that Elton Williamson liked to have the pleadings Friday afternoon to take home with him to study over the weekend before a Monday trial.

"Did you find the missing fifty-four cents?" Elton asked.

She grinned. "I sure did. I screwed up and entered fifteen-twenty-eight, when the check was really for fifteen-eighty-two. Voila, fifty-four cents found!"

"You're too much of a perfectionist, Fran," Elton said. "Thanks for your help." The phone went dead.

In the glow of the compliment, she sipped her coffee and smiled, as the events of the night before filled her mind. Finding the elusive fifty-four cents in the petty cash fund had been satisfying, but not nearly as satisfying as convincing Chaundra to come home with her last night. She'd gone to find Chaundra, and they had talked. She had avoided being accusatory, as Dr. Martinelli had recommended, and it had worked. Chaundra had come home with her. They had talked until early in the morning, since they had so much to rebuild. *I should call to see if she's still there.*

A knock on her open door brought Fran back to present. "Yes?" She looked up.

Tim Anderson peeked around the door. "You got a moment?" he asked.

"Sure," she said. "Come in."

Tim Anderson was in his mid-fifties, the youngest of the senior partners. His angular face was ruggedly handsome and set off by a curly mass of brown hair that showed signs of graying. His thick, bushy eyebrows hooded his brown eyes. At six foot six, he was the tallest of all the partners. Tim had joined the firm as senior partner while Fran was transitioning to office manager, so Fran didn't know him as well as she did the other partners.

Tim closed the door and walked toward her. "Don't get up," he said as he eased into her guest chair, crossed his right leg over his left knee, and adjusted the crease of his trouser leg.

"Sorry to just barge in," he said, "but I need a special favor." Tim looked around the room. He was as aware as Fran of the regular sweeps for listening devices made by the firm's security company. Even so, Tim was definitely being careful.

"Whatever you need," Fran said.

"I need you, personally, to get the Carlos Guerrero file with his will and estate papers," he said in a low voice. "Make a copy of it, and then bring them both to my office without anyone knowing what's going on."

Fran lifted her eyebrows. "You want the original file *and* a copy?"

"Yes."

"What's up?" Fran asked.

Tim looked from side to side. "Someone found Carlos dead this morning."

"He's dead?" Fran's forehead wrinkled into a frown. A disquieting thought flashed through her mind. She calmed herself and asked, "What happened?"

"I don't know any of the details," Tim said. "Right now, all I know is that Hermosa called me and told me about it. Then, I'd no more than hung up from talking to her, when a Pierre County sheriff's detective called me. She asked me to keep it as quiet as possible, but, as is normal, they want information about heirs and other interested parties. You've been through this before, so I'll let you handle it—discreetly."

"The sheriff called?" she said. "It must be serious."

Tim nodded. "Since the sheriff is investigating, we're assuming it's a homicide."

"Do they have any suspects yet?" Fran asked absently as she jotted *C Guerrero file* on her notepad. "Did you handle his will?" she said.

"It's still early, so they don't have any suspects. Yes, I did his will, soon after I joined the firm. It was routine, so it went into the filing system from Marge. Now I want you to dig it out."

"Should I give it to Marge?"

"No. She's not in the loop right now. Bring the files directly to me. You're the only one in the office who can walk past Marge into my office." Tim winked at her and grinned.

All the clerks and secretaries who worked on the sixth floor, amid the senior partners' offices, reported to Fran administratively. She rarely tried to pull rank on any of them. She glanced at the clock on the wall. It was 10:25. "Okay," Fran said. "Give me an hour or so."

"There's no real rush," Tim said. "Sometime this morning will be okay. Just avoid attracting attention. I'm going to meet the sheriff's detective at one o'clock, in the lobby of the law center."

"Is there something more involved than just that fact that you were the attorney who did his will?" Fran asked.

Tim nodded. "Carlos Guerrero is Hermosa's great-uncle," he said, pursing his lips. "I thought you knew that."

"I didn't know that," Fran said. "I'll get the files ready and bring them to you."

*　　*　　*

Kurt Maxxon, After Lunch

As usual, Alexander had lunch delivered at high noon, and, as planned, we had just reached a break point in the presentation of tax management by Lyle Hendricks of Hyatt, Ward, and Bainbridge. I was always happy with Alexander's handling of lunches for board meetings, since I don't drink. In the past, some board members had suggested lunch at restaurants with a lounge, but they'd lost that vote. Alexander, and most of us, liked the lunch break to be finite, controlled, and to include the opportunity to contact offices to keep up with business. Today, for the first time, I wanted to call somebody—I called Penelope to see how the boys were faring.

Penelope assured me the boys were still there and doing fine. She and the boys had played Clue, Monopoly, and checkers. She'd made them sandwiches from a can of SPAM that was in the kitchen of the drivers' lounge and bread she kept in her office. "How's the board meeting going?" she asked

"Kinda dry," I said. "About what I expected. The next two discussions will be tedious."

"You have to stay for it all?"

I grinned. "Probably don't *have* to, but I will, since the boys are okay."

"You are a real trooper," she responded. I could hear the chuckle in her voice.

I heard a door bang, and loud voices, and I knew the boys had just entered her office. Penelope cuffed the phone, but I could hear her gently shushing the boys.

"Are they bothering you?" I asked

"Get serious, Kurt Maxxon. They're just being normal boys. No bother."

"You sure?"

"I'm absolutely positive," she said. "You'll have to tell me how you got them."

"That's a long story," I said.

*   *   *

As the meeting droned on, I wondered if I could stay awake. Boredom and lack of sleep never mix well in my brain. Fortunately, Lyle Hendricks had set up his presentation screen at the opposite end of the table from me, and all the board members' eyes faced in that direction. No one noticed the couple of times I nodded off, that I knew of.

My mind wandered back to Thursday afternoon. Meeting the boys. Getting to know them. Trying to decide how best to help them and satisfied with my decision to defer doing anything until I could talk to Christina and Marguerite. As the afternoon passed, the boys had relaxed and settled in, after I found a spare picnic table in the track's storage area and dragged it next to my camper. In short order, the boys had transformed it into a fort, using a couple of blankets from the back of my truck.

We'd driven over to the Trattoria in my truck.

"This is a cool truck," Jacob had said.

"Yeah, man," Joshua added, "it's a diesel, huh?"

"Yes, it is," I'd said. "I need it to tow my car's trailer and haul that camper." I pointed with my chin to the camper sitting on its stilts.

Carlos had taken to the boys as if they were long-lost grandchildren and had endeared himself to the boys, especially after they had eaten his personally prepared *pappas rellenas*—potato balls stuffed with special seasoned meat. Then the boys sampled some of my fried banana dessert with other fruits and chocolate syrup, as well as the *cuatro leches* cakes.

"This is a very ritzy place," Joshua said.

"I'm full," Jacob said. "That food is very, very good."

These boys are budding gourmets, I thought.

* * *

Tammy McPherson

Tammy kicked off her spike-heeled shoes, as she closed the door to the condo and let the cool air calm her down. She opened the coat closet, set her briefcase on the floor, and then checked her hair in the mirror next to the entry door. Walking toward the wet bar in the far corner, she unbuttoned her blouse, swung out of it, and draped it over the back of an easy chair. She leaned down to look at the bottles on the shelf under the bar and chose a twenty-one-year-old Scotch whisky. She dug ice cubes from the bar's refrigerator, a highball glass from above, and filled the glass nearly full.

On her way to the sofa, she stopped to check her hair again in the mirror next to the bar, and then turned sideways to view her shape. "You need to cut back on the carbs, hon," she said to the mirror, and she walked to the sofa, littered with pillows. In a practiced move, she grabbed the remote, clicked on the stereo with its easy-listening CDs, and wiggled into the pillows, holding the highball glass carefully so as not to spill it. She sipped on the drink and then relaxed into the pillows.

"Things are going to work out just fine," she said aloud. "Sergeant Hoppy didn't act like she suspected anything." *Have they had time to get a rap sheet on me?* "Hoppy didn't talk as though they know who I am," she whispered.

I should never have let Carlos put my name on that damned emergency call list.

"Because you're in charge of the girls," Carlos had insisted.

He and Ernesto were in charge of everything else. Carlos didn't want to appear involved with anything other than the restaurant.

But that had been before Carlos discovered the money she'd stolen. How the hell had Carlos found out about her time in prison? Had he told anyone else about it? When they'd argued about it, he'd said he wasn't going to turn her over to the cops. He didn't want the exposure.

Did Carlos leave any tracks?

Did I leave any tracks this afternoon?

She replayed the afternoon interview with the sheriff's lead detective. Tammy's name was on the management list for the Trattoria, so, naturally, she got a phone call. She'd arranged a solid alibi for the night before, so there was no suspicion at this point. She let the entire alibi story play out in her mind.

Then her mind pulled up the events of the last several months. Carlos had seemed agitated about something, and, at one point, seven months ago, he'd told her to run the operation herself. "Keep me out of it," he'd told her. "Keep the money you and the girls collect in the safe in your office," he'd instructed her.

Who else knows about the money?

The girls. Of course, the girls know about the office. *I doubt any of them know exactly how much money there is.*

The only other possibility was Rachael Mellon. *She knows more than I do about Carlos' operations. Rachael knew about the office and how much money Carlos kept.* Carlos never talked about it, and the details were never clear, but Tammy knew there had been something between Carlos and Rachael—something financial that wasn't good. Tammy believed that, at one time, Rachael had somehow cheated Carlos out of some money, and Carlos had been trying to get it back. Carlos kept everything about his operations in the shadows, so there was no way for her to find out. Carlos handled the money and kept the books for all his operations. That was the other question: *Where the hell are those damn ledger sheets?*

She'd searched the office, including Carlos' office, after she'd picked the lock. She found another $245,000 in cash, which she'd stashed in her briefcase, bringing the grand total of cash to over $425,000—which was now sitting on the floor of the coat closet. Under the guise of being a businesswoman, Tammy always carried a hand-tooled leather briefcase to let anyone who watched her think it natural to see her carrying it. She'd found all the loose cash, but she still hadn't found Carlos' ledger sheets.

I've got to find those damn ledger sheets.

She remembered Carlos' disinterest in discussing his business books, when she'd asked about his lax attitude toward loose cash lying around. "I keep the ledger sheets pretty accurate," Carlos said. "I put the checks and credit card forms into the bank every day. The loose cash, I take the ledger sheets to the bookkeeper, and she does the books. She tells me how much cash I should have, and I round it up, fill out a deposit slip, and put the cash in the bank. That's how it works. It's worked that way for years now."

Then a few months later, she had needed fifty thousand dollars to get herself out of a bind and gone looking for loose cash lying around. She'd discovered that Carlos had recently swept it all up and put it in the bank. So she had had to take the money the best way she could find.

"All you gotta do now, hon, is pack up and quietly get out of town, and all that money is yours."

Whoa. Not so fast, her mind screamed. *You need to develop a plan. How do you cover the move so no one asks any questions? You can't just up and disappear. With Carlos dead, everyone will be watching. Go slow, and act like you're just moving on.*

Tammy drained her glass and realized she needed to eat something before she drank much more whisky. *Is there anything in the fridge to eat?* She struggled to her feet, unbuttoned her slacks, slid them down over her thighs, and then kicked them off. She padded to the kitchen door, stopping to view her hair in the mirror next to the kitchen door. She turned and went to the master bedroom, opened the closet door, and stood for a long time viewing her body in bra and panties. She turned sideways and then turned to view her rear end. *Dammit. Time to diet again, hon.*

She returned to the kitchen, rummaged in the refrigerator, and decided to make a tuna salad sandwich. She picked up jars of mayo and relish, dug a can of tuna out of the pantry, and found the last two slices of bread. She set the finished sandwich on the dining room table, mixed a new Scotch and water highball, and sat down to eat.

Where should I go? Several places flashed through her mind. *Uh-uh, those are places people who know me would tell the cops about.*

"I need to go somewhere no one would ever suspect," she said aloud. "Where? How do I move the money? Don't let anyone know you got the money."

Just don't spend too much for a while. Live the way I have been. Fortunately, Carlos owns this condo, so I don't have to worry about getting rid of it. His estate will kick me out, anyhow. Even if I could afford the rent, they'll charge for this place; his niece, Hermosa Anderson, will be the executor of his will, and she does not like me any more than I like her.

"Figure out where to go, hon," she said aloud.

The briefcase came to mind. *Is it safe to have that much money around?* If Carlos left tracks, would they be able to connect her? Would they come looking for her and the money?

"I never realized how much money flowed through Carlos's hands," she said to herself. "And then, last night, he had the gall to refuse to give me the cut I deserve." She turned and smirked, her hands on her hips, as she visualized Carlos last night. "Well, buddy, I've got it all now. How about them apples?"

A plan started to gel in her mind—a temporary, workable plan that would allow her to stay in touch and watch the mystery stymie everyone. It would give her time to develop an escape plan to get away with all the money, while not giving herself away. She could hide in plain sight.

She stood up from the table and moved quickly to the bedroom. She threw underwear, tank tops, shorts, and toiletries into her old hiking backpack, gathered her jewelry into a plastic sandwich bag, and checked to make sure she hadn't forgotten anything she'd need tonight or tomorrow morning. She pulled the briefcase from the coat closet, opened it, snuggled the bag of jewelry into it, closed it, and locked it. She paused for a moment, looking around the room. *Ritzy digs, hon. Too bad you gotta leave 'em.*

As she reached for the doorknob, her phone rang. She froze and waited for her voicemail to answer. Sergeant Hoppy's voice came over the speaker, "Ms. McPherson, this is Sergeant Janice Hoppy, with the Pierre County Sheriff's Office. I have a couple of additional questions for you. Could you call me at …"

"Dammit," Tammy muttered. "What the hell has she come up with now?"

Tammy hurried down the stairs and turned to go out the door to her black Mercedes parked just outside. But she stopped. She stood for several minutes and then moved to the house phone on the wall next to the door. The phone number of the taxi company most of the girls used was scribbled on the wall above the phone, and Tammy dialed it.

The Mercedes was registered to Guerrero Food Services, so it would be gone by tomorrow. But she could watch it to see if the cops were onto her. If they did come looking, they'd find it and figure she'd left town.

During the twenty-minute wait, Tammy paced continuously from the front entrance to the back entrance, each time hoping to see a taxi in front when she returned. Eventually the taxi arrived, driven by a Middle-Eastern man who spoke English just well enough to pass a driver's test. She was glad she going to the airport, since he understood that word and knew where it was. At the airport, she paid him and walked into the ticketing area carrying the backpack and briefcase. She waited several minutes, making sure no one was following her or watching her—other than the occasional businessman who gave her a quick once-over. Then she walked out of the baggage claim area door and to the taxi stand. She climbed into the first taxi in line, told the driver she wanted to go to the Speedway Hotel Complex, and gave him the address when he asked.

I'll only have to walk three blocks from there.

CHAPTER FOUR

Friday September 8

<u>*Kurt Maxxon and the boys, Afternoon*</u>

Lyle Hendricks ended his presentation with the offer to take questions after a short break. I stood up, walked to the end of the table, thanked Lyle for his presentation, and told him I had to leave and the main people he should deal with were Alexander and Ivan. I waved to Alexander and the other board members, as I made my way to the door.

I drove to the track, while formulating a plan to take care of what I had to do.

The boys were shooting pool in the drivers' lounge, using a step stool that Penelope had found. They lost interest when I walked in and came to crowd around me, shouting questions: "How'd it go?" from Joshua, and Jacob asking, "Where we goin' for supper?"

"You hungry?" I asked, spreading a frowning and goofy smile. I love the way kids let their body language talk for them.

Both boys bobbed their heads vigorously.

"Before supper, we need to get you two some new clothes and shoes."

The boys looked at each other, then at me. "Why?" they said together.

"Because you both look scruffy," I said.

"Before we eat?" Joshua said, even before he wondered what "scruffy" meant.

I stopped to think about it. "Well, if you're as hungry as you look, then maybe we should eat before we get the new clothes."

"Yeah," they shouted.

"Yeah, what?" I said.

"Let's eat first." Jacob jumped up and down at each word.

"Okay," I said. "Where do you want to eat?"

"How about Sam's place?" Joshua offered.

The name didn't ring a bell. "Where's it at?"

"Over by where we used to live," Jacob told me. "Over on Roosevelt Boulevard."

Joshua added, "And easy to get to."

"What's this guy Sam got to eat?" I asked.

Both boys giggled in unison.

"Sam be a woman," Joshua said, visibly shaking with laughter. "But she's a good cook."

"Momma used to take us there for supper," Jacob reported, "when she have extra money. When she work extra hours, they pay her more for it."

Joshua looked at Jacob. "That's called overtime," he said gently.

"Oh, yeah, I didn't remember," Jacob frowned and chewed his lower lip.

"Okay," I said, "what's good to eat at Sam's?"

"She makes big, big Sloppy Joe sandwiches," Joshua said, spreading his hands about a foot apart. "An' she gives them to you with French fries and coleslaw."

"I like the coleslaw," Jacob said.

"I like the fries," Joshua returned.

"It all sounds good to me," I said. "Let's go."

When the boys were strapped into the passenger seat, neither of them could easily look out the windshield. Joshua was next to the window and could see out that way. Joshua started talking once he recognized buildings, as we drove east on Roosevelt Boulevard, the main east-west thoroughfare. As we sat waiting for a light to change, he scooted forward on the seat and looked over the dash. "Auntie Jean, she lives in that building," he said, pointing to a complex of four-story shabby looking apartment buildings on the opposite corner. "We live there too, for a while," he said.

"Where did you live when your mother disappeared?" I asked.

"It's a few blocks up ahead, just before we get to Sam's," Joshua answered.

Before the light changed, I helped the boys change position, so they were sitting on their knees with the seat belt still holding them in, but they could see out the windshield. With both boys able to see ahead, they set up a constant chatter about memories of various businesses.

"That guy, he don't like kids," was the report by Jacob on one convenience store.

"Lady in that bakery, she like kids," Joshua said. "She give us toasted raisin bread and cookies every once in a while."

A few blocks later, I saw the sign announcing a public works improvement to an apartment complex so old most of the color and lettering had faded away. I instantly knew that was where the boys had been living when their mother disappeared. The buildings were brick, but neglect had led to dilapidation everywhere. Entry doors hung open and askew, probably not closable. Plywood covered several windows. Piles of bricks, probably two buildings' worth, covered a vacant lot.

"That's where we lived, way back there," Jacob said, a tinge of excitement in his voice, as he pointed to the farthest building.

Joshua said. "There's another family living there now."

"I know." Jacob sounded defeated. I wondered if the façade of strength was about to break. But Jacob recovered quickly. "I didn't like the place, anyhow," he said.

"There's Sam's," Joshua brought us back to reality as he pointed to the sign a few blocks ahead. Brick storefronts in various states of disrepair lined both sides of the street. I'd never had reason to be in this part of Carpentier Falls in my many travels to the city to race or on other business. My first impression, however, was that I never wanted the boys to live here again.

On the corner, surrounded by an asphalt parking lot, stood a decaying diner, probably built in the 1950s, when diners were so popular. When the boys and I pushed through the front door, it squeaked louder than the heralding cluster of bells hung on the handle. A walkway ran the entire length of the building, with a low eating counter with barstools along the left side, and a row of booths along the right, next to the windows. Behind the eating counter was a high counter holding drink machines, coffeemakers, an ice machine, and shelves of glasses and coffee cups.

Every barstool seat had rips and tears, many showing a white streak of the cotton backing through the vinyl. Some seats showed puffs of cotton where some idle hands had picked away at the tear, and duct tape covered a few seats in several places. The seats of the booths looked even worse. Years of cigarette burns showed along the edge of the counter and booth tables. I remembered a few years before, when the city council had adopted an ordinance forbidding smoking in public eateries, the howl from several small-business owners who claimed they would land in bankruptcy court if the law went into effect. I wondered if Sam had been one of them.

It wasn't the supper hour yet, which probably explained why only one booth was occupied. A couple of African-American teenagers huddled over large cola glasses. An odor of burnt grease overwhelmed everything else in the room.

The boys scrambled onto barstools and in unison, shouted "Hi, Sam."

A heavyset African-American woman, of indeterminate age, turned from cutting tomatoes and looked at the boys over the rim of her glasses. I wondered how the woman had ignored the racket of two boys running down the aisle, chattering all the time, and clambering up onto barstools opposite her.

After a long moment, Sam said, "Where you two been?" She looked around, not paying any attention to me. "Don't you know we've been worried sick 'bout you two? Where you go? Why not come see Aunt Sam? Where's your mother?"

"Dunno," Joshua said.

"What?" Sam's eyes grew huge, and she looked around the room again.

"She gone," Joshua said. "She went to work one morning an' didn't come home that night."

"Lord a'mighty," Sam said. "You boys been staying with Aunt Jean?"

"Kinda," Joshua said. "We staying with Mr. Kurt, now," he added.

Sam's focus settled on me, as Joshua turned to look up at me.

"Where have I seen you before?" Sam asked.

"He be famous," Jacob said, apparently happy to be able to get into the conversation.

"He drive race cars," Joshua said.

I nodded.

"Uh-huh." Sam turned to deposit the knife she was using on the cutting board. "You boys want Sloppy Joes?"

"Yeah," the boys yelled in unison. "Mr. Kurt want one too," Joshua said.

Sam went into the back room, which I surmised was the kitchen. I turned and scooted into the booth opposite the boys, who climbed off their barstools and crawled into the booth seat across from me. I looked around, spotted a booster seat in the corner, and went to get it for Jacob. Sam returned with two large glasses of milk and set them in front of the boys. She looked at me, and I said, "Iced tea, please." Sam started to walk away, but there was a commotion at the front door, as it squeaked and chimed open. Sam stopped and watched an older couple wobble in and sit down at a booth near the door.

"Hello, Lorraine, Zeke," Sam shouted. The woman waved acknowledgment. Sam walked down the diner behind the counter, filled two glasses with water, and walked around the counter to the couple's booth. She stood and chatted with them, while they perused the menu.

It was early evening, so I hoped the place would continue to fill up. A large crowd would mean the restaurant's food quality was excellent for the price.

Sam chugged up the aisle and into the back, and I wondered if she was running the place by herself. Then a twenty-something woman wearing jeans and a T-shirt from a "Hard Rock Café" appeared from the kitchen door, tying on an apron as she walked. She was tall and thin, with braids hanging down each side of her face. I could tell from her cheekbones and eyes that she had some Native American heritage in her.

"Hey," she said when she saw the boys. "Haven't seen you guys in a while."

"Hey, Lavena," Joshua said. "We've not had the money to eat here."

"Ah, that's too bad. Your mom sick, or something?" Lavena said.

"She gone," Jacob said.

"Gone? Gone where?"

"Dunno," Joshua said.

Lavena's face hardened. "You boys been staying with Auntie Jean?"

"Kinda," Joshua said again, looking at me to bless his fib.

Then Lavena looked directly at me. "You're Kurt Maxxon, aren't you?"

"Yes," I said. "Are you a race fan?"

"My boyfriend, Artie, is," she said. "He goes to every race there is."

"Mr. Kurt a big star," Jacob said.

"I know," Lavena said. "How'd you guys get hooked up with Kurt Maxxon? Artie would give anything to sit and talk with 'The Colonel.'"

"Artie be Sam's kid," Jacob said.

"We spent all day today at the track," Joshua offered, straightening in pride.

"Cool," she said.

I pulled out my wallet and dug out one of my KurtMaxxonRacing. com business cards. On the back of it, I printed PIT PASS and signed my name. I handed it to Lavena and said, "Give this to Artie. He can come to my pit before Sunday's race. I'd like to meet him."

"This is awesome," Lavena said. "Can I come, too?"

"Sure—"

"Me and Jacob will be there, huh, Mr. Kurt?" Joshua interrupted.

"Oh, sure," I said. "I'm betting Maurey Kennedy will need you guys to help during the race."

"Sam took your order, didn't she? You all want Sloppy Joes, right? What'll you have to drink, Mr. Maxxon?"

"I told Sam iced tea," I said.

Lavena delivered my drink and then went to the booth where Lorraine and Zeke sat. She took their order, prepared an order tab, and went to hang it on the rotary.

Sam huffed out of the kitchen with a huge round tray of plates. She set the tray on the table of the booth next to ours, and distributed plates to each of us. The Sloppy Joe sandwiches were huge. The plate of French fries would have fed the high-school football team, and there was at least two pints of coleslaw in a bowl.

The boys dug in, and I knew they were enjoying the food, because they weren't talking. I wondered if I was going to be able to eat the entire sandwich, French fries, and coleslaw. But I did. The boys were so hungry they each ate a giant wedge of chocolate cream pie. I passed on the pie.

We left Sam's, and I drove further east on Roosevelt Boulevard, to the Eastside Shopping Plaza, and into JCPenney. Before we left the store, each boy had two new pair of jeans, three new shirts, six pairs of skivvies, six pairs of socks, a new pair of pajamas, a new pair of Nike running shoes, and new sheets to line their sleeping bags.

I'd decided the ratty sleeping bags would probably do until we decided how to handle the boys' living arrangements. In any event, I didn't think they would need new sleeping bags any time soon.

On the drive home, the gaiety of the evening evaporated when I told the boys that as soon as we got back to the camper, they were going to shower and put on the new clothes. They liked the idea of the new clothes.

"Why we need to shower?" Joshua asked.

"So your new clothes don't get dirty," I said.

"We can sleep in these ole clothes," Jacob offered.

"No. You need to sleep clean," I said. "That means taking a shower, putting on your new pajamas, and sleeping in your sleeping bags, with clean new sheets." I hoped my grandfatherly manner would win them over.

"Okay," Jacob said, nodding at Joshua. "Let's do it for Mr. Kurt."

After a shower, the boys, in their new pajamas, sat with me at a picnic table in the drivers' lounge. I'd found a box of instant hot chocolate and a bag of miniature marshmallows in the cupboard, left by the same driver. They told me about the times they had gone to Sam's Diner before, with their mother. They told me about Auntie Jean, who lived in the first complex they did.

I thought the boys might be wearing down, so I suggested we go over to the camper. I hoped to put them down and get to bed. But, as the boys sat on their sleeping bags, with new sheet lining, Joshua said, "Tell us some stories 'bout when you be at war over in that place."

War stories are not good fare for kids you are trying to put to sleep. So I told them about some of the funny things that had happened on the aircraft carrier Brad and I flew on and off from. The right storyteller could probably make some of those things into a fairy tale. I'm not much of a storyteller, but I did the best I could. The boys had a tough time grasping the size of an aircraft carrier, even after I compared it to the twenty-story Valley Insurance building in downtown Carpentier Falls.

"That high off the water?" Joshua asked.

"And where I slept was below the water level," I told them.

"You have to climb a lot of stairs?" Jacob asked.

"I used the elevators," I confessed.

Before I got to the time I tripped in the galley line and sent food flying all over, I realized both boys were sound asleep.

Dodged another bullet, Maxxon.

CHAPTER FIVE

Saturday, September 9

<u>*Kurt Maxxon and the boys at practice, Morning*</u>

When the boys asked where we were going for breakfast, I told them I wanted to go to Maple's Pancake House. The boys seemed excited and interested in a new restaurant.

"Is it good?" Jacob quizzed.

"Sure is," I said.

"They got more than pancakes?" Joshua asked.

"They have French toast," I said.

"That's what I want," Jacob said.

"They also have blueberry pancakes and strawberry pancakes."

"Strawberries on pancakes?" Joshua said.

"Yes. With whipped cream on top."

"That don't sound very good," Jacob said, wrinkling his nose.

'You don't like strawberries?" I asked.

"Not on pancakes."

"Okay. How about blueberries?"

"Not ever had them," Jacob said.

"Yes, we have," Joshua interjected. "A long time ago."

"I don't remember," Jacob said.

"Man, you sure forget a lot," Joshua said, shaking his head.

"He was probably too young to remember when some things happened," I said, hoping to cheer Jacob out of the fearful look he'd let spread over his face. "You are old enough to remember those happenings, Joshua, but Jacob was too young." My musings apparently soothed Jacob, and they didn't faze Joshua. I drove silently.

Maple's Pancake House is difficult to drive to. By the time Carpentier Falls grew around it, the city leaders had adopted a city-block plan consisting of east-west and north-south roads. As a result, Maple's occupies an isolated triangular-shaped piece of property on a three-block long stretch of the old road that parallels the river.

Over the years, Maple's Pancake House has become an institution in Carpentier Falls. The owners, and many others, claim it is the longest continually operated eatery in the valley, having been founded in 1826 by Tyrone Maple. It operated as a tavern and stagecoach stop, until the railroads drove stagecoaches further west. In 1863, the diners of southern sympathies and the diners of northern persuasions got into a fight inside the tavern. A candle or two knocked to the floor burned the original log cabin and a clapboard addition to the foundations.

The descendent at the time, Sylvia Maple Gavoure, decided not to rebuild until the war was over. Sylvia died, however, shortly before Lee's surrender at Appomattox Courthouse, and her heirs got into a squabble between the southern and northern sides of the family. Rebuilding didn't commence until 1872.

If you merely subtract out the nine years of closure, Maple's still is several years ahead of the nearest competitor, Weir's Diner, opened in 1855. Some detractors also subtract the thirty years, plus or minus, that Maple's served as a tavern. Many modern people associate tavern with beer joint, where the only foods available are peanuts, popcorn, pretzels, and potato chips.

History junkies, like me, know that taverns were a whole lot more than merely rest stops where weary travelers could find a meal and a bed. They often became the center of the community. Maple's was, for most of its early existence, "out in the sticks," because it was five and a half miles upstream of the great falls, where a shallow ford allowed wagons and stagecoaches to cross the river. Even so, Maple's was a valuable meeting place for many local groups.

The clapboard building, finished in 1873, forms the base of the complex, with three add-ons made at various times. The original building is now mostly a museum of Maple's history, full of antiques, photographs, memorabilia, and heirlooms. The kitchen addition is the newest, having been a total remodel of the original about thirty years ago. The north dining room, added in 1927, and the south dining room, added in 1948, allowed seating for an extra two hundred people. On Saturday and Sunday mornings, there is a waiting line of customers, despite the extra space. Maple's converted from a family restaurant to a pancake house in the 1980s and for several years was open for breakfast and lunch only. They switched back to full service in the late 1990s.

When we arrived, the sun was already bright and the air was warming. However, a high-pressure ridge to the west of town was bringing in cool, dry air from the north. The weather people on TV were predicting hot, humid weather later today and into tomorrow— race day. I helped the boys out of the truck. When we walked into the entryway, a matronly woman gathered menus from a rack. "How many will there be?" she said, looking at her seating chart.

"Just the three of us."

We followed her to a table for four, and she laid menus in front of three places. She went to the corner of the room and returned with a booster seat for Jacob. I lifted him up into it.

"Our special this morning is strawberry pancakes with a side of bacon," the woman said. "A server will be with you in a minute." She walked back toward the entryway to intercept a group of men coming through the door.

"I want the strawberry pancakes," Joshua announced.

"I want regular pancakes," Jacob said.

I also ordered the strawberry pancakes special.

"My friend, Christina, is coming this afternoon," I told the boys. "And she's bringing my little dog, Beau."

I noticed the boys look at each other nervously.

"Is he mean?" Jacob asked.

"No. Beau is very gentle. He likes kids."

"A dog attacked Jacob," Joshua reported.

"Where?" I asked.

"In the projects. Somebody's wild dog," Joshua said, as Jacob held up his arm to show scars I had not noticed before. "They never found the dog."

"I had to have a bunch of shots," Jacob said, patting his stomach. "They hurt."

I was familiar with the rabies treatments humans had to endure if the authorities couldn't find and test a suspect animal.

"I bet that was hard and hurt a lot," I sympathized with him.

Being the center of attention brought Jacob out of his funk. Our food arrived, which also helped. Joshua chose strawberry-flavored syrup. I asked Jacob what flavor he wanted: maple, blueberry, boysenberry, or strawberry.

"Strawberry," he said.

"What we do today?" Joshua asked.

"I need to practice. You guys can time my laps. I'll show you how to do that."

"That be cool," they said together.

*   *   *

Joshua and Jacob rode with me in Nikki from my garage to the track, even though they had to stand up and hold on to the cross bracing while I drove slowly. I parked in the first pit space, since the assigned pit stalls wouldn't be available until after the qualifications in the afternoon.

I stationed the boys behind the concrete barrier wall and showed them how to use my wrist chronometer as a timer. I pointed out the timing mark on the wall across from the pit, which is a red vertical stripe.

"When the nose of Nikki crosses that mark, you press the start button, like this," I demonstrated. Both the boys were eager to learn. "When I come around again, and the nose of Nikki crosses the line the next time, you push this button to stop the timer." I gave the chronometer to Joshua.

"It's heavy, huh?" Joshua said, hefting the watch in his right hand. I knew Jacob would hold the watch in his left hand. *So alike as brothers, yet so different.*

I watched Joshua as he pushed the start button. Then he fumbled to adjust the watch in his hand, so he could push the stop button. Eventually, he decided it was going to take two hands to operate the timer. After a half-dozen starts, stops, and resets, I said, "Okay, let Jacob see if he can do it."

Jacob's eyes grew big, and he grinned. I handed him the chronometer and eased it down to let him get the heft of it.

"Heavy," Jacob agreed. Since he wasn't quite as dexterous as Joshua, it took him longer, but he eventually became reasonably adept at handling the timer with both hands.

Then I showed both boys how to read the time in seconds. In the end, I suggested that Joshua operate the timer, then both of them read the time, and Jacob be responsible for writing the time down on the clipboard I'd brought along. That was acceptable to both of them. I put on my skid lid and climbed into Nikki, started her engine, and waved to the wide-eyed boys, as I pulled away. "It'll be interesting to see what your times are," I said to Nikki. "The boys will probably get a couple of laps about right."

I got Nikki up to speed, and we made our first lap. As I approached the timing mark the first time, I saw the boys heads follow me to the mark and then, as Nikki's nose passed the mark, their heads bobbed down to start the watch. At the end of each timed lap, their heads would bob down to stop the watch. I could only imagine what the two boys did as they discussed the number of seconds and Jacob recorded the number. The boys went through the same routine for each timed lap.

I'd planned on running ten laps and checked on the boys each time I passed by the pit stall. I was the only one on the track, and Nikki was purring with contentment. The times should be among Nikki's best, but I worried the boys might not give me accurate readings.

Since the boys were thoroughly enjoying themselves, I made it to lap 6 before my mind strayed. It replayed the events of Friday morning—first with the boys finding Carlos, and then, finally, the revelation at the board meeting about betting on the SRVSCRA races being conducted at the Trattoria. I was convincing myself that gambling had been the main reason for Carlos's death.

I've known Carlos for eight or nine years, mainly from racing each September, and a few other visits to the Trattoria, simply because I like Cuban food. Carlos was always happy, friendly, cordial, and seemingly, an upstanding businessman.

Did I miss any signs?

Was I looking for any signs?

It wasn't robbery. Carlos still had his Rolex on his wrist. Damon Hertz told me Carlos's wallet had still been in his pocket, with $350 bucks, and nothing missing. Did the killer not know the value of the Rolex watch?

As I came out of turn 3, Nikki's rear end got loose, and I corrected, letting up on the gas pedal and steering into the slide. Nikki fishtailed a little and then straightened out nicely. I accelerated into the long, arcing straightaway between turn 3 and turn 1.

The racetrack is what they call a "tri-oval." If you look down on the track from ten thousand feet, it looks like the letter D, with a bend, or dogleg, in the straight side of the letter. The start/finish line is midway along the long arcing front runway, and then turn 1 is a fairly sharp curve, banked to allow speeds of about sixty-five miles per hour—if you're careful. From turn 1, you go into a "short shoot," or a short, straight leg of the dogleg. Turn 2, between the short shoot from turn 1 and the short shoot into turn 3, is banked to allow speeds of about eighty-five mph. Then turn 3 is identical to turn 1—no more than sixty-five miles per hour. The main grandstand is along the long arcing runway of the D, and then bleacher seats line the two dogleg short shoots. The pit stalls are opposite the grandstand, on the inside of the track along the long arc. Pit stall number 1 was only a few yards from turn 1. So, as I approached the target mark on the wall for the boys to time me, I was slowing down to go into turn 1. That would make it easier for the boys to see me cross the mark.

I saw the boys behind the wall as I passed the pit area. I'd forgotten whether this time past was the start of the lap or the end of the lap. It really didn't matter to me. My mind was racing around the universe, while I herded Nikki around the track. The boys were having fun timing my laps.

Nikki was having fun—she was roaring like a lion and running like a gazelle.

"You're doing great, Nikki," I yelled over her noise and the wind whistle. But, going into turn 3, she suddenly shuddered, got loose, and slid sideways. I corrected the best I could, but the steering wasn't working right. I had no control, and I crunched the brake pedal. We barely missed sideswiping the concrete wall, and we screeched to a stop. In the aftermath, I sat for a few minutes, my heart pounding, and I finally caught my breath. I decided against just sitting still on the track. Plus, I didn't want the boys coming out of the pit area to see what had happened to me. I cranked Nikki. She didn't start on the first and second crank. But she fired, hesitantly, on the third crank. As I rolled forward, a loud thump, thump, thump rattled the whole car, telling me we had a flat right front tire. It could have caused the skid. Or it could have happened during the skid.

We limped into the pit area, where I saw Dave Kellogg's number 4 Ford Taurus parked in the lead stall.

I stopped Nikki several yards behind Dave's car, and I then realized Dave was out of his car, sitting on the concrete wall talking to the boys. I shut off Nikki, took off my skid lid, and climbed out. I would have to go get a tire and put it on, so I could drive Nikki back to her garage.

"You can't go very fast when one of your tires is flat, Co'nel," Dave said, laughing.

"It's just flat on the bottom side," I said, enjoying his jest.

"That's true," Dave said. "You got yourself a new pit crew, huh?"

I walked toward him to shake hands.

"Pretty good one, too," I said. Jacob was dancing around, eager to show me how he had written the numbers. I reached over, picked him up, and set him on the barrier wall. Then I helped Joshua climb up to sit on the wall.

"You guys want to time my laps?" Dave asked.

Both boys' eyes swung to me. "Sure," I said, "We've got time."

"You want me to run over and get ya a spare and a jack?" Dave asked.

I nodded, "If you would."

Dave took the key to Nikki's transporter and roared away toward the garage area. When he returned, I told the boys to stay behind the wall, where they could time Dave's laps, while I changed the tire.

"Good deal," Dave said. "I'll suppose I'll have to pay the co'nel a coupla bucks to rent his chronometer—maybe he'll share with you guys." He grinned, swung his skid lid onto his head, walked to his car, and climbed in.

I told the boys to get down off the wall, but then I noticed that Jacob was standing on a pallet they had found at the back of the pit area. I hadn't paid attention, and I felt bad about that. I relented and walked toward the boys.

"As long as you stay on the wall, you can sit up here," I said, lifting Jacob onto the wall. Joshua climbed up next to him. "But you can't get down on this side." I remembered the clipboard Jacob had handed me, which I'd laid on the wall. I scanned down the list. Every entry was in the thirty-five-to-forty-second range; those were reasonably good times for me during practice, but, more importantly, they showed that the boys were fairly accurate in their timing.

We watched for Dave to come around, and Joshua pressed the start button right at the mark. When the blue car came around again, Joshua stopped the timer perfectly. I nodded approvingly, to let both of them know I was proud of them, since I didn't want to distract them. The two boys discussed the reading and settled on thirty-five seconds. They followed the same process for each lap. I jacked Nikki up and changed the flat tire.

Dave ran ten laps and then pulled into the pit stall behind Nikki. I helped Jacob down off the wall, and Joshua jumped down. Jacob ran to Dave and handed him the clipboard. Dave looked at the times and grinned. "Boy, you guys are goo-ood!" Dave said. "All those times look great, especially the thirty-two-second one."

"I pushed the buttons," Joshua said proudly, "and just as the nose of—ah— what's the name of your car?"

Dave laughed out loud. "Molly," he said.

"I wrote the numbers down," Jacob shouted, beaming at Dave's praise.

Dave started toward his car, stopped, and turned to me. "Did I really have a thirty-two-second lap?" he asked.

"I watched them working, and it's mighty close to that," I nodded. "Did you have Maurey Kennedy build that engine for you?" I teased and chuckled.

"I wish," Dave said. He took his wallet out of the dashboard cubbyhole and walked over to me. He fished out a five-dollar bill and handed it to me. "Split it any way you want, Co'nel," he said. "They're a good pit crew."

Dave and I looked over to the boys to see two pairs of eyes dancing. "We're proud of you," I said. "Should I just tear it in half and give a piece to each of you?"

"No!" they shouted in unison.

"We gonna wait until you get change, then give each of us two bucks, an' you get a dollar for your watch," Joshua declared.

"Okay," I said, knowing I'd give each of them two and a half. "Let's climb into Nikki and get off the track. Who's up for some cool refreshment?" I asked, thinking about the Tasty Cool place up the street from the Trattoria.

"Me!" Jacob shouted.

"Me!" Joshua bellowed louder.

"Me, me, huh?" I teased. "How about you and me?"

"Okaaaaay," Jacob said. "We want some, please."

Several times during the last two days, memories of Kurt Jr. had filled my mind—wonderful memories—and now it seemed I had the chance to relive those crazy, off-the-wall, impromptu activities I had experienced with Kurt Jr. I suddenly realized I was enjoying every minute of it. The boys were polite and well-mannered. A caring mother had obviously taught them those wonderful qualities.

Where had that mother gone?

Where was the boys' extended family?

And thinking about Kurt Jr. made me miss his mother—a lot.

CHAPTER SIX

Saturday, September 9

<u>*Kurt Maxxon and the boys, Lunch*</u>

I'd set up a lunch appointment with Cliff Ramsey several months ago. As I always do, I called to confirm if we were still on. Cliff chuckled and said, "Would I forget lunch with Kurt Maxxon? Not likely."

I told Cliff I was bringing my new pit crew along.

"This I got to see," Cliff said, and I knew he was smiling.

Cliff and Becky Ramsey are longtime friends of mine in Carpentier Falls. They own and operate Ramsey Collectibles, Inc., a business well known throughout the valley. They're especially prominent in the northeast region, where Carpentier Falls is the largest city. The stamp part of the business is the bailiwick of Sylvester James Prendergast, Becky's older brother. Affectionately known by friends, family, and clients as Silly, he joined the business upon his return from Vietnam in 1968. He brought an insatiable love for postage stamps from around the world and quickly added value to the business.

Rebecca Louise (Prendergast) Ramsey is the doll collector and antique specialist, and she was the Carpentier Falls comrade-in-arms of my late wife, Vicki, and her Raggedy Ann and Andy doll collection. Since Vicki passed away, Becky has rounded up a couple of Raggedy dolls I can't refuse to add to Vicki's collection. Christina Zouhn, the third *amiga* in all of Vicki's local forays for Raggedy dolls, was coming to town later this afternoon.

Cliff is the coin component of the business, which has been my main interest over the years, since I'm an on-again, off-again, longtime coin collector. As a young lad, I focused my collecting on dimes, developing a keen attraction to the Mercury dimes. Once I became slightly affluent, my quest became mint-state "full side band" Mercury dimes. Depending on the year and mint mark, these can cost more money than I want to spend, so I had no illusions of ever having a complete collection of them. Cliff just about always comes up with at least one coin of interest.

Issued in 1916, it is officially known as the "Winged Liberty Head" ten-cent piece, because the obverse image depicted the mythological goddess, Liberty, wearing a Phrygian cap, with wings added to symbolize freedom of thought.

Despite the rationale offered by the mint people, most people associated the image with the Roman god Mercury, known as the "messenger god," who flitted from place to place. Thus, his depiction in mythological art often showed his "winged" helmet to facilitate flight. Other artwork gave Mercury his flighty capabilities with "winged" sandals.

To a few of us modern-day collectors, the obverse image is not the most important feature of the coin, however. The key feature we look for is the bands that encircle a bundle of sticks (sometimes thought to be arrow shafts) on the reverse side of the coin. The design includes three sets of bands. The most desirable coins show distinct "side bands," and pristine uncirculated models with full side bands command some steep prices.

The value of any coin is predicated upon its scarcity. And scarcity results from the number of coins still available to collectors. Some year/mint marks had low production numbers to start with. Other year/mint marks had low production numbers, but a lot of people hoarded them, which means there are ample supplies available. But the real culprit in the scarcity of full-side-band Mercury dimes is simply the complicated design. During production of the winged Liberty dime, the dies used to punch the coins speedily gummed up with metal in the machines used to stamp the design. I've seen estimates that less than one hundred of the coins produced by new dies resulted in full-side-band coins. Most of the time, those coins simply went into general circulation.

The total number of full-side-band winged Liberty dimes in existence, for all year/mint mark combinations, is comparatively low. Finding the good ones is a quest almost as elusive as winning races. Cliff Ramsey has been looking for the best models for years, and for the last dozen years he has been looking for them for me, at prices I can afford.

Besides his coin expertise, Cliff is also a great storyteller. I always sit fascinated when he starts an "I remember the time ..." story. This guy has been everywhere, seen everything, done whatever he wanted to, and likes to talk about how it all went down. Occasionally, Becky interrupts his storytelling with, "Now, Cliffy, you know that's not the way it was ..." but she'll usually just sit and listen like the rest of us.

Last year it was the story about their neighbors on either side. On one side was a retired schoolteacher who had a champion Border collie, named Mamie, which she planned to breed and sell the pups. On the other side was an ex-truck driver who had a mixed breed, named Romeo, who roamed the neighborhood without much fuss. Romeo's bloodline contained boxer, shepherd, and some other hounds. When Mamie turned up pregnant, the indignant schoolmarm declared that Romeo was the father. She made rather derogatory remarks about Romeo, his owner, and the owner's insensitivity to the other dogs in the neighborhood. She threatened to sue, and she would have taken Mamie to have an abortion, if she could have afforded it. So, for several weeks, Cliff and Becky sat between their feuding neighbors, trying to be indifferent, but sympathetic to both parties.

Eventually, Mamie birthed a litter of three puppies, all of whom looked very much like Gus, the basset hound three doors down and across the alley.

Did the schoolmarm forgive Romeo? No—she claimed it was Romeo who taught Gus how to wander the neighborhood with impunity.

Cliff and I nearly always meet for lunch at Ruby's Lobster Shack, since it's halfway between the racetrack in the southwest part of Carpentier Falls and Cliff's shop and home in the northeast part of town.

As we rode toward the restaurant, I asked the boys if they liked seafood. They looked at each other, then looked at me, and said in unison, "Never had it before."

The sun was fading behind clouds that were thickening from the west. The air was warm enough to cause shimmering on the horizon, but a gentle breeze moved the air enough to keep it reasonably comfortable.

"Seafood is good," I said. "You'll see." I knew the boys were open to trying a new eating establishment.

"This another fancy place?" Jacob asked.

"Not really," I said. "It's different." I caught the boys looking at each other with worry lines on their foreheads.

Once inside the building, I let my eyes adjust and searched for Cliff. He and Becky were sitting at a round table near a window in the shape of a porthole. The boys trailed behind me, taking in the sights and sounds of the Lobster Shack. The main dining room is done in traditional fishing nets, plank floors imitating the deck of a fishing boat, and pictures, paintings, and sculptures on the walls depicting fishing ships from the time of Moby Dick to the present.

Cliff stood up and walked around the table to shake my hand and survey my pit crew. "They look hardy enough," he said. "They any good at changing tires?"

"They watched that this morning," I said and watched two pairs of eyes look from Cliff, to Becky, and then back to me. "Next time I plan to let them do it by themselves."

I watched a cloud of fear wrinkle the boys' foreheads. I winked at them, hoping they would realize I was not serious.

"Do they collect coins?" Cliff asked.

"Not yet, but maybe in the future."

Becky stood, walked to the boys, and knelt down to be on their level. "I'm Becky Ramsey," she said. "What're your names?"

"I'm Joshua Lawton," Joshua said. "This is my brother, Jacob."

"Joshua and Jacob, I'm glad to meet you," Becky said, shaking the boys' hands. The boys had found a new friend in Becky. They watched as she stood and helped them into their chairs, even going to get a booster seat for Jacob. Cliff and I sat down. The waiter arrived, and the boys ordered Coca Cola. We three adults ordered coffee. We brought each other up to date since our last visit a few months earlier, when I had come to Carpentier Falls to meet with the county commissioners on some traffic easements the racing association had requested. The boys were the subject of our discussion for a while. The boys responded to questions from Becky but seemed unable to answer any of Cliff's queries.

I ordered the boys a seafood combination platter I figured would give them each enough to eat even if they didn't like some parts of it. I ordered my normal surf and turf; Cliff and Becky both opted for crab legs. When the waiter came to the table to help Cliff and Becky don their bibs, the boys stared wide-eyed and then started giggling.

"What's so funny?" Cliff asked, with a goofy grin on his face.

"We never seen grownups wear bibs before," Joshua chortled.

"We wear them all the time," Cliff said. "It helps keep my shirt clean."

"And, he really needs one," Becky said.

"We gotta wear one?" Jacob asked.

"No. You guys are getting shrimp and crab legs already cracked and some other good things."

After we finished our food, Cliff hauled a large three-ring binder out of his briefcase. It was stuffed with sheet protectors containing photographs of coins, arranged so you could view both sides of each coin. He had some very nice-looking Mercury dimes, and I would have loved to say, "I'll take them all." But reality always keeps me walking the straight and narrow, so I picked two coins that fit within my budget. "I'll run by Monday afternoon to pick them up," I said.

"I'll knock a hundred bucks off that 1916-S," Cliff said.

"What's a 1919-D going for now?" I asked.

Cliff shuffled through some notes. "Somewhere north of forty-five thousand dollars."

The eyes of both boys flew open. Then they started to blink rapidly.

"How much?" Joshua said.

"They are very expensive," I said, hoping to stem their surprise. "About fifty thousand."

"Fifty thousand dollars," Jacob mimed.

I bobbed my head.

Cliff smiled and looked at Jacob. "You want me to get you one, or do you want two?"

Jacob cowered a little, and said, "Don't got that much money."

"Maybe someday," Becky said.

Joshua eyed Cliff suspiciously. "How come you charge so much for a dime?"

That gave everyone a good laugh.

"I'll explain it to you later," I said. "You guys want dessert?"

The boys opted for pecan pie with ice cream. We adults opted for another cup of coffee.

"Did you know Carlos Guerrero?" I asked Cliff.

"No. Ate at the Trattoria several times, so I know who he was, but we never met," Cliff said.

"I met him at a fundraiser one time," Becky said. "He sat at the same table as me for lunch. He was pleasant enough, and he bid high on several auction items."

"Anything new about his murder?" Cliff asked.

"Not that I know of," I said. "I imagine the cops are digging for evidence."

"Do you know the name of the detective in charge of the case?" Becky asked.

"It's the sheriff's department," I said. "I haven't heard any more from them."

"I thought the racetrack was in the city limits," Cliff said.

"The racetrack is," I said. "The strip mall that includes the Trattoria on the east side of Speedway somehow has kept out of the annexation campaign."

"That's right," Cliff said. "I read something about the taxes on several of those businesses being way behind. The county auditor made a big deal about that last fall just before the election."

"Didn't do any good," Becky said. "The same old bunch got reelected."

Cliff put his notebook into his briefcase. Before he closed the briefcase, he picked up and handed me a business card for an insurance agency north on Adams Street. The name on the card was Gordon Michaelson, Agent. The card named the insurance company and a slogan, and I was reasonably sure the agency catered to farmers and rural people. "You should try to meet this guy," Cliff said. "He's doing a lot of his own shopping for coins now, and he collects full-side-band Mercury dimes, like you do."

My frown must have been revealing, because Cliff looked at me and said, "Oh, don't worry; I'm not giving up on you buying from me. But some of the better stuff you'll need from here on might just be a little cheaper if you go get them yourself."

"Okay, how much of my time will this take?"

"Well, that depends on how you look at it." Cliff handed me a tabloid newspaper entitled *Coin World*. "Take this, and look through it. You'll see display ads and classifieds in the back, for mail-bid auctions. It's not like going to estate auctions or other scheduled sales. With mail-bid auctions, you can fill out the bids at midnight and mail them off the next morning. They just have to be in by the closing date."

I knew I was frowning more than I like to do. "How do you protect yourself from getting scammed?"

"First, you choose reputable dealers," Cliff said. "It's a lot easier than you might think. Like I've told you from when we first met, you need to join the American Numismatic Association. They have lists of dealers. They have a grading service, the NGC, the Numismatic Guaranty Corporation. You should always buy coins with NGC grading. If it turns out the NGC didn't grade the coin, the dealer will usually give you a refund."

"I'm not a real trusting animal when it comes to coin dealers." I noticed the boys' faces swinging toward me.

"That's why I suggest you talk to Gordon," Cliff said. "He was just like you. But he started slow and, over the last couple of years, has gotten into it big. He's added some excellent pieces to his collection on his own, at a lot less cost than if I had to go find them for him."

"Okay," I said. "I'll try to get up with this guy Gordon Michaelson. Get his take on shopping for coins on my own."

Cliff looked at the boys. "Did I tell you about the pet store guy next door to me?"

I'd visited the pet store next to Ramsey Collectibles to buy toys for Beau. The boys were staring at Cliff, waiting for his story.

"Yeah," Cliff continued. "The guy next to me traded this navy captain a parakeet for a parrot. He put the parrot in his store, and the next morning the parrot started cursing a blue streak. My friend next door didn't like that. So he told the parrot, 'You keep swearing like that, and I'm going to put you in the freezer to cool your heels.' Well, the parrot sat there for a few minutes, and, when another customer came in, he started swearing again. So, my neighbor, true to his word, put the parrot in the freezer. After a few minutes, he let the parrot out of the freezer. 'Do you understand now what happens when you swear?' my friend asked the parrot."

The parrot looked at him for a long time and then said, 'What'd that damn turkey say to you?'"

It took me a couple of beats to understand, but the boys were already belly laughing. Becky wore her normal poker face while listening to Cliff's stories.

After the laughter, the boys finished their desserts and were getting antsy. "Have you found any new Raggedy dolls for my collection?" I asked Becky.

She wobbled her head. "I haven't seen anything worthwhile lately. But I haven't been all that active, either."

"They diagnosed Janie, our youngest granddaughter, as being autistic," Cliff said, giving Becky a worried look. Becky's eyes betrayed her concern.

"They know a lot more about autism today than even a few years ago," I said. "I think I'd rather my granddaughter have autism than a lot of other conditions." I hoped that I was giving it a proper perspective, but the subject pretty much ended our lunch.

* * *

Chaundra Dunkin

Chaundra carried her coffee cup to the breakfast nook and slid into the seat opposite her mother, who was engrossed in the morning newspaper. Her terry cloth robe was too warm, but she hadn't known who would be in the kitchen. "Where's Gordon?" she said to the newspaper curtain.

"Gone to a breakfast meeting for something or other," a voice said from behind the newspaper.

Chaundra sensed something had changed about her mother. Maybe she had overcome the childish infatuation with Gordon. Chaundra wondered if that would happen with time. She wiggled out of the robe, sliding it down to where she was sitting on it, and sipped her coffee.

Her mother shook the paper to change pages. "You sleep well?" her mother's voice came from behind the newspaper.

"Yeah, pretty well."

"It's nice to be home, isn't it?" the voice behind the newspaper said.

Chaundra stared at the newspaper curtain between herself and her mother. Carpentier Falls Furniture had a full-page, full-color ad featuring sofas and recliner chairs. "It's okay."

The newspaper curtain folded. "Just okay?" her mother said.

"I can't talk to a newspaper," Chaundra said.

"Oh. Oh …" her mother flustered. "I'm sorry. But I read the newspaper every Saturday and Sunday morning."

"I know that, Mom. But maybe we could talk about a few things."

Fran folded the newspaper into a neat section and stacked it on the other sections lying nearby. "Look, baby, I'm ecstatic that you are home. That you haven't gone back to that dreadful business … that career … that profession … that *whatever*."

Chaundra sighed softly. "I'm glad I'm out of that business, too. But I'm not sure I feel comfortable about what lies ahead."

"What lies ahead, baby, is that we—Gordon and I—are going to help you get an education, finish high school, and get into college."

"Gordon told you he'll help me?" Chaundra said.

"Gordon has always said he'd do all he can to get you through college."

"I didn't know that," Chaundra said, wondering whether this new information was a real change of heart on Gordon's part or something her mother had never bothered to mention before. Either way, it changed her opinion of Gordon slightly.

"Gordon will go with you to talk to the high-school counselor, whenever you're ready," her mother said.

Chaundra liked the overall idea, but she started to worry about how involved her mother and Gordon were going to be. Her preference would be that they help her get into—and through—school, but she didn't want them dictating how she did things, or when, or why. And she definitely *did not* want Gordon Michaelson going with her to talk to the counselor.

"Don't worry, baby," her mother murmured, "it's all going to work out for the best."

The best? Chaundra thought. *For you and Gordon? Or for me?*

*   *   *

Kurt Maxxon and the boys

I helped the boys out of my pickup and we walked to the camper. I'd parked outside the RV lot, since there is only room for one vehicle in the RV spaces, and I knew Christina and Beau would park near the campsite.

A half dozen RVs had set up in the lot while we were at lunch, and another driver was backing his travel trailer into a space. I considered putting the umbrella up over the picnic table. Then, because of the stiff southerly breeze, I decided I didn't want the hassle of repeatedly correcting the umbrella's position. The table would be in shade after six o'clock anyway.

The boys crawled under the second picnic table I'd dragged from the storage yard for them to use as their tent, while I sat in the shade of the cab-over part of my camper. My new camper has an air conditioner mounted on the roof, but I rarely run it, except when we leave Beau at home in it. Just as I was about to set up a jar of tea to brew in the sun, I noticed a shadow approaching the camper and looked up to see Jimmy Davison. Suddenly, I felt the conflict Carlos' death had brought to this race. Jimmy drives the number 89 Ford Taurus, sponsored by Carlos's restaurant, the Trattoria. He is also Carlos's great-nephew, and, as a result, Friday morning's events flooded my mind.

"Hi, Colonel," Jimmy said. "How you doing?"

"Just fine," I replied, watching the boys peer out from under the picnic table to see who I was talking to. They'd built a fort and were playing at fighting off an Indian attack.

Carlos had never talked much about himself, other than tidbits in his evolution from a short-order cook to a full-fledged chef—but he had talked about his family. His great-niece, Hermosa Anderson, and his great-nephew, Jimmy Davison, dominated the family stories. I could hear the pride in his voice every time he spoke of these two, and I knew from his stories that they also doted on him. Hermosa's parents were both Cuban, and her father was a Guerrero. After her parents fled to the United States when Castro took over, Hermosa went to law school, where she met and married Timothy Anderson. Carlos proudly showed me pictures of their three beautiful children, who each have their father's striking blue Swedish eyes and faces framed by their mother's dark hair.

Carlos's niece, Estella Guerrero, had married an Irishman named James Bryan Davison, whom she met when he was a U.S. Navy radioman aboard a ship that put into Havana harbor in 1956. James Bryan left for six months, to finish the tour he was on, and then returned. They married in Havana, and James Bryan started arranging to move Estella to Jacksonville, Florida, his next duty station. Jimmy was born in Ocala, Florida, in January 1958, which made him an instant U.S. citizen.

Jimmy is an inch shorter than I am and has dark auburn hair and green eyes. That day, he was wearing blue jeans, with a light blue Western shirt, and a white cowboy hat. He is so slender, I worry that he might not have strength to finish the race, but he gets by. His nickname around the tracks is "The Crooner," since he is a songwriter and singer of some note.

"I need some advice," Jimmy said, without apology. He sat down on the bench of the picnic table. He was in the sun, but it didn't bother him. He'd inherited his mother's Caribbean hue, and he apparently had trouble keeping women from fawning over him.

"What do you need?" I asked.

"You think it's appropriate for me to run Uncle Carlos's car Sunday?"

"Why not?"

"Wouldn't it be disrespectful?"

"No," I said. "Hell, no."

Jimmy's eyes grew large. "I've never heard you swear before, Colonel."

"I'm sorry, Jimmy," I said; I realized I'd startled Joshua and Jacob also. "I think you should race Sunday, and I think you should win it for Carlos."

"My mother called this morning," he said and then stopped, looking toward his wife, who came sauntering toward us. "She didn't think I should."

"I'm not one to trump your mother, Jimmy. Carlos was very fond of you. He loved racing, and he'd want you to race, and win."

"I haven't had a win in my career yet," he said. "The car's good; I just usually figure out a way to lose."

"Well then, now is the time to figure out a way to win, partner."

Jimmy's wife, Vinnie, short for Vinita, stopped behind Jimmy. Vinita Ignacia Hernandez Davison was the perfect match for Jimmy. She was of Cuban heritage, the same height as Jimmy, and still sported an hourglass figure after bearing two children. She was wearing a yellow tank top with matching shorts, which served to highlight her skin tone, black hair, and brown eyes. Vinnie is a clinical psychologist at the local medical center. After she heard the end of our conversation, she said, "Hermosa told me she wants to talk to you, Jimmy."

Jimmy started to get up, looking apologetically toward me and reaching for his cell phone. "She may not want me driving the car any more," he said in a small, hurting tone.

I felt bad for Jimmy. The events of the weekend were obviously taking a toll on him.

Vinnie stayed him with her hand on his shoulder, saying, "Oh, I think it's something else, Jimmy. Hermosa didn't demand you call her right now. It was more general, like 'the next time I see him' kind of request."

Jimmy straightened up, a sudden determined look on his face. "What time is qualifying?"

"I think they'll start about five," I said. "I'll do a ten-minute meeting and then Penelope will draw the numbers out of the ammo box. There'll only be a dozen drivers qualifying, from the looks of things, so that'll only take thirty minutes or so."

At Carpentier Falls we use an old ammo box that was dug up when they excavated to build the new racetrack. The land had been a government ammunition depot during World War II, was decommissioned in the middle 1950s, and was donated to Pierre County. The county commissioners decided to build the replacement for Pumpkin Hollow Raceway on the land.

Carpentier Falls has had a racetrack since the late 1920s, when moonshiners and bootleggers got together annually to discuss souping up their cars to outrun the local county sheriffs, state police, and federal revenuers. The original racetrack was on a farm owned by one of the moonshiners, who used one-fourth of his land to raise pumpkins for the local jack-o-lantern trade and the rest for corn to make white lightning. To get to the track, people had to drive through the pumpkin patch, so the track came to be known by various names: Pumpkin Patch Run, Pumpkin Road Raceway, and others.

The new racetrack, finished in 1960, was dubbed Pumpkin Hollow Raceway and changed in 1975 to Pumpkin Hollow International Speedway after a major enhancement. The ammo box has been part of the drawing of numbers for all the racing leagues that use the new racetrack.

I glanced at my watch. "Maurey Kennedy will roll in any minute," I said.

"Yeah, I need to check my car, too," Jimmy said. He led Vinnie toward their motor home in space 6.

I thought the boys had dozed off, but the minute I stood, they flew out from under the table. "Let's mosey over to the garage," I said. "Maurey should be coming soon."

We walked to the garage, and I opened the door. The boys helped me push Nikki out of the garage onto the apron. I lifted and propped the hood up.

Each boy clambered onto a fender to ogle the engine packed into the compartment.

"What be the horsepower?" Joshua asked.

"About five hundred," I said.

"Man. That's a lot," Joshua said.

"How fast will she go?" Jacob asked.

"This track we can probably get up to about 110 miles per hour in the front part of the track."

"Our grandpa had a fast car," Joshua said, frowning as he searched his memory. But then he clammed up, as if he'd said something he wasn't supposed to.

"Who was your grandpa?" I asked.

"I don't remember," Joshua said. "Mama told us about him."

Maurey Kennedy arrived in his pickup. He took two toolboxes from the back and walked toward Nikki.

The boys shied back from Maurey, who is a magnet for small children, especially boys. I introduced everyone all around, and Maurey shook their hands. "You guys mechanics?" he asked. Both boys shook their heads.

"What be a mechanic?" Joshua asked.

"A guy who fixes cars," Maurey said. "You know, uses wrenches and screwdrivers."

"I can't use a wrench that's too heavy," Jacob declared.

"We don't need any big wrenches for Nikki," Maurey said as he leaned in to attach wires by alligator clips to various places.

"What do those wires do?" Joshua asked.

"Before I can tell you that," Maurey said, straightening up and grinning at me, "I gotta swear you in as official pit crew members."

"Okay," the boys said in unison.

Maurey proceeded to administer an ad-libbed oath of allegiance to the checkered flag and grease and tune-up equipment, and then he declared the boys official pit crew members. "You'll have to pay your own dues, though," Maurey concluded.

"What are dues?" Joshua asked.

"Money you have to pay to be a member." Maurey was having so much fun with this, I wondered how he kept from laughing till he cried.

"I'll pay their dues," I said.

"There you go; the boss is already taking care of you," Maurey said.

"Okay." Maurey held up a test meter. "This reads the computers in the engine," he said.

"There are computers inside the engine?" Joshua's eyes widened.

"There's a couple of computers for fuel, a couple for oil, and a couple for cooling in there," Maurey said and smiled at each boy.

"How you learn to fix them engines?" Jacob asked.

"You go to school for that," Maurey said. "It takes about three years."

"I wanna do that," Jacob declared. "I go to school and become like Mr. Maurey."

"Okay, buddy," Maurey said. "Just as soon as you finish high school, you call me, and I'll help you get into the Ford Motor Training Program."

"You want to do that too, Josh?" Jacob asked.

"I think I want to learn to fly airplanes," Joshua said. "Like Mr. Kurt."

"Oh, yeah," Jacob said. "I forgot about that. That be cool, too, huh?"

"You can't do any of that until after you finish high school," I said. "So you have plenty of time to make up your mind."

Jacob relaxed.

"How soon we get to high school?" Joshua asked.

I felt like I was explaining something analogous to "the shin bone is connected to the leg bone; the leg bone connected to the knee bone," etcetera. I said, "You have to finish grade school, then middle school, and then high school." I hoped they would understand.

"That be a long time," Jacob said.

"You can't get a job till after you finish high school, anyway," Joshua said. "Ain't that right, Mr. Kurt?"

I bobbed my head with exaggerated motion. "That's right, Joshua."

Hopefully, I'd planted a seed that would grow into a desire to finish high school and then go beyond.

CHAPTER SEVEN

Saturday, September 9

<u>*Kurt Maxxon and the boys, Afternoon*</u>

As we walked back to the camper from the garage, the boys chattered about how cool Maurey Kennedy was and how they'd helped him "tweak" Nikki.

"We be the pit crew," Joshua declared as we walked.

"Yo, man," Jacob added and turned around to walk backward, looking up at me. "What did Mr. Maurey call us?"

I stopped walking, worried that Jacob might trip and fall over backward. Joshua surged ahead, then realized he was alone, and turned to see what was happening. Fortunately, Jacob stopped also. "He called you the pit crew *extraordinaire*," I said.

"Yeah. That's it," Jacob shouted. "We be *that kind* of pit crew."

We made it to the camper, and the boys dashed to their special hidey-hole under the spare picnic table. I'd just unlocked the camper door, when I saw Christina come through the gate, drive to my driveway, and park her ivory Lincoln. She slid out of the driver's side and walked around the car to lift Beau down to the ground. I walked quickly toward Christina. When Beau saw me coming, he made a beeline to me, and I bent down to pet him. He is always happy to see me and give me his sloppy welcome kisses, which makes me feel good. Christina spoils him rotten when he stays with her, so it feels good to know he still wants to be with me and my harsh, pragmatic way of living.

As I calmed Beau down, I looked over my shoulder to see what the boys were doing. I could hear *vroom* and *squeal* and *screech* coming from under the table. They must have been playing at racing cars or something. When I looked back, I saw Christina open her trunk lid and reach to lift out her ice chest. "Let me get that," I said, handing Beau to her. I carried the ice chest to the camper. My mind, however, worried about the meeting of Beau with Jacob and Joshua.

Beau's tail started wagging, which caused his whole body to wiggle, and he started yapping, wanting down. I took Beau back from Christina and walked to the picnic table. A split in the curtain showed two faces, both with large brown eyes and frowns on their foreheads, who had been following our voices. I decided to make a frontal assault on the problem. "Come on out, boys," I said.

The boys emerged from the other side of their table and walked timidly around it. They stood looking at Christina and me, and then their eyes fell on Beau.

Christina walked up beside me. "And who are these boys?" she asked.

"My new pit crew," I said and switched to a formal introduction. "Christina, this is Joshua Lawton, and the other boy is his brother, Jacob. Boys, this is Christina Zouhn."

"Are they replacing Maurey?" Christina said, forcing down a smile.

"No. They're his assistants."

Seeing new playmates, Beau began to wiggle so severely I hoped I could contain him. He gave a low *gurruff* of frustration, just as he did when I wouldn't let him do something he wanted to. It wasn't a bark, and it wasn't a growl. In fact, I haven't heard Beau growl at anyone since he was a very young puppy, when he did growl a bit angrily at Detective Marty Fisher in Kings Rapids. All the other growls were just mild noises of irritation; his training has given him a pleasant disposition.

Both boys looked at Beau with apprehension, but Jacob's eyes were full of fear. I returned to the picnic table and sat down, putting Beau on my lap. Nonplussed, Beau started an even more agitated wiggle, his tail banging against my belly.

"Okay, guys, come over and let me introduce you to Beau."

"You two are mechanics?" Christina asked.

The boys looked at her, then me, bewildered. "Nawh," Jacob said. "We be the pit crew ex—ex—what did Mr. Maurey call us?" Jacob asked, looking to me for help.

"The pit crew *extraordinaire*," I said. I realized Christina was trying to make them relax and I sensed that as long as Beau was in my lap they felt more secure. They approached slowly, and Joshua moved his hand slowly, in a fist, to allow Beau to get a sniff of him, before he petted Beau. I eased my grip a little and Beau wiggled more. Beau, of course, loves to have his ears scratched, so when you pet him he jerks his head so you don't miss the ears. Beau's move frightened Joshua, and he jumped back a little.

"He just wants you to scratch his ears," I said, demonstrating.

Joshua moved back close enough to scratch Beau's ears and neck. "C'mon, Jake," Joshua said, "this one's real friendly."

"Dogs have a keen sense of smell," I said. "And I think they can sense when people are friendly to them."

Jacob moved a little closer. Like most boys, he was mesmerized by living animals, and he didn't want Joshua to have all the fun. After several minutes, Jacob timidly reached out to scratch Beau's ears. With the first touch, he jerked back when Beau swung his head. But Jacob recovered quickly and, from then on, he moved more boldly. Of course, Beau loved having found two new buddies.

Christina opened the ice chest. "I sun-brewed this tea while Beau and I were out running errands this morning. I knew you'd enjoy it." She filled a glass with ice cubes from the chest, spun the cap off a quart Mason jar full of tea and filled the glass. She was right about me enjoying it. And I could see at least three more Mason jars in the ice chest.

Christina asked, "When did you hire this pit crew *extraordinaire*?"

"It's a long story, so I'll start it later," I said. "Maybe we can come back here after dinner so you and I can chat about that subject."

"Works for me," Christina said. "What time are the qualification runs?"

I looked at my watch. "In a half-hour, or so."

*   *   *

We left Beau in the camper, with the air-conditioner running. Christina and the boys went to the pit area of the track, while I went to the drivers' lounge to facilitate the drivers' meeting and oversee the drawing for qualifying runs. There were fourteen drivers wanting to qualify, which would determine the first fourteen positions for Sunday's race. The remaining entrants would line up alphabetically, according to their last names. If your last name was Aardvark, you stood a good chance of starting the race in the fifteenth position. If your last name was Zyla, it was a good bet you'd be starting in the last position.

To my surprise, one of the drivers (not Jimmy Davison) asked for a moment of silence in honor of Carlos Guerrero. I granted that request without hesitation. I gave the drivers a pep talk about their upcoming qualification runs and our race tomorrow. Then Penelope drew our numbers out of the metal ammo box set on the table. My draw was a fifth start in the qualifying runs. I walked to the garage, pushed Nikki out onto the apron, closed and locked the garage door, and cranked Nikki. She fired on the first crank, so I knew she was anxious to run. When our time came, Nikki performed admirably. She took the corners in stride, only getting a little loose in turn 1 a couple of times, and she screamed down the straightaways. Because of her performance, we captured the number 3 position to start tomorrow's race.

I'm not fond of starting races in the number 1—or the *pole* position. I actually prefer starting a race around the fifth position. For that reason, I always compete in the qualifying laps to improve my chances of starting in the front half of the pack. If I didn't run the qualifying laps, and started where M, for Maxxon, would fall alphabetically, that would put me back twentieth or so.

Some drivers say, "If my car is running right, I can win the race even from the last position." And there probably is a grain of truth in that. But, I'm not so pragmatic. I like being more proactive. There is a method to my madness, as I like to say.

*   *   *

Tammy McPherson

Tammy closed the briefcase, wrapped it in the spare blanket, and stuffed it onto the small shelf in the closet. She'd added $750 from last night's action, and she'd add even more than that tonight. She'd take the briefcase back to the train station tomorrow morning. She worried about keeping the cash in her room even for one night, but the housekeeper had cleaned the room earlier, and no one should bother it.

She sensed the real danger was the missing money from Carlos's office. If Hermosa or the cops went looking for it, whoever had the money would become their prime suspect. Would they get a search warrant to look through her stuff? So far, Sergeant Hoppy had not asked Tammy for a new address, so no one knew where she was living.

Hoppy apparently believed Tammy still resided in her old condo. But the cops probably already knew that Carlos owned the condo she lived in, because of property deeds. Her biggest worry was the ledger sheets Carlos had kept as part of his books. *Where had Carlos stashed those damn ledger sheets?*

Carlos was adept at not leaving tracks. He kept books—one set for show and one set for real. But Carlos had a penchant for not entering cash items into either set of books when they happened.

Those damn ledger sheets could put me back in jail.

The room was closing in on her, and she needed to get out of the room. She'd take a quick shower and then decide whether to go to Dino's Bar or the Speedway Grill and Lounge. They were an equal distance away, one east and one west. She stood and patted her hair, as she walked past the mirror on the wall above the beat-up old dresser. She glanced in the closet, trying to decide which dress to wear.

Her cell phone rang. She looked at the number and punched the talk button.

"This is Mac, darlin'," the voice said. "You and I got it on a couple of weeks ago, and I'd like an encore."

"How soon?" Tammy asked.

"I was thinking we could meet at Dino's in about an hour, have a drink, then go to your room."

"That'll work," Tammy said.

She hung up and walked into the bathroom. She patted her hair, as she looked into the dingy mirror. She opened her cell phone and speed-dialed a number.

"Capri Motel."

"Yes, this is Tabatha Harris. I need to use a room about seven. One-twenty-five. Okay. Thanks."

Tammy decided a short soak in a hot bubble bath was the way to go.

*   *   *

Kurt Maxxon, Christina and the boys

The vote was four to zero in favor of supper at the Plantation Restaurant, a huge old antebellum home a few blocks southeast of the downtown area. It always reminds me of Tara, in *Gone with the Wind;* the wait staff dresses as if they are on the set of the movie. There is a Scarlett O'Hara, and a Rhett Butler, running around, as well as other characters from the movie.

An addition at the back of the old house nearly triples the dining area and has a room devoted to the movie. There are photos of Vivien Leigh, Clark Gable, and all the others, along with black-and-white posters from the era.

The menu represents its heritage. Southern fried chicken, obviously, catfish and hush puppies, shrimp jambalaya, a flavorful crawfish casserole, and a unique recipe for escargot are the main items on the menu. The restaurant enchanted the boys, being a place they'd never been to, and Jacob surmised it was "a fancy place."

The maitre d' said, "Hello, Mrs. Zouhn, Colonel Maxxon. Four for dinner?"

I nodded, and he led us to a corner table next to a window, where he placed huge, colorful menus in front of each setting. The dining room was about three-quarters full, but I knew other diners had likely filled the addition to near capacity.

A waitress arrived and offered booster seats. Jacob accepted one, while Joshua sat up straighter to show he could dine without one. Then the waitress assumed her station next to me and asked what we would like to drink.

Christina ordered a mint julep, I ordered a Diet Coke, and the boys chose milk.

"What's good tonight?" Jacob asked her from his new perch. The rest of us stared at him; Joshua's mouth was agape.

The waitress suppressed a laugh but couldn't stop a wide grin from spreading across her cheeks. "I think, sir, you'll find the fried chicken quite delightful, and the crawfish casserole is very good tonight."

Jacob stared at her and a frown creased his forehead. "Okay," he said, and the waitress left. "What's a crawfish casserole?" he asked.

"Crawfish are like shrimp, just a little smaller and tastier," I said.

"They be crawdaddies," Joshua said, "like down at the river."

Jacob wrinkled his nose. "Ugh. They always are muddy."

I continued studying the menu, even though I was familiar with it and had tried all of the main items. The last few visits I'd feasted on the crawfish casserole. Christina was studying the salad section of the menu. The boys were looking around the room. I looked at the children's menu, which featured smaller portions of all the main entrée items. There were a few combination plates, and the one that caught my eye was the plate with chicken and catfish, with sides of hush puppies and French fries.

"Why didn't you have a mint julep?" Joshua asked.

"I don't drink that stuff," I said. "I just drink Diet Coke, iced tea, and coffee."

"What we gonna eat, Mr. Kurt?" Jacob asked.

"You guys like catfish?" I asked.

"Never had it," Jacob said.

"We have, too," Joshua said. "Remember that time Mama took us to the fish fry at that church down the street?"

"I don't 'member," Jacob said, shaking his head.

The waitress arrived and distributed our drinks. "You ready to order?" she asked.

I nodded to Christina, who ordered two children's plates of chicken and catfish, and a grilled chicken Caesar salad for herself. I ordered the crawfish casserole.

*   *   *

The boys picked at the catfish and devoured the chicken, hush puppies, and French fries. Christina consumed most of her salad, and my plate was clean enough to go right back on the shelf. I shared a bite of my crawfish casserole with the boys, and, while Joshua didn't care for it, Jacob declared the bite delicious and wished he had ordered it. The waitress bussed the table, and the boys chose Georgia mud pie à la mode, while Christina and I declined dessert.

While Christina started to tell me about her meeting on Monday, her gaze strayed over my shoulder, and I turned to see what she was watching. Mike Collins walked up, and I stood to shake his hand.

"Have you heard about Rachael?" Mike asked in a low voice.

I shook my head.

Mike looked at Christina and then to the boys. I said, "Christina, this is Mike Collins; he graduated high school with me and the Rachael he just mentioned."

Christina nodded. The boys just stared.

Mike said, "Let's step outside and talk."

I followed Mike to the smoking patio, and we took seats on the edge, where there was a fresh breeze blowing in.

"Rachael is in jail," Mike said before he was fully seated. "For killing Carlos Guerrero."

"Rachael?"

Mike nodded. I didn't have to ask how he came by the information; Mike is a bail bondsman who owns a fairly large bonding service near the county jail.

"I recognized you sitting there. I'd forgotten this is race weekend, and I thought you might like to know. You asked about her history a few years back."

I nodded again and wished I'd brought my coffee cup, although Mike had also come out without a drink. I asked him, "When was she arrested?"

"Yesterday afternoon—late, I think."

"You have any of the details?"

"Not much," Mike said. "What I've heard is mostly circumstantial. The sheriff probably isn't releasing everything. What little the sheriff is letting out is that they have a skillet they're reasonably sure is the murder weapon, which they found near the dumpster. Rachael's fingerprints are on the skillet. There was a Trattoria take-out box in her fridge, with the remains of an omelet that match the scraps of egg in the skillet. And Rachael was sleeping off a drunk when they went to question her."

"Damn," I said. "If they found the skillet near the dumpster, it would be near where they found Carlos. So there might be a connection."

"Carlos's body was near the dumpster?" Mike asked.

I bobbed my head.

"I didn't know that," he said. "How did you know that?"

"I … was there," I said, hoping not to sound like a braggart. "The two boys at my table in there found Carlos, and they came and got me. We called 9-1-1."

"Double damn," Mike said.

"Maybe I should talk to Damon Hertz," I said, thinking aloud.

"The sheriff's investigator?"

I nodded.

"Why?"

"Rachael isn't the type."

"I'm not sure I'd get involved with Rachael, Kurt. I've told you that before, and now I think it makes even better sense to just walk away and leave her to her own devices."

It sounded like pretty good advice.

*   *   *

Tammy McPherson

Tammy hadn't spent as much time in Dino's as she had other places in the immediate area, and she realized, as she walked in, that it was uncomfortably dark inside. The only lights were the beer signs that covered the three walls opposite the bar. Four concealed lights above the shelf area behind the bar, and spotlights above the mixing area, gave the bartender just enough light to mix drinks.

She stood a moment to let her eyes adjust. As she walked to the first empty booth, several sets of eyes followed her, as she made sure her figure was on display. She gracefully slid into the booth. As she always did, Tammy took her makeup mirror from her purse and, under the guise of checking her makeup, she checked out all the people behind her. Mac should be along any minute, and then she would feel a lot more comfortable.

She noticed the man talking on the pay phone in the corner near the front door and her instincts went on high alert. She looked at the small rectangular table below the wall-mounted pay phone, which was positioned to allow people to write notes while talking. The man sat with his chair leaning back, animatedly talking with the free hand, so engrossed in his conversation that he apparently hadn't seen Tammy enter the bar. The table wobbled as he moved his hand. The man looked so familiar that Tammy felt a chill run up her spine. *Where have I seen that guy before? Where's Mac?*

Another woman entered the bar, and this time the man on the telephone followed the swinging hips as they walked, until his eyes came to Tammy sitting alone in the booth. The man's eyes locked onto Tammy, and the hair on her neck stiffened.

"Ya want something to drink?" the scantily clad waitress behind her asked, startling Tammy out of her reverie. "Oh! Yes, thank you," she said. "A vodka Collins."

The man kept his eyes locked on her; he was sitting still, like a cat ready to pounce. *Was the guy a cop?* The waitress set the drink on a round paper coaster advertising Miller Beer.

"You meeting someone?" she asked.

"Yes."

"You want me to start a tab?"

"Yes. But we won't be long." Tammy hoped the man's eyes would go somewhere else. They didn't. *Damn. Where the hell is Mac?*

People came and went from the bar, and every time, after they'd blocked her view of the man, she would discover him still staring at her. She checked her makeup again to see how the people behind her had rearranged themselves. She thought about Mac. Whatever his real name, he was well off, even though he liked this dingy bar to meet. She knew his type. She doubted Mac was a married man and getting some extra on the side. If she had to guess, she'd say Mac worked hard at his business, and, when he took a break, he wanted a woman.

She glanced towards the man. He was still there, focused on her. *C'mon Mac. Get here.*

The door swung open, and Mac walked in. Stopping to let his eyes adjust, he spotted her and walked to the booth. "Hi, Tabby," he crooned. "How are you?"

"I'm just fine," she said.

Mac slid into the seat across from her. Tammy looked quickly at the man on the phone. He was studying the back of Mac's head. The waitress arrived. "A vodka Collins," Mac told her.

Tammy wished she had just stood up, thrown a few bucks on the table, and told Mac she wanted to leave. The man on the phone had returned to studying her.

The waitress brought Mac his drink. He threw down half of it in one tilt. Tammy remembered the last time she had met Mac. He hadn't wasted a lot of time with drinks. One drink and they had been on the way to her room. He tilted the glass a second time, and she started to relax. She sipped enough of her drink to make it worth paying for, before Mac reached into his pants pocket and extracted a roll of bills. He stripped off several and threw them on the table.

"You ready?" Mac said and slid out of the seat.

Tammy followed Mac to the door, keeping Mac between her and the man on the phone. When she got closer, she was sure she had met him somewhere, but she couldn't remember where or when. The man was hanging the phone up, as they walked out the door.

Mac started to turn to the left, but Tammy took hold of his arm and led him to the right, into the alleyway next to Dino's. They moved down the alley to the back-door alcove into Dino's, and Tammy led Mac into the alcove. She peered around the corner and saw the man from the phone walk past the alley opening at a fast pace.

"That guy on the phone was a cop," Tammy said.

Mac shrugged and lifted an eyebrow. "Oh, yeah."

"I'm pretty sure he's undercover CFPD."

"Well, he can go find his own woman," Mac said, smiling and wrapping his arms around her waist.

Tammy led Mac in a longer, circuitous route to the Capri Motel. Mac hung in the shadows, while she went into the office. In well-practiced moves, Tammy handed the ancient owner of the motel a twenty-dollar bill and got a room key. She went out, and Mac moved beside her.

"What room do we have?" Mac asked.

"On the end. Number 125."

They walked to the room, and Mac took the key from her and opened the door. The room was clean and smelled of French perfume. For the next two hours, Tammy performed well. She sensed that Mac enjoyed himself. But most of the time she was racking her brain. *Where have I seen that guy before?*

*   *   *

Kurt Maxxon, Christina and the boys

When I returned to the table, Christina was telling the boys about her job as the school district's administrator.

"How many kids?" Joshua asked.

"Only about three thousand," Christina said. "Albertstown is a small town."

"That be a lot," Jacob said.

"You guys ready to go?" I asked the table.

Christina helped Jacob out of his booster seat and set him down on the floor. We made our way out the front door, and I felt a few drops of rain. We made it to Christina's car without getting too damp.

"Were we supposed to get rain?" I asked Christina after we'd piled into her car.

"I don't know. I haven't seen a weather report for days."

"How come?"

"The TV quit working, and I haven't done anything about it."

"The boys may have to stay with you tonight," I said.

"Where?" Joshua asked.

"She's got a room on the fourth floor at the Speedway Hotel."

"The Speedway?" the boys said in unison.

"She pretty rich, huh?" Jacob said.

Christina and I choked back guffaws.

"Beau, too?" Joshua said.

"Beau likes to stay with me, in the camper," I said, hoping Beau wouldn't misbehave and prove me wrong.

I took my cell phone out of its holster and speed-dialed the local NOAA pilot's weather number. I put the phone on speaker, and we listened to the computer voice give the surface winds, direction and velocity, the winds aloft, and tell us the ceiling was at five hundred feet. Thunderstorms to the southwest were moving toward us, and those storms might produce quarter-sized hail. The severe weather would last most of the night and into the early morning hours. I worried about delays or cancellations of the race. I also thought about going to the Speedway Hotel myself.

But, in the end, I stayed in the camper and sent the boys and Beau with Christina to spend the night in her room at the Speedway Hotel.

CHAPTER EIGHT

Sunday, September 10

<u>*Kurt Maxxon with Christina and the boys, Morning*</u>

Christina, Beau, and the boys came to get me for breakfast about seven o'clock. After rain most of the night, with occasional gusty winds and small hail, the sky had cleared, and all was calm. The boys had enjoyed Grandma's Café on Friday morning, and, with the help of Christina, outvoted me to go there. I knew Christina wasn't merely catering to the boys' wishes, since she loves the Raggedy Ann and Andy dolls as much as Vicki did and Grandma's is the epicenter of doll collecting in Carpentier Falls.

We trooped into Grandma's and took a large, circular booth in the far corner of the dining room.

"Man, this place be too cool," Jacob said, louder than normal, as he scudded into the middle of the circular seat. Joshua followed him and then pushed Jacob a little further around.

"Yeah, man," Joshua chimed, after annoying his brother. "And the food is excellent, too."

I choked down a chuckle at Joshua's perceptiveness. I went to get a booster seat for Jacob and helped him into it.

The boys bantered back and forth about the merits of having a ham-and-cheese omelet versus ordering ham and eggs.

"Both got hash browns," Joshua said.

"Yeah, but on the omelet, they put cheese on it all," Jacob countered. "I like the cheese."

"With ham an' eggs, you get more ham," Joshua declared, "and more spuds, too."

When the waitress came to take our order, both boys ordered ham and eggs, with their eggs broken yolks and hard.

I ordered the legendary Farm Boy's Special. It consisted of three plate-size pancakes, made from their own recipe of squash-and-blue-cornmeal batter, three fresh, double-yolk eggs, three slices of thick apple-wood-smoked bacon, and three sausage patties the size of saucers. It's only slightly different than the Hungry Man's Breakfast, which features two of everything, plus grits and gravy.

Christina ordered a bowl of oatmeal and a dish of fresh fruit.

"You not hungry?" Joshua asked Christina.

"I'll be just fine," Christina said.

"She eat like a bird," Jacob said.

"She's skinny, too," Joshua said,

I glanced at Christina, who seemed to be taking it in stride.

"She's not skinny," I admonished. "She's very well proportioned."

"Like a big girl s'pose to be, huh?" Joshua said, moving his hand in an hourglass shape.

I paused and said, "Uh, yeah, I guess so."

Christina gave me a *thank-you* look.

After the waitress clanked and banged all the plates in front of us, we ate in relative quiet. The boys were becoming more sophisticated in their eating, mainly, I supposed, because they were no longer worried about when or how the next meal would come. Christina and I chatted about her plans for her upcoming trip to Little Rock. She had meetings here in Carpentier Falls on Monday morning, and then she and a friend would drive to Centralia to fly to Little Rock Tuesday morning. During our conversation, the boys kept us entertained with their banter and questions.

I was so engrossed in my little world that I almost didn't notice the gambler I'd overheard Friday morning. He was sitting alone at a table near the front door, sipping coffee and reading the newspaper. I excused myself from our booth and, carrying my coffee cup, walked over to the man's table. At my approach, the man lowered the paper, glanced at me, and said, "Hello, Colonel Maxxon. I was just reading about the race today. You're starting number 3, huh?"

I nodded, and he leaned forward, as we shook hands. "If you don't mind," I said, "I'd like to ask you a couple of questions."

The man pursed his lip and gestured toward an empty chair. "Oh, sure, you want to sit down? My name is Dick Schaeffer, by the way."

"I'm pleased to meet you," I said, sitting in a chair opposite him. "Last Friday morning, I couldn't help overhearing you and another man talking about being at the Trattoria the night before."

"Oh, sure. Yeah, that's something, ole Rachael knocking Carlos off," he said, holding his cup so the waitress could refill it. I did the same.

"You know Rachael?"

"Oh, sure." Dick sipped coffee and then watched the cup back to the saucer. "She came around a lot."

Since she was a boozer, it made sense, although I had to wonder why she would go to a high-class bar like the Trattoria, rather than one of the neighborhood dives nearer to where she lived. "Why was she at the Trattoria?" I asked.

"To see Carlos. Rumor has it that she loaned Carlos some money. But Carlos couldn't pay her back, because he was being blackmailed by some woman who had his baby years ago. I never really bought in on that theory."

"Was she there Thursday night?"

"Oh, sure, she was there. But she left early, I think. She didn't stay too long."

"What did she do while she was there?"

"Sat near the bar," Dick said, grabbing his coffee cup, "drinking."

"Doesn't the bar close at 10:30?"

"Oh, sure, on the restaurant side. But there's a cash bar in the meeting rooms. It's open as long as there are people around." I nodded understanding. "From what I overheard, I surmised you might be talking about gambling going on at the Trattoria." I paused to see if I had touched a nerve. When Dick didn't react, I continued, "And then I have another source that tells me there may have been betting on the car races going on at the Trattoria. Do you know anything about that?"

"You working with the police?"

"No. No, I'm just making some inquiries," I said. "If there has been betting on the races there, then it behooves me, and other drivers, to be careful about going there. I'm the president of the SRVSCRA, and I'd just like to know what's going on."

"Oh, sure," Dick said, nodding his head. "I never bet on the races, but there's a bookie at the Trattoria, usually, I think Friday nights, taking bets on football games, basketball games, you name it. College and pro. He makes book on the car races at the track, too. Me, I just play a little poker, that's all. I don't get into anything else."

"How does it all work?" I asked. "I mean, it's mainly a restaurant, right?"

"Oh, sure," Dick said. "Thursday, Friday, and Saturday nights, Carlos lets 'em use the meeting rooms. They set up tables for poker, mainly. There is a blackjack counter over near the bar. And I've seen guys on their knees in the corner, shooting craps. That's too hard on my old knees," he said, chuckling to himself. The bartender was kinda in charge of the whole operation."

"Was Carlos there, too?"

"No. Carlos never came in while the gambling was going on."

"But he knew it was happening."

"Oh, sure. Hell, even the cops knew it was happening."

I glanced at Dick to see his expression. Calm, unafraid. "So the cops knew there was gambling at the Trattoria, but they didn't do anything about it."

"Nawh. Why should they? It was pretty much just friendly, local games. No one ever complained about it." He sipped coffee for a minute. "Well," he said, "that ain't quite true, either. One time a woman complained to the police that her husband had lost all the grocery money there one Saturday night. The police turned it over to the sheriff's department, since it's in the county. They leaned on Carlos to not let guys like that in. Carlos, he leaned on the barkeep. It got tough to get in for a while."

"Just the old-timers that Carlos knew?"

"Well, those the barkeep knew." Dick quieted as the waitress neared with the coffeepot and accepted another refill. I shook her off. "Carlos stayed away and just let the house get the drink and snack business. But it was usually the same bunch of people. You know, it was rare when someone new showed up. And someone already there had to vouch for them."

I searched my memory and recalled the conversation. "If I remember correctly, your friend mentioned something about his girl didn't show up. Mind telling me what that was about?"

"Oh, sure," he said. "There were call girls that came to the Trattoria to meet up with some of the guys. I never used them, but LeRoy was a regular customer. His girl didn't show up Thursday night, so he had to just go home and go to bed—alone."

"Was the prostitution in any way connected to the Trattoria?"

"I can't say, for sure," Dick said. "I never really paid any attention. But if I was forced to guess, I'd say Carlos probably was around the edges, just like the gambling. But you really need to talk to LeRoy about that."

"Who is LeRoy?"

"LeRoy Kitchens," he said. "The other guy you heard talking Friday morning."

"Would you tell me how to contact LeRoy?"

"Oh, sure," Dick said and dug out his wallet. He fished out a slip of paper and gave me LeRoy's phone number.

"Is it all right for me to tell LeRoy I talked with you and you gave me his number?"

"Oh, sure. Go ahead. Me and LeRoy work at the packing plant south of town from four to midnight. We work Saturday through Wednesday nights. He's out of town today. You can probably get hold of him tomorrow about three in the afternoon."

I thanked Dick for the information and went back to the booth.

"That guy was here the last time we was," Joshua said.

"He was," I confirmed. "I needed to ask him some questions."

"You be a detective?" Jacob asked.

"No. I'm just an interested bystander," I said.

Christina gave me a quizzical look that warned me she wanted to know what was going on, when the time allowed.

We drove to the track, and I opened up the camper. Beau was happy to be free again and even happier that the boys were back to play with him. Beau tried to wear out the boys by claiming three tennis balls at once. Of course, Beau didn't win that game, since he always had to leave two of the balls behind, as he chased the third one thrown, but he was having fun.

Christina went in to clean up the camper, which was her standard procedure whenever she got near it. Lately, I've had a clean camper on the second and fourth weekends of the month.

I saw Maurey Kennedy's white truck drive back to the garage, so I put Beau inside the camper and told Christina I was taking the boys to the garage. We walked toward my garage. There were several other drivers working on their cars in the garages, as well as even more who didn't rent a garage but worked on their cars in the general area between the RV lot and the garages.

We saw Maurey unlock the garage door and walk in. The boys and I arrived, and we pushed Nikki out onto the apron. Maurey lifted the hood, propped it open, and then walked to his truck. When he returned, he had two car ramps, which he set next to the fenders, so the boys could stand on them. Then he went for his toolbox and the test equipment.

The boys each walked up a ramp and marveled at the view they had.

"These be pretty neat, huh?" Joshua said.

"Where'd you get them?" I asked.

"Down at the parts store," Maurey said, looking at me as if I were a dunce.

"We have them in our store over in Centralia," I said.

"Yeah, but we needed them *now.*"

"Okay." I can tell when I'm in a battle not worth fighting.

Maurey checked Nikki over and declared her the winner. "No need to run the race—right there's the winner."

The boys looked at Maurey.

"Mr. Kurt said you gotta run the race, or else it not be worth the trouble for all the other drivers to come here," Joshua said.

Maurey looked at me, raised his left eyebrow, and then said to the boys, "That's right. And you boys should remember what Mr. Kurt tells you."

"Go ahead and fire her up," Maurey said.

The boys both swung to look at me. "We gotta move back, like Saturday," Joshua said to Jacob. I nodded and climbed into the cockpit. The boys moved back. I went through the process of starting Nikki.

For the next several minutes, Maurey fussed over Nikki, while the boys and I watched. Using a tiny screwdriver, Maurey made adjustments here and there. Then Maurey straightened up and sliced his right hand, with two fingers saluting, across his throat. I moved to lean in and shut Nikki off. The boys rushed to my side, standing on tiptoes to look into the driver's compartment. I lifted Jacob into the seat again and watched as he replayed the first time, left hand on the steering wheel, right hand on the gear shifter. He yelled a couple of *vahroooms* with gusto. I lifted Jacob out and lifted Joshua in. He repeated his first time also.

"She's ready to win this one," Maurey declared while toting his toolboxes back to his truck. He would drive into the pit area of the track and set up for the race.

"Who are your helpers?" I heard a familiar voice ask, and I turned to see Terry Grossman walking toward the garage. Marguerite walked beside him. The boys watched them approach.

"They are my pit crew extraordinaire," I said, smiling broadly, as I shook hands with Marguerite and then Terry.

"They look like they can handle it," Marguerite said. She looked at Joshua and then Jacob. "What's your name?" she said to Jacob. Jacob cowered back a little. "He be Jake," Joshua said.

"And what's your name?" she asked.

"I'm Joshua," he said.

"Jacob and Joshua," Marguerite said. "Those are nice names. What's your last name?" she asked.

"Lawton," Joshua said. Jacob nodded.

Marguerite said, "You live near the track?"

Joshua looked at me.

"We need to talk about that," I said to Marguerite. She frowned slightly, as I continued. "Joshua and Jacob, this is Marguerite and Terry Grossman, from Kings Rapids."

Both boys beamed. A little respect never hurts.

"Marguerite is the chief of police in Kings Rapids."

The boys' eyes flew open. "The chief of police!" Jacob stammered.

I bobbed my head.

"A cop," Joshua said, eyeing me suspiciously.

Marguerite smiled.

"How many cops work for you?" Joshua asked.

"Ninety-three," Marguerite said.

Joshua's eyes grew even larger. "That's a lot."

"Kings Rapids is a big city," Marguerite said. "Bigger than Carpentier Falls."

Terry walked around Nikki as if able to sense any problems she might have. He'd watched Maurey make that walk several times, and

I think he wished he was as adept as Maurey. "Is Nikki going to win today?"

"Naturally," I said. "She's ready, and so am I."

"Christina at the camper?" Marguerite asked, lifting her head in that direction.

"Yes. She's expecting you."

Marguerite left and walked briskly toward the camper. The boys helped Maurey get the ramps into the back of his truck. We watched him drive toward the track passageway.

Terry, the boys, and I walked back to the camper. It was nearly time for me to go to the drivers' lounge to facilitate the drivers' pre-race meeting. For September, the temperature was reasonably mild. Upper 80s. Good racing weather. The track had been in pretty good shape during the qualifying runs yesterday, and, while several drivers had run practice laps into the evening and early this morning, I doubted the track had changed much. One driver had blown an engine leaving the pit area and spread oil on the approach to the track. The maintenance people had worked most of the morning putting down Oil-Dri, scrubbing, and vacuuming it up.

As did most of the drivers, I carried my race rags in a duffel bag and put them on just before the race started. I'd left the duffel bag in Nikki, and I would change by closing the garage door.

When we got to the camper, Terry walked to the ice chest and dug out two cans of Budweiser. He opened one, handed it to Marguerite, and then opened the second one for himself. Since they started visiting us at several races around the league, Christina has learned to cater to Terry and Marguerite's fondness for beer.

At the *whoosh* sound of the first beer can opening, I noticed that Joshua and Jacob exchanged fearful glances. *I'd have to find out the reason.*

To avoid distractions, the drivers had agreed years ago not to bring their children to the pre-race meeting. Neither of the boys understood why such a rule could exist, and I explained that rules existed because someone took unfair advantage of a liberty. I left the boys, Christina,

Marguerite, and Terry at the camper and made my way to the drivers' lounge.

Before I entered the drivers' lounge, I glanced back toward the camper and saw the boys were off again playing fetch with Beau. I felt relieved they had not taken the meeting rule personally. Christina, Marguerite, and Terry were sitting at the picnic table watching the boys. Terry was draining his beer. He'd agreed to take the boys over to the pit area and turn them over to Maurey, who should be all set up and could pay attention to them. It wasn't unusual for drivers to have their children in the pit area, especially those whose wives helped time them and so forth. The kids were okay as long as they stayed behind the concrete wall and out of the way of everyone else. If children strayed even close to danger, however, they and their mother would have an escort to the stands for the rest of the race. It's dangerous enough for the drivers.

The SRVSCRA likes kids, when they aren't in danger of getting hurt. I've started a program of having drivers go to various schools around the valley to talk to the kids about safe driving. Nearly all the drivers, owners, and sponsors support the program. Young children around the racetrack are always a worry for me—and for all the SRVSCRA officials.

CHAPTER NINE

Sunday, September 10

Kurt Maxxon, Pre-Race

I was sitting on the pit wall, trying to stay cool and doing my mental relaxation calisthenics. My late wife, Vicki, had been a geography whiz, so when I first started racing, she'd ask me stupid questions, like: "In what state is New York City?" Then, when I started competing seriously in the SRVSCRA, Vicki started teaching me the capital cities of the fifty states. Now, a dozen years later, I sat mentally going through them, eventually getting to: Charleston, West Virginia; Madison, Wisconsin; Cheyenne, Wyoming. It wasn't exactly like a hypnotic trance, but it did give me a clear-the-brainwaves-of-trash feeling.

Maurey and the boys were puttering with Nikki. Maurey had shown the boys how to check the tire pressure in all four tires and write it on the chart. Maurey explained to them how the right front tire would be the one doing all the work, so it needed a little extra pressure. The rear tires needed lower pressure, so they would help keep the car from slipping in the turns. Joshua and Jacob both hung on every word Maurey uttered.

"We be the pit crew, extra … something, huh?" Joshua said.

"Yep. The pit crew extraordinaire," Maurey said.

Joshua and Jacob were beaming, watching and emulating Maurey.

He'd rounded up two extra handheld timers for the boys to use. Both boys were ready to record my lap times and do other things Maurey asked of them.

Maurey had somehow rounded up a Texas Rangers ball cap for each boy. "To keep your head cool," Maurey told them, pointing to the sun, which was bright and directly overhead. The rain that had fallen most of the night had ended about five this morning and had cooled the air to a comfortable temperature for the fans. I surveyed the grandstand opposite pit row and saw most of the seats occupied. If the bleachers on the back straightaways had as many people, we would have a crowd of forty to fifty thousand people. A crowd like that means an excellent purse, or prize money, for the first five finishers.

The crowd noise died down, as the track's announcer requested attention to the colors and a local vocalist doing a creditable rendition of the Star-Spangled Banner. After an invocation given by a local Methodist minister, the crowd noise rose again. Three dozen cars without mufflers roaring to life would drown out their noise.

When the call came to start our engines, the boys stood on tiptoes and gawked into the dark cockpit. They jabbered about things I couldn't follow. Before I did anything else, Maurey shooed the boys over the pit wall and followed them. I then switched on the electrical system, turned on the fuel pump, and levered the starter switch. Nikki fired on the first crank, which was a sure sign she was ready to run.

When we moved to follow the pace car, Maurey gave his standard two-finger salute, which the boys quickly emulated as well as they could. I blew a kiss to my missing wife's spirit standing behind the wall, as usual, and then touched a kiss to my fingers and planted it on Nikki's dash. "You ready to run?" I asked Nikki.

I thought I heard a very clear "You bet."

I was in the third position, behind Hermann Nordstradt, in the number 88 Ford Taurus, on the pole, and Sean Forester, driving the number 29 Pontiac Grand Prix. Running behind me were Jeffry Depeuw, in the Number 25 Dodge Intrepid; Richardo Romez, in the number 85 Chevy Monte Carlo; and Vince Jackson, in the number 60 Dodge Intrepid. Jeffry Depeuw, nicknamed "the Skunk," for reasons I had yet to learn, was a rookie driver who was on his way to a great future in auto racing.

During the first half of the heat, I didn't pick up on the boys standing behind the wall of my pit stall. The racing was intensely competitive, and I couldn't take my eyes off the track long enough. But, later, when we had settled into a follow-the-leader, more relaxed pattern of racing, I caught glimpses of them holding their timers and violently clicking at the precise moment I crossed the number 27 line marked on the outside wall. Even the most experienced timer never caught the exact times. The idea of timing during a race is to note the relative time between me and other cars ahead or behind me.

I pulled into the pit for the rest period between the first and second heats. I noticed that both boys sported blue shop rags hanging from the right hip pockets of their new blue jeans—just like their mentor, Maurey Kennedy. I had to chuckle at that discovery. They probably had them there at the start of the race, but I had been too focused on relaxing to notice. I really chuckled about halfway through the break. Maurey did his signature mopping of his bald pate, brow, and neck with his blue shop rag, and of course, the boys swiped at their hair, foreheads, and necks, just like Maurey.

Maurey and the boys checked the tire pressure in each tire and recorded it on the clipboard. Maurey decreed the right front tire needed a little more air, and he showed the boys how to add air, about two psi at a time. Then they let some air out of the left rear tire. Nikki was ready to go for the second heat.

There had been some position changes behind us, but the first seven cars were running in the same order at the end of the first heat as at the start of the race. Maurey told me that, out of the twenty-nine starters, two had dropped out of the race due to mechanical problems. Even though it was September, the heat didn't affect the race the way it had in many other races. Of course, in the cockpit, the temperature was always extremely uncomfortable. I'd sweated enough to thoroughly soak my Nomex racing suit.

*   *   *

Christina Zouhn

Christina knew Terry Grossman, and Kurt's other friends, were high up in the stands to see as much of the racetrack as they could. Joshua and Jacob were with Maurey Kennedy in Kurt's pit stall, clocking lap times and helping wherever they could. She also knew that Marguerite, like herself, came to the races to satisfy the man in her life, not to watch the race. The second heat was just underway, with Kurt running in the third position, a place he liked to be at this point in the race. Christina decided it was time to have the heart-to-heart talk with Marguerite, since she'd promised Kurt she would. The crowd roar made it difficult, but she would manage.

"What do you think of the boys?" Christina asked as she sat down.

"They're adorable," Marguerite answered. "But I'm terribly concerned about their future."

"As are Kurt and I," Christina said, glancing toward the track, as the crowd roared. She watched the cars come into view around the third turn. Kurt was still running third, so whoever the crowd was cheering was further back in the pack and of no interest. She turned back to Marguerite.

"What is Kurt thinking to do with them?" Marguerite asked, keeping her focus on Christina.

"First, he wants suggestions from you and Terry, and your help. I'm reasonably sure he does not want to just turn them over to the social services people here in Carpentier Falls. There have been so many horror stories about social services in the newspaper, and Kurt's worried about them falling through the proverbial cracks. Plus, there's the issue of keeping them together. The boys have already told Kurt that if they are split up to different homes, they'll just run away any chance they get."

Marguerite nodded. "It's tough placing siblings together in foster homes. In Kings Rapids, we do have a couple of foster families that have done it, but it's always chancy."

"Kurt would like the four of us to sit down this evening and discuss what we think is best for the boys, and then figure out how to do it."

Marguerite grinned, "If you asked Terry right now, I'd almost bet he'd say, 'Hell, I'll take 'em home with me.' But I think our first efforts should be to find their mother, or some family. If we can't do that, then I'd be agreeing with Terry."

"I agree finding relatives is important, Marguerite," Christina said, "but what makes you think they're abandoned children?"

"There are several things that make me feel that way," Marguerite said. "Mainly, they were on their own here in Carpentier Falls, living under bridges. They obviously have no connections here. The boys also seem fearful of something, perhaps an abusive father. Where did their mother go? Why? I'm very concerned about them for those reasons and many others I've seen in my years of law enforcement."

"We have to discuss who takes charge of them. They could become a burden. Do you and Terry have time to manage them—with school and all, and the demands of your job and Terry's business?"

"It probably would be easier for us than most," Marguerite said. "The city employee's children's center is on the first floor of my building. The older children go to school from there and return there in the afternoon. The important thing about that arrangement is the boys would be under control at all times."

"That's a good point," Christina said, letting her face lighten. "I'm amazed you and Terry have already thought this through so far, but I'm happy you have. Kurt will be, too. We can discuss our ideas tonight."

"Yes," Marguerite agreed, quietly bowing her head. "Terry and I have seen stray kids in our business. As singles, we didn't feel we could do much about them. Since we got married, we've tried to help in several situations, and most have worked out well. When we met the boys this morning, and Kurt told us their story, well, Terry and I both knew we were going to have a part in this."

"Your support will make Kurt feel so much better," Christina said. They watched as Maurey Kennedy led the two boys up the steps to them.

The two boys flopped down into empty seats.

"These two pit crew guys are plumb tuckered out," Maurey said. "And there's not much left to do in the pits. So they said they wanted to come over here to watch the rest of the race."

"We're happy to have you join us, Joshua and Jacob," Christina said.

"Mr. Kurt's leading," Joshua reported.

"He gonna win by a lot," Jacob added.

Christina smiled. "That's great."

Maurey excused himself and went back down the steps to the pit area. The four of them watched the race in silence.

Eventually, Marguerite asked, "Do you boys have any idea where your mother went?"

The boys looked at each other. "No, ma'am," Joshua answered reluctantly. Marguerite smiled at him. "We need to find her, don't we?" she said gently.

Both boys brightened. "Think we can?" Jacob asked.

"We're going to try," Marguerite said. "I think I know a little about how to do it. If I don't, well, Mr. Terry sure does."

"That'll be great," Joshua shouted above the sudden crowd noise, clapping his hands.

"Can you tell me how tall your mother is?" Marguerite asked.

"About the same as Mrs. Christina," Joshua said.

Knowing that children's perceptions of adults change as they grow older, Marguerite guessed the boys' mother was a petite woman. "Can you tell me what color of hair she had?" she asked.

"We got a picture," Jacob said.

"A picture of your mother?" Marguerite said.

"Yeah," the boys said almost in unison.

"Can I see it?" Marguerite asked.

"Sure. It be in our box, under the picnic table by Mr. Kurt's camper," Joshua said.

"Can we get it now?" Marguerite asked.

"Yeah," Joshua said. "I'm tired of racing."

"Me, too," Jacob chimed in.

Christina led Marguerite and the boys out of the grandstand and through the passageway to the RV lot. The boys ran ahead and shot under their picnic table fortress. They emerged just as Christina and Marguerite arrived, and Joshua handed Marguerite a small, two-by-three, mall kiosk picture. Marguerite studied the photograph. "That's your mother?" she said. Both boys bobbed their heads. "Yeah," Joshua said. Christina had noted that Marguerite's face clouded as she looked at the picture.

Beau barked softly from inside the camper, so Christina opened the door and let him come down the steps to join the crowd. He bounced around from person to person, sniffing at each to make sure he knew them. After receiving a friendly pat from each, he strolled over and laid down in the shade under the picnic table with his head cradled in his front paws.

"Do you know how long ago this picture was taken?" Marguerite asked.

"Last year," Joshua said.

"Where was it taken?"

"In the mall," Joshua said.

"In Carpentier Falls here?"

"The place Mr. Kurt took us to buy these new clothes," Jacob said.

Joshua bobbed his head. "Out past where we used to live."

Christina stood and said, "The race is about over. Let me go over to the track. You boys stay here with Mrs. Marguerite."

The boys climbed under the picnic table and started scratching and petting Beau.

"They are darling little boys," Marguerite said as she walked with Christina to the RV area gate. When they were out of earshot of the boys, Marguerite said, "I've seen their mother's picture somewhere. Possibly on a wanted notice or something like that."

"I hope not," Christina said, over her shoulder, as she hurried toward the track.

*   *   *

Kurt Maxxon, Sunday Race

We started the second heat running pretty much in the same order—until lap 19. Whitney Rasmussen, running the number 71 Ford Taurus in the twenty-second position, blew a tire and went hard into the wall on turn 2. I was on the opposite side of the track when it happened, and when I came around, under the caution lights, I saw how crumpled up the car was. I hoped Whitney hadn't suffered any serious injuries. As I came around the next time, the hydraulic jaws had pried the roof up enough that I saw Whitney climb out, apparently none the worse for the experience.

From that point on, the second heat felt punctuated by severe mishaps. On lap 25, two cars tried to occupy the same space coming out of turn 3, which sent both spinning into the infield. The twelfth-place number-10 car, driven by Mason Smith, was too damaged to return to the race. The thirteenth-position number-77 car, driven by Don Percy, eventually returned to limp around the track to get a finish.

In the reordered restart, nothing changed in the first five positions, but six through ten became a lap-by-lap tossup.

When I rolled in for the break between the second and final heat, I was soaking wet and tired. *You may be getting too old for this stuff, Maxxon,* the left side of my brain said. *Bullshit,* the right side of my brain said. *This is fun. Driving a hundred miles per hour around the track is neat. Remember the six-hundred-mile-per-hour flights? Over Vietnam? Over Kuwait?*

Whenever my mind starts mixing metaphors, or experiences best forgotten, like Vietnam and Kuwait, I always try to regain control as quickly as possible. As I stopped in my pit stall, I realized the boys and Maurey Kennedy were springing into action. I had duties to perform during this stop, too, and I did remember to leave the engine running, so Maurey could do his intensive listening and analyzing routine with the hood up.

The SRVSCRA rules only allow you to raise the hood for nonemergency checks during the break between the second and final heat. Every car on pit row had its hood up. Maurey always checks Nikki stem to stern during this break, asking her how she feels. "How are things working? Are there any problems?" And he listens to her responses.

I climbed out of the oven-like cockpit and stood watching Maurey instructing the boys on being master mechanics. Maurey listened to Nikki's engine. The boys cocked their heads to listen. Maurey walked to one side and leaned in to listen more intently. The boys galloped behind Maurey, and, again, cocked their heads to listen. But Jacob gave me a *what-are-we-listening-for?* look.

After a few minutes, Maurey slashed his fingers across his throat, and I went over, leaned in, and shut Nikki down. Then I went to my normal task of changing tires, while Maurey leaned into Nikki's engine compartment and started adjusting screws and other things. The boys hung with Maurey. I had to fill Nikki up with gas.

Maurey and the boys finished tweaking Nikki. "Okay, young lady," Maurey crooned to Nikki, "You've got this one in the bag. You're going to win it; just be patient and do what Kurt asks you to." He leaned out from under the hood, grasped the braces, and closed Nikki's hood. He latched it shut and then grabbed the blue shop rag from his hip pocket to wipe his hands. Two small pairs of hands grabbed their blue shop rags from their hip pockets and wiped their hands clean.

I laughed so hard it might have relaxed me more than reciting the state capitals. The three of them looked at me as if the heat had affected my brain.

I hadn't paid any attention, so I didn't realize until we lined up to roll for the restart of the third heat that Jimmy Davison had moved his number-89 Trattoria car into the tenth position. The third heat began uneventfully and moved along at a rapid pace through the first ten laps. I was still running in third position, which was fine with me at this point in the race. Then problems came, with a blown tire that resulted in a seven-car mix-up. The SRVSCRA has a mandatory three-lap caution rule, so even minor mishaps slow down the race. But, in this one, the seven cars had severe damage, and it took five laps to get it all cleaned up.

On the restart at lap 16, after the long delay, I caught both Nordstradt and Forester asleep at the switch, and I vaulted past both of them into the lead position. Even though it was only lap 17, I decided to assume the winning mentality early.

All but one of the front-running ten cars had changed positions, like the scattering that happens when the music stops in musical chairs. Only Hermann Nordstradt, in the number-88 car, kept his second-place spot. All the rest jumbled themselves into a new running order, with me in the lead.

When you're running in the pack, you stay focused mainly on the track and cars in front of you. When you become the leader, you have to split your focus between the empty track ahead of you and the cars trying to run you over from behind.

We ran laps 16 through 23 in nearly single-file formation. Then, in turn 1 of lap 24, someone caused a pileup that took out two more cars. Between wrecks and attrition, I estimated that only fifteen cars were still running, counting the wounded number-77 car.

In the rearview mirror, I saw the car painted with the distinctive Cuban flag's red triangle and white and blue stripes. Jimmy Davison, who had started in the eighteenth position, had just moved into the seventh position. I grinned with satisfaction. "Go for it, Jimmy," I yelled above the roar of Nikki's engine.

In lap 37, Drew Westlake, who had moved up to the fifth position, saw an opportunity going into turn 3 to go low and slingshot himself into the second position. Jimmy Davison had been drafting Drew closely for several laps; he apparently saw the same opportunity, and he stuck to Drew like glue, moving into the third position. Jimmy and Drew were both driving an exceptional race, and I nudged Nikki a little and said, "Those two boys are going to give us a run for our money."

As I came out of turn 3 on lap 39 and accelerated down the long, arcing straightaway ahead, a smoky spinning car headed for the infield caught my eye in the rearview mirror. Sean Forester's number-29 car came to a dust-enshrouded stop about the same time I arrived in the area. I could tell from the way it happened that Sean had lost his tires; he would probably call it a day.

The yellow caution lights came on. We'd get a three-lap breather. We'd restart the race on lap 42, which meant we'd have eight laps of the hardest racing all day to get to the finish. "Are you ready?" I shouted to Nikki. She responded with a leap forward.

My Nomex suit felt like lead. My skid lid was compressing my sweat-soaked head. I wanted to take a nap or something—anything other than being on this track right now, leading the race with two talented young drivers challenging me.

Are you ready, old man? my brain asked.

You better believe he's ready! Someone said in my head.

"It's just you and me, Nikki," I yelled above Nikki's roar. "Let's do it."

As we came out of turn 3 toward the start/finish line to restart at lap 42, I surveyed the cars running behind me in my rearview mirror. I suddenly felt pleased that Jimmy Davison had his number-89 car in the third position—and even more pleased to see my old friend, Eugenios Christofides, the Greek, running his number-114 car in the tenth position. We restarted without excitement and ran follow-the-leader for the next four laps. In lap 46, cars started passing one another so fast, I couldn't keep up with who was doing what to whom. The cars immediately behind me in, the second through fourth positions, tagged along behind me as if I were pulling them by chains. When Rocky Balloossah's number-2 car went almost sideways and then straightened out, I tensed, waiting for the yellow lights to come on. I relaxed and felt relieved when they didn't. We only had four laps left to go, and if the yellow came on now for anything trivial, the fans would be furious.

The cars behind me continued to reorganize themselves occasionally. My main focus was on the number-89 car now running in second place, and the number-60 car running a close third. They looked to be teaming up against me, so I would have to be careful on each of the turns. They could not take me on the straightaways. Everyone in the league knew my engines were the best that could be had, built by Maurey Kennedy exclusively for me, and damn hard to beat flat-out down a straightaway. The turns, however, were a whole different story.

We started the final lap with me in first, Jimmy Davison in second, Vince Jackson in third, Oscar Danielson in fourth, and Eugenios Christofides in fifth—the money positions. In turn 1, Vince Jackson tried to slingshot low to pass me and Jimmy from the third position, but he didn't make it before we were on the short shoot straightaway between turns 1 and 2. Jackson and I raced each other, and I pulled three-quarters of a car length ahead, on engine alone. As Jackson slowed me down in my draft, Jimmy went high and was able to pass Jackson and me. Jackson and I raced each other, giving Jimmy an advantage. Since I had the middle line, Jackson had to ease up and fall in behind me going into turn 3. Danielson took advantage of the draft and dived low to slingshot past Jackson into the third position.

We were a hundred and fifty yards from the finish line, and Jimmy Davison couldn't go any faster. I thought about passing him, and probably could have, but I eased up slightly on the gas pedal and followed Jimmy Davison across the finish line a car length ahead of me.

Jimmy had just won the biggest race of his life—his first in the SRVSCRA—but, more importantly, a big one for Carlos Guerrero.

"Way to go, guy," I yelled to Jimmy as I cruised past him on his victory lap. I doubt he heard me, though; it looked to me as though he was laughing and crying at the same time, while pounding the hell out of the steering wheel.

That's exactly what I would have been doing.

*　　*　　*

Christina Zouhn

The crowd noise ebbed and roared, as the cars flashed past different sections of the grandstands. Christina returned to her seat and distractedly watched. Marguerite's words occupied her mind. "I've seen their mother's picture somewhere, possibly on a wanted notice or something like that." The noise level increased and then died away.

Suddenly realizing that the race was over, Christina hurried toward the winner's circle, where she expected Kurt would be arriving any minute. The dense crowd slowed her. After she made her way through the crowd surrounding the circle, she realized it wasn't Kurt's car being guided into the center. It was the number-89 Trattoria car, driven by Jimmy Davison.

Christina moved back to the edge of the crowd and looked down into the pit area. The red-over-white number-27 car was sitting in Kurt's pit stall. She jogged the rest of the way and arrived to find Kurt just getting out of his soaked Nomex racing suit. Maurey Kennedy was helping him. Kurt had removed his crash helmet, and his face and head were red, flushed, and sweaty.

"What happened?" she said between gasps for air.

"He gave the race to Jimmy," Maurey growled.

"I did not," Kurt said. "I screwed up. I was in the wrong gear to accelerate out of turn 4. That's all. Jimmy did it all right."

"Right," Maurey said. "You want me to pull Nikki home and get ready for Jamesboro?"

"If you would," Kurt said. "I'm going to stay in town here to see how the Carlos Guerrero thing works out."

"You probably thought that would surprise me, huh?" Maurey said, letting a wan smile break his stern set of lips.

Christina looked at Maurey. "You have Gatorade?"

"In the truck," he said, waving a hand at his pickup parked near the pit stall. As she approached the pickup truck, Christina noted that Maurey already had hitched Nikki's enclosed transporter behind it. She dug two containers of lemon Gatorade from an ice chest on the floor of the truck bed. As she walked back toward the two men, she realized that, when it came to racing, and especially *their car*, Nikki, Kurt and Maurey shared the same goals.

Kurt took one of the Gatorades and drank it down without stopping. Christina took the lid off the second and handed it to him. Kurt took a long draw and then said, "I've got to go down and congratulate Jimmy. Thanks for hauling Nikki home for me, Maurey. I'll see you in a couple of days."

Christina walked with Kurt toward the winner's circle. She knew losing didn't bother Kurt as much as it did many other drivers. When he won, Kurt was gracious. When he lost, he was even more gracious. However, she doubted Kurt Maxxon had ever been in the wrong gear, no matter where he was or what he was doing. Something else had happened here, and she sensed it was something Kurt didn't want to talk about—*now or ever.*

CHAPTER TEN

Sunday, September 10

Kurt Maxxon, Evening

In the hubbub at the end of the race, I led Christina, and we made our way to Jimmy's pit to congratulate him on his win. As we shook hands, he said, "You're all invited to the celebration party at the Trattoria."

I paused for a heartbeat and then decided, *What the hell? There's nothing wrong in me accepting.* "We'll be there," I said.

"Bring anyone you want," Jimmy called after us as we walked away.

Back in my own pit, I told Maurey about the invitation to the Trattoria. Maurey bowed out and accepted responsibility of getting Nikki home to Albertstown, so he could "start getting her ready for Jamesboro in two weeks." I accepted congratulations from all who offered them; I then left Nikki in Maurey's hands and started toward the drivers' lounge. Then I realized the boys weren't around.

"Marguerite and Terry are with them," Christina said, "watching them play with Beau over at the camper."

I wound my way to the lounge, showered, and put on clean, dry clothes. While I showered, I realized I hadn't paid much attention to the people in my pit. Had I invited everyone?

Once again, I fell back on my chief backup, Christina Zouhn. If I'd missed anyone, I was sure she would invite those who should be there. I was relying more and more on Christina for order in my life.

We had a couple of hours, so I relaxed, unwound from the race, and rehydrated my body. Marguerite and Terry excused themselves to go to their hotel and change clothes for dinner. Joshua and Jacob romped with Beau, using both picnic tables for their games.

*   *   *

I might have dozed off during the short ride to the Trattoria, if it hadn't been for the boys chattering in the backseat. Christina wheeled her Lincoln MKX deftly around the people, through the gates, and over to the Trattoria's parking lot. Except for the bits of yellow POLICE CRIME SCENE tape fluttering here and there outside the building, everything was normal. The restaurant had not officially reopened for business yet. A sign posted near the front door stated the restaurant would reopen on Tuesday evening, September 12, and a NEW HOURS decal on the door indicated the restaurant would now be open Tuesday through Sunday, 4 PM to 10 PM.

Ernesto Vasquez met the four of us as we came through the main door, just as he had done for the guys Thursday night. "Right this way, Mrs. Zouhn, Colonel Maxxon, Joshua and Jacob," he said, remembering us all, and he led us toward the largest meeting room. I watched the boys' eyes widen at the new respect they were receiving. Both boys warily eyed the table in the main dining room where Investigator Hertz had questioned them last Friday morning.

Hermosa Anderson, Carlos's grandniece, came out of the kitchen area and walked toward us.

"I'm so glad you came," she said, walking with us into the room. "I would like a word with you and Jimmy alone, a little later, if you don't mind."

"I don't mind," I said.

Hermosa said, "Thanks," and whisked back through the door.

Only a few people had arrived and were milling around in the room. Most of them I didn't know; I assumed they were Jimmy's relatives and friends. I spotted a bar in one corner, and I asked Christina if she wanted a drink. "I might have a white wine, later," she said. "But not right now."

The boys were abnormally quiet, sitting on their chairs like little gentlemen, but taking in all the activity around them. I gained new respect for Christina when I realized she had them under her control. Their crisp new pants and shirts still showed creases, and the colors were brand-new bright. I spotted an ice chest full of cans and went to get sodas for us. I got a can of Diet Coke for myself, a can of Diet Pepsi for Christina to hold her until she wanted wine, and a can of regular Coke to split between the boys. When the staff finished setting out a table of appetizers, I filled two plates with a wide variety of items and set it in the middle of the table, then proceeded to eat away at them. The boys tried a few items and decided they liked the fried cheese sticks, barbecued wieners, and buffalo hot wings.

"Save room for supper," I warned the boys, and my eyes moistened slightly as I remembered the many times Vicki had said the same to our two children as they grew up.

Christina nibbled at the broccoli, carrots, and quesadilla wedges. I was proud of myself for learning her favorite foods.

The first of my friends to arrive was Eugenios Christofides. Affectionately known as "The Greek" around the racing circuit, he is every part of the moniker. He immigrated to the United States from Greece when he was seventeen. He drives the number-114 Buick Century, sponsored by his employer, Maplewood Transfer and Storage. I hadn't seen him after the race, but I had heard him singing in the shower when I entered the locker room. He was gone by the time I finished. I was glad he had accepted an invitation to the party. He came roaring into the room, escorting a stately woman, and he walked straight toward me.

"You drive helluba race, today, my friend," he said, in his loud Greek voice. "Is bad you lost."

I looked at the lady with Eugenios.

"This is Valestra Zwoblowski," he said. "She was mother-in-law to me till Helena killed in car wreck." He screwed up his face. "Hell, she still mother-in-law to me, I guess." He laughed. Valestra laughed with him.

"You still good boy," Valestra proclaimed.

Valestra was short, maybe five foot two, and thin, not skinny. She had an angelic grandmother's face, framed with white hair, worn bouffant. Her eyes were dark blue and augmented her perpetual smile. She was wearing a tan one-piece jumpsuit, trimmed with brown piping, and canvas shoes. When she looked at Eugenios, I sensed they had worked to keep their relationship cordial, even respectful of the wife and daughter they had lost.

Christofides is medium height and solidly stout. While mild-mannered and mostly soft-spoken, he appears brutish, mainly because of his fierce brown eyes, unruly black hair, and a massive black walrus-style mustache that dominates his face.

"They got Ouzo?" he asked, pointing his chin toward the bar.

"I don't know," I said. "Would you like me to get you and Valestra some?"

"I get," Christofides said. "Val not drink Ouzo. She Polack, drink beer." They laughed as they walked toward the bar.

Don Epperley came strolling in. Don is a retired Kings Rapids lieutenant detective—the one before Terry Grossman took the position. Mutt Sparks had introduced me to Don a year after my first win in Kings Rapids. Don had retired at age sixty, essentially because of excruciating pain in his shoulder. This was from a gunshot he took while shielding an innocent bystander who'd been caught in the crossfire of a shootout with two drug dealers. A year after I met Don, he had a pair of surgeries that finally relieved the pain. Don became a much nicer person to be around.

At seventy-something, Don may be the oldest in my circle of close friends. He's taller than me, six foot four, and outweighs me by a hundredweight, at least. His brown eyes are bright and determined, and he wears a constant smile that makes you wonder what he's thinking or has just gotten away with. Like many guys his age these days, he's decided a shaved head is easier to care for than a haircut.

From the beginning of our friendship, Don has made it clear he is comfortable with designators such as "black man" and "negro."

"Don't call me an African-American," he warned early in our friendship. "My family has been in this valley for a long, long time. None of the relatives I've met or heard about came from Africa. They've all been right here in the valley."

"Have you seen Mutt lately?" I asked him now.

"He's coming," Don replied and headed for the bar to get a Scotch and water.

I hadn't seen Mutt at the track—before the race or after. I'd wondered if he had come, because I knew he was caring for Alisa Sharpe. From Don's remark, I surmised that Mutt was in town and had been at the race.

Terry and Marguerite Grossman had decided to come to the party, and I greeted them warmly when they came into the room. I wanted Marguerite's advice on what to do about the boys and hoped both of them would help me with the decisions I needed to make quickly.

I'd met the Grossmans before they were *the* Grossmans. Terry Grossman was the lead detective on the Rusty Gallegar case in Kings Rapids. I had met him a year earlier at the Law Enforcement Officers' Pro/Am Golf Tournament in Centralia. I had met Marguerite two and a half years ago. At that time, she was Marguerite Vinssant, Acting Chief of Police.

When Christina and I received our invitations to Marguerite and Terry's wedding, I knew something was going to have to give. Marguerite was the new chief of police. Terry was a lieutenant detective in the department. The rules against nepotism forbade him from working for his wife. Which one would give up his or her position with the police department?

When Christina and I arrived for the wedding, I knew how the decision had gone. Terry was the new owner of a well-known private investigation company in town. His name was on the business page of the *Times-Democrat*.

In the time since, that company had grown and prospered.

Marguerite is a statuesque and graceful African-American woman. She wears her salt-and-pepper hair cropped close to her head in an attractive business-comes-first style. Tonight her almond-shaped eyes sparkled in the light, and she had a special glow about her. She was wearing dark brown pedal pushers with a pink tank top. The only jewelry she wore was a pair of gold stud earrings and a pink and gold broach in the shape of the ribbon for breast cancer awareness. Her diamond engagement and wedding rings showed they were more than one carat each.

Terry is a "Caucasian male," as Marguerite says, taller than me by several inches, but the same weight. His eyes are dark brown and piercing. His salt-and-pepper hair is always razor cut and trimmed at the ears. He is also an ex-marine. Today he was wearing tan Dockers and a dark blue polo shirt. He and Marguerite were wearing matching New Balance running shoes.

Terry's cell phone rang, and the Grossmans excused themselves to the relative quiet of a far corner of the main dining room.

I was picking through the remains of the appetizers on our table, when I heard Christina's breath catch, and I followed the gaze of her widening eyes. Mutt Sparks stood just inside the doorway to the room, looking around.

My heart skipped a beat.

Standing beside Mutt, her hand on his shoulder for support, stood Alisa Sharpe. My eyes moistened, and I looked at Christina, who wore her natural smile.

I'd also met Alisa Sharpe in Kings Rapids. She had been the prime suspect in Rusty Gallegar's murder, because she was his ex-live-in lover, and he'd kicked her out of his apartment the weekend before his murder.

After Alisa's experience in jail, she'd decided to go through the local community college's police science course. She'd finished that program early and with straight A's. Marguerite had been instrumental in getting her hired into the department. Alisa had gone through the police academy with flying colors and immediately joined the force as a patrolperson. *Alisa is one of the best new cops I've ever had,* her division sergeant had written on her six-month review.

I'd heard that Alisa was a favorite partner to every cop she worked with.

During a high-speed chase with a robbery suspect, who was spraying magazine after magazine of 9 mm Uzi bullets into crowds along the streets, Alisa had suffered severe injuries. Alisa's partner had been driving the patrol car, and, after a split-second discussion weighing the safety of innocent people, they decided to take the guy out. They made a move to ram the fleeing car in an open space. Their move sent the suspect's car spinning out of control, but in its wild bouncing and rolling, the shooter kept shooting. A spray of bullets came in through the shattered side window of the patrol car. One slug hit the driver; he lost control, and the car careened into a bridge abutment. Another slug hit her partner's radio mike, sending shards into Alisa's face as the partner doubled over. In the following crash, Alisa sustained life-threatening head injuries. For several days, all of us who knew Alisa prayed she would make it. Then, when word came she would live, we prayed she would make a full recovery.

This was the first time I'd seen her since the accident. Alisa walked slowly, following Mutt. I saw that her right eye had cotton padding and tape over it. Mutt walked slowly toward me, leading Alisa. I stood and gripped Mutt's hand when he held it out to me, but my total attention was on Alisa. She moved so I could bend down to give her a gentle hug. I moved carefully so as not to bump the bandaged eye.

"You really are Kurt Maxxon," Alisa said, smiling, mimicking the first time we had met, when I visited her in jail, and she had greeted me with the same words.

I hoped the water in the corner of my eyes wasn't evident. "I'm so proud of you," I said through pursing lips. Christina moved beside me and helped me deal with the emotion of the moment by taking Alisa in a motherly embrace.

Mutt and Alisa are an odd pair. Mutt is a nickname for Rudolph Michael Sparks, a six-foot-seven slender man with a comb-style moustache. At one point in his career, he had had a squat, stocky photographer on his team, and the rest is obvious. Even today, Mutt reminds me of the Mutt and Jeff comic strip I loved as a kid.

Alisa is a petite woman, five foot four, with hazel eyes, a pug nose fitted into her oval face, and dimpled cheeks. She has carrot-colored hair, which, the first time I met her, made me think of the Kewpie doll my sister still has on her bed.

Christina held Alisa and led her to a chair. Don returned from the bar and handed Mutt a tall, dark amber glass. Mutt took a deep draft from it and moved to stand behind Alisa's chair.

"Why'd you let Jimmy win?" Mutt said to me in a low voice.

"I didn't *let* him win."

"Bullshit, Maxxon. You had that race won, and you let up so Jimmy could win," Mutt said sharply.

Don sat down next to me and said, "What'd you do, Mutt, file your report before the race was over?"

"No. Dammit," Mutt seemed full of fight.

"Calm down, Mutt," I said. "I simply blew it when I tried to accelerate out of turn 2, wrong gear, and I spun my wheels. I lost the position," I said.

"Is Kurt Maxxon getting too old to race cars?" Mutt growled. I looked at him, puzzled by his frustration.

"Mutt, please," Alisa said with an edge in her voice.

Mutt swung to look at Alisa, studied her for several moments, and said, "Sorry, hon." The fight left him.

I suddenly realized that Alisa and Mutt were acting like an old married couple. Alisa was living in Mutt's house, ostensibly on the unused second floor. I had won the race in Kings Rapids last June, and we'd had a small victory party afterward. I'd noticed then that Alisa and Mutt were hanging together all the time. I commented to Christina that they looked like lovers and secretly congratulated old Mutt.

Marguerite and Terry Grossman came back into the room and walked toward our table. When they spotted Alisa, they went directly to her. Marguerite bent down to embrace the seated Alisa. Terry waited and then embraced her when Marguerite stood up. "You are doing magnificently," Marguerite said. The group rearranged chairs so they were all sitting close to Alisa. Mutt seemed a little agitated, but he realized he would lose if he protested. He stood behind Alisa's chair.

Don was the one who brought us all to the question of the day. "What did the board say?" he asked Alisa.

"I'm done," Alisa whispered.

Don nodded understanding. "They couldn't do anything else, Leezy. You're better off for it."

"It's my right eye," Alisa said. "I'm completely blind in it."

Everyone at the table groaned in unison, because we all knew what that meant. Cops have to have two good eyes. The board might cheat a little on dexterity in arms, legs, or shoulders. I looked at Joshua and Jacob. They were quietly following the conversation, and I wanted to make sure they understood. "Alisa was a cop who was in an accident while chasing a bad guy," I said to the boys. "She's just now getting better." Both boys nodded. "She be a pretty girl," Jacob said.

The entire table laughed, with a release of tension. "Hell, yes," Mutt roared. "The prettiest one I'll ever lay eyes on."

Alisa shook her head and blushed. "You guys," she squeaked. Then she swung to focus her good eye on me. "Where's Beau?" she asked.

"Probably sound asleep on a bed at the hotel," I said.

"I didn't think the Speedway Hotel allowed pets," Alisa said.

"They don't," Mutt said. "Unless you're Kurt Maxxon."

"Beau was with Christina Zouhn, not me," I said.

"In a room on the drivers' floor, arranged for by Kurt Maxxon," Christina said with a smile.

"It helps to be famous," Marguerite said.

"I'm hungry," I said as I gazed around the room. I realized it was nearly full. Jimmy had arrived and was being swarmed by his admirers. He roamed among them, accepting handshakes, pats on the back, and kisses from many women. At one point I saw him search the room, and, when he found me, he motioned me to join him. He walked toward a small podium in a corner. I excused myself from the table and made my way through the crowd to meet Jimmy. Hermosa Anderson beat us to the podium, where she fiddled with a microphone and then spoke into it, "Ladies and gentlemen, if I could have your attention, please ..."

The cacophony of voices slowly quieted. Hermosa moved the microphone up to speak: "And the winner is, Jimmy Davison, driving the number-89 Trattoria Restaurant car, winning by an eyelash over the famed Kurt Maxxon, in the number-27 car. Great race, guys." Jimmy walked up and Hermosa hugged him. She then handed him the microphone.

Jimmy said, "I don't know if I really won or not; I think the great Kurt Maxxon let me win it. But, whatever happened, I came in first, and that makes me very, very, happy tonight. It's my first win, and it came in the Trattoria car, and it feels greeeeaaaaat!"

The crowd roared, whistled, and applauded loudly.

As the noise died down, Jimmy said, "Thank you all so much, for sticking by me through all these races. I want Kurt to say a few words, and then the waiters will be around to take your orders. Order whatever you want; it's all on the house." Jimmy handed me the microphone.

"Don't sell yourself short, Jimmy," I said. I noticed an echo, so I moved the mike away from my mouth. "You ran a great race, and you won it, fair and square. Take it to the bank. And I hope you win a lot more races in the future. Thanks, everyone," I handed the mike back toward Jimmy, but Hermosa interceded.

"You may have noticed the sign out front," she intoned. "The Trattoria will remain open, but only as a dinner restaurant, open Tuesday through Sunday nights. Many of you are used to having breakfast and lunch here, and we're sorry you won't be able to do that in the future. But, with Uncle Carlos gone, Ernesto and I have decided to just serve dinners. Thank you for your past patronage, and we hope you will come in often in the future."

As Hermosa trailed off and mounted the microphone on the podium, a half dozen waiters spread to each of the tables and started taking orders for dinner. Menus were already on the tables. Several groups, including my circle of friends, rearranged tables into cozy groupings. At our oversized table, two waiters arrived to take dinner orders. The boys seemed lost in the events. "Can we get them potato thingies we had last time?" Joshua asked.

"I'll see," I told them. "They're not on the menu. If we can't, we'll find something you guys will like."

Marguerite had moved so she was sitting next to the boys. "What do you boys like?" she asked, looking at each separately.

"I like hamburgers," Jacob said.

Marguerite smiled. "What else?"

"Anything with hamburger," Joshua agreed.

"And cheese," Jacob added.

When I told the waiter the boys would like pappas rellenas, he said, "Let me check with Dominique."

I ordered *boliche*. Christina chose a Cuban salad plate.

After a while, the waiter came back to tell us Dominique had what he needed to make pappas rellenas. "They'll be right out," he promised.

"What are pappas rellenas?" Marguerite asked.

"A special potato ball stuffed with a spicy ground beef mixture," I said.

"They're hamburger in a potato," Jacob said with a wide grin.

"Okay," Marguerite said. "Can I try one?" she asked the waiter.

"I'll bring you some, ma'am," the waiter said, and he left.

Marguerite turned to me and whispered, "I'd better find that recipe."

I looked at Christina, and she smiled. It had definitely been worth the wait to let those two have a say about the boys.

*   *   *

Tammy McPherson

Tammy had lined up clients for several of the girls still working for her. There had been two requests for Chaundra; both of them had accepted other girls when they were told Chaundra was unavailable. Where in the world had Chaundra gone? She hadn't heard from LeRoy, but another girl had told her Chaundra also had not shown up for her appointment with him on Thursday. *Damn that Carlos—if I had only been paying attention to the girls instead of arguing with him.*

Just before the last call, Barbara had phoned to tell Tammy there was some kind of party going on at the Trattoria. Barbara and her client had driven past it, and it had been swinging pretty good. At first Tammy let that information slide past her, even thinking that if there was another call, she'd consider talking the caller into accepting her for the evening. Or she might even dress up and visit the Speedway Grill.

But, as she sat staring at the TV set, she started wondering what was going on at the Trattoria. Maybe it was some kind of a wake for Carlos. But the obituary had listed the wake for next Tuesday evening and the funeral Wednesday morning at eleven o'clock. "What's Hermosa up to now?" Tammy asked herself aloud. She wondered what they could possibly be partying about. Carlos had only been dead three days.

Tammy dressed in a short red skirt with white piping and snuggled into a white tank top. As she applied her makeup, Tammy checked herself in the mirror, patting her auburn hair back into place and approving, with minor reservations, the body that the tight-fitting garments revealed. She would check out the action at the Speedway, and maybe Dino's, if she felt like it. But then she stopped and sat down. "What's going on at the Trattoria?"

Having developed a plan, Tammy walked to the Speedway Grill but didn't go in. She dialed the cab company and asked for a cab at the Speedway Grill.

When the cab arrived, she gave the cabbie the address of the Trattoria and sat wondering what she would find when she got there. There was still plenty of time to get to the Speedway and get "picked up" if someone with the right money was there. If there was no one at the Speedway Grill, she could wander over to Dino's and take on a lower-paying client.

At the Trattoria, Tammy told the cabbie to park in the dark corner of the lot and wait for her. She slipped out of the cab and took a circuitous route to the back, where she could peer through windows that opened into the dining room as well as the meeting rooms. The gaiety she saw inside the restaurant startled Tammy. She saw Hermosa being the quintessential host; Ernesto was escorting people to tables; several waiters and waitresses were scurrying about; and she saw Jimmy Davison. Then she saw the banner strung across the room: CONGRATULATIONS ON FIRST WIN. Tammy recognized several of the race drivers. *Carlos is dead. Why have a celebration party for a driver?*

She thought about going back to the cab the same way she had come, but then decided to look in the kitchen. She was about to crack open the kitchen door, when Dominique came through it with a bag of trash. "Hello, Tammy," Dominique said.

"Hi, Dominique. I was driving by and saw the action and was wondering what was going on."

"Ah, Jimmy won his first race this afternoon. They're all celebrating."

"Carlos would be proud of him," Tammy said. "Well, I guess I'll keep moving. Good night, Dominique." She walked quickly back to the cab. She'd wanted to find out what was going on, but quietly. Now, dammit, Dominique had seen her. Would he go running to Hermosa?

He didn't know how Hermosa and Tammy felt about each other, did he?

The cab ride back to the Speedway Grill went quickly. Tammy prepared her explanation of why she had been at the Trattoria, in case Hermosa confronted her about it. *I was just driving by and saw the lights. "What were you driving?" Oh, ah, well, I was actually in a cab.*

Back at the Speedway Grill, Tammy paid the driver and was walking toward the door, when her cell phone rang.

"I'd like to hook up with Candy tonight," the voice said.

"Candy is unavailable tonight, sir. Could I interest you in someone else?"

"No, thank you." He hung up.

Damn. Where did that girl get to?

CHAPTER ELEVEN

Monday, September 11

<u>*Kurt Maxxon, Early Morning*</u>

Joshua and Jacob elected to stay with Christina in her room at the Speedway Hotel again, which proved to be a good choice, since the weather was not ideal for sleeping under the picnic table next to my camper. When I'd walked from the camper to the drivers' lounge to shower earlier, the air had been humid and I could see fog in the night-lights to the south of the garage area.

When I returned to the camper, Beau jumped off the bed, skipped down the steps, and went out to do his business. I poured a cup of coffee and set it on the picnic table, then put food and water out for Beau. After he ate, Beau went off to inspect the perimeter of the RV lot to see if anything had trespassed on his territory while he slept. At the corner to the outside road, he nosed for several feet, went to a point position, studied the ditch on the other side of the fence for several minutes, and then moved a few feet down the fence. Something decided against trying to outlast him, and I heard rustling in the weeds of the ditch. Probably one of the feral house cats that live around the track, subsisting on mice and voles.

Beau lost interest and went on down the fence line to finish the inspection. Eventually, he came back, jumped up on the bench seat next to me, and lay down.

"Did that wear you out?" I asked him.

He rolled his eyes up to look at me.

"Are you sure the neighborhood is safe now?" I said. His tail thumped against the seat.

The sun appeared, peeking over the misty eastern horizon. I decided the fog would burn off quickly. I had over an hour to kill before I was to meet Christina, the boys, and the Grossmans for breakfast. We'd decided to meet at the restaurant in the Speedway Hotel. Their buffet breakfast offered a variety of food, enough to satisfy Christina and me. For the next few mornings, I would be enjoying the buffet, since I planned to take a room at the Speedway this afternoon. I can live in the camper three nights, four max, and, after that, I need a king bed and a little space around the bed.

I'd pack my suitcase before I left for breakfast and stow it in the back of my truck.

"You want to go up and stay at Buster's place?" I asked Beau. His ears perked up, and he sat up to look at me.

Buster is Jerome Pierpont Jennings. He bought the farm he lives on from an elderly aunt, the older sister of his father, whose husband's family had homesteaded the place in the late 1890s under the Homestead Act of 1862. "I've loved this farm since I was a little boy," Buster told me when he took me on tour the first time.

Beau and I had visited Buster in the spring, during the off-season, when I'd come to Carpentier Falls for a regional meeting of the Auto Parts Store Owners Association. When I called Buster to tell him I would like to meet him and Roxanne for dinner one night, I told him I would have to put Beau in a kennel. Christina would be out of town at the same time and unable to keep him.

"Hell, bring Beau up here. Roxanne and the girls will watch him for you." Since I always feel kennels are like jails for my four-legged family members, I'd decided to take Buster up on his offer. I took Beau up to Buster's place the night before. End result: Beau loved the place, loved Buster's two daughters, Charlene and Michelle, and their two border collies—Hercules and Aphrodite—who accepted Beau even though he didn't have a Greek name. And, with a twelve-acre fenced-in yard, the three dogs had a field day romping and rollicking, which wore Beau out.

"You can play with Hercules and Aphrodite, and see Charlene and Michelle." Beau's ears twitched. He seemed to remember who I was talking about. "We'll go up there today, so you can stay a few days, okay?"

Beau gave me a small, "Gruff."

I packed what clean skivvies remained in the drawer into the suitcase I keep in the camper. I hung the one clean shirt I had left and took empty hangers in the dirty clothes bag, since the Speedway had a small guest laundry in the basement. I had enough for only one load, but I always wash my jeans separately. My wife, Vicki, had never washed dark and white clothes together. I didn't go that far, but I'd had bad experiences with jeans coloring other clothes, especially when the jeans were new. Both pairs of jeans were almost new. My one pair of dress pants was dark blue, so I was safe there.

I stowed and tied down everything in the camper, so I could just back under it, lower it down onto the truck bed, and roll whenever I got ready to leave town. I couldn't get out of town fast, however, since I had to go through the two-step process of turning the camper around, the reverse of when I set it up. Beau sat on the bed, encouraging me to hurry.

"If we leave now, you'll have to sleep in the truck longer," I crooned. "That's why I'm not in any big hurry. We still have forty-five minutes before we're to meet Christina and the boys."

At the mention of the boys, Beau's ears shot straight up. "You like those boys, don't you?" I thought Beau bobbed his head, but maybe the camper shifted at that moment.

Beau proved to be too antsy for me to put up with, so, a few minutes later, I loaded him into the passenger seat, stuffed my clothes and suitcase into the backseat, and we drove to the Speedway Hotel. I spotted Christina's Lincoln, as I cruised through the lot looking for a parking space. As I walked toward the door, I spotted Terry Grossman's Cadillac Escalade. I turned to see if Beau was standing up against the dash, as he usually was when I closed my door and walked away. He wasn't, so he must have curled up and gone back to sleep.

*　　*　　*

Tammy McPherson

Tammy walked into Dino's and looked around, after her eyes had adjusted to the darkness. Only a few booths had customers at this hour, and half a dozen men squatted on barstools. She had woken up at five thirty, her worries about what Hermosa was doing causing her to have a bad dream. After a couple of hours of wild thoughts about Hermosa looking for her and finding her, she had decided to contact Hermosa on her own, up front. *In your ear.* She stood looking at the telephone on the wall.

She moved slowly to the table under the wall phone and pulled the chair so her back was to the door. She had coins in her hand, but she waited. Then, with a determined look, she loaded coins into the slot and dialed the number she had scribbled on a sheet of paper.

"Hello," she heard Hermosa Anderson say.

"Hermosa, this is Tammy McPherson. I wanted to call to tell—" She grimaced as she listened to the tirade on the other end. She knew Hermosa had a fiery temper. When Hermosa eased up, Tammy continued, "Yes, well, I thought you should know that I have vacated the condo, and the car is in the parking lot there."

She smiled when Hermosa told her they had already had the car towed back to the lease company and changed the locks on the condo's

128

doors. She nearly chortled when she thought about anyone trying to get to the back door of the condo, it being a sliding glass patio door onto the cantilevered terrace on the fourth floor of the building. Then came the inevitable questions.

"No, I don't know where Carlos put the books. He never told me."

"No, I don't know where the petty cash fund went to. Ernesto would be the one to talk to about that."

"No, I don't know where the operating cash went to." She hoped her voice didn't betray her lie.

"No, I didn't kill him," she said, with an edge to her voice. "I don't have any idea who killed him. The last time I saw him was early Thursday morning." Once again, she prayed her voice stayed steady.

She listened again. She said, "Thank you," and hung up, silently swearing at Hermosa.

Tammy looked toward the bartender, who was wiping glasses with a blue and white towel and stacking them on the bar. Each corner of the room had televisions tuned to the local morning news, weather, and traffic show. The local weatherman stood in front of a weather map, pointing to features only he could decipher.

It was too early for booze, and she was tense from too much coffee. A *long walk will be best to calm these jitters, hon.* She stood, pressing the wrinkles out of her skirt, and walked out the door.

That went better than I thought it would.

*   *   *

Kurt Maxxon, Christina, the boys, and the Grossmans

I was about twenty-five minutes early, so I grabbed a newspaper on the way to the dining room, in case I had to kill time waiting for the others. But, when I walked into the room, I saw the gang at a long table. The boys clambered off their seats and dashed toward me. Jacob arrived last, since he had to negotiate the booster seat. "Hey, guys," I said.

"Hey," they shouted back in unison.

"We're hungry," Jacob said. "Good thing you got here now."

They led me to the table, and I sat at the end, opposite Terry. Joshua sat next to Christina, and Jacob sat next to Marguerite. The menus sat in a neat stack at the side of the table. Jacob and Joshua had placemats with puzzles and two crayons in front of them.

"We all decided to have the buffet," Christina reported. "I knew that's what you would have."

"Why didn't you start without me?"

Marguerite didn't look at me, but she growled, "We're trying to teach the boys good manners."

Self-inflicted head slap. "Okay. You guys ready?" I said, starting to stand up. But Christina shook her head and gave me a hard look.

"What?" I said.

Christina paused for several beats and then said, "Are you gentlemen ready to eat?"

"Yeah," the two "gentlemen" shouted in unison.

Christina smiled, but I knew she was planning more training.

Everyone at the table stood with me. Christina herded Joshua, teaching him how to put food on his plate, while Marguerite did the same with Jacob. I followed Terry down the line, hoping he would load the plate up, since I intended to put about the same amount on my plate as he did on his. Fortunately, Terry is also a big eater. We loaded our plates and lugged them to the table. We ate in relative peace, since the boys were hungry.

After we finished eating, we sat chatting over coffee and hot chocolate. The boys, however, were getting wiggly. Being inside a building is not their idea of fun, and listening to four adults talk about life in general makes it even worse. Christina suggested they go out to my truck, get Beau, and go for a walk around the hotel grounds.

She didn't have to ask twice. Both boys flew off their chairs and were heading for the door before Christina could stand up.

After Christina and the boys had left, Marguerite said, "I took the picture to the CFPD this morning, and we sent it to the crime lab in Centralia. Then I called Brad Langley and asked him to help me expedite it. He said he would."

"Did you tell him I met the boys?" I asked.

"No. He didn't need to know that right then," she said with a confident smile.

"Oh. Okay, did you tell him about the boys?" I asked.

"Yes, I did. I told him Terry and I were taking them to Kings Rapids with us this morning."

That revelation didn't surprise me, nor did it concern me. Marguerite and Terry were the ideal people to take the boys into their care—and off my hands. Christina surely couldn't, since she had her plans to go to Little Rock, and she wouldn't be back until Thursday afternoon. I wanted to stay around Carpentier Falls, even though I hoped to be home by Thursday. I had no reason to stay in Carpentier Falls—other than my uneasiness with Carlos's killer. *Rachael wasn't the type.*

"What time are you leaving?" I asked.

"We're packed and ready to roll," Terry said. "We'll load up and hit the road shortly after breakfast. We thought it would be good if you talk to the boys and suggest they go with us for a few days. We can do some preliminary work from Kings Rapids. Then I can run over here to dig for leads. I might call you to do some legwork for me here," Terry said, "if you're still around."

"I can do that," I said.

"Is there anything the boys will need?" Marguerite said. "If there is, we need to take care of it before we leave."

"Their sleeping bags are in the back of my truck. We can get them out now," I said.

"I think it best if they don't take them," Marguerite said. "I'd prefer they sleep in the spare bedroom upstairs, in beds, not outside in the yard. That way we can keep an eye on them."

Terry nodded agreement. "Besides, if they camped in the back yard, I'd have to sleep out with them, and my old bones aren't interested in campouts anymore."

An hour later, we gathered on the veranda in front of the hotel. I had talked to the boys and they seemed eager for the adventure of staying with Terry and Marguerite. I'd asked if they wanted to take their sleeping bags and stuff with them, and both shook their heads.

"We won't need that stuff till we get back with you," Joshua said. "You keep it with you, so we always got it."

"Okay."

Christina said her "goodbyes" early, leaving for her nine o'clock meeting in downtown Carpentier Falls. The boys piled into the back of the silver Escalade, and I said good-bye to Marguerite and Terry. As Terry slid behind the wheel, he asked, "When is Carlos's funeral?"

"I think someone mentioned Wednesday morning," I said. "I need to check. You want me to let you know?"

"It's not necessary. I was just wondering, since I figured you'd be staying here until at least then, or until you solve the murder." Terry's eyes betrayed his humor. I could tell he was having a hard time keeping from laughing out loud. Marguerite nudged him and shook her head, smiling.

"I'm not thinking about the murder," I said and wished it were true.

I stood and watched them leave; then I glanced toward my truck. I saw Beau standing on the dash. I needed to get him up to Buster's place. Then I'd call Hermosa to confirm the time of Carlos's funeral. After that, I might go to the library and relax with a good book for a little while. At least four of my favorite mystery writers had released new books in the last few months, and I had fallen even further behind in my reading.

*   *   *

Tammy McPherson

She'd walked nearly an hour—glad she had worn comfortable shoes. Her head was much clearer, and she was craving some action. She decided she would take a taxi to the area of the condo complex and walk around the edges, to see what was happening. She might even visit the Trattoria again.

Since the restaurant had become a dinner-only establishment, there would be few, if any, people who knew her at this time of day. Hermosa had stopped the gambling, which didn't bother her. She'd kept several of the girls working, since her cell phone was the number all the clients had. She used the Capri Motel as control central. All but a couple of the girls were pretty independent. Kaleen was a foreigner, who really didn't understand the prostitution business. She gave away more product than she charged for. But she was still a money-maker.

Tammy wondered again what had happened to Chaundra, her "most requested" girl. She hadn't heard a word from the girl since Thursday, when Tammy had called her to meet her usual Thursday-night client, LeRoy. Another girl had told Tammy she'd seen Chaundra leaving with a woman in a car and that she hadn't come back to meet with her client. Tammy had no confirmation either way. LeRoy hadn't called to complain. She had thought about tracking down Chaundra Friday morning, but with all the activities surrounding Carlos's death, she'd forgotten about it. The last two days, Tammy had left messages on Chaundra's cell phone. She hoped nothing bad had happened to the girl. She could have just turned off the phone, or she could be out of range of a tower. Chaundra was so young, and she was naïve. But she had rapidly become the favorite girl of several men, who asked for her specifically. *Naivety has its benefits,* she thought. *But where is she? Is Rachael trying to muscle back in?*

As she rode in the taxi, Tammy wondered if Carlos's books had turned up yet. The cops had scrubbed every inch of everything associated with Carlos, and they more than likely had found them, but they were keeping awfully quiet about it. If the cops had the books, how long would it be before they had someone analyze them? Not only would that show there was a lot of cash missing, but it would also mean big trouble for her—if they had already checked her record.

I've got to find those books. Carlos was maddeningly casual with cash. Carlos handled checks and credit card items promptly. But cash was Carlos's downfall. The books would show the money she had taken earlier this year.

Tammy paid the cabbie and walked the three blocks to the condo complex. For a fleeting moment, she missed living in this luxurious building and the comfortable condo. *Easy come, easy go*, her mind said, dismissing the discomfort that welled up in her chest.

She walked around the buildings next to the condo and entered the ramp down to the garages below. Carlos had a garage on the second level below the building. She recalled when Carlos had had a sprained ankle, and she had gone to his garage to get his car, so he wouldn't have to walk from the elevator. *What about Carlos's garage? Did he store anything of value there?* She walked down the ramp and hoped she wouldn't have to leave too fast. She probably wouldn't have time to use the elevator, and to run up the ramp was more than she could do physically.

When she rounded the wall, she saw that Carlos's garage door was up and the room empty. On the front wall of the garage were two shelves and a metal workbench with a center drawer and two side drawers. The concrete walls of the garage were unfinished. Tammy flipped on the light switch. The twin overhead fluorescent lights flickered on and brightened. The remote door opener was the only loose object in the room. Tammy picked it up and inadvertently punched the close button. The door began grinding down, which panicked Tammy. She quickly punched the open button. The door stopped about half closed, hesitated, and then started going up. Tammy blew out a breath. She watched the door climb back full open. But she saw a flash. "There's something taped to the top of the door," she murmured.

Tammy tried to reach the door, but she was too short. She walked briskly out and looked around the garage level. Across the driveway, an open door revealed the caretaker's tools he used in the yard: shovels, rakes, hoses, and a wheelbarrow. She ran to the wheelbarrow, wheeled it under the door, and cautiously climbed up into it. The flash proved to be a key taped to the top of the door. She looked to make sure no one was watching and ripped it loose.

"Just like Carlos to do something like this," she said aloud as she turned the key over several times to inspect it. "What do you open?"

She slipped the key into her pocket and climbed out of the wheelbarrow. She returned the wheelbarrow and then quickly searched the drawers. They were empty. She thought about taking the remote, but why?

Tammy rode the elevator to the ground level, where she got off to look around. Satisfied that no one knew she was around, she returned to the elevator. She wondered if Hermosa had changed the entry codes. She punched in the code for the elevator to go up to the penthouse level. It worked, and she rode up.

She got off the elevator and walked to the door that had been Carlos's condo. She twisted the knob. Locked. Suddenly she regretted having gripped the locked knob. She dug a tissue out of her fanny pack and wiped the knob furiously.

A chill shook her, and she swung her head from side to side, looking, listening. In the landing, she felt exposed and vulnerable. *I've got to get out of this building.* She walked quickly to the stairwell and began to run down the stairs. About midway down the first flight, she realized she was making so much racket that people might wonder why she was running down the stairs. She went down the two remaining flights as quietly as possible, and, as she exited the stairwell on the first floor, she nearly bumped into Sergeant Hoppy standing in front of the penthouse elevator. Two uniformed deputy sheriffs stood with Hoppy. Before she could react, Sergeant Hoppy said, "Hello, Mrs. McPherson. How are you today?"

"I'm—I'm fine," Tammy said.

"I was going to stop by your condo in a little while," Hoppy said.

"I was just on my way to a doctor's appointment," Tammy said. "What do you need?"

Hoppy backed away from the elevator. She handed a key to one of the deputies and said, "Go on up and open the condo. I'll be right up."

Tammy wondered if the question was personal and Hoppy didn't want to ask it in front of the two men. But Hoppy said, "Did you know anything about the cigarette operation Carlos started?"

The elevator door opened, and the two men got on. Tammy stood for a long time, a worry line forming between her eyes. "I've never heard anything about cigarettes," she said. "Why do you ask?"

"Someone told us Carlos might be dealing in untaxed cigarettes," Hoppy said. "We haven't verified it either way. I was just curious. Thank you for your cooperation, Mrs. McPherson."

As she walked to the front door, Tammy fingered the key in her pocket and decided to find out what she could about the key.

She called a taxi from the pharmacy on the corner and told the cabbie she wanted to go to Hank the Locksmith, in the strip mall just north of the Trattoria.

When they arrived at the locksmith's shop, Tammy told the cabbie to wait for her, and she went inside.

Hank was puttering at his workbench along the back wall of the room. He stood when she entered and walked toward her. "Hi, Tammy."

"Hello, Hank," she said as she handed him the key. "Can you tell me what this key fits?"

Hank looked at the key. "Number is L189. If I had to guess, I'd guess a lockbox."

"A lockbox? What kind of lockbox?"

"The metal, fireproof boxes people buy for home and office."

Tammy took the key back from Hank. "Did Carlos have a lockbox like that?"

Hank shook his head. "If he did, I didn't know about it. All I ever did for Carlos was change locks in his condo and office building. The restaurant once, a long time ago."

"How big a box would it be?"

"They come in different sizes, from small, like six by six, up to twenty-four by twenty-four. There are several different brands, but they all use the same locks. That key might open a thousand lockboxes in Carpentier Falls alone."

Tammy returned to the cab and settled into the backseat. She gave the driver the address for Dino's on Roosevelt. *A lockbox, huh? Carlos had a lockbox somewhere. That's probably where he kept the ledger sheets. So, where in the hell would Carlos have kept the damn thing?*

During the drive home, Tammy stared at the buildings whizzing by, reviewing the events of the day. She'd phoned Hermosa and stood up to her—essentially, *in your ear Hermosa*. She'd learned that Carlos had a secret lockbox. *And Sergeant Hoppy thinks I'm still happily living at my old address in the condo. This has been a pretty productive day, hon.*

*   *   *

Kurt Maxxon

As you follow the Swift River northeast from Carpentier Falls, the bluffs transition into a plateau, which becomes steeper, with considerably more layers of shale and sandstone exposed in the road cuts. Ridge Road is an asphalted two-lane road that meanders along the crest of the river bluffs up and over the plateau. It announces several gravel side roads with well-marked signs, and the various farm driveways with mailboxes.

Buster Jennings's farm is in a bowl-shaped hollow, high up on the plateau north of the river. According to Buster, it's 160 acres of prime farmland, although I doubt the soil overburden anywhere on his land is more than a foot deep. He does have thirty acres of corn that produces quite well, fifty acres of hay, and the rest is devoted to pasturage for horses. Buster's wife, Roxanne, brought three horses to the marriage, while Buster contributed the 160 acres to feed them. Buster's parents did some farming on a smaller spread closer to Carpentier Falls, while they owned and operated a seed and feed store on the northeast side of town. When his folks retired and moved to Florida, Buster's sister got the folks' farm and Buster got the feed and seed business, which he still operates.

A dilapidated mailbox on the edge of Ridge Road, leaning severely windward, heralds Buster's place. Since Buster gets his mail in a post office box, the mailbox hasn't been used for decades. The gravel driveway back to Buster's farmstead is about three-quarters of a mile long, and meanders through pine and hardwood forests. There are several rock outcroppings, usually topped by struggling red cedar trees that have rooted in a crack full of dust. The fences are wood, and Buster gives them a fresh coat of white paint every three years.

Once you break out of the trees and see Buster's spread, you realize just how secluded the place is. An artesian well about halfway up the steep hill behind the farmstead sends a steady flow of water into a three-acre lake. The overflow from that lake flows down the hill and forms a creek that eventually feeds into the Swift River, about three miles downstream.

The lake serves as a centerpiece for the original farm buildings. The original dwelling house is now a remodeled visitor's lodging, used by Buster's many relatives who come to visit him. Buster built his current house in 1981. It's a rambling ranch with about four thousand square feet—five bedrooms and six baths. Buster chose to use native fieldstone and brick in its construction, with two fireplace chimneys and simulated cedar-shake shingles.

The horse barn, built shortly after the house, was a ten-stall structure, with architectural themes that matched the house. Roxanne, and their daughters, Charlene and Michelle, acquired six horses. Then Roxanne decided to board other horses, and when the total number of horses nearly filled the barn, Buster added on to it, so the total number of stalls went to twenty-two. A couple of years after that, they added a separate building for the tack, hay, feed, and supplies. Currently, they board an even dozen horses for other people.

When I drove to Buster's place today, Beau sat passively on the passenger's seat, watching the land go by and sniffing out the side window once in a while. I wondered if Beau was having second thoughts about staying at Buster's. As I turned into Buster's driveway, however, Beau knew where he was and started his signature wriggling with excitement. When I parked in front of the house, Charlene and Michelle came romping out, followed by Hercules and Aphrodite. Beau didn't wait for me to let him down; he leaped from the seat all the way to the ground and dashed to join the two border collies and then enjoy the girls' welcoming pats and ear rubs. Roxanne came out of the kitchen door while the girls pampered and spoiled Beau.

Beau looked at me as if to tell me he was looking forward to a long visit; then he turned and ran off with the other dogs. I relaxed, knowing he was in good hands.

As I drove back toward town, my cell phone jangled. I hesitated to answer it, worrying that Brad Langley had heard about my involvement with the Carlos Guerrero murder. I looked at the caller ID and saw it wasn't Brad. So I answered it. The female voice introduced herself as Sergeant Hoppy, with the Pierre County Sheriff's Department Major Crimes Investigation Unit. That didn't ring a bell with me, but her being able to get it all out without taking a breath impressed me. She said she would like to talk to me about the Carlos Guerrero homicide.

An investigator had interviewed me early Friday morning and I suspected a detective would eventually want to get my side of the whole story. They hadn't come around very fast, however, and I worried they were being a little cavalier about letting evidence and witnesses grow cold. I had no way of knowing how compelling the evidence against Rachael was. Maybe she had confessed. At any rate, I felt the detectives were finally doing their job.

I agreed to meet with Sergeant Hoppy in her office at one thirty. Christina and her friend were to meet me for lunch at eleven thirty, at Ruby's Lobster Shack. I'd go directly from lunch to the law center.

I noticed my suitcase in the rearview mirror, as I drove to Ruby's. If I forgot to go to the hotel, the suitcase would remind me.

Christina and Ruth Higgins, her friend, were at the table when I arrived.

"I took Beau up to Buster Jennings's place," I told Christina.

"He likes that place, doesn't he?"

"He didn't even notice when I left," I said. "He's very comfortable there, with the girls and the other dogs."

"That's good," Christina said and went back to chatting with Ruth, bringing me into their conversation occasionally. Ruth glanced at her watch and prepared to leave, saying, "I'm late for a doctor's appointment," and then she left.

I told Christina about Sergeant Hoppy from the sheriff's office calling me and that I had an appointment to talk with her.

"Janice Hoppy?" she asked.

I shrugged, not knowing Sergeant Hoppy's first name.

"That's great. I'll go with you," Christina said, surprising me.

We arrived at the law center a little after one o'clock, told the receptionist we were there to see Sergeant Hoppy, and sat down to wait. About five minutes later, a medium height, stout, Native American woman came down the hallway. Her long black hair, braided into a single strand, hung nearly to her waist. Her dark eyes reflected the fluorescent lighting. She wore the greenish-brown Western-style uniform of the sheriff's office, with a gold badge above the left breast pocket. As she came into the waiting room, she stopped, and a wide smile spread over her face.

"Christina," she said joyfully.

I watched as the two women embraced in greeting.

"Janice," Christina cooed. "You look great in that uniform. I'm so proud of you."

After they stepped apart, I caught a glimpse of Janice's nametag over her right breast pocket. The first name was Janice, but the last name had at least a dozen letters in it.

Then Christina stepped back, made eye contact with me, and said, "Kurt, this is Janice Hoopaneewanda, also known as Sergeant Hoppy."

"Pleased to meet you, ma'am—" I stuttered, "—um, Sergeant."

"Just call me 'Hoppy,'" Janice said to me. "That's what most people call me; it saves me from having to spell my name a hundred times a day."

Hoppy led us down a hall to a spacious conference room, which was relatively quiet even with the door open. She pointed out chairs for us to sit in, walked around the table, and sat down behind a pile of files, papers, and a tablet. She dug a pencil out of a satchel on the floor and then turned to face Christina.

"It's been a while since I've seen you," Janice said to Christina.

"I don't get over here that much anymore," Christina said. "I'm working more hours now than when I worked for a living."

I wanted to ask how Christina and Hoppy knew each other but decided Christina would fill me in on that later.

"I work such odd hours," Hoppy said. "It gets tough at times, just taking care of my husband and the kids. It seems like the only time I leave Pierre County is if I have to go somewhere for a depo or something."

"When did you make sergeant?" Christina asked.

"A year ago June." She took on a confident look. "So far, I've hung onto it."

"You've got all it takes to be a detective," Christina said. "They won't find a better person than you."

Hoppy beamed, and then swung her gaze toward me. "So, Mr. Maxxon, once again you've discovered a homicide. This makes how many now? Three?"

Her knowing about me caught me off-guard. "Masonville and Kings Rapids," I said. "Not a habit I really want to get into."

"Your reputation precedes you. And that's the reason I wanted to talk to you," she said, maintaining direct eye contact. "I've heard you're pretty good at solving murders, when the cops didn't get it right to start with. However, in the Guerrero homicide, I think we've got it pretty much right. Pretty overwhelming evidence."

"Do you mind sharing what makes you so sure Rachael killed Carlos?" I asked, hoping not to turn her off.

"I'm not prepared to share *all* the information we have with you," Hoppy said. "I will share what I can if it will keep you from going off on your own, in case something turns up that changes your mind. That work for you?"

"Yes. I'm not interested in doing anything with the case. If you've got the killer, that's all I want."

Hoppy studied me for several beats and then slipped a file folder from the pile, opened it, and laid it on the table. She shuffled through the pages to a particular one. "Okay. Carlos died as a result of severe blunt force trauma to the craniocervical junction and collateral injuries—a blow apparently delivered by a cast-iron skillet. The lab guys have absolutely connected the skillet to the wound on Carlos, which was the killing blow. Time of death was between two o'clock and four o'clock. It looks like the victim could have lived up to two hours after the blow."

I sat impassively. I thought Mike Collins had said *they theorized* it might be the skillet. "They *know* it was the skillet?"

"Rachael had apparently made herself an omelet in the kitchen of the Trattoria," Hoppy said. "She ate some of it, Carlos came in, and they argued. When he took a bag of garbage to the dumpster, she followed him, slugged him with the skillet, threw the skillet toward the dumpster, and went back inside. She put the remaining omelet into a Trattoria carryout box and went home. She was probably half smashed all that time. We literally have an omelet crumb trail from murder scene to Rachel's house and her fingerprints all over everything in between, including the skillet."

"It doesn't sound good for Rachael," I said.

Hoppy shook her head. "Did you know Carlos Guerrero?"

"Yes, I did."

"How well?" Hoppy asked.

"Well—from eating most of my meals in the Trattoria the weekends I came to Carpentier Falls to race," I said. "I like Cuban food. Carlos was always friendly. He had a lot of race drivers frequent his place. But, just last Friday, the board of directors for the SRVSCRA warned me that there might have been betting on the races going on at the Trattoria. Do you know anything about the gambling at the Trattoria?"

"What do you know about it?"

"I talked to a guy Sunday morning. He told me about the games being played. He told me there were bookies there occasionally, taking bets on football, basketball, and the races, too. My interest was simply the betting on the races, after what the board told me."

"Who'd you talk to?"

"Dick Schaeffer," I said, hoping I wasn't violating a trust.

Hoppy clicked keys on her computer keyboard. "Richard Schaeffer," Hoppy said. "We talked to him once about gambling at the Trattoria. Nothing open on him now. He works at the packing plant south of town."

"So, about the gambling at the Trattoria?"

"The department knew about the gambling. The FBI came in looking to see if it's big enough to be of interest to the mob, or if the mob was the guiding force. We've monitored the weekend gambling, looking for any connections to organized groups. As long as none of them turned up, or appeared to be snooping around it, we treated it as just a friendly, local bunch of people playing cards."

"They played for money," I said.

"If we busted every group playing cards for money, we wouldn't have time to investigate burglaries, robberies, rapes, murders, or anything else. And we'd fill our jail with otherwise decent citizens."

"It doesn't bother me, if it doesn't bother the sheriff's department." I paused, wondering if I should tell Hoppy about the boys and the fact that their mother had disappeared from Carpentier Falls. I decided not to, since the boys had left with Marguerite and Terry for Kings Rapids.

"So you're going to let us do the detective work, right? No independent amateur sleuth stuff, right?" Hoppy said, bobbing her head for emphasis.

"That works for me," I said.

"That's good," she said and then looked at Christina. "I assume you'll help me keep him from going off on his own?" Hoppy said to her.

"I can try," Christina said. "But I'm leaving tomorrow morning, and he'll be here all by himself."

Hoppy returned to looking at me. "Do you know Rachael Mellon?" she asked.

"Yes, I do."

"How? What's your interest in her?"

"She and I graduated high school together," I said. "In fact, we were going steady when I left to go to Georgia Tech. We've not been close all these years." I suddenly realized I might be saying things Christina didn't know about. But there was no reason to keep it secret.

"Damn," Hoppy muttered, deep creases folding her forehead. "Do you know about her past?"

"Most of it. Bad marriage. Divorce. Two bad kids. Booze. That pretty much sums it up, right?"

"Close," Hoppy said. "Then there's the money she skimmed from Carlos, and her attempts to extort money from him lately."

I suddenly regretted my bravado at even claiming to know Rachael. "You've got evidence for all that?"

"We have an informant working with us on it. We've still got some digging to do, but I think we know where to look."

After the interview, I drove back to Ruby's, so Christina could get her car. Mike Collins had been absolutely right in warning me to stay away from Rachael. At one point I said, "Damn, I had no idea Rachael's life had gone so bad."

"That's because you always root for the underdog," Christina said.

I hate it when other people know my inner secrets, especially those I worry about the most.

I left Christina at her car, saying, "Good-bye, and have a safe trip." Then I drove to the Speedway Hotel and parked in one of the *Registration Only* spaces, because of the packed parking lot. I wondered if it were just day meetings, or if there were a significant number of them staying at the hotel. When I asked the desk clerk if I could get a room, he gave me a startled look. He said, "Why, certainly, Colonel Maxxon. We always have room for you."

He punched computer keys in an automatic pattern, studying the screen. You can have the Presidential Suite or the Bridal Suite," he said. "Your regular rate."

"What's the difference?"

"Just the name. They're identical except for the name."

"I'll take the Presidential Suite."

"Very good, sir." He tore off a computer-generated form, put it on the counter in front of me, and asked me to initial the rate at the top and sign at the bottom. I noticed they had my truck information already filled in, current license number and all.

CHAPTER TWELVE

Monday, September 11

Kurt Maxxon, Afternoon

I took my suitcase and clothes to my room. The king-size bed looked inviting enough to take a nap, but I've never taken naps and wasn't about to start now. I piled my dirty clothes on the floor of the closet, trying to decide when to do laundry. I pulled the change out of my pocket and realized I needed more quarters for the washing machine and dryer. That made it easier to put off doing the laundry.

I dug the wad of notes out of my shirt pocket and leafed through them, looking for the phone number of LeRoy Kitchens. I saw the business card for Gordon Michaelson, so I dialed his number first. He answered, told me Cliff Ramsey had called him, and suggested we meet at the Speedway Grill and Lounge Wednesday afternoon about five o'clock. "I've got a Kiwanis thing at seven," he said. "You can go to that with me, if you like."

I told him I'd think about it and hung up. Then I dialed LeRoy's number, hoping I wasn't waking him up earlier than his usual time. LeRoy sounded bright and chipper and assured me he had been up for a while. The questions I had in mind at the time I probably could have asked him on the phone. As a manager of people, however, I know that the give-and-take of a face-to-face interview usually produces far better results. I asked if I could run by and ask him a couple of questions before he left for work.

"Sure," he said. "Ole Dick tole me you'd talked to him. I probably can't add much to what he tole ya."

"You never know," I said. It was a ten-minute run to LeRoy's house, a small bungalow in a 1960s development about midway between the track and downtown. I saw the door was open, as I walked up onto the small concrete stoop. I pushed the doorbell and heard LeRoy yell, "Come on through; I'm out back on the patio."

The house had a single-car garage, and the living room and kitchen were to the left of the entry door. A wall to the right had a hall leading to three bedrooms and a bathroom. I walked across the house to the sliding screen door leading to the patio. It was hot and muggy inside the house. If he owned an air conditioner, it either didn't work or wasn't on. A high-pressure ridge had passed through Carpentier Falls overnight and stalled out just to the east, pumping hot, moist air up from the Gulf of Mexico.

LeRoy sat in the shade of a yellow umbrella, at an octagonal metal picnic table with glass top. He had scattered the morning newspaper on top of the table. He waved me out and stood to shake my hand. LeRoy was in his mid-forties, no more than five foot five, but his head was an elongated oval set on top of a long neck, which had the effect of making his body seem smaller. He was prematurely balding, and he shaved the stubble short. His ears stuck straight out from his head, like flower petals. His eyes were dark brown, large, and sparkled with what I usually ascribed to pure mischief. His nose had been broken several times, and it angled in two directions. His grip was the firmest I'd encountered in a while.

"Pleased to meet you, Mr. Maxxon," he said. "Dick tells me you're quite a race driver. I don't follow the car races that much. Bet on the ponies once in a while."

"At the Trattoria?"

"No. I go over to Farmers City to the horse racing track there," LeRoy said. "I get the handicap sheets and a program, and I spend a lot of time handicapping the horses. You know, so I can pick the winners. That's why I'm so wealthy." His mouth cracked into a toothy grin, showing an upper and a lower incisor missing.

"Do you know the bookie who took bets on the car races at the Trattoria?"

"Nah. I didn't know him. Dick was trying to describe him. I don't think either one of us ever heard his name. Dick says he shows up a couple times a month, mostly making book on football and basketball."

"Was Carlos responsible for the gambling at the Trattoria?"

"Yeah, well … probably. I never saw him in the room while we were playing. But, hell, he let us use his room."

"Was there a cover charge to get in?" I was fishing for clues.

"Nah. Carlos made money off the cash bar and snacks. Several guys, like Dick and me, got there early enough to eat dinner. The barkeep had to know ya, before ya could play. If the barkeep didn't know ya, then someone already in had to vouch for ya. But no cover charge."

After I had exhausted my interest in the gambling, I wanted to know about the girl who hadn't shown up. I said, "You said something about a girl not showing up. What was that all about?"

"Yeah. Well, since my ole lady took the kids and ran off with our insurance agent a couple of years ago," LeRoy paused, "I been known to buy a little sex, now and again, rather than go out chasing it. I know I might get lucky and get it for free, but working the crazy hours I do, I don't get much chance. It's easier to just call and have a girl meet me."

"So you use a call-girl service?"

"Yeah. I guess that's what you'd call it."

"Are the girls working at the Trattoria?" I asked, frowning a little.

"Nah, they always came there to hook up with me, usually by taxi." LeRoy took a sip from his coffee cup. "Damn," he said. "My bad manners. Ya'll want a cup of coffee?"

"No, thank you," I said. "So, you just called, and a girl would show up?"

"Yeah. I had a phone number. The same woman always answered and took my order. She was the 'madam,' I guess they call them."

"Could you ask for a specific girl?"

"Yeah. And a few months ago, I did. I started asking for Candy. She was sweet and awful damn good in bed. Rumor has it she's the favorite of ole Reggie Claymore, our illustrious congressman. Hell, he's eighty years old, so I doubt he can wear her out," LeRoy said, with a wink and a chuckle. "I hope I'm still going strong when I'm eighty."

"But Candy didn't show up Thursday night?" I asked.

"Somebody told me they saw her get in a car and leave a few minutes before my meetin' with her," LeRoy said. "She mighta got a better offer. Maybe ole Reggie showed up. I don't know. I *do* know her real name isn't Candy. I saw her underwear, and other clothes, one time, lying on the chair in the motel room. Her bra and panties, at least, had *Chaundra Dunkin* stenciled in them like they do when ya send your laundry out. I used to, but been doing my own lately."

I wanted to remember the name, so I repeated it. "Chaundra Dunkin stenciled into her clothes?"

LeRoy nodded, emptied his cup, and swung around to get up. "I'm goin' to get another cup. Sure ya don't want one?" he said, as he stood up and moved toward the kitchen door.

"I never turn down coffee," I said, "if it's not too much trouble."

"It's already made, and still fresh, too. You need cream or sugar?"

"Just black, thanks."

"Good," he said. "I'm not sure if I got any sugar, and all I have is milk." He stopped just before he slid the screen door open. "Another thing ..." LeRoy frowned as he paused. "Candy couldn't have been much more than sixteen or seventeen years old." He disappeared into the kitchen. After a few minutes he reappeared, carrying two mismatched mugs of coffee.

"How old does a girl have to be to be a—what, a call girl?" I asked.

"It ain't how old she has to be; it's like—and I never thought about it before just now—but what's the age for statutory rape around here?"

"I have no idea," I said, having never thought about the subject before in my life.

"I hope it's sixteen," LeRoy said.

"Did these girls work for Carlos Guerrero? Was Carlos involved in any way?"

"I don't know," he said. "But if I had to guess, I'd say he probably was."

"Do you know the woman who is the madam?"

"No. I might recognize her voice if I ran into her. But I doubt it."

"You work at the same place as Dick Schaefer?"

"Yeah, we both work the same shift, four to midnight, Saturday through Wednesday. Been doing it for seven years now. Ole Dick's been doing it for twelve."

I left LeRoy and drove back to the hotel. I had worried about Carlos's reputation and whether he had had a hand in the gambling and, now, the prostitution, associated with the Trattoria. So far, however, it was probable that Carlos knew what was going on, but was only letting others do their thing. I hoped that was all.

When I got back to my room, I tried to decide whether to do my laundry then or wait until after supper. I'd passed Marcelles Steak House on my way back from LeRoy's, and it was like a magnet. Eating alone in a fancy steak house was always a little embarrassing to me, but Marcelles opened at five, and there were usually only a few couples eating there at that hour. There was always a chance they might be race fans and know I'd lost my wife a few years before.

The thought of a thick, juicy Kansas City strip steak was the tiebreaker. I took a quick shower and dressed to be ready to leave at five. Christina called just as I was combing my hair, to tell me she and her friend were at the airport in Centralia and would be boarding in a few minutes. She worried about me being alone in Carpentier Falls. How was I doing? What was I going to do for supper?

I told her of my plans for Marcelles; she said she wished she were going with me and bid me good-bye when they called her boarding section. I went to my truck and drove to Marcelles.

* * *

Chaundra Dunkin

Chaundra studied the woman across the desk from her. Then she looked again at the sheet lying in front of her on the desk. She took a deep breath. "I don't want to come back to high school here," she said. "I want to go the GED route."

"That's fine," the counselor said. "I can get you set up for that. Do you want to do that this evening?"

"If—if I could," Chaundra said. "I know it's late, but I'd like to show it to my mother when she gets home from work. She and my stepdad are going to Nashville this coming weekend. So I'd like her to do whatever she has to do tomorrow or Wednesday, so she can plan and pack Thursday and Friday."

"I'm pretty sure we can," the counselor said. "There's an advisor at the community college until about seven each evening. Can I reach you on this cell phone number?"

"Yes."

As Chaundra approached her new Ford Mustang, she walked around it, admiring its shape and the black with silver trim, remembering how proud Gordon had seemed when he took her to the car lot this morning to pick it up. *Maybe Gordon hasn't been the problem.*

She started to open the car door but stopped to watch a boy walking toward her.

"Hey, Chaun," the boy said. "Is this your car?"

"Oh, hi, Quig," she said. "Yes, it is," she let her pride slip into her voice.

"You must have hit it big. I've been wondering where you went. Haven't seen you around for a while."

"I've been working out of town since I dropped out of school last year. Lotta hours, you know, never got back here except weekends."

Quigley Carmichael nodded. "You coming back to school? That what you're doing here now?"

"Not coming back to school here. I'm going into the adult program at Community College."

"You dating anyone?"

"Yes, I'm really into another thing altogether. I'm not on the market."

"That's too bad," he said. "I always liked you a lot, and I thought we were getting along good. I had a tough time accepting it when you just up and dumped me."

"I'm sorry, Quig," she said. "I didn't mean to hurt anyone. I had some real problems that I couldn't handle, so I just bailed out."

"I knew you were having problems, what with your mother and all," Quigley said. "But you coulda talked to me, though, not just go off and leave me."

Chaundra let her mind wander back to the days when she had decided to go into prostitution and the problems that were overwhelming her then. Her mother. The divorce from her dad. Her mother's indifference to her problems—about boys—and about her increasing interest in other girls. "Like I said, Quigley, I'm sorry about what I did."

"Who is the other guy?"

"You don't know him," she said, looking away quickly. "He—he lives out in the country, on a farm. He—uh, he graduated from East a couple of years ago."

"What did I ever do to you?" Quigley gave her a hard look.

"Quigley, please. Leave it alone. It's over. I'm sorry about what I did. But there's nothing I can do about it now. So, please, just let it go, and leave me alone."

"Okay," he said in a pouty voice. He walked away.

Chaundra got into her car and drove away quickly. *I didn't need that. That's exactly why I chose the adult ed program.*

* * *

Kurt Maxxon

As I walked out of Marcelles Steak House, the heat and humidity hit me like a sledgehammer. I climbed into my truck and cranked the air conditioner up to high, while I left the door open. I was glad Beau was up at Buster's place and I didn't have to worry about him. I didn't like leaving him alone in the hotel, and I sure didn't want to leave him in my truck. Even with the windows cracked, the temperature inside was sauna-like and probably deadly.

Back at the hotel, I gathered my dirty clothes into a pillowcase and headed for the laundry room. Then I remembered I needed quarters and went back to the front desk for change. I'd just gotten the washer going, when my cell phone jangled. It was Marguerite, and I dreaded what she was going to tell me.

Marguerite was in her business-as-usual mood, and was succinct. "Brad Langley and the state lab are almost certain the boys' mother and the woman found stabbed to death in Marysville are the same woman. But they still don't have a good ID, and, until we do, I don't want to tell the boys. Both of them insist their last name is Lawton, and they don't know where they lived before Carpentier Falls. Did they tell you anything at all that might help track down their past?"

"I'm sorry, Marguerite," I said. "I've already racked my brain. I can't come up with anything that might help."

With freshly cleaned clothes, I returned to my room and brewed a pot of decaf coffee. I sat down at the desk with my writing tablet and recorded highlights of my conversation with LeRoy. I stopped and flipped the tablet to a new sheet. Now, with the news that the boys' mother was most likely dead, I felt a new need to run their past down. I wrote "Auntie Jean" at the top of the page. The boys had mentioned her several times when talking about their life since they'd arrived in Carpentier Falls. They'd showed me the complex she lived in when we drove past it on our way to Sam's Diner last Friday night. If my memory was working right, the boys had said she lived in apartment H-6.

Auntie Jean might be the person to fill in some blanks.

The boys and their mother had lived in the same complex, so Auntie Jean probably knew their mother. And, perhaps, just maybe, their mother had told Auntie Jean about their past. I wondered if the boys had told Marguerite and Terry about Auntie Jean. I should have mentioned that to Marguerite, and I promised myself I would the next time I talked to her. If Terry was going to come to Carpentier Falls to investigate, he could use a spotter running interference for him. I could do that.

I watched the ten o'clock news to see what the weather was going to do. The forecast was for heat and humidity again tomorrow, with a slight possibility of rain through the day, and a better chance during the night.

I turned the air conditioner down and went to bed.

CHAPTER THIRTEEN

Tuesday, September 12

Kurt Maxxon, Morning

I had breakfast at Grandma's, polishing off her famous big breakfast at a leisurely pace and then admonishing myself for not eating healthier. While I ate, I wrestled with what I should do. I could just bide my time until Carlos's funeral on Wednesday, then go get Beau, and go home to Albertstown—let the chips fall as they might. No matter how I sliced and diced it, the authorities appeared to have a pretty solid case against Rachael. There was no good reason for me to stay in Carpentier Falls, other than to see how the case unfolded and maybe do a little investigating of my own.

The morning's light fog had started to ease, even as I finished breakfast and was sipping my last cup of coffee. It was going to be another hot and humid day, with mostly sunny skies and light and variable winds. The only real winds blowing were inside me, where my naturally curious mind and unrelenting mental energy erupted every time some part of me whispered, "Cool it. Just leave it alone. Go get Beau. Go home."

Joshua and Jacob came to mind. The boys didn't deserve what they were getting, and I hoped that between myself, Christina, Marguerite, and Terry, we could get them through it without too much damage to their emotions and future. I decided to implement the plan I'd generated last night just before I fell asleep—talk to Auntie Jean to see what she knew about the boys and their mother. That would keep me busy and not interfering with Sergeant Hoppy's investigation into Carlos's murder. If and when Terry Grossman came to Carpentier Falls to investigate, I'd have done some of the legwork for him.

The complex was on Roosevelt Boulevard, about where I remembered. Thinking about the boys' mother caused me to miss the entrance to it from Roosevelt. I turned the corner and drove into the Ash Street entrance.

I drove into the parking lot that had a sign indicating it was the Roosevelt Complex and parked near the building the boys had pointed out. They had mentioned she lived in apartment H-6, if I remembered correctly, and there was a faded letter "H" visible near the top of the building. A city worker was mending a pipe railing down the concrete stairs, and he watched me climb down out of my truck. He eyed the truck as I walked toward him. "I don't think I'd be leaving a truck like that parked here too long, mister." I scanned the parking lot. Around the edges were three cars on blocks without tires and two burned-out hulls—the remains of cars stripped for everything valuable. "How long have I got?" I asked him.

"I'll be here another hour fixin' this pipe. Who you lookin' for?

"Auntie Jean—"

"Apartment H-6, right through that door, and up to the fourth floor, then left," the man said as he walked to his pickup truck for another tool.

"Is she home?"

"Auntie Jean is always home."

I pushed my way through the heavy metal entry door and climbed the three flights of dirt-covered stairs, feeling justified for eating a big breakfast. The landings and floor corners reeked with the smell of urine. Empty cigarette and condom packs were on the stairs and in the hall. I found apartment H-6 and rapped on the door. There was noisy movement inside. After a long time, I heard security chains bang against the door, the click of a deadbolt, then a knob being twisted, and the door squeaked open a crack. I could see the left eye of an African-American woman.

"Whadda ya wan?" the woman asked.

"I'd like to talk to you about Joshua and Jacob Lawton," I said, trying to ignore the odor emanating from the apartment.

Her breath caught, and I could see her eyes were thinking. "Dem boys in tro'ble?"

"No, ma'am," I said, breaking eye contact, hoping she would not feel threatened. I tried for a pensive look, unemotional. "But I need some information about their mother."

"She in tro'ble?"

"We don't know, ma'am," I fibbed slightly, since I wasn't absolutely certain of her fate. I hoped God would give me a little leeway. "But she's disappeared," I said, wanting to maintain her interest. I decided against telling Auntie Jean we thought she was dead.

"Dis'peared." The woman opened the door and looked around. "Whar de boys?"

I looked into a cluttered apartment. "They're safe and secure," I said. I realized the woman was standing with the help of a battered aluminum walker.

"Whar?" she demanded, and her face told me she would not be put off.

"They went to Kings Rapids yesterday," I said. "They're staying with friends of mine there."

"Sum whitey got 'em?"

"Not exactly," I said, wondering how this was going to play out. "Look ..." I realized I didn't know this woman's name. "Ma'am, I'm sorry, but the only name I have for you is Auntie Jean. I'm Kurt Maxxon. What is your name?"

The woman relaxed a little. The fight was leaving her.

"Jeanette," she said. "Jeanette Trossler. But de boys, dey always call me Auntie Jean."

"Mrs. Trossler—"

"You jes call me Jean," she said, leaning into the hall to look down it in both directions. "You might as well come in—the whole buildin' knows you here talkin' to me by now." She backed into the apartment.

I followed her. She closed the door behind me, clicked two mechanical locks, but left the three chains hanging open. The apartment was about the size of a single-car garage, with a bathroom walled off in the back right corner. Next to it was an open kitchen, with a worn and leaning chrome dinette table and one chair.

The front room had a couch that was probably a foldout bed, but I suspected Jean slept on it the way it was. A small rabbit-eared TV sat on a rickety utility table. Jean had probably rummaged them out of dumpsters somewhere. There was a salvaged wood nightstand with a too-tall lamp on it. Cardboard boxes filled with junk cluttered the remaining space.

Jean was about five foot five and quite heavy. A head of wild, dull gray hair highlighted her dark chocolate-colored skin. Her dull hazel eyes perched over pudgy dark cheeks. She had a hooked nose that bent toward the right side of her face. Her mouth drooped on the right side, and a track of saliva leaked from the corner.

Jean shuffled to the couch and plopped down into it. I walked to the kitchen, brought the dinette chair to the living room, and sat down.

"Irene dis'peared?" she asked.

"Is that her name?'

"De boys' mother named Irene," she said. "You didn't know dat?"

"No, ma'am," I said. "She was Irene Lawton?" I repeated the name.

"Uh-huh. How'd you get the boys?'"

"I found Joshua and Jacob last Thursday … at the racetrack—"

"Way down der?" she said, shaking her head. "Wha' dey doin' down der?"

"They were looking for food—"

"Why dey don't come heah?"

"I don't know, ma'am. I suspect—"

"Dey come heah near ev'ry day. We have PB en J sam'witches. Dem boys love PB en J sam'witches."

To give the boys peanut butter and jelly sandwiches had to be a sacrifice for this woman. "The police may come around to talk to you—"

"Don' wan no police coming heah."

I might be the only person the boys had told about Auntie Jean. If they told Marguerite and Terry, hopefully it would be Terry who came to talk to her. In the meantime, I wasn't going to say anything about her. Again, I was hoping for a little forbearance from God. "Do you know who Irene Lawton dated, went out with, or about—"

"She not date nobody while she live heah," Jean said. "She not do nuttin 'cept work and take care o' doze two boys."

"Where did she work?"

"Don know wha' comp'ny was. She put t'ings togeder, you know, she sit at one place all day long an' put parts into sumt'ing. I tink she say make some kinda boxes. She tell me, 'It boring as hell,' an she cut her fingers most ev'ry day. Turr-ible job," she said, drawling out the word "terrible."

"How far did she drive to work?"

"Irene got no car. She walk ev'ry whar."

"So she worked on an assembly line within walking distance of here," I said. "Do you know what direction?"

"Dat way," Jean said, pointing west.

"What apartment did Irene rent?"

"I don' know. Dey live in the odder building over der," she said, pointing to the north. "Never been der."

"Did you see Irene often?" I asked.

"When dey live heah, I did. She come over ev'ry now en again. But then they had to move, en I not see her again, mebbe once."

"They had to move—why?"

"Sumbuddy stole her purse. Got all her money, for de rent, food, ev'ry t'ing. Irene, she try to make it, but den she say she can't do it no more. She go ren' a place in dem slum projects a few blocks east of heah. She an' de boys put der clothes in groc'ry sacks and left. She say, 'Now, I gotta walk o'er a mile to work.'"

"Were the boys here a lot over the last few weeks?"

"Sure. Dey come heah ev'ry day. I watch 'em."

"You babysat with the boys during summer vacation?"

"Shor nuff. I luv dem boys like my own," she said, and I could tell the words were coming right from her heart. "When Irene disappear?"

"I don't know for sure, but it has been several weeks."

"Good Lawd," Jean muttered. "De boys come heah ev'ry day, even weekends. Dey stay till dark, den go home." She frowned, and her eyes moved from side to side. "Whar dem boys bin stayin'?"

I thought about evading the question, but guessed Jean wouldn't let me. "The boys have been living under a highway bridge," I said.

"Unner a bridge," Jean spat, her eyes widening. I wondered if she had heart problems, because she lost her breath.

"Are you all right?" I asked her.

"I'm out of med'cin."

"What kind of medicine?"

"Blood pressure. Heart."

"Why are you out of medicine?" I asked. "Do you have the money?"

"Not righ' now. Welfare check due tomarra. I can't go get it myself."

"Who gets your medicine?" I asked.

"The boys been gittin' it for me de last little while. If dey don', James, he git it."

"James lives in this building or the other building?"

"Dis one. He come up and ax me, 'You need anyt'ing Auntie Jean?'"

"He calls you Aunt Jean, too?"

"Ev'ry body call me Aunt Jean. You can too, effn' you wan."

I smiled. Jean was old enough to be my great-aunt. Jean returned my smile. A new thought crossed my mind. "Is there an elevator in this building?" I asked.

"Yeah. But it quit workin' a few months back," Jean said. "Dey always takes 'bout six month to get it fixed. Daz why I don' go no place. I kant get back up dem stairs."

I nodded my understanding. I wondered when the last time was she'd been out of the apartment but decided not to ask. "What can you tell me about Irene? When did she and the boys arrive in Carpentier Falls? Where did they come from?"

"Can't say whar dey cum from. Donno dat. Dey move heah abow two year ago, springtime, mebbe. Irene, she not talk much about before dat. De boys looked like dey been beat up on when dey firs move heah. Lot of scars and stuff. Pore 'ittle Jacob, he got a crooked leg, ya know. Got it busted sum'how and not righ'ly fixed."

I hadn't watched the boys while they showered in the locker room. They both always had jeans on when I saw them.

"Maybe Irene took the boys and ran away from an abusive father," I said, frowning. "Maybe she was hiding out here, but the father found them?"

"Mebbe."

A new twist. I also realized I hadn't questioned the boys that much about their life before Carpentier Falls. The few times we had talked about it, I'd decided the boys' memories of their lives were kind of muddled. That might be due to their being so young and not paying attention, or it could be that their mother had drilled into them an ability to not want to get it right.

I stood up and carried the chair back to the kitchen. "Where's your empty medicine bottles?" I asked.

"O'er der on the sink," Jean said, pointing toward the kitchen. "Wha' you do?"

I picked up five medicine vials, from a pharmacy a few blocks east on Roosevelt, and read the labels. One was a statin drug. There was also a blood thinner, a beta blocker, a calcium channel blocker, and one I didn't recognize. I suspected it might be a prescription NSAID. "You take a baby aspirin, too?" I asked.

"Yeah. But, I got nuff of dem."

Not an NSAID, then.

"You need any groceries?"

"I got sum crackers, peanut butter, grape jelly, and SPAM left. Need bread."

I got Jean's medications and stopped at the grocery store in the same strip mall. I wondered if I could get James to help me carry the ten bags of food I'd bought; while also hoping I wasn't spoiling Auntie Jean. If she became used to eating the foods I do, she would never survive on her meager social security check. Social Security and Medicare—even with Medicaid, don't cover much these days.

*   *   *

Tammy McPherson

Tammy cracked the door and surveyed the area outside the motel room. She slipped through the door and walked west on Roosevelt for several blocks. At a pawnshop, she stopped to inspect something in the window, while checking the people on the street around her. Satisfied she didn't see anyone suspicious, she walked back east on Roosevelt, past the motel to the coffee stand, where she stopped and ordered a cup of coffee. She sat on a bus bench sipping it, as she surveyed the people moving around her.

Then she quickly crossed the street, hurried down the alley, and ducked into an alcove, where she waited while she caught her breath. Satisfied that no one was tailing her, she moved to the cross street and made her way to the train station seven blocks away. She sat in the station for several minutes, watching the few people who moved around in it. Finally, Tammy dug her briefcase out of the locker and carried it to a stall in the ladies' rest room, where she laid it flat on the toilet seat, entered the combination, and clicked the case open.

She took an envelope from her bra, put it into the briefcase, and then closed and relocked the lid.

Tammy stood in front of the mirror, patting her hair into place and checking her makeup. She left the rest room and walked around the train station for a few minutes, carrying the briefcase, in normal businesswoman mode, paying attention to the few people milling around in it. But no one showed interest in her or the briefcase. Most of the people were railroad workers she'd seen before. Then she chose a new locker, put the briefcase into it, entered the quarters required and took the key.

As she always did, Tammy found a seat—not close to the lockers, but such that she could watch the lockers. She always worried someone had rigged the locker to open it without a key. The constant concern about using the briefcase as a safe-deposit box surfaced again. Should she get a real safe-deposit box at a bank? That would require that she open an account with the bank, however, and what would happen if she had to leave town faster than she planned? The train station was open twenty-four hours, seven days a week.

A man walking toward her jerked Tammy's attention back to the present. He was one of the private security people who patrolled the station. She stiffened. The man stopped in front of her. "Excuse me, ma'am, is that your blue Mercedes parked outside the front door?"

"Uh ... no. No, I'm walking."

"Sorry to bother you, ma'am," the man said, walking away. "It's in the fire lane, and we're about to tow it."

Tammy let her breath out. *Why are you still sitting here? The security guard had seen her here. He would remember her. Cops and security guards are all trained to observe details. That guard could identify her and tie her to the briefcase. Maybe she needed to put the money into another container. Maybe a suitcase. Yeah, a suitcase ... a suitcase with wheels on it.*

The combination of fifty- and hundred-dollar notes, plus the briefcase, weighed nearly twenty pounds. *It'll be nice to wheel it around rather than carry it.*

With over four hundred thousand dollars in the briefcase, was leaving it in a locker at the train station a good idea? How could she keep it safe? She recalled one of her girls had told her she'd bought U.S. Savings Bonds regularly. "They're safe and easy to carry," the girl had said. "In case you have to leave town in a hurry."

Tammy calculated that if she bought one ten-thousand-dollar bond at one bank, it would take over forty banks, because someone in government scrutinized transactions over ten thousand dollars. She should probably buy five-thousand-dollar bonds. That would mean she'd have to deal with over eighty banks. Not a chance, her mind told her.

She worried that if she visited even a half dozen banks, someone would notice and get suspicious. Would the U.S. Treasury Department notice? *Probably not too quickly. Eventually, for sure, but not fast enough to slow her down. What name should I use? Deborah Lynelle Glassmayer, my Christian name? Tamara Lynelle McPherson, my professional name? Tabatha Christianson, my most commonly used alias? Or should I come up with another name?* She wondered if she'd have to show a social security card. If she did, that would squelch the whole idea. But most advisors today recommended you didn't carry your social security card on you. Banks typically just asked you for your social security number and accepted it verbally.

Tammy put the locker key into her wallet pocket, and she saw the lockbox key. Her mind wondered back to that key. *Where would Carlos keep that lockbox? I'm sure that's where the ledger sheets are.*

Then Sergeant Hoppy's mention of untaxed cigarettes came to mind. The girls had been the only thing of interest to her at the time. *Lord knows, they kept me busy enough. Where would Carlos keep the cigarettes? If he had a secret storage place for them, that's probably where he kept the lockbox.*

Tammy started to put her wallet back into the fanny pack she wore around her waist, but she stopped and opened another section. *If you open a bank account you'll definitely have to show a driver's license.* She dug her license out and studied it. It had expired six months ago.

Damn good thing I checked that. Should I risk renewing it? I don't drive that much anymore. How do you plan to get out of town, hon? Train? Drive?

Dammit.

*   *   *

Kurt Maxxon

Jean's apartment complex was a group of eight buildings that occupied a four-square-block area north of Roosevelt and west from Ash Street. Roosevelt is the main east-west drag through Carpentier Falls. The north-south streets are alphabetical with various topics, and this part of town is trees. The east-west streets originally ran from A to R, before postwar developers started carving streets that didn't run on a square grid and were named by the developer's wives or girlfriends. Roosevelt would be M street if the scheme hadn't been broken. I drove slowly west on K Street, past various commercial and industrial businesses, and looked down the side streets, but nothing looked to be a company that assembled something that would cut Irene's fingers. *Did Auntie Jean say she cut her fingers every day?* Oak Street was the next major north-south street, twelve blocks west of Ash Street. I turned south on Oak, idling along. Nothing looked promising. I went south, crossed Roosevelt, and turned back east on O Street. I planned to drive along Roosevelt on my way back to the motel. Most of the businesses were distributors of various and sundry hardware and materials.

Five blocks later, at the corner of O Street and Juniper Avenue, I saw the sign on a building for Arnold Toolboxes, "The Strongest Toolboxes in the World." I took a chance, parked in a "visitors" space, and went in.

The receptionist asked how she could help me. I asked to speak with the personnel manager. She asked my name, then punched a number, and spoke into her headset. She had stopped talking for only a moment, when a door across the open entry area opened and a smiling woman came toward me. She was a healthy thirty-something who looked as if she did aerobics at least three times a week and the other days something else to keep her shape. Her hair was red, parted in the middle of her head, and hung to the middle of her back. Her eyes were emerald, and she had a pronounced assemblage of freckles on a pleasant oval face. Her blue tank top and hip-hugger jeans highlighted her figure.

As she neared me, she swung her hand out to me, "Colonel Maxxon, I'm so happy to meet you in person." She paused. "I follow car racing," she added, as if to cover her obvious excitement. "I'm Beverly Warrenton, Employee Relations. Please, come into my office."

I followed Beverly into a cluttered office. She pointed toward a chair in front of her desk and swung around to sit down in her chair. "How can I help you?"

"Well, I'm flying blind, but I was wondering if Arnold's ever had an employee named Irene Lawton?"

Beverly's eyebrows lifted, enlarging her eyes. Some of the emerald was coming from tinted contact lenses. "Are you a friend of hers?"

"Sort of," I said. "I just—"

"Let me get Kenny in here," Beverly said, holding up a hand like a cop stopping traffic. She reached for a phone and spoke into it. "He'll be right in," she added and fell silent. A few minutes later, there was a rap at the door, and Beverly said, "Come in."

A gray-haired man of medium height, in a three-piece blue serge suit, blue button-down shirt, and conservative blue-and-red tie, walked in and came toward me. He was a couple of inches taller than me, with a marathon runner's slenderness. His oxford brogue shoes gleamed.

"This is Kenneth Arnold," Beverly said. "He's the owner."

"Colonel Maxxon. I'm very pleased to meet you," the man said as we shook hands. "Call me Kenny, like everyone else does."

"He's asking about Irene Lawton," Beverly said. "He's a friend of hers."

Kenny motioned for me to sit down as he did. "And what would you like to know about Ms. Lawton?"

"I'm trying to figure out what happened to her," I said.

"How well do you know Ms. Lawton?" Beverly asked.

"Not well at all," I said. "I'm coming to the game late. I do know she had two little boys, and they've been living under bridges and stealing food to get by. I ran into them last week."

"Damn," Kenny said, frowning and pursing his lips.

"Irene's last name is not Lawton," Beverly said, glancing at Kenny, who nodded approval for her to tell all.

That took me by surprise. "What is it?" I asked.

Beverly continued, "The social security number she gave us turned out to be for an Irene Faye Wallace. Naturally we did some checking, to determine if it was real or a stolen ID. A driver's license issued to Irene Faye Wallace two years ago, here in Carpentier Falls, has her picture on it. She would have had to turn in an old license to get the new one, so Wallace is probably her real last name. We have no idea what she was doing or why she was using another name."

"And then, she just didn't show up for work one day," Kenny added. "We didn't look into this until that happened. Then, all of a sudden, we had a mystery on our hands. We've never had anything like this happen before."

"When did that happen?" I asked.

Beverly dug out a file folder from her desk drawer. "August third—a Thursday—was her last day," Beverly said, reading from the file. "She was here Wednesday, the second. Next day, she didn't show up for work and no word about why. We've not heard a word since."

"Did she have any friends here at work, people she talked to?" I asked.

"Not close ones," Beverly said. "She was a loner, and working on the assembly line doesn't allow a lot of socializing. At break times and lunch, maybe. We talked to all our people, and there wasn't a lot of information about her. She had two boys. She was having financial problems. She had to move into the city's poorest project. That's about all anybody knew about her."

"Do you have that address?" I asked, thinking of Terry Grossman investigating.

Beverly scribbled the address on a note sheet and handed it to me.

"She didn't talk to anyone about where she came from, or why?"

"Nothing we could learn," Kenny said.

"Did you call the police about this?" I asked.

"No," Beverly and Kenny said together. They looked at one another, and then Beverly said, "We didn't have any reason to call them the first few days. I mean, we've had employees leave and not call us for several days. Then, after a while, we figured that if something had happened, the police would contact us. But they never did. So we just wrote it off as a disgruntled employee who went off and found another job."

"Does that happen often?"

"Not very often," Kenny said. "But it has happened to us before. Generally, our employees are happy, and most of them have been with us for several years." Kenny swung around to face me. "Colonel Maxxon, we'd just as soon none of this hit the streets. Nothing nefarious, I assure you. We're prepared to help all we can to find Irene. But we have other issues we have to deal with."

"We always have to deal with illegals," Beverly said. "It's a real problem for small businesses, in addition to all the other mandates from the government. At the time we hired Irene, we had just finished the addition to our building, and we hired fifteen new people in a short time. We did the best we could to screen them. But, still, if this gets out, everybody with a dog in the immigration debate will start bugging us. We try to run a nice, quiet little business."

"I understand," I said.

"Are you in charge of the boys?" Kenny asked.

"Sort of," I said. "But I sent them to Kings Rapids to stay with friends of mine there: Marguerite and Terry Grossman. Marguerite is the chief of police in Kings Rapids, and Terry is an ex-homicide detective."

Kenny raised his eyebrows. "Pretty high-powered baby-sitters."

"Yes, well they both took to the boys."

"We have Irene's two final paychecks," Beverly said. "We—"

Kenny said. "Maybe we could reissue the checks to Irene Wallace and her boys' names. Let me talk to my attorney and CPA about doing that. If we can do something like that, would you get the checks to the boys?" he asked.

"Yes, I will. I'll be going to see them in a few days."

"Beverly, would you follow that up?" Kenny asked.

I gave them one of my KurtMaxxonRacing.com business cards after I scribbled my cell phone number and room number at the Speedway Hotel on it.

Kenny walked with me to the parking lot. "You drive a pickup truck, don't you?" Kenny asked.

I pointed to my truck. "That's it right there."

"A Ford F-450 crew cab," he said. "Christ, that's only a few ounces short of a semitruck."

"Yes, well, it hauls my cab-over camper and tows my car transporter for Nikki."

"Nikki is your racecar?"

"A Ford Taurus."

"If you could use a couple of Arnold toolboxes," he said with a broad smile, "I'll make you a great deal. Factory-direct price, so to speak."

I looked at the billboard along the fence of the parking lot, which showed a utility truck with shiny Arnold custom-built boxes. "That the kind of toolboxes you make?"

"Yes. We make boxes for pickup beds, but we do more for commercial repair trucks. That's where our expansion has been the last decade or so."

"You replace the pickup bed with a big box with all kinds of drawers and doors, that the kind?" I smiled.

"That's the kind."

I told Kenny that my camper precluded me having anything other than carry-on toolboxes, but that I would recommend his toolboxes to anyone who would listen. "And maybe," I said, "We could do some kind of custom arrangement for my auto parts stores to get you some business."

Kenny handed me one of his business cards. "Let's do that," he said as we shook hands. "It'll be profitable for both of us."

I climbed into my truck and started to twist the ignition. Something in the pile of camping gear in the backseat caught my eye. When they'd left for Kings Rapids with Marguerite and Terry Grossman, the boys had asked me to watch over their sleeping bags and other personal effects. I had agreed to stow the stuff in my parts store in Centralia. The only thing they'd taken with them was the picture of their mother, which Marguerite had promised she would get a frame for.

So I could turn, and see plainly, I undid my seatbelt. I realized the boys had also left their little metal treasure box—with the little key in the lock. Now, that's trust.

I reached back to move the box, so it wasn't visible from outside the truck. I'd feel terrible if someone broke in and stole it on my watch. It seemed heavy for a box with a few papers in it.

*　　*　　*

When I entered my motel room, I noticed the cleaning people had left me a hefty pile of coffee bags. So I brewed a pot of coffee. No sense having to run to the lobby every fifteen minutes. I sat at the desk and took out a writing tablet. I jotted notes of my interview with Aunt Jean. After several false starts and wadded up sheets thrown into and around the wastebasket, I finally got on a roll, and I kept going until I figured I had most of it on paper.

Then I wrote the questions that popped into my mind:
Where did Irene and the boys live before Carpentier Falls?
Was the boys' father abusive?
To the boys?
To Irene?
Did the father find them?
Did the father take their mother—had he harmed her? Killed her?

Why did he leave the boys alone?

After thinking more about what Auntie Jean had told me, I jotted to the right of the fifth one: *He might not have been able to catch the boys.*

The boys had told me a lot about themselves, but only the latest, what's happening now, stuff. What about their past?

The box.

Did their treasure box hold answers to any of my questions? I worried that I was violating the boys' trust. *Does that box have the same sanctity as a young girl's diary?* I smiled as I remembered when my twelve-year-old daughter, Vanessa, had accused Little Kurt of reading her diary. "Dull as wood swords," nine-year-old Kurt had quipped. "Daaaaddy," Vanessa had wailed. I debated all this for a few minutes, and then I went to the truck to get it.

I put the box on the desk, and sat looking at it for several minutes. After a lot of internal debate, I opened it.

The top sheet was a birth certificate, for Joshua Wyeth Wallace, born September 23, 1994, at the Evandale General Hospital. Mother was Irene (Lawlor) Wallace. Father was Randolph H. Wallace.

"Irene Lawlor Wallace," I said aloud. *That social security number came back for an Irene Faye Wallace*, I remembered Beverly Warren saying.

The next sheet was a birth certificate for Jacob Michael Wallace, born September 21, 1996. Parents were the same, Irene and Randolph Wallace.

The next sheet was a sheet of heavy parchment paper folded to envelope size. I gently unfolded it to see a college diploma. The Regents of St. Mary's College in Evandale had awarded Irene Faye Lawlor the degree of Bachelor of Arts in Human Relations.

Irene Faye Lawlor? Irene Lawlor Wallace?

A picture started to form in my mind.

The last piece of loose paper was a marriage certificate, showing that Randolph H. Wallace had married Irene Faye Lawlor on July 17, 1993, in the Living Memories Wedding Chapel in Evandale.

At the bottom of the box was a thick, brown clasp envelope, jammed full and heavy. I figured it was photographs and set it aside to look at later.

I dialed Terry Grossman's number on the room phone. His secretary answered, and when I asked for Terry she told me he was in a meeting. I gave her my name and number and hung up. My stomach growled, and I started debating where to go for lunch. The salad bar/buffet in the hotel seemed to be the most convenient, especially now that I had an envelope of pictures to go through.

I hadn't made a decision on lunch when my cell phone rang. It was Terry.

"What's up?" he asked.

"That was fast," I said.

"When Kurt Maxxon calls, I know it's important," Terry said. "I learned that lesson well in the Gallegar case."

"I know the identity of the woman found dead—unfortunately, the boys' mother."

The tone of my voice must have frozen Terry. He waited several beats and then said, "Yeah?"

"Okay, here's the connection," I said, pausing to take a breath and rearranging the papers in front of me. "Irene Faye Lawlor, L-A-W-L-O-R, graduated from St. Mary's College in Evandale, with a BA in Human Relations in May 1994. She apparently didn't change her name at the college when she married Randolph H. Wallace on July 17, 1993. I've got her degree in my hand." I switched papers.

"Joshua Wyeth Wallace," I continued, "born September 23, 1994, at the Riley County General Hospital in Evandale. Parents were Irene and Randolph Wallace. Jacob Michael Wallace was born September 21, 1996, at the same hospital. They're from Evandale."

"How do you know all this, I ask, grinning?" Terry said.

"The box the boys had, with the picture of their mother in it. They left it in my truck. I just was looking in it. There's an envelope jammed with pictures, too."

"Hang onto it," Terry said. "Marguerite will want those pictures."

"Okay," I said. "Also, I talked to a lady the boys told me about, Auntie Jean. She lives in the apartment complex they lived in for a while. When the boys first mentioned her, she didn't seem important in the case. But then I got to wondering, so I decided to go talk to her—"

"Just for the fun and grins, right?" Terry said. "Is this in CF's projects area?"

"No. Irene and the boys apparently tried to avoid the projects," I said, "and they probably would have. But someone snatched Irene's purse, and she lost all the money she had. After that, she had to move over to the projects about eight blocks east. If you've got a pencil, I'll give you the address."

Terry copied the address and then read it back to me. He had it right.

"The boys mentioned an Auntie Jean," Terry said.

"After talking to her, I came away with a whole different perspective of how this thing played out. I'm wondering if the real story goes something like this: Irene took the boys and ran from away from an abusive husband or father. If she was hiding out, she'd have had to train the boys to become Joshua and Jacob *Lawton*. They probably made the switch easily, if they'd been abused, especially if Irene told them it was a way to get rid of the abuse."

I stopped talking and waited for Terry to comment.

"Keep talking," Terry said. "Christ, you may have just solved another murder, sitting in your armchair, two hundred miles away."

"Not much else I can add," I said, looking at the stuffed envelope lying on the sofa where I'd left it. "No armchair, however," I said, thinking of my comfortable recliner at home.

"Let me call Marguerite and get her going on this information," Terry said. "If she needs to, she can call you, right?"

"Oh, sure."

"I'm going to say it again, Maxxon—I'm glad you're on our side."

"How are the boys doing?" I asked.

"They're settling in real well. They like having separate beds and each has his own chest of drawers. Jacob says to Marguerite, 'Now we gotta buy more clothes to fill up the drawers.'"

I chuckled. "Joshua's the more dexterous of the two, but Jacob is definitely the wittier."

"We're going to enroll them in school tomorrow morning. Both boys seem anxious to get back into school. But, you know, they're a little skittish about it, too."

"Well, now we know what lies ahead for them. I'm glad you and Marguerite are there to help them through all this."

"We're on it, Colonel Maxxon. And we thank you for all your help."

We hung up, and I sat for several minutes trying to fathom what it was going to be like for the boys to learn their mother was—for sure—gone forever. Then my thoughts turned to *Where is their father?* Was he the kind who would step in and take the boys and raise them?

But ... had he been abusive to them? Was that why they were in Carpentier Falls? How could we find him? And then, the worst thought of all: *Was he the one who did Irene in?*

Damn.

CHAPTER FOURTEEN

Tuesday, September 12

<u>*Kurt Maxxon*</u>

Talking to Aunt Jean, finding where Irene worked, finding more information about Irene and the boys' past and their real names made me almost giddy. Then, learning that the boys were doing well gave me a totally satisfied feeling, like I get when I win a race in the last fifty feet. I decided to celebrate with a special lunch. *Do something new and exciting, Maxxon,* one side of my brain whispered. *Yeah, let's go find a new joint—some old greasy spoon,* the other side yelled. Whenever both sides of my brain are in agreement on something, I *always* pay attention.

I drove west on Roosevelt. The morning's light fog had burned off, and the sky was clear and blue, but the high-pressure ridge to the east of Carpentier Falls had stalled and was funneling warm, moist air into the region. I idled along, studying the signs and buildings on both sides of the street. There were the representatives of all the national chain stores hawking hamburgers, pizza, fried chicken, seafood, sub sandwiches, and Mexican food. I was about to turn around and drive north on Speedway, when a sign ahead caught my attention. It was a twenty-foot-high imitation of a Saguaro cactus plant heralding a run-down joint called Hector's Taqueria.

It was new—to me.

It looked as though it might be—different.

The area was obviously of diverse ethnicity. Across the street was a run-down Vietnamese grocery, and next door was a Thai restaurant. The parking lots for both eateries were behind the buildings, carved out of a weedy wasteland. The cloudless sky with the sun directly overhead seemed to be superheating the air. I parked the truck and walked around to the front door.

Behind the counter I could see what had originally been the kitchen for a diner, fifty years ago. A huge oven, grill, and griddle lined the far wall. A dozen skillets and pots hung from the ceiling. Smoking deep fryers sat to one side of the stove. Two commercial-sized microwave ovens were above the stove on the other side. While it probably could pass a health inspection, it looked like it had a scrubbed grease and grime coating.

It definitely qualifies as a greasy spoon.

Ten tables were in the dining room, all but two occupied. On either side of the order/pickup counter were stand-up tables, each with four men standing at them, eating. I noted that all eight men were wearing suits, and their shoes were expensive, high-polish brands.

The menu was a worn blackboard mounted on the wall above the counter. I studied the menu and had a tough time deciding on only three items. Behind the counter, a Latina woman attempting to pass as a teenager had turned some of her naturally black hair into a peroxide multi-toned red to blonde. She had three earrings in each ear, a loop through her left nostril, and an assortment of earrings around her left eye. She smacked her bubble gum as she chewed it. "Ya ready?" she said, pencil poised above an order pad.

"Let me have a Taco Special, a Beef Burrito Special, and a Beef and Bean Tostada," I said.

"Ya want a drink?"

"Iced tea."

"We don't have iced tea. Beer or Coke."

"Diet Coke."

She blew a half-dollar-sized bubble, popped it back into her mouth as she took my money, made change, and turned toward the kitchen area. I walked to the pickup station, expecting someone to materialize and prepare the food. The bubble gum girl hustled around the kitchen area preparing my food. She put some of it in the deep fryer, some of it in a microwave oven, and dug the fixings for the tostada out of a refrigerator hidden from view. She assembled the tostada on the counter.

A group of three men straggled in and stood waiting at the order station, watching as the bubble-gum girl finished my order. "Be wit 'cha in a sec," she yelled as she brought the tray to me at the pickup station, turned, and walked toward them.

I chose a table, feeling a little guilty about sitting at it alone. After I'd tasted the food, I sensed the place would soon fill with wall-to-wall people. Hopefully, I could eat and get out before the crowd arrived. My only disappointment was the amount of tomato the bubble-gum girl had put on my tostada. It could have used twice as much—I needed the lycopene.

You did good, Maxxon, both sides of my brain whispered in unison, as I climbed into my truck. I thought about running by the track to see if Penelope had the final numbers from the race ready. She normally mailed them to me on Tuesdays, but I had told her I'd run by to pick them up. I decided to call Penelope to check—and realized my cell phone was lying on the desk in the room. So I retraced my route to the hotel. When I retrieved my phone, I had one voice message.

The message was rather cryptic: "Kurt, this is Hermosa. I found some things that Uncle Carlos labeled for you only. Please call me at the Trattoria, or come by for supper, and I'll give them to you. Thanks."

Since I had just finished a huge lunch, supper didn't have much appeal to me yet. I dialed the track but got a busy signal. I kept trying the track and kept getting the busy signal. I'd returned to my writing pad, and added some new notes, edited some existing notes, and read them all over again. The sun came out brightly and the room lit up. Suddenly, my recurring claustrophobia kicked in. I had to get outside. So I went down, got in my truck, and drove to the track.

At the track, Penelope looked up when I walked in and said, "How are those boys doing?"

"They're doing just fine," I assured her. "I talked to Terry this morning, and they'll be starting school tomorrow morning."

"Is the school close to where they live?"

"Actually, Marguerite takes them to the law center with her each morning, to the public employees' day care center. They go to school from there and then return there."

"That's handy, huh? I'm happy you guys are taking such good care of them," Penelope said.

They're definitely in good hands. A lot better than sleeping under a picnic table next to my camper. By the way, I put that extra table back in the storage area. I'd like to leave my camper where it is until I go home."

"That's okay," Penelope said. "Next weekend is the local ARCA race, and there'll only be three or four RV spaces used."

When I asked about the busy phone, Penelope discovered she had knocked the phone off the cradle and hadn't heard it bleeping at her. She had the reports ready.

As I climbed into my truck, I realized I'd not found the complex where the boys were living when their mother disappeared. Terry probably wouldn't need to come to Carpentier Falls now that I'd pretty well filled in all the blanks, and the trail led to Evandale, not here. I left the track, meandered around so I avoided the downtown area, and drove out east Roosevelt Boulevard. The boys had pointed out the complex on our drive to Sam's Diner last Friday. I drove into the complex, and thought it was strange that there was no sign identifying the place. The buildings were even more dilapidated than those in the Roosevelt Complex. If there were any glass windows left in those buildings, you couldn't see them from where I sat. I could see three openings where entry doors had once hung. But there were no doors now. Trash, single items and bags of it, littered the grounds. The parking lot had several cars in it, some on blocks without tires, a few with all four tires flat, and a couple of burned-out hulls. There were no people out and about, even though several thousand souls lived in the buildings.

There were no numbers showing on the buildings, but I was sure the building I sat staring at was the one the boys had pointed out as the one where they'd lived. I couldn't remember the apartment number I'd just read to Terry, and I decided I had no reason to find out. The sun went behind a black cloud, and the sky darkened, spreading a sense of raw despair over the scene. Suddenly, a teenage Latino boy, tall and lanky, came running out of the open door of the building. He was waving a large semi-automatic weapon in his hand. He ran toward my truck. His eyes were wide, his mouth twisted in anger. I lunged at the door-lock button. The locks clicked as the boy reached the front fender. Adrenalin flooded my body. The engine was still running. I could put the truck in reverse and roar away before the boy could do much damage other than break the side window glass. But he could shoot me even as I drove away. I gripped the gearshift lever anyway, ready to take my chances. But the boy raced past me, crossed the parking lot, leaped high up on the chain-link fence, scrambled over it, and then disappeared down the street.

What the hell are you doing in this part of town? my brain screamed.

A Latino father and son raced out of the door, and I froze again. They raced past me, clambered into a battered old Honda Civic, and sped across the lot toward the street. A small boy, probably no more than three or four years old, trotted out of the building and stood on the sidewalk at the parking lot, watching the car disappear out of the lot. He looked around, spotted me sitting in my truck, and walked over to look up at me. I rolled the window down.

"What's your name?" I asked the boy.

"Jesus."

"Hi, Jesus," I said. My name is Kurt."

Jesus nodded acceptance.

"Who were those men? Do you know them?"

"My pa and my brothers."

"The boy with the gun is your brother?" I asked in disbelief.

"Alejandro," he said, nodding. "Mama says he's a bad boy."

A heavyset woman came running out of the door. The terrified look on her face eased when she saw Jesus standing talking to me. She walked toward us. "You no supposed to be out here alone, Jesus," she said. She took Jesus' hand and turned to go back into the building.

"Is there a problem?" I asked, pulling out my cell phone. "Should I call the police?"

"No. Please no call police," the woman pleaded. "Rico will talk to Alejandro."

"But, he's running with a gun. What if he shoots someone?"

She shook her head. "No bullets in gun," she said, and she turned toward the building. "We don't need no police here."

With my heart still banging inside my chest, I drove back to the hotel, trying to rationalize the incident. How many stories had I heard of young teens killed by "empty guns"? As I walked to the elevators, the bar drew my attention. I reached to punch the elevator call button and hesitated. A shot of Scotch whisky suddenly sounded good. It would calm my jangled nerves. I swallowed the saliva my taste buds had generated at the thought. I walked into the bar and found a booth where I felt insulated from the world. The waitress was busy gathering a large order of drinks for a big, round table, occupied by what had to be a group of the meeting attendees playing hooky from their duties.

I sat thinking about what a shot of Scotch would taste like. It had been twenty-six years since my last drink. But then, memories of the life-changing incident flooded my mind.

It was the fall of 1980. We'd been practicing air-to-air combat maneuvers all day in black, rainy skies. Our squadron leader made us redo several routines, unsatisfied with our performance. We were rapidly approaching the maximum number of hours we could fly, when he finally gave us the word to give up for the day. After securing our aircraft and debriefing, Brad Langley and I, along with several of our squadron-mates, decided to have a beer at the officer's club. One drink led to another, and then the bartender shut us off. So, we moved our party to the lounge in an off-base bowling alley. About four thirty the next morning, our next-door neighbor found me asleep in my pickup truck parked in the driveway, and she made so much noise she roused me. I couldn't remember how I'd gotten there.

She told me Little Kurt had slipped and fallen down the steps while getting off the school bus during his second-grade field trip. He'd banged his head on the pavement, and they'd rushed him to the hospital in serious condition. Vicki had frantically tried to find me—and couldn't. After sitting the night with Vicki, the neighbor had just left the hospital, to get ready for work. Now she ordered me to scoot over, and she drove me to the hospital. I can still see Vicki's eyes when I came running into the emergency room's waiting area. The terror. The love.

Vicki didn't scold me. She walked into my arms. "He's going to be okay," she whispered—and then crumpled and cried. I cried with her. I swore to God I would never, ever, touch another drop of booze.

And I never had—*until now?*

The waitress arrived at my booth. "What can I get you?" she asked.

I looked at her for several beats. "A Diet Coke," I said.

The waitress couldn't hide the frown that spread across her face. She studied me for a while and then said, "Are you okay?"

"Just reliving a bad experience in my life," I said.

"Bad enough you don't want a drink?"

"It was bad enough that I quit drinking—cold turkey—twenty-six years ago."

The waitress pursed her lips, swung around on her heel, and walked to the bar. She brought me a tall cocktail glass full of Diet Coca-Cola, with a slice of lemon in it. "Good for you," she said. "I've seen so many people lost in booze, and it isn't pretty."

She was a very perceptive person.

I left her a hefty tip.

*   *   *

When I got to my room, I called the Trattoria. Hermosa answered and I asked, "Do I need a reservation for supper?"

"Kurt Maxxon never needs a reservation in this establishment," Hermosa said.

"Has the menu changed?"

"Not much. We have a new head chef. Dominique replaced Carlos, but Dominique did most of the cooking anyhow. I assumed you knew that."

"I did," I said. "I'll be there about six."

I dug out my writing tablet and read the notes again. There was a sharp rap at my door, and I wondered who it could be. I walked to the door and looked through the peep glass. A tall African-American woman, wearing a suit with skirt, stood waiting; a uniformed CFPD officer stood next to her. I opened the door. She was only a couple of inches shorter than me, pleasantly built, with black hair, now mostly gray, brown eyes hooded by penciled-on eyebrows, and a nose that hooked up at the end. Her smile had a red coating of lipstick.

"Mr. Maxxon," she said. "My name is Agatha Cochrane. I'm with the Pierre County Child Protection Services. I understand you have two young boys living with you, and I'm here to determine their status."

The hair on the back of my neck stood up. I stepped back and motioned the pair into the room. The cop stood near the door, supposedly disinterested. Mrs. Cochrane moved to the guest chair near the desk. I sat down at the desk.

"The two boys are in Kings Rapids," I said.

"Are the children from Carpentier Falls, Mr. Maxxon?"

"No. They're from Evandale," I said, hoping God would overlook my charade.

"Evandale?"

I debated telling Mrs. Cochrane the whole story—mother gone missing, later found dead—but eventually decided to avoid as much detail as possible.

"Are they back with their parents?"

"No."

"Who are they staying with in Kings Rapids?"

"They're staying with good friends of mine, Marguerite and Terry Grossman," I said. "Marguerite is the chief of police in Kings Rapids."

Her face eased a little. "I know Marguerite," she said, staring directly into my eyes. "There's more to this than you're telling me."

I nodded. "A lot more. But ... I'd prefer you talk to Marguerite about it."

She stood abruptly and walked toward the door. "Thank you, Mr. Maxxon." The cop moved to open the door for her, and they disappeared out the closing door.

I thought about calling Marguerite to warn her but decided we were merely performing a compassionate rescue of two little boys who were only guilty of wanting to eat regularly.

And, if Marguerite got into a shootout with Mrs. Cochrane, I already knew who I was going to put my money on.

$*$ $*$ $*$

Chaundra Dunkin

Chaundra could barely contain her excitement as she walked toward her car. The advisor had told her she could take the GED courses needed to get her high-school diploma *and* enroll in first-year college courses at the same time. "You only need three GED sections," the advisor had told her. "And you can take three or four credit courses besides that."

Chaundra had all the paperwork filled out; all her mother had to do was make out a check for the tuition and expenses. At this point, Chaundra decided she would use her own money, if her mother balked at all. She noted that she had parked the Mustang almost dead center under a bright parking lot light. It had been dusk when she arrived; now it was a starless night.

As she neared her Mustang, Chaundra caught movement out of the corner of her eye. Suddenly, Quigley was beside her.

"Hey, Chaun," he said in a low voice, and she backed away from him. She could tell by the way he slurred his words that he had been drinking. When he wasn't with her, she'd never minded if Quigley drank—he constantly skimmed the near-empty bottles of vodka from his mother. Chaundra had always refused to go anywhere with Quigley when he had been drinking. Now Quigley stood between her and the door to the Mustang. He was swaying, so it wouldn't take much to knock him out of the way. And Chaundra had learned some valuable tricks on how to handle rough men very quickly from the other girls.

"Ah, hell, Chaun," Quigley slurred. "I loved you so much. I wanted you so bad. I want you now so bad." He swayed backward and fell against the car but remained upright. "I need you. Give me a little love. Get in the backseat with me, please."

A car door banged nearby, and Chaundra looked around the parking lot. She saw a taxi pulling away from the loading zone and a woman walking toward them on the sidewalk. She turned back to Quigley. "Go home, Quig, and take a cold shower. I'm not available to you anymore."

Quigley swayed again and started to walk away, but he teetered and fell forward. The woman walking on the sidewalk saw him fall. "What's with him?" she asked, having stopped moving.

"He's stone drunk," Chaundra said.

"Chaundra? Is that you?" The woman walked closer, stepping into the halo of light.

"Hi, Terri," Chaundra said. She and Terri embraced, and a warm sensation spread throughout her. "What are you doing here?"

Terri backed up a half step but continued to hold Chaundra's hands. "Tammy called me and told me to meet a guy here outside the library and do him in the basement. Apparently, he's a professor or something. All Tammy said was to make sure he's got the money first."

Quigley stirred and tried to get up, but he fell back down. "Let's get him over on the grass," Terri suggested. The two girls manhandled Quigley several yards and laid him on the grass. Then they walked back toward Chaundra's car. "You walking or riding a taxi?" Terri asked.

"That's my new Mustang right there," Chaundra said, pointing to the car.

"That's yours?"

"Present from my stepfather."

"Damn nice of him," Terri said with a grin.

"He's a lot different than what I thought. My mother ... well, I think she was a lot of my problem."

They stopped at the car. Terri turned to face Chaundra. "I've missed you, Chaun," she whispered.

Chaundra swallowed hard. "I've been missing you, too."

"There's a motel down the street a couple of blocks," Terri offered. "They do rooms by the hour."

"What about your trick?" Chaundra said.

"Fuck him."

"Get in," Chaundra said. "Let's go."

*   *   *

Kurt Maxxon

After Mrs. Cochrane's departure, I stood leaning against the kitchen counter, letting my heartbeat and breathing calm down a little. And, once again, I thought about going down for a shot of Scotch, but it subsided quickly. I looked around the room. My writing pad was on the desk, along with the clasp envelope full of pictures from the boys' box. I sat down and undid the clasp, which broke off from wear.

I looked inside the envelope. Instead of photographs, it was full of old newspaper clippings and other memorabilia. I hauled the entire pile out and laid it on the desk.

The top piece was a folded newspaper. It took me a minute, but I realized I was looking at a photograph of Mickey Lawlor congratulating me after I'd beat him during the last lap of the Evandale race several years ago.

Mickey Lawlor was a legend in the SRVSCRA, having won more races than anyone before or after him. To this day, I savor my win over Mickey Lawlor in 1995, because it was my first win at the Evandale racetrack. The caption to the photo said it all: *Upstart beats Mickey Lawlor by a bumper.* The article did mention my name later and told how Mickey was going for his one-hundredth win. I was the upstart kid, in my third season in the league, and I had my first win over a seasoned veteran who already had ninety-nine.

Mickey did get his one-hundredth win a few weeks later, in Carpentier Falls, in fact. Sadly, Mickey died in a multicar pileup on one of Atlanta's freeways the following winter. I went to his funeral in Evandale, along with half the people of that town, Riley County, and all the SRVSCRA drivers, officials, and associates. His death in Atlanta that winter meant he'd never run in front of them again. I'd never thought of it that way before, but now those thoughts flooded my mind.

I sat staring at the yellowed newspaper in front of me. The decade between now and the time of that photo flooded my mind with vivid memories of other races at Evandale. Mickey Lawlor and I had raced each other to a near draw at Maplewood. But Mickey had won that one. He had faked me out, and I lost because of it. He was a great race driver—and an even greater friend.

It didn't take me long to make the connection between Mickey Lawlor and Irene Faye Lawlor. In another newspaper photo, I saw Mickey Lawlor standing next to his Chevrolet Impala, holding a young girl in his arms, who was identified as his daughter, Irene. Other photos showed a maturing girl, always identified as Irene, or Irene

Faye. I wondered if Irene had thought ill of me for beating her father at a crucial time. She would have been a grown woman by the time of the race, judging from the chronology of the memorabilia I was looking at.

I realized the room had gone dim, and I walked to the window expecting to see rain. A flash of lightning confirmed that while it wasn't raining at the moment, it would be soon.

I decided it was close enough to six o'clock to leave for the Trattoria. I could cheat a little. I went down and climbed up into my truck. Then I sat for several minutes before I twisted the key. Going to the Trattoria for Jimmy's celebration dinner had been easy. We had all been coming off the adrenalin rush from driving in a race, or rooting for your favorite driver in the race. For some reason, however, going to the Trattoria for supper this evening seemed a little more difficult—it was generating all manner of memories. But I fought them down and drove to the restaurant. Ernesto Vasquez greeted me, with the usual, "Good evening, Colonel Maxxon—right this way."

He showed me to a corner table next to the window. A winsome young waitress in pure white waitress garb arrived even as Ernesto turned to leave. The new wait staff uniforms indicated a desire to upgrade the Trattoria into four- or five-star status. "My name is Valerie, Colonel Maxxon, and I'll be your server tonight," she sang. "Would you like an iced tea to start with?"

I was a known quantity at the Trattoria, there was no escaping that. "Yes."

Valerie headed for the kitchen.

Hermosa swept in from the larger meeting room and came to my table. I stood as she approached.

"Thank you for coming," Hermosa said. I pulled a chair out for her to sit in. She looked at me for several beats, and then she accepted.

"You look worn out," I said, having debated whether to be honest or polite.

"God, what a mess," Hermosa said. She looked around the main dining room. "I had no idea what it takes to keep this place going."

"I can imagine," I said. "Anything I can do to help you?"

Ernesto was seating other couples and groups in the main dining room.

"Not that I can think of right now," Hermosa said. "Can I reserve the right to redirect later?"

"Absolutely," I said. "I'm always ready to help."

"Thank you," she said. "Uncle Carlos kept a scrapbook of key visitors and events of the Trattoria. It's a rather large book, and there's one large section devoted to you and your racing exploits. Uncle Carlos left a note for me to give the scrapbook to you first, so you can extract anything you'd like to keep. As the executer of his will, I want to comply with his wishes as much as possible, and I want to get it all settled as quickly as possible, too.

"Oh, yes …" she said, "I almost forgot. There's a letter for you, too." She walked briskly to the kitchen. When she returned she handed me a rhino-skin ten-by-twelve envelope marked "Personal and Confidential.

"The scrapbook is out in my car, so, when you're ready to leave, just have Ernesto come get me, and I'll go out and give it to you. Enjoy your dinner, Colonel Maxxon. And, by the way, it's on the house."

"I always paid Carlos for my meals," I said.

"Next time, you pay," Hermosa said as she stood and walked toward the kitchen.

With my curiosity piqued, I had a devil of a time eating supper—mouth-watering *rabo encendido*, or Dominique's version of Cuban oxtail stew, which I dearly love. When I finished eating my stew, I caught Hermosa in one of her orbits around the nearly packed dining room. She led me to her car parked near the kitchen door and handed me a scrapbook from her front seat. It was normal size, twelve by twelve, but at least six inches thick. As I studied it in the light from the kitchen, my heart skipped a beat. The cover was red and white fabric, quilted together in a checkerboard design. Centered on the cover was a color eight-by-ten photo of me being greeted by Carlos at the Trattoria the first time I had met him. It instantly brought back a flood of memories.

"This is incredible," I said to Hermosa. "There has to be at least four hundred pages in here. How in the world did Carlos find the time?"

"He loved racing," Hermosa said. "You were the closest thing to a personal friend in racing. He also enjoyed the fact that you liked his cooking. And, you were the reason he decided to sponsor the 89 car."

I hoped Hermosa didn't see the sheen coating my eyes. I needed to just take the scrapbook and go to my truck. The scrapbook was enticing, but I resisted the urge to go through it in the truck, and drove to the hotel.

I lugged the heavy scrapbook to my room and laid it on the desk, ready to dig into it after I brewed a pot of coffee. I stood next to my desk chair, waiting for the coffee to finish, and studied the scrapbook on the desk. Suddenly, an eerie feeling caused me to pause. I wasn't *that* big of a commodity in the racing world. As I pondered that thought, a chill ran down my spine. *What else is involved here?*

I got my nerves calmed down as the coffeepot gurgled to closure, filled a cup, and sat down at the desk. I set the scrapbook aside after taking the large envelope from it. I studied the envelope for a brief moment, then tore it open, and started reading.

> To My Dear Friend, Kurt Maxxon:
>
> I write this letter to you only because you are the one person I trust to handle it confidentially, discreetly, and objectively. I pray nothing I tell you in this letter will change your attitude toward me. I truly hope nothing I've done in my life will reflect on my family, especially my niece, Hermosa Anderson, and my nephew, Jimmy Davison. I have tried to make peace with God and other folks. I ask you to handle this letter so that the truth becomes known without harm to them. You may be reading this letter because

I died of natural causes, which is what I pray has
happened (I just had a scare from lung cancer, which,
while it proved benign, made me start thinking
about my mortality). But if I died for other reasons,
I will have the peace of mind in knowing that you
are looking after Hermosa and Jimmy's security. The
cause of my death might have something to do with
my past.

My past has always been a problem for
me. I was an operative in the Havana mob before I
graduated high school. I went through university on
wages paid me by the mob. It was my connections,
however, that allowed me to get out of Cuba when
Castro and his thugs took over, with my wife, my two
children, and my life savings. But then the Miami
mob executed my wife and two children when they
couldn't find me for an accusation that later proved
to be false. But the damage was done. I have heard
since, from relatives, that several of the mob members
responsible have died in mysterious ways, and a few
have mentioned my name as a possible revenge killer.
I've not done any revenge killing, although it crossed
my mind years ago.

I have been illegal all the time I've been
in the United States. When I came to the valley, I
needed a new social security number with the local
numbers on it, to avoid attracting attention. I found
the purveyor of illegal social security numbers was
Mr. Forest Claymore, the local congressman. Forest's
son, Regnault, has followed in his father's footsteps,
in both old and new illegal enterprises and election to
congress.

The letter's opening grabbed my interest better than the best novel I'd ever read. But, before I'd become totally hooked, my cell phone jangled. I retrieved it from the nightstand. It was my daughter, Vanessa. We chatted about the grandkids' progress, what she had been doing, familywise, and her career as a personal trainer at a fitness center. As we talked, I was reading Carlos's letter, and it was very intriguing. Eventually, after I had talked to my grandkids, Vanessa ran out of news and things to talk about and said, "We love you, Daddy. Good-bye Daddy," in a singsong voice. Anxious to get back to the letter, I mumbled, "I love you all, too." She hung up. I took up Carlos's letter again.

I came to Carpentier Falls to start over, but I couldn't find many ways to make money, other than the rackets. I finally settled on providing women to greedy men, which I did for many years. I have profited mightily from other people's greed and lusts, and the ladies have prospered as well. I think no one was ever hurt by this activity.

Since the Trattoria came into existence, I have allowed friendly gambling in the meeting rooms. I never gambled with them. The house never took anything other than the profits we made on the concessions we sold. That was why the sheriff's department wasn't eager to bust anyone.

Before this letter gets too boring, I ask of you a favor. I owe a woman $60,000 that I borrowed to help me launch a cigarette importing operation a few years back. I owe her that money. I've been putting money into an account for her. I have no idea when you will read this letter, or if you will read it. But please direct her to the Carpentier Bank downtown. The account is in my name with her, Rachael Mellon, as beneficiary.

Rachael Mellon! The name arrested my attention. I'd known Rachael had problems, but I'd never imagined how big, and who she was dealing with. "Oh, dear God." I bowed my head. "Lord, help me handle this mess right," I whispered. I returned to reading the letter.

> She should be able to get what is in the account without any trouble. Then I'd like you to convince Hermosa Anderson, my executor, to pay Rachael whatever the balance is to make up the $60,000 I owe Rachael.
>
> Now, for some useful information that I will allow you to decide what to do with. I've been paying Regnault Claymore $10,000 per month in blackmail to keep quiet after he found out about my girls a couple of years ago and he demanded a cut of the action, or he would rat me out.
>
> As you probably guessed when I mentioned the cigarette business, the cigarettes came from offshore, untaxed. But that operation took too much of my time, and so many people wanted the cigarettes, I had to get rid of it—to who is not important.
>
> As you know, I have kept a scrapbook of items about the Trattoria. You have been one of the more prominent and frequent celebrity visitors to my restaurant, so there is a special section in the scrapbook about your racing career in Carpentier Falls. I would like you to look closely at the clippings about the 2002 race. I've made some notations you will find interesting.
>
> Go in peace, my trusted friend. I know you will do what you can to rectify my wrongs. Thank you for your friendship all these years.

Carlos Guerrero

In large, bold, hand printed block letters across the bottom of the letter, Carlos had written:

I'M NOT TRUSTING TAMMY MCPHERSON SO MUCH THESE DAYS. I FEAR SHE IS UP TO NO GOOD.

I remembered when Carlos had had to have the biopsy of a mass in his left lung two years ago. He'd told me about it when I was in town for the September race, having had it five weeks before. That gave me a rough date for when the letter had been composed, or last revised. In the margin, next to the note about Tammy, Carlos had scribbled "5/25," which probably meant that he'd added it on May 25. I assumed the note had been added this year. Hermosa had said she'd found the letter in Carlos's desk at his condo, so there was no way to tell how long ago he had added the note. *But is that important?*

I glanced at the alarm clock on the nightstand and realized I needed to go to Carlos's wake, at the funeral home a few blocks east on Roosevelt.

The rain was holding off, but the heat and humidity made being outside uncomfortable. Just the walk from motel building to my truck soaked my shirt.

After I'd paid my respects and circulated among the other mourners, I decided I didn't know enough of them to hang around. I drove back to the hotel, brewed a pot of decaf coffee, put on my pajamas, and returned to Carlos's letter.

I read the letter through several times. I sat at the desk and doodled some notes on my writing tablet. All I was doing was delaying the inevitable. After it had rattled around my brain a thousand times, I picked up the phone and dialed Mike Collins.

When Mike answered, I asked, "Do you think we can bail Rachael out of jail?

"They arraigned her, but I think it was just so she could enter a plea," Mike said mechanically. "You could probably get a lawyer to set up a bond hearing. A court-appointed kid represented her. Will they grant bond? That'll depend on the judge you get. The judge will look at the danger she would represent to the community, and the level of flight risk."

"Would you do the bail bond?" I asked and then added, "I'll guarantee it."

"I'll post the bond, if you personally guarantee it, Kurt. "But," he said, "I'll say it again: if I were you, I'd leave the whole mess alone. Not get involved with Rachael Mellon."

I hung up and dialed Hermosa's cell phone, hoping she was back at the Trattoria from the wake.

After pleasantries, I said, "I need a favor, and I realize this may not be the best time to ask for it."

"What is it?" Hermosa said, and I thought her voice was calm.

"I need a good lawyer to set up a bond hearing for Rachael Mellon."

There was a long pause, which I had planned on. "She killed Uncle Carlos and—you want her out on the street?" Hermosa said, her voice breaking.

Dammit, Maxxon. Hermosa is already stressed enough with the death of Carlos. Why the hell did you come up with this hare-brained idea? Find another lawyer.

"I don't—I don't think she killed Carlos," I stammered, hoping to console her emotions.

"Is this another one of the famous Kurt Maxxon gut feelings?"

I chuckled slightly. "Probably." Suddenly I was back on earth. I hoped Hermosa was, also.

"You know, something has been bothering me about this whole affair …"

"What's that?" I prompted, after what seemed like a long time.

"Uncle Carlos always had a ton of cash lying around. He was terrible about depositing cash in the bank. But, so far, I've found no cash at all. Not in his office, not in his condo. And only fifty bucks here at the Trattoria. There hasn't been a cash deposit to the bank for four months. The sheriff tells me that when they arrested Rachael, she didn't have any money in her house. And, quite frankly, they don't believe she was sober long enough to hide it anywhere."

Another long pause. "What else?" I said, trying to prod her into continuing the conversation.

"Maybe the motive was robbery," Hermosa said slowly. "There's probably a huge amount of cash gone."

"Any way to tell how much?"

"We can't find Uncle Carlos's books, no records of any kind."

"That's strange," I said. "I don't think a business as successful as the Trattoria could get by too long without records of some kind." I tried to remember his letter. *Had Carlos said anything in the letter about where he kept the books?*

"Let me talk to Tim," Hermosa said, her voice gaining strength. "See what he thinks. He'll probably take it on, since he's just like you, always enjoying a challenge. You want him to call you still tonight? It'll be eleven before he gets here."

Even though Carlos's letter was intriguing and had compelled me to seek Rachael's release, the day was catching up with me. I hesitated a moment, considering the stress Hermosa and Tim had gone through. "Tomorrow morning will be fine," I said.

Reading the scrapbook about my race in 2002 could also wait until tomorrow morning. I climbed into bed and tried to go to sleep. As usual, my mind was rummaging through all the information I had gathered so far. *And then, the scrapbook ...*

Eventually, I fell into a deep slumber.

* * *

Jim Overturf

Hermosa Anderson

Hermosa sat at the table just outside the kitchen doors. The restaurant was quiet, all the diners gone until tomorrow, and all the wait and cooking staff had gone for the night. She sipped on her rum she'd mixed herself, a little stronger than what it should be. The first few days had gone well, she told herself. The people who had frequented the Trattoria before were coming back, even with Carlos gone. Hermosa had promised Tim she would only give it three months. If it didn't look as if would pay off, she would close it or sell it off.

Tim had not called yet, and Hermosa surmised he had decided to stay over in Centralia after a long day in court. They both always agreed it was best to stay overnight, rather than try to drive home when you are exhausted.

How do I broach the question of representing Rachael Mellon? The more she thought about it, the more she wondered if Tim would take the case. *Should I argue for Rachael?*

Hermosa remembered a few years before, when Uncle Carlos and Rachael had had some kind of relationship she'd never understood. It wasn't romantic, and Hermosa more than once had wondered what Carlos and Rachael had going, and why.

Should I help her now? Try to get her out of jail?

The sheriff had pretty compelling evidence that Rachael had killed Carlos. The motive was a little nebulous, and Rachael had a reputation as a drunk.

Why should I help her get out of jail?

Kurt Maxxon asking for her help was a strong reason, but not an overpowering one.

Rachael is a woman who needs help—a woman who probably doesn't stand a chance in hell of getting a fair trial with some young, inexperienced attorney from Legal Aid representing her.

Her cell phone chimed. It was Tim. He was in a hotel in Centralia and would drive to Carpentier Falls early the next morning. He would be in time for Carlos's funeral.

When she asked Tim about representing Rachael Mellon, Tim asked her if she wanted it. "Yes, I definitely do," she said.

"I'll be talking to the office next," Tim told her. "I'll get a paralegal started on it first thing tomorrow morning."

After they ended the call, Hermosa sat finishing her drink.

You're doing the right thing, Herma, she heard a voice whisper in her mind.

Uncle Carlos's favorite diminutive of her name made her start. *Okay, this is spooky. Time to close up and head home.* Hermosa got up, swallowed the drink, and left, locking the doors behind her.

CHAPTER FIFTEEN

Wednesday, September 13

Kurt Maxxon, Morning

My internal alarm clock went off about four thirty, and, after a few minutes of planning my day, I got up, brewed a pot of coffee, showered, dressed, and turned on the local morning news, weather, and traffic show. With a fresh cup of coffee, I stood at the desk and opened the scrapbook. Carlos had organized the section about me so that stuff could be added at the end. That meant that the 2002 race Carlos had specifically mentioned in his letter to me would be about a third up from the back of the section.

The first page was a color photograph of me standing next to Nikki in the pit stall at Carpentier Falls track. I was in the number-2 stall, so that was probably the 1998 race. The next article was the photo of me beating Mickey Lawlor for my first career win at Evandale. Carlos's scrapbook had similar contents to the boys' envelope with their mother's father, Mickey Lawlor. So, to quote Yogi Berra, it was kind of déjà vu all over again—newspaper clippings and photos, as well as other articles from racing magazines and tabloids, and pictures of me at the Trattoria before and after different races. Carlos had hosted several victory parties for me over the years, and, as I leafed through the pages, the memories of each one came winging back into my mind.

Then I felt my chest constrict, and I thought my heart had exploded, as I realized I was looking at photos with Vicki standing next to me. And then my mind filled with memories of Vicki. I was missing her worse than I had for a long time. So I quickly flipped pages, until I realized I was looking at 2002 items. I'd finished third in that race, but there was a large photo of me congratulating the winner, Eugenios Christofides. It took a few minutes before I realized there was some writing on the white part of Nikki in the photo.

Storage room #14

5916 No Cypress St

Lock combination = KM's birthday

Metal lockbox

Take care of the papers in it.

Thanks, Carlos

I looked at the lettering on the photo several times and then wrote the information on my writing pad. I filled my coffee cup again and dug out my map of Carpentier Falls. Fifty-ninth and Cypress was at the north city limits, in the north-central part of Carpentier Falls.

When I'd finished my coffee, I took my writing pad and went down to the truck. I drove to the storage building on the east side of Cypress, just north of Fifty-Ninth Street, and found unit number 14. I opened the combination lock in only two attempts. It was a ten-by-twenty storage unit with a roll-up metal garage door. The sun was fully above the horizon, casting shadows into the room, but a layer of dark clouds was about to engulf it. The room was empty, except for four boxes that once had been full of cigarette cartons. An unopened package of cigarettes was on the floor, under a shelf. On the top shelf sat a metal fireproof box the same size as a large file box.

I lifted the lockbox and realized it was fairly heavy. I set it on the floor and reached under the shelf for the package of cigarettes. I didn't know what I was looking at, since I'd never smoked, but it seemed to me that cigarette packages usually had a tax stamp of some kind on them. The cigarette pack in my hand was Marlboros, but there was nothing resembling a tax stamp on it. I tried to remember what Carlos had said in his letter and chastised myself for not bringing the letter with me. He'd mentioned that Rachael had lent him money to do something with cigarettes—but what? Start a cigarette business? That didn't sound right. The more I tried to remember the letter, the less I was sure what it said. I decided to simply wait until I got back to the room and read the letter again.

Having made that decision, the next thing that came to mind was: *Where's the key to the box?* A key slot was on the side of the lid. I felt around the box, turning it on one side to see if there was a key. Instead of the key, Carlos had taped a handwritten note to the bottom of the box. *See the stuff about the 1999 race in the scrapbook.*

Damn. A posthumous scavenger hunt orchestrated by Carlos. I shook my head. Oh well, this might be fun to see the mind of Carlos working diabolically.

Back in my room, with a cup of coffee from the lobby, I flipped through the pages of the scrapbook to the 1999 race. I almost thought I'd missed something, until I came to the newspaper item with a photograph of the mayor presenting me with a key to the city. In the margin of that photo, Carlos had written *key to lockbox = top/center my garage door*. I drained the cold coffee in my cup and reached for Carlos's letter. Carlos had borrowed money from Rachael to "launch a cigarette importing operation."

I was suddenly on alert again. For the first time, I worried where Rachael had gotten fifty thousand dollars to be lending out. It could have been insurance money from Lloyd's accidental death in an industrial accident. Satisfied with what I knew so far, I decided to drive to Carlos's condo.

My truck was too high to clear the garage ramp's low height, so I walked down the ramp. I knew Carlos's garage was on the bottom floor of the building, because he had complained about that many times. When I got down to the bottom level, I saw four garages, all with their doors open. Three were empty, with nothing of value on the walls or shelves. One had a car in it. If you don't keep anything of value in a garage, and you lock your car, there is no reason to close the garage door, let alone lock it.

I decided the occupied garage with a car in it probably wasn't Carlos's and started with the next one. Nothing on that door. The next one yielded the same result. I saw a garage door opener in the last garage, and I remembered Carlos had told me about having to have the opener code changed. This probably was Carlos's garage. I felt along the top of the garage door and found nothing. No key, at least, although the inside lip of the rubber seal was sticky. I wasn't tall enough to get a good view, so I went out and looked around. One room was open; it contained tools and a wheelbarrow. I decided I could borrow the wheelbarrow and walked into the room. When I entered, however, I saw a stepladder in a corner. I carried the stepladder to Carlos's garage and climbed up on the first step, giving me just enough height to let me see a clear indentation where the key had been taped.

I frowned. Who had taken the key? The sheriff's deputies? The cops could have scoured the garage and could have the lockbox key. If so, there was no danger. On the other hand, someone else might have the key and want to find the lockbox—at any cost.

Maybe you better start taking this whole matter a little more serious, Maxxon, someone whispered in my ear. I thought of the lockbox sitting on the floor behind the seat in my truck. *What's in the box?* Carlos obviously had taken extreme measures to assure that not just anyone got into the lockbox.

Was someone watching me right now?

I decided to take the elevator up to the ground level and exit the garage from a different direction. I might be able to spot anyone if they were watching my truck. I got off the elevator and stood in the shadows to let my eyes adjust. The early sun had risen above the layer of clouds, and, while they didn't portend rain real soon, they would, as they thickened and started roiling. I looked out at the parking lot and saw a man edging the sidewalk in front of my truck. He seemed innocuous, but I hung back until he was down at the end of the parking lot. He kept going. I walked to my truck and made sure the lockbox was still behind my seat.

I glanced at my watch. It was quarter to seven. In air-to-air combat training, you learn to throw the enemy off by doing the unexpected. My original plan had been to have breakfast at the buffet in the hotel. But now I decided to do the unexpected and also take anyone who might be tailing me into territory unfamiliar to them, but familiar to me. So I meandered around the streets of Carpentier Falls, watching the rearview mirrors, and eventually arrived at Sam's Diner. I parked, went in, and claimed the same booth the boys and I had sat at last Friday night.

An older Native American woman was hustling around the diner, taking orders, delivering meals, and cleaning tables. I sat down and was watching her, when Sam came out of the kitchen and walked to me.

"Where are the boys?" she demanded.

"They're in Kings Rapids," I said, "staying with the chief of police and her husband."

Sam looked toward the waitress and then back. "Is that Marguerite Vinssant, the one on the news a few months back?"

"She was. Now she's Marguerite Grossman."

"Humph," Sam sighed. "You know her?"

"She's a good friend of mine."

"The boys like her?"

"They sure do. And they'll be starting school over there this morning."

Sam studied me for a long time. "What do you want for breakfast?"

I hadn't looked at the menu yet. "Just some eggs and sausage, with hash brown potatoes and whole wheat toast."

"How many eggs you want, and how do you want them cooked?"

"Three. Over easy, please."

Sam left for the kitchen, and the waitress came toward me with a steaming mug of coffee. "You need cream?"

I shook my head.

Because I felt she was more emotionally involved with the boys and Irene, I hadn't told Auntie Jean that we suspected that Irene was dead. I decided to tell Sam, however, to see what her reaction was.

When Sam came back, she set a heaping plate of food in front of me—enough to feed three people—still steaming hot. Sam left to take care of a customer standing at the cash register. I dug in. As I ate, I watched the waitress refill coffee cups and Sam working behind the counter. I finished eating and set the plate to the side. The waitress came to refill my coffee mug and asked if I wanted anything else. I shook my head. Sam came to my booth with a cup of coffee in her hand and slid in across from me.

"Why are the boys staying with the police chief in Kings Rapids?" she asked abruptly. "What's going on, Mr. Maxxon?"

"Sam," I started and then paused to organize my thoughts. "They found a woman stabbed to death in Marysville, a town north of Kings Rapids, several weeks ago. They think it might be Irene Wallace, the boys' mother."

Sam stared at me, and her mouth opened.

"Joshua gave Marguerite a picture of Irene last Sunday, and Marguerite sent it over to the state police in Centralia for lab comparisons. Everyone is pretty sure the woman in that picture is the same woman found stabbed to death."

Sam's eyes squinted a little, and I decided she was blinking back tears. "Okay," she said in a low voice. "How'd you get so interested in the boys?" she asked.

"Well, that's a long story," I said. "Let's just say, I figure the boys have been dealt a pretty tough hand. They didn't deserve it. And they deserve to get some real help, not just what some local social worker thinks they should have."

Sam's tension eased, and she nodded. "They are good boys. They never gave their mother one ounce of difficulty. They weren't like a lot of the kids running around the projects."

"Were they going to school regularly?"

"Oh, sure," Sam said. "Their mother made them go to school come hell or high water. She was a real stickler for getting an education. And the boys got pretty good grades. I think Irene helped them with their homework."

"Irene had a college degree," I confided. "From—"

"She did?" Sam said. "I always thought so. She talked like she did. I mean, that girl talked like the people on TV; you know, her words made sense, and she used some big words, too. I always wondered if she didn't have a good education."

"She must have been on the run," I said, letting my thoughts come out without the limitations of logic. "She worked on the assembly line over at Arnold Toolbox. She should have been working as a personnel manager somewhere. Makes me think she was just getting by, waiting for something. What?"

"One time," Sam squinted, remembering, "maybe the second or third time they come here for supper, Jake said something like, 'Daddy's not going to hurt us again, huh, Momma?' And Irene said something like, 'No, Jacob, he isn't.' But I don't remember another thing they ever said out of the ordinary."

"Was there ever a man with them? A father? A boyfriend?"

No. Always just Irene and the boys. Irene never talked about their past to anyone. Even Auntie Jean didn't know what caused Irene to be alone with the boys."

"You know Auntie Jean?"

"Oh, hell, yes. She's the one who told the boys about my Sloppy Joes. She sent the boys over here to get sandwiches for them to have at her place one time, and I tell the boys, 'Don't stop along the way, or the sandwiches will get cold.' Jean called me after and told me the boys ran all the way home, and the sandwiches were hot as ever."

Sam emptied her cup and scooted out of her seat. "I gotta get back to cooking," she said and walked toward the kitchen. Just before she disappeared into the shadows of the kitchen, Sam turned and eyed me. "I'm glad you're taking care of them boys. You're right. They have a tough time ahead of them. Thank you, Mr. Maxxon."

The waitress arrived to fill my coffee cup, but I waved her off. "I'll take my check now," I said. She went into the kitchen. When she returned, she said, "Sam say breakfast on the house."

I nodded appreciation and left a tip big enough to cover it all.

When I left Sam's, it was nearly eight o'clock. Carlos's funeral was at eleven. I drove toward the track, because I remembered seeing a locksmith's sign in the strip mall just north of the Trattoria. As I neared, the Hank's Lock and Key sign came into view. I parked and carried the lockbox into Hank's store.

Hank met me about halfway between the door and the counter. He said, "Hello, Kurt Maxxon. How are you?"

He knew me, but I sure didn't know him. But I was glad to make his acquaintance.

Hank looked at the lockbox I was carrying and said, "Whatcha got there?"

I explained that this lockbox was Carlos's, and he had asked me to deal with it. I told him I couldn't find the key and asked if he could open it. I set the lockbox on the counter.

Hank moved closer and looked at the key slot. "L-189," Hank said. "I can open it, but, I know who has the key."

"Who?" I asked, hoping it was the sheriff.

"Tammy McPherson. You know Tammy, don't you?"

"I don't think so," I said. "I've heard the name, though."

"She was Carlos's event planner, or something like that."

The name had set off alarms and sirens, since Carlos had mentioned her name in his letter, as a postscript.

"You want me to call her and have her get the key to you?"

"No. I think we better not let her know I have the lockbox, right now, if you don't mind. But I need to get it opened, so I can deal with whatever is inside, per Carlos's special request of me. Then, I'm going to turn it all over to the sheriff's department."

Hank moved to his workbench across the back of the room and returned with a huge key ring of spare keys. He looked at several, and then took one off the key ring and handed it to me. "I'd prefer you leave and open the box somewhere else. That way, I'm not involved in any way. There is a code of ethics for locksmiths. I only break that code once in a great while. If you don't mind, Kurt."

I didn't mind. "How much do I owe you?" I asked.

"All you owe me is you don't tell sheriff where you got the key to open the damn thing. I don't want my name mentioned in any way."

I carried the lockbox out to my truck and set it on the floor of the passenger's side. I glanced around to make sure no one was watching me. I unlocked it and took the contents out—two stacks of ledger sheets wrapped with huge rubber bands. I put them back into the box, locked it, and drove back to the hotel, trying to decide when to go through the ledger sheets—before or after the funeral. *After* won by a wide margin. I got a luggage cart to haul the lockbox to my room.

I made some notes on my writing pad about the events of the morning. At ten o'clock, I was ready to go to Carlos's funeral. It would only take me ten minutes to drive to the church, so I went to the lobby for another cup of coffee. Back in my room, I drank coffee and read the newspaper. At ten thirty, I left to drive to the Blessed Sacrament Catholic Church eight blocks west of Hector's Taqueria.

During the drive to the church, I started to reflect on my decision to help Rachael Mellon get out of jail. My reservation was whether I should be involved at all. My gut feeling told me one thing, and my brain told me something else. Over the years, however, my brain has learned that, in arguments with my gut feelings, the brain lost about 80 percent of the time.

I parked my truck at the back of the parking lot. The lot was nearly full, and parked cars lined both sides of the streets for blocks around. The sun had given up for the day, and the clouds were growing darker by the minute. How long before it started to rain was now the question—not *if* it would rain.

I walked to the front of the church, where clusters of people were chatting and milling around. I recognized several prominent businesspeople, city council members, county commissioners, and other dignitaries. There were quite a few law enforcement officers scattered around.

When Brody Wagoner, the mayor, saw me, he ambled over. Brody has always reminded me of Boss Hogg of the *Dukes of Hazard* TV show. He looks like him, he talks like him, and I strongly suspect he operates like him. Brody is short and squat, balding, and wears a white three-piece suit all the time. "Glad you could come, Kurt," Brody blustered as he shook my hand. Then he leaned in close, and, in a conspiratorial voice, said, "Have you figured out who killed Carlos yet?"

I let a smile cross my face and in a low voice said, "I'm positive it wasn't the butler."

"I was just curious," Brody said and turned to leave.

"Mr. Mayor," I said, a little louder than I had planned, and I noticed heads in nearby groups turn toward me. Brody stopped, turned to look at me, and walked quickly back to me.

"You never call me Mr. Mayor unless you've got a problem of some kind," Brody said.

"I have a serious problem, Mr. Mayor," I said in a low voice. "A very good friend of mine lives in the Roosevelt Complex, Building H, and the elevator quit working last month. That means my friend can't go anywhere, since she has problems going up and down the stairs, and she just sits in her apartment. Can you get that damn elevator fixed, so my friend can go out to get groceries and her medicine?"

Brody looked at me for a long time, his mouth grinding. He then said, "Kurt Maxxon has a very good friend living in the Roosevelt Complex?" He paused, and his nose wrinkled slightly.

I nodded and stared him down.

Brody took his cell phone out of the holster on his belt, opened it, punched a speed-dial number, and waited. "Burt, will you check out the elevator in building H at the Roosevelt Complex? A very influential person has a good friend living there, and she needs the elevator." He listened for a few moments and then said, "Okay. Thanks." Brody looked at me. "Done," he said, and he ambled toward another knot of men.

I wound my way toward the steps leading up to the church door. Several people greeted me, and I responded. I climbed the steps and walked into the cathedral-like church. At the front, people knelt in prayer, while others sat in pews. Hermosa sat in the front pew, along with several other people, who I surmised were Carlos's family. I stood at the back, watching. Jimmy Davison and his wife came in and walked past me, not paying attention, to join Hermosa in front. I decided to go offer my condolences again and then sit toward the back.

Hermosa stood as I approached, and she took my hand in hers. She was emotionally on the edge, but still in control. "Thanks for coming, Kurt. Carlos liked you a lot, and so does all of his family."

"Thanks," I said.

"We'd like you to sit with the family," Hermosa said. "Uncle Carlos would like that."

"Okay" was all I could say.

"Tim will be along any time now," she continued. "He had a paralegal do the pleading for Rachael's bond hearing this morning. It's probably already filed with the court. He'll talk to you about it when he gets here."

"Thank you. I'll pay for it all."

"Don't worry about the money," she said, turning and pointing to the pew directly behind her. "You sit there," she said, and then she sat back down.

The building started to fill with people, and I turned to watch them taking seats behind me. I recognized a few more people, but, for the most part, they were all strangers. Tim came striding up the aisle, just as the priest was walking toward the pulpit. He leaned down to kiss Hermosa and moved to sit next to her. As he looked around, he recognized me and nodded. The priest intoned a prayer.

Carlos's relatives occupied the first four rows of pews, with exceptionally close friends included. It was a good-sized group, and I felt honored to be included but worried what the board of directors might think about it. The service had just gotten underway, when a flash of lightning lit up the room, and a loud clap of thunder rumbled the building. Was that a sign of what the board of directors thought of my being here?

The service, a typically Catholic long affair, was one of the better ones I've been to. Burial was in the old cemetery a half mile down a dirt road. This was where the original church had stood for a century, until a tornado had caused extensive damage in 1985, and the replacement church was built in its current location.

The rain had held off until just as the graveside service ended, when it started to sprinkle. Nearly all the attendees scrambled for their cars. I walked toward my truck. Tim Anderson caught up with me and asked if he could catch a ride back to the church to get his car, since he'd ridden over in the family car. Once in my truck, Tim said, "We filed the petition for Rachael's bond hearing this morning. We should know when it will be this afternoon. The only time I can handle it is tomorrow morning. If it's afternoon or Friday, Hermosa will have to handle it."

"That's great," I said. "What do you think the chances are?"

"It'll depend on the judge we get," Tim said. "Have you got a bail bondsman lined up?"

"Mike Collins," I said. "He's an old friend of mine."

"Mike's a good one," Tim said.

We arrived back at the church, and I pulled up behind Tim's Escalade. He opened the door and, as he got down out of my truck, he said, "Someone from my office will let you know the time." He moved quickly to his car and got in. I drove out of the parking lot. Then it dawned on me. I had made a lunch date with Pearce Livingston at McCoy's Spaghetti Factory for one o'clock. I had about fifteen minutes.

*   *   *

<u>Chaundra Dunkin</u>

Chaundra parked her Mustang in the city's parking ramp and ran down the ramps, rather than wait for the elevators, which were notoriously slow. She dashed the half block to the sandwich shop and rushed in. Her mother was sitting at a table in the middle of the room, munching on a sandwich.

Chaundra walked to her mother and leaned down to embrace her. Fran acknowledged her and kept on eating. Chaundra knew she only took thirty minutes for lunch most days, and she was already near that limit. So she eschewed getting a sandwich, even though she was hungry. She sat down.

"When you didn't come home last night, I got a little worried you might have gone back to your old … uh, profession. When you called me this morning, I was so relieved." Fran looked away.

Chaundra wondered whether she was truly emotional or doing her thing.

"I ran into an old friend, and we got to talking, and, pretty soon, well, it was too late to come home, so I stayed at her place."

"Her place?"

"Yeah. Her name is Terri Browne. We've been friends for a long time."

"I don't remember you mentioning her before."

"Well, you probably don't know very many of my friends, Mother."

"I suppose," Fran said. "What did you need to talk about?"

Chaundra dug folded sheets of paper from her fanny pack and handed them to Fran. "I'm all signed up for the adult ed program at the community college. These are copies for you. I just need a check from you for $350 to pay for it."

"I don't have to sign anything?" Fran said.

"Nope. It's all done. I just have to pay for it."

"Okay," Fran said as she dug a checkbook out of her purse. "That's the Pierre Community College?"

"That's it," Chaundra said. "Three hundred and fifty bucks."

Fran scribbled on the check and tore it out of the checkbook. She handed it to Chaundra. Do you need money for books or anything else?"

"I will next week," Chaundra said. "I figured I can put them on my VISA card, and then you can pay the card next month."

"That'll work," Fran said. "I've got to get back to work." She stood and bent to kiss Chaundra on the forehead. "You'll be home tonight?"

"Yes."

"All right, baby. I'll see you this evening."

"I'm going to get a sandwich," Chaundra said as she stood. She watched her mother move through the crowd to the front door. She moved to the order station and ordered a pastrami on rye with Swiss cheese.

That her mother had accepted her explanation of the night before so easily relaxed her. Next, she worried about Terri dealing with Tammy. Tammy had a way of making sure her girls didn't ditch their clients at the last minute without regretting it. She thought about calling Tammy and trying to explain why she had ditched LeRoy last Thursday night. But she didn't want anything more to do with Tammy. She'd turned off her old cell phone and thrown it into a dresser drawer. She had a new cell phone and didn't want Tammy to know that number. If she called Tammy using that phone, Tammy would be able to read the caller ID number.

Chaundra was going to talk to Terri later this afternoon to see what Tammy had done to her. Last night, she and Terri had talked about getting a room together and Terri giving up the business. Terri wanted to, but she needed the money. Maybe they could find something for her to do that would give her an income.

Maybe.

CHAPTER SIXTEEN

Wednesday, September 13

<u>*Kurt Maxxon, Afternoon*</u>

If Pearce Livingston has a choice of where to meet anyone for lunch or dinner, it's going to be at McCoy's Spaghetti Factory. Whenever I'm in Carpentier Falls on business other than race weekend, I always try to have lunch with Pearce, and, since I'd decided to stay over, I called Pearce to set up a lunch date. He was free Wednesday.

Pearce is another one of the people I met when I first returned to the valley after retiring from the Marine Corps and deciding to buy an auto parts store. At that time, he owned two stores in Carpentier Falls; now he owns six. Pearce had been a manager of one store in the legendary Brian Jeevers' auto parts stores empire. When Brian retired, Pearce bought out the store he had managed for Brian. Then he added a second store, and a third, and so on. Brian Jeevers mentored me in both the purchase and management of my store.

I arrived at the parking lot and waited for a torrential downpour to ease up. In spite of being five minutes early, I wound up ten minutes late to the table. I also arrived slightly damp. Pearce was sipping a Manhattan cocktail and talking on his cell phone when I spotted him. He ended his call and reached across the table to shake my hand. He's a little shorter than I am, but about a foot greater in girth. Over the years, he's complained bitterly about putting on weight, but he does nothing about it. His round head seems to sit on his shoulders, with undersized ears and nose. Bushy eyebrows arch over his hazel eyes. He'd be a good poker player with his happy, serene face.

"You're probably still wearing the same size pants as when I first met you," he said.

"Not really," I said, remembering last November when I had tried to get into my old dress blues uniform, just for the fun of it. Christina had agreed to accompany me to the annual Marine Corps birthday bash in Centralia, and I was thinking I'd show it to Christina. It turned out that if I were going to show Christina my old uniform, I would need to have the waist let out a little. Happily, it wouldn't have to be much, less than an inch. Maybe I'll do that sometime in the future.

When the waitress arrived to see what I wanted to drink, I ordered a Diet Coke.

"Still drinking that belly wash?" Pearce chided.

"Still am."

He emptied his Manhattan and ordered another when the waitress delivered my Coke.

We both settled for the lunch special of spaghetti and meatballs, with a generous slice of garlic bread on the side. The lunch special was only $8.05, so it wasn't a huge meal. Pearce was bemoaning the ten pounds he'd put on in the last few months. The realities of weight gain were apparently starting to sink in, because Pearce only ate about three-fourths of what was on his plate, while I cleaned my plate with only a twinge of guilt.

McCoy's has an item on their dinner menu they call the Tex-Mex Plate. The description on the menu makes me think of the Cincinnati area's Five-Way Chili. It's served as a heaping platter of spaghetti, along with bowls of chili, chopped onions, kidney beans, and grated cheese on the side that allows you to mix your own concoction. The only problem with the Tex-Mex Plate is that it's enough food to feed four people. Every time I come to McCoy's, I think about talking Christina into accompanying me for dinner some Saturday evening. If she would eat about a fourth of it, I could probably do a lot of damage to the rest, and then we could get a doggie bag to take some home for a snack.

After our meal, the waitress bussed the dishes. Pearce ordered a Drambuie, and I ordered a cup of coffee. Pearce had confided in me several months before that he was having marital problems. I hoped he would bring me up-to-date on that issue. His wife, Lillian, had never enjoyed socializing, and so, when Vicki and I had come to Carpentier Falls and met Pearce for lunch, Lillian had only come with him a few times.

"How's Lillian doing?" I said, hoping to move through it quickly, especially if they had already separated or divorced.

Pearce squirmed noticeably in his chair, "I've got prostate cancer," he declared.

I jerked to look at him. "Damn," was all I could say, and I asked, "How bad is it?"

"I guess it's pretty bad, but they say it's controllable," he said, matter-of-factly. "They're pretty optimistic they can knock it down. Next week I start external radiation treatment, which is every morning for a week. Then, the following week, they install a radioactive bullet next to the prostate and let it burn the bad cells to death."

"You'll be glowing in the dark." I said, hoping the levity would ease the tension I sensed in his voice.

"You know me," Pearce said, "I like to shine."

We both chuckled, and I sensed Pearce was actually dealing with it better than I had first thought. "So, how are things going with you and Lillian?"

"Well ... you already knew she was ready to leave me," Pearce said. "I don't know. It's like I told you a while back; it was just a strange deal. Neither one of us was seeing other people. I think after we got the kids through college and out on their own, it was just routine, nothing new—we just got tired of waking up to each other every morning."

For a fleeting moment, I wondered if that would have happened to Vicki and me and quickly decided it wouldn't have. Where Pearce and Lillian Livingston had probably woken up to each other nearly every morning for forty years, Vicki and I had had several months of separation every couple of years, while I was on overseas tour of duty, during most of our married life. "Is she staying with you?"

"Oh, yeah. She's in the nurturing mode with this cancer business. She's a good woman. We're getting along real good now."

"So how long are these treatments going to last?"

"Doctors are talking about several months. They're saying the first couple of cycles will either prove that it works or we gotta do something else."

"If I can do anything—"

"There's one thing I need you to do, Kurt."

"Sure, what do you need?"

Pearce massaged his forehead with his left hand and looked away.

I waited for him to work out what he wanted to say.

"It's our grandson, Kurt," he said in a low voice.

I studied Pearce's face, trying to read what was coming.

"I know you've been touring the valley talking to high-school kids about safe driving and being good citizens."

I nodded. "I do what I can."

"He's seventeen, into drugs, thinks he knows everything there is to know, won't listen to anyone. But he's a good kid, I think. And, he's rooted for you many years now. Hell, the kid worships you."

Pearce shut up abruptly and sat staring into his liqueur.

"Is he here in Carpentier Falls?" I asked.

"No. He was hanging out with a bunch of hippies over on the east side of town. The cops raided the place couple of weeks ago and busted them all for possession and using and everything else they could think of. He's over at the youth training center, west of Farmers' City."

"I don't know if I can get in to see him there, but I'll try," I said. "If I need help, I'll call a friend of mine in the state police. What's his name?"

"Pearce," he said. "Pearce Chauncey Livingston, the fourth."

I gave him a sidelong glance to make sure he wasn't stringing me along.

"I'm Pearce Chauncey Livingston, the second," he said and then smiled. "My father was Pearce Chauncey Livingston, Senior, but I didn't like being a junior. So, I took on the moniker of "the second," and then named my son Pearce Chauncey Livingston, the third."

I'd met Pearce after his children had flown the nest. I knew he had a son and a daughter, probably a few years older than my children. And I also knew that his daughter was a veterinarian in Ford Junction, and his son was a superintendent for a major construction company in Centralia. That was another source of bitterness in Pearce that his son had not wanted to follow in his footsteps. But how many sons do that in today's world?

"I'll see what I can do and talk to him as soon as possible. It'll be next week or so before I can get over there," I said.

"He's always said he wanted to drive race cars," Pearce said with a smile, "ever since he met you with me about ten years ago. You remember that?"

I didn't remember it, but I have managed to hide my ignorance of questions like that by changing the subject. "Does he own a car?" I asked.

"Not his own. His folks have three cars. But then, Pearce four, as we call him, was busted for drunken driving six months after he got his driver's license. He's been walking ever since. That may be why he took up with that bunch he did. But that's water under the bridge. If you'd talk to him, maybe get him interested in a racing career—God, that would be great."

"Can't promise you anything, Pearce, other than I'll try."

* * *

I left McCoy's and drove back to the hotel. I stopped in the lobby to get a cup of coffee.

I realized my cell phone was ringing, as I pushed through the door, and I answered it, expecting to hear Christina's voice. It was Marguerite Grossman.

"We solved the—"

"Is it Irene?"

"Yes."

My stomach did a flip. I fought for air and swallowed hard.

"With the info you gave Terry, we called Evandale PD. They tracked down former neighbors, who told them how Randolph beat Irene and the boys, quite badly. They all figured she'd taken the boys and run. They didn't know where. Apparently, Randolph then beat hell out of the cousin who drove Irene and the boys to an aunt's house near Carpentier Falls. He found out where she was, stalked her, and then grabbed her as she was walking home from work one evening. He's told the state guys some of it, but there's still a lot we need to work out. Times. Places. Travel routes. Witnesses."

"Dammit," I said, my stomach churning with emotion for the boys.

"We put out a *Be On the Look Out* for Randolph Henry Wallace, and Brad's guys picked him up leaving a Maplewood bar last night. Get this, the murder weapon was lying on the backseat of his car."

"Damn," I said. "He still had the weapon?"

"Yeah. A big, ugly butcher knife. Irene's blood all over it."

"Damn," I said. "Not real smart, is he?" Then my stomach tightened, when I remembered the boys. "How are Joshua and Jacob?"

"So far, they're fine," Marguerite said, and I could detect she was hedging a little.

"Have you and Terry told them about their mother yet?"

"Not really," she said. "We hinted at the possibility last night, and they seemed to accept it. This evening we plan to take them to the pizza parlor for supper and then talk to them when we get home. They're getting used to living with us, and Terry mentioned adoption to me this morning, so we're both on the same page and ready to pursue that route."

My stomach eased. "I'm glad you guys are doing that. That would be good for them," I said. "Have you heard from Child Protective Services in Carpentier Falls?"

"Who?"

"I have the card somewhere … here it is: Agatha Cochrane, Pierre County CPS."

"I know her," Marguerite said, and I detected a tinge of hostility. "I'll call her. How is the Carlos Guerrero case progressing?"

"I'm really not involved," I said, hoping God wasn't recording my fibs. "They think they have the killer in custody, but I'm not so sure she did it."

"Oh, oh," Marguerite said. "You don't like their suspect?"

"No."

"Have you told them you don't like their suspect?"

"No."

"Why not?"

"Because I'm just not that sure of myself yet."

"Is this *the real* Kurt Maxxon, I'm talking to?" she said. "It sure as hell doesn't sound like it. You're telling me you're just sitting on the sidelines, watching a suspect you don't think did it stay as their main focus?"

"For right now, I have to."

"Brad Langley said he's going to call you," she said.

The hairs on the back of my neck stood erect, and a cold chill ran down my spine. *What was Brad going to say?* Suddenly, I didn't want to talk to anyone.

Marguerite thanked me for my help and hung up. I wondered if I shouldn't turn my cell phone off.

So far, I didn't think Brad knew about my involvement in the investigation into Carlos Guerrero's murder. Brad and I have a long history: good the first thirty years and not so good the last few years.

Our history began when we met as entrants into the flight training school at Pensacola Naval Air Station. In a "it's a small world, isn't it?" moment, while chatting as we stood in line, we determined Brad was from Farmers' City, approximately thirty miles northeast of Centralia, and I was from Albertstown, about twenty miles southwest of Centralia. Brad had graduated from Lehigh as an aeronautical engineer, with four years of NROTC credit; I had graduated from Georgia Tech as an aeronautical engineer, with four years of NROTC credit. We had both opted for the aviation program offered by the United States Marine Corps.

After we met, we were roommates and classmates through most of the early flight schools and other training programs that led to fighter pilot status, graduating with our "wings," and then becoming combat ready. Brad and I drew the same squadron of A-6E Intruders. Every time I moved up in rank, Brad followed soon after. If he moved up first, I followed him in short order. I was the best man at his wedding. He was my best man when I married Vicki. I am the godfather of his two children. He's the godfather of my two children.

I made the rank of major nine months before Brad did. When he made that rank, we arranged a meeting to celebrate. At that meeting we celebrated, and we commiserated that if we were going to advance any further, we would have to go through the Naval Command College at the Naval War College in Newport, Rhode Island. I was ready to just say, "I'm happy as Major Maxxon," even thought it was tongue-tying to pronounce. Brad changed my focus, however, when he said, "I'll bet you a hundred bucks I get through command college before you do."

The challenge was on.

I wound up paying Brad the hundred dollars—but secure in the knowledge that I was scheduled to start command college six months later.

Brad retired from the Corps three years before I did, not by choice, but due to health problems, aggravated when he made a bad approach to a carrier while practicing flattop landings. His tail hook missed the wire, and, as he tried to wind the engines up to go around and try again, the winds ran against him, one engine flamed out, and he went into the drink. The exercises were being conducted off the coast of Oregon—even in September, the Pacific Ocean that far north is extremely cold.

It only took about twenty minutes to fish Brad out of the water, but those twenty minutes damaged nearly all of the old man's joints, loaded with arthritis beforehand. So Brad retired after twenty-three years of service. He applied for a gravy position on the Valley State Police Department and got one. But Brad wasn't interested in "just being taken care of," so he worked his butt off—as he always had, in everything he undertook—and he progressed up the proverbial ladder so fast, none of the younger people saw him streak past them.

The room phone ringing brought me out of my reverie. I answered it, expecting to hear Brad's gruff voice. "Hello," I said, trying for my meek, ready-to-listen voice.

"I had a minute between breakout sessions, and I wondered how you were doing," Christina said. "Are you all right?"

"I'm fine," I said, laughing.

"What's so funny?" Christina said. I could visualize her frowning.

"I was expecting Brad Langley. He told Marguerite Grossman he was going to call me."

"How are the boys doing?"

"They're fine," I said. "The police are sure the dead woman in Marysville is the boys' mother. And, worse yet, it was their father who killed her."

"Good Lord," Christina said. "That's terrible. Do the boys know?"

"They'll know tonight after a pizza party," I said. "I'm glad it's Marguerite and Terry, and not you and I, having to deal with it."

"Marguerite is perfectly capable of handling it," Christina said. "She is very astute in dealing with people. And she will do wonderfully with the boys."

"Yes. And the rest of the story is that Marguerite and Terry are talking about adopting them."

"That's wonderful. It doesn't surprise me, though," she said.

"I may try to get over to Kings Rapids next week to see them."

"Make it Monday, and I'll go with you."

"Okay. Monday it is."

"Any more on Carlos's death?"

"No," I said. "I'm not doing much, other than nibbling around the edges." I wondered if I should tell Christina about trying to get Rachael out of jail. I decided against that for now.

"I know Hoppy appreciates all the help you can give her. You are a very good amateur sleuth. How long are you going to stay in Carpentier Falls?"

"Probably 'till Friday."

Having Christina's vote of confidence made me relax. I gazed around the room and saw Carlos's scrapbook lying on the desk. Then I spotted his lockbox sitting on the sofa.

"I gotta go," Christina said. The line went to dial tone.

I moved to the sofa and sat down next to the lockbox. I unlocked it and took the top stack out, undid the rubber bands, and shuffled through them, studying them as I did. I did the same thing with the second stack. I decided I needed a good CPA to look at them and tell me what they thought about them. And then I remembered my good friend and racing compatriot, Eugenios Christofides, telling me that his niece was a CPA, somewhere in the Carpentier Falls area. I grabbed my cell phone and found him in my contacts list. I dialed the number.

Eugenios told me his niece lived ten miles southwest of Carpentier Falls. She was currently working out of her home, while nurturing her ten-month-old baby son, Eugene, and "CPAing" for several large businesses in Carpentier Falls. He would call her and ask her to help me. He gave me her phone number.

*   *   *

I left the ledger sheets lying all over the sofa cushion, got up to get a cup of coffee, moved to the desk, and stood reading the open sheet of the scrapbook. It was the same picture of Mickey Lawlor congratulating me for beating him that I'd seen in the envelope of memorabilia from the boys' box. Irene Lawlor Wallace—dead. She had been the daughter of a great race driver. Had she been a fan?

Now that I knew who Irene Lawlor Wallace was, I knew how Joshua had known me when I captured them in the drivers' lounge. He must have at least gone through the stack of clippings, probably since his mother had disappeared. The stack must have some significance to Joshua. Why lug them around, otherwise? Mickey had shared his hopes and dreams for his daughter with me during pre-race socializing. I did a quick mental calculation and decided Mickey had probably been alive for Joshua's birth but gone before Jacob came along.

My cell phone jangled.

It was Brad Langley, who said, "I like the way you operate, especially when you work with local agencies to solve murders."

"Thank you."

"I see your name popping up in the Carlos Guerrero case," Brad said, and I tensed. "You're working with Sergeant Hoppy. That's good. Keep up the good work."

"Thank you."

"Why the hell didn't you win Sunday?"

I almost said 'Thank you" again, but stopped just in time. "I was in the wrong gear."

"Yeah, sure."

"I screw up once in a while," I said, adding a chuckle to my voice.

"Yeah, I know that, too," Brad said. "Well, the whole state appreciates your help with the Irene Wallace case. You did good. Do what you can to help Sergeant Hoppy with the Guerrero case. When you get a chance, let's get together for supper."

I hung up with a great weight gone. I breathed a giant sigh of relief.

*   *   *

Tammy McPherson

The new roll-along suitcase was sitting in the motel room closet looking innocently ordinary. Tammy had gone to the airport and bought it from a dealer there. Then she'd retrieved a torn routing luggage tag from a trash can and taped it to her new suitcase—so the carrier of the cash now looked like just a traveler's suitcase.

On the taxi ride back to the motel, she'd worried more about where the lockbox was than the cash in her briefcase. The key to the lockbox in her wallet coin pocket occupied her attention.

She'd gone to the train station, retrieved the briefcase, and lugged it back to the motel, where she'd transferred the cash from the briefcase to the new suitcase. The backpack she'd used to pack her clothes when she vacated the condo sat next to it, looking beat up and ancient. In an impulsive decision, she determined that tomorrow she'd go back to the airport and buy the remainder of the set—and chuck her old backpack.

Tammy felt the money was safer now, here in her motel room. It would be nice if she could figure out a way to make it totally secure, like savings bonds—but, for now, that was out of the question.

Her cell phone rang. The voice said, "I'd like to have Candy meet me tonight."

"Candy is not available, I can send Kaleen."

"Where's Candy? I've called three times now, and all you tell me is she's not available. What the hell happened to Candy?"

"Quite frankly, I'm not sure. If you want a companion tonight, I can send Kaleen. If that's all right?"

"I suppose," the man said. "Yeah, send Kaleen."

Tammy hung up; satisfied she had her most worrisome girl at work. The next girl would be Barbara.

Where did Rachael hide Chaundra?

Why did Carlos hide the lockbox so I can't find it?

Did Carlos have evidence against me he didn't want me to see?

* * *

Kurt Maxxon

I went down to the Speedway Grill and Lounge a little early. When I'd nearly fallen off the wagon the day before, I'd noticed that the bartender was Jake Hanasman, who had worked for Carlos for several years. He was a race fan, who, over the years, had rooted for several drivers and was currently rooting for Jimmy Davison. I liked Jake for his bartender's wisdom and advice. When I walked in and sat down at the end of the bar, he poured a cup of coffee and brought it to me.

"Howdy, Colonel Maxxon," he said, setting the cup in front of me. "Meeting someone?"

"Do you know Gordon Michaelson?" I asked.

"Sure do," Jake said. "You meeting him?"

"Yes. I don't know him, though. So when he arrives, help us meet up."

"I can do that," Jake said. He moved back to the middle of the bar.

The only other patron was a man sitting on a stool at the bar. "Who was the woman Schmitty just left with?" the man asked.

"Her name is Tabby Harris, aka Tammy McPherson," Jake said. "She comes in here occasionally—sometimes to meet men, other times trying to get picked up."

"Nice ass," the man said.

"She is a classy broad," Jake said. "Better than Schmitty has hooked up with for a long time."

"Schmitty's into those women: call girls, hookers, whatever. I hope one of them don't roll him."

I listened to the conversation with passing interest, but the woman they were talking about didn't register. My coffee mug was about empty, when a short, heavyset man came through the lounge's door.

Jake yelled, "Hello, Gordon. Colonel Maxxon is here to meet you," he pointed to me at the end of the bar.

Not the most subtle introduction I've ever enjoyed, but it worked. Gordon Michaelson walked up to me, and we shook hands. He was about five foot ten, with a pretty hefty girth. His round face was jovial, with a totally bald pate and a pug nose. He wore aviation-shaped glasses with gunmetal frames that had turned dark in the sun, so I couldn't see his eyes. He was wearing a dark blue, expensive sports blazer, a light blue shirt with white collar, sans tie, and dark tan pants. I followed him to a booth along the far wall.

"I don't follow racing that much," he said as he scooted into the booth seat. "But I keep track of the important events in Carpentier Falls, and the annual SRVSCRA race is an important event in the chamber of commerce's schedule."

"That's good to hear," I said. "Not everybody is a race fan, Gordon. And we learn to live with that."

Jake walked to our booth with what looked to be a gin and tonic for Gordon and a fresh cup of coffee for me.

"You drinking coffee?" Gordon asked.

"That's about the strongest I drink," I said with a grin.

"I thought all the race drivers were beer guzzlers," Gordon said.

"Not true," I said, offering a smile to appease him. He didn't need to know why, when, or how I'd sworn off alcohol.

Gordon imbibed half of his drink and said, "Cliff Ramsey tells me you're a collector of full-side-split-band Mercury dimes who wants to get more serious about them."

"Yes. Well, I want to look for coins for my collection that Cliff and other coin dealers in the valley just don't have. He mentioned you had done the same and that I should talk to you about how you did it."

"I hear you," Gordon said. "I used Cliff and other dealers to find me nice specimens for several years, but over the last year, I've gone out on my own and started doing some mail bidding, and I've looked at several serious auctions. I've been acquiring some nice coins. I bid on a half-dozen coins with the idea that if the coin proved to be better than the one I already had in my collection, I'd deal the one in my collection. I've got these three," Gordon said as he reached into the pocket of his suit coat. He handed me three gleaming coins sealed in plastic coin holders by the ANA grading service.

I took the coins and studied them. "I guess that's why Cliff wanted me to meet you," I said. "I want to do the same."

"It's going to take more time," Gordon said as he emptied his drink. He waited to catch Jake's attention and signaled for a refill.

"I've got a little time," I said, hoping it wasn't going to become too time-consuming. I handed the coins back to Gordon. "I already have these dates and mint marks in my collection," I said. "And, quite frankly, I think the ones I have are better looking than those."

"That's good," Gordon said.

Jake brought Gordon a fresh gin and tonic and me a new mug of coffee.

Gordon and I discussed coins, and he promised to bring me names, addresses, phone numbers, and pertinent information, so I could branch out into the world of coin collecting on a level I hadn't known existed. We set up a dinner date to meet at the Kin Folks Restaurant when he was next in Centralia on business.

Gordon asked, "Are you married?"

"No," I said. "My wife passed away three years ago from ovarian cancer."

"I'm sorry," he said. "I just remarried a couple of years ago. Wonderful woman. She's been upset the last few days. I don't know if it's because of the Carlos Guerrero murder or the problems she's had with her daughter."

Once again, I thanked God that my daughter, Vanessa, had made it through adolescence to married motherhood without causing any major problems to Vicki and me. "Daughters can be difficult," I said, hoping to present a neutral stance.

Gordon nodded agreement. "My first wife and I had a son and a daughter who we put through college and married off without any problems. But Fran is fifteen years younger than me."

"How is she involved with the Carlos Guerrero murder?"

"Fran is the office manager of Williamson, Mayer, Henry, Petersen and Anderson, a law firm in downtown Carpentier Falls."

I know Tim Anderson," I said. "He's married to Hermosa Anderson, Carlos Guerrero's great-niece."

Gordon shrugged, picked up his new drink, and took a healthy swig. "You want to go to the Kiwanis thing with me?"

"I think I'll pass," I said. "I've got some things I need to get done."

Gordon tipped his drink and emptied it. He stood up and threw a twenty-dollar bill on the table, and I followed him out of the lounge. We parted company in the lobby of the hotel with the promise that we would keep in touch with each other.

* * *

I called Andrea Christofides. She told me she was in town for a meeting and could stop by the hotel about seven thirty. That made it easy for me, so I decided to go down to the Speedway Grill for dinner.

When I arrived, about half of the booths were empty. Jake waved to me, as I slid into a booth.

"You here for dinner?"

"Yes. I know what I want," I said. "I already looked over the menu while I waited for Gordon."

A skimpily dressed girl arrived and asked what she could get me to drink.

"Iced tea."

"Excuse me," she said, her eyebrows springing upward.

"I'd like iced tea."

She turned and walked back toward her station at the bar. Jake handed her a tall glass of iced tea. She talked to him, looked at me, and then, with a shrug, brought the glass to me. "What'll you have?"

"I'll have the Reuben sandwich basket."

I watched the nearest TV set showing the nightly news and read the closed captioning as best I could. By the time I finished eating, the place was full, with a waiting line at the door.

I rode the elevator up to my floor, gathered the ledger sheets into two piles, as they had been in the lockbox, reinstalled the rubber bands, and went back down to the lobby for my meeting with Andrea Christofides. She arrived at 7:25, and, as usual, she knew me from pictures in the newspaper, but I wouldn't have known her from Eve.

We chose a quiet and reasonably isolated grouping of chairs and sat down. I put the two stacks of ledger sheets on the coffee table in front of us. Andrea picked up the smaller stack of ledger sheets and leafed through them, studying them. Then she did the same with the larger stack. When she finished looking through the sheets, she laid the stack back on the table.

"Well, it's obvious that Carlos had one set of books he allowed the world to see," she said, pointing to the smaller stack. "And a set of books for his real operations," she said, pointing to the large stack. "The problem will be to decipher what the codes represent. Do you have any idea what Carlos was into?"

"I'm not sure I know what all he was into," I said. "But I've heard about gambling, illegal cigarettes, and prostitution."

"It would take several hours to sort these ledger sheets into accounts for each of the code names," Andrea said. "The real set," she pointed to the bigger stack, stops June 30, which is probably the end of the second quarter. The bogus set ends just a few weeks ago. So, there are some additional sheets somewhere. Do you know where they are?"

"I have no idea," I said. "Carlos was adept at hiding things."

"One thing that pops out at me is that there are a lot of cash entries here," she said as she ran her finger down one of the columns. She paused and then said, "The deposits to the bank accounts don't seem to add up."

"What does that mean?" I asked.

She looked up at me and pushed her glasses up on her head. "Well, it could mean several things. One, it could mean that, while Carlos was meticulous about recording the cash, he wasn't so meticulous about putting it in the bank. Two, he could have been converting it to his own use, with the idea of paying it back. Or, three, he could have been paying extortion or blackmail."

"It was blackmail," I said. "I think he mentioned something like ten thousand dollars a month."

"Ten thousand a month wouldn't cover all these cash entries."

"You mentioned he might have been converting the money for his own use. He could do that, couldn't he?"

"Well, he could, but after it has been fully accounted for. In other words, whoever does his books would go through the double-entry process of putting the dollars into an 'undeposited funds' account and crediting the cash account when he deposited the cash in the bank. After that, he could use the money in the bank account any way he, or any partners he might have had, saw fit. But to do it before it is fully tracked isn't kosher and might even be considered suspicious."

I thought about that for a minute. I couldn't imagine the details of many cash entries like that, when my auto parts stores didn't have nearly so complicated an accounting system.

"Look here," Andrea said, as she viewed the fourth ledger sheet in the stack. "There's something wrong here."

I looked at the entry next to her index finger. Nothing looked bad to me. I looked at her, puzzled. "What do you see?"

"First there's been an erasure and then an overwrite. It looks to me like something originally written thirty thousand dollars was changed to eighty thousand dollars. The memo line says 'new car.'"

"That's strange," I said. "But how did you spot that?"

"That's not the proper way to make a change to an existing entry," Andrea said. "I see a lot of book entries, Mr. Maxxon, and I can tell when something's wrong—especially when it appears that it's a different person's writing. Look close, here," she said, pointing to another entry. "Here's an eight written by Carlos … and here's another. Now, look at the entry for eighty thousand dollars. The person making the overwrite wasn't as interested in copying Carlos's handwriting of numbers as much as they were intent on making the three look like an eight. The problem they had, though, once they erased the original three, was that they couldn't follow the original lines. It is definitely an altered entry, maybe a forged entry. Do you know what kind of car Carlos drove?"

"He drove one of those little Mercedes cars," I said. "Probably cost thirty thousand, because he traded for new every two years."

"So, someone doctored this entry to cover for another fifty thousand dollars. Maybe someone embezzled fifty thousand and they covered it up to keep Carlos from finding it on his ledger sheets. Do you know who had access to these ledger sheets? Do you know who his bookkeeper is?"

"No, maybe Hermosa knows."

"I doubt it," Andrea said. "If Carlos was running two sets of books, he obviously had to have someone who would keep his books and also keep quiet."

"That's certainly possible."

"Yes, and I'd bet you'll never find the real books. So, these ledger sheets are probably all that will be available to the executor of his will to probate his estate. My opinion is that these ledger sheets are quite valuable, Mr. Maxxon, and I'd be showing that entry to Hoppy," Andrea said, pointing to the doctored eighty-thousand-dollar entry. "Hoppy can get an official copy of whatever she needs and then turn the ledger sheets over to the executor of Carlos's will. I suggest you turn these sheets over to the authorities and let them figure them out."

"I just wanted to see if they told us anything outright," I said. "If something pointed toward who would want to kill Carlos."

"Whoever changed that entry might make a good suspect," Andrea said. She shook her head. "The entry doesn't tell us much, other than the dollars involved. We won't be able to tell much until someone can figure out the codes. Then maybe they can tie them to real people. Did Carlos ever mention any names to you?"

"A couple," I said, "in a confidential letter to me. I'd prefer giving them to Hoppy first."

"I understand," she said. "If one of his side businesses was the cause of his death, then the sheriff needs to know that."

"Thank you."

Andrea stood and pressed the creases of her pants with her hands.

"I'll take them to Sergeant Hoppy tomorrow morning. Maybe she can come up with the missing sheets and figure out what they mean," I said.

"Is she the lead detective on the case?"

"Yes. Do you know her?"

"She's the best detective in the sheriff's department."

I agreed with that, too.

To my offer to pay her, Andrea shook her head. "Let Uncle Gene win a race once in a while."

"I'll try," I said, and she left.

I carried the stacks of ledger sheets back to my room. *Where are the current quarter's sheets?*

When I got to my room, the phone was ringing, but it stopped before I could push through the door. I watched to see if the message light would start blinking. When it did, I dialed the voicemail. It was Tim Anderson, telling me they had been able to get Rachael's bond hearing on the docket for tomorrow afternoon. Hermosa would call me in the morning with a time for the hearing.

Why doesn't that cheer you up? a voice in my head asked.

CHAPTER SEVENTEEN

Thursday, September 14

<u>*Kurt Maxxon, Morning*</u>

After I set the coffeemaker up, showered, and dressed, I poured a cup of fresh, fragrant coffee and started to sit down at the desk, ready to peruse Carlos's scrapbook. The on-again, off-again thunderstorms fired up with a loud clap, and I could hear the rain beating down on the roof above me. Instead of sitting down, I walked to the window, pulled the drapes open, and stood watching the rain pouring down. It was going to be a gloomy day. I replayed the morning the boys had discovered Carlos's body, letting the events since then stream through my mind.

I'd had a fitful night. Rachael's bond hearing had made me toss and turn until four thirty, when I decided I might as well get up and do something. I felt more tired than I had last night.

"Why are you feeling so ambivalent about this?" I asked my reflection in the window.

A myriad of reasons why the judge would deny Rachael's bond flooded my mind. Very few reasons for a successful result made it through my black mood. In my humble opinion, Rachael was incapable of harming anyone. *Would the judge be able to see that in her? Would the DA present something about Rachael I didn't know?*

The evidence against her is strong. Is it actually what happened?

I replayed the most salient parts of my involvement with Rachael in high school as well as I could with the nearly forty years in between. Rachael Lynn Bradshaw had been the girl across the street. We went to elementary school together, and we discovered each other in our junior year of high school. We had a two-year high-school romance, went too far, but thankfully didn't do any real harm. I'd left Albertstown for Atlanta and Georgia Tech in August of 1962. I don't really remember my feelings about leaving Rachael; there were dozens of other emotions involved. There was the thrill of leaving the nest, the uncertainty of being away from that nest, the worry about future grades, and a dozen others. My four years at Tech included a couple of other women. I'd gone directly from Tech into my career in the Marine Corps.

Thinking back on it, I think Rachael and I both sensed my leaving for Tech meant we would never be together again. Rachael and I never really tried to maintain contact. Her father had moved her and the family to Carpentier Falls shortly after I left, and the quick trips I made home for Thanksgiving and Christmas never allowed time to track her down. Somehow, our young love faded into, "Oh, yeah, we did that."

A couple of years later, I heard Rachael had married Lloyd Mellon. Lloyd had been two years ahead of us in high school and after graduation had gotten a job as a laborer for a major construction company in Centralia. I figured Rachael had her life settled.

I flew home to attend the twenty-fifth class reunion in 1987. It was a quick trip, since I had to get back to Newport, Rhode Island, to start Naval Command College. Vicki didn't come with me. During that trip, I met Rachael and Lloyd. Rachael was still very attractive, but I distinctly remember being glad I was married to Vicki, the mother of Vanessa and Kurt Jr., and being very anxious to get home to her.

The year after Vicki and I moved back to the valley, I read in the *Police Blotter* that Rachael Lynn Mellon had been arrested for DUI in Centralia. The article gave her address in Carpentier Falls. Without mentioning anything to Vicki, I covertly talked to Sue Creighton, the woman who had coordinated the class reunions for three decades, and she gave me Rachael's address and phone number. Sue told me Mike Collins, another classmate, lived a few blocks away from Rachael. I contacted Mike, under the guise of catching up, to pry out of him all I could about Rachael. He gave me an abridged version of Rachael's problems: nasty marriage, worse divorce, two sons, both in prison for murder, and her biggest nemesis—booze. I empathized with her, but I decided against contacting her, helped by Mike's admonition, "Rachael Mellon is bad news, Kurt. Probably best to stay away from her."

I puttered around the hotel room, checking notes and making sure I had everything for Sergeant Hoppy organized. I'd gone through all the coffee in the room and made a trip to the lobby for more.

I called Sergeant Hoppy to see if she would be available this morning. She said she would be back in her office about ten o'clock. She didn't seem all that interested in the scrapbook or the ledger sheets.

I sat down at the desk with two capped cups of coffee. I looked at the scrapbook and debated whether to take it to Hoppy or to keep it. It was an interesting book, and I wanted to go through it page by page someday. However, I decided to give it to Hoppy, but only if she promised to return it to me when it had served its purpose to her. That might be the soonest I'd have time to go through it thoroughly anyway. Carlos had spent a lot of time putting it together over the years.

I hadn't taken the time to look at anything other than the section on my racing career and the references Carlos had made about the lockbox and its key. I hadn't even looked completely through my section. I turned the scrapbook over, so I could start at the back, and I realized there was a wide gap between the sheets. I let the sheets flop open.

There were several ledger sheets.

"Aha!" I breathed. "This book is a great place to hide stuff."

Most people going through the scrapbook would probably skip the section on Kurt Maxxon's racing career. Except Kurt Maxxon, of course.

* * *

Tammy McPherson

Tammy hung up the phone and sat on the edge of the bed staring at it. When Sergeant Hoppy had asked her to come in and sign another release form, Tammy had instantly wondered what was coming down. *Has Hoppy dug up something against me? Is she just luring me into a trap?* For several minutes she thought about just packing and leaving town. She could get on a northbound Amtrak train about noon or a southbound train about five o'clock.

Tammy turned her focus to the three new suitcases jammed into the tiny closet. The smallest one held the cash. The other two were empty, but she calculated she could get everything she'd kept in the other two. *Where do I go? Up to Saint Louis? South to New Orleans?*

She decided to bathe and dress. She had plenty of time, since it was only eight thirty. *Does Hoppy know where the lockbox is? Was that what she found against me? Something Carlos left in it?*

She let her focus blur as her mind wondered.

"Maybe I can get Hoppy to tell me if she has the lockbox," she said aloud. "If Hoppy has the lockbox, maybe she'll share with me what's in it—let me look through it. And maybe I can sneak the ledger sheet I altered out and destroy it."

Tammy began rehearsing her approach. "Carlos and I shared this lockbox, putting important papers into it. But I haven't been able to locate it since Carlos's death. Did the sheriff's take possession of it? If they did, can I look to see if some of my important records are still in it?" *That should work.*

It might be smart to go to Hoppy's office, sign any form she has, and make my pitch about the lockbox. She walked into the bathroom and ran bathwater.

Stop being so paranoid, hon. If the cops knew what you'd done, they'd have already come and got you. They've got Rachael. Why would they be looking at you?

Tammy called for a cab and arranged her room so it looked innocently like a tourist's room. Then she rehearsed her spiel about the lockbox again.

* * *

Kurt Maxxon

Hermosa had called to tell me that since it was a late addition to the docket, Rachael's hearing would probably be midafternoon. As I walked from my truck toward the law center, carrying the scrapbook, the ledger sheets, and the envelope with a copy of Carlos's letter, I wondered if I should even mention the letter to Hoppy. I pondered what Carlos had written in his letter, trying to formulate a way to broach the subjects with Sergeant Hoppy.

I sat down on a bench nearby when I saw Hoppy's office door was closed. I stared at the floor, trying to decide what course of action to take. I'd heard and read the name Regnault Claymore several times, and then LeRoy Kitchens had mentioned him as still cavorting with prostitutes. I raised my eyes to the ceiling, but movement brought me back to reality. A woman came out of Sergeant Hoppy's office and was walking toward the entrance. I recognized her as a woman I'd seen at the Trattoria several times, but I'd never been introduced to her. I stood up, followed her out of the main entrance, and watched her cross the concrete sidewalk to a cab parked at the taxi station. I moved so I could read the number of the cab. Number 0027. That would be easy to remember—the same number Nikki had painted on her side. I went back in and headed to Hoppy's office.

Hoppy was standing outside her office door when I returned, and she invited me in. "Who was the woman who just left here?"

Hoppy studied me for several beats, then sat down in her chair, and pointed to a chair in front of her desk. She lifted her right eyebrow, and said, "Her name is Tammy McPherson. She was third or fourth on the emergency call list for the Trattoria."

"Oh," I said, nodding, "that's why she looked familiar to me." I sat down in Hoppy's guest chair. I'd heard the name Tammy McPherson enough lately, and now I had a face with the name. "Since we're sharing information, I have some for you."

Hoppy leaned back and tented her fingers with her elbows on the chair arms. "Okay," she said, "is this about the scrapbook?"

"I'll get to that in a minute," I said. "First, a surprise, at least it was to me. Carlos was an illegal alien."

Hoppy's eyebrows lifted slightly. She wrinkled her lips. "That's good information. How did you find that out?"

"He left me a letter. I brought you a copy. I have the original in a safe place." I laid the copy on her desk.

"Why can't I have the original?"

"It might be useful to Rachael's defense."

Hoppy picked up the letter and held it poised to read. "All right, does this letter have anything to do with Carlos's death?"

"I don't know, but it's got some very interesting information in it." I leaned back and crossed my right leg over my left. "There are a lot of facts there, and Carlos apparently thought he might meet an untimely demise. I don't exactly see myself as the local confessional."

Hoppy skimmed through the letter, and I watched her eyes brighten when she read certain parts of it. "Holy … Mother of Jesus," she said, and she returned to the top of page one to read the letter slowly.

I waited while Hoppy read the letter, stopping and going back to start a section over several times. "Very … interesting," she said, and laid the sheet on her desk.

"You knew about the gambling," I said. "Anything else in the letter you already knew about?"

Hoppy pursed her lips and looked at a spot over my head. "We knew about the cigarette operation, and we're about ready to take it down."

"What about the prostitution?"

Hoppy leaned back into her seat and looked at me for a long while, her face blank. "We had no information that the Trattoria was a base for any kind of prostitution."

"It probably was operated from another place," I said. "It looks like Carlos has been running a ring for years. But I doubt you can tie it to the Trattoria."

"Hmm," Hoppy digested my statement. "I wonder if this is how Tammy McPherson fits into the puzzle?" she said.

"It wouldn't surprise me." I let her information work through my mind.

"She's been fairly cooperative," Hoppy said. "We lost contact with her last weekend. She resurfaced a couple of days ago. She came in to sign some forms today."

Damon Hertz appeared in Hoppy's doorway and knocked lightly. Hoppy looked up. "Have you got a minute?" he asked.

Hoppy nodded, "Come on in. I think you know Kurt Maxxon?"

"Oh, yeah," Damon said, looking at me as if I were an afterthought to his mission. "How are you, Colonel Maxxon?"

This guy will go far, I thought, pleased he had used my racing nickname. He has a great memory and finesse to match. "I'm fine," I said, smiling and nodding my head.

Damon had a file folder in his hand. "I need you to sign this arrest warrant." He handed the folder to Hoppy, who read for a few minutes before scribbling her name on the warrant.

Hoppy handed the folder back to Damon and said, "If you've got a few minutes, Kurt has found some information that might have a bearing on the Guerrero homicide."

Damon pulled a straight-back chair toward the desk and straddled it. He looked at Hoppy quizzically.

"Hasn't anyone informed you of Kurt Maxxon's unique ability to find out information that solves murders?" Hoppy asked.

Damon frowned, as his head jerked toward me. "No," he growled.

"It's nothing personal," Hoppy said, laughing. "Kurt was just telling me he's pretty sure Carlos was running a prostitution ring. He

239

might have had Tammy McPherson fronting it to keep suspicion from himself."

"Where did he run it from?" Damon said.

"We don't know," I said. "He owned an office building a few blocks from the restaurant, with luxury condos upstairs."

Damon nodded as if he knew about the office and condos.

"Have you talked to Tammy McPherson as part of your investigation?" Hoppy said. She handed Carlos's letter to Damon. "At the bottom, Carlos wrote he didn't trust Tammy."

"Not yet," Damon replied. "Since we have the Mellon woman in custody, I've been concentrating on other cases. I did go out to her condo once, but she wasn't home. I haven't had an opportunity to go back out there." He read the letter through, grimaced, and handed it back to Hoppy. "If Carlos owed Rachael money, they might have argued about it, and she killed him during the argument."

"That's possible," Hoppy said. "But, not the most overwhelming motive I've ever heard."

"Another bunch of information you might find useful," I said, opening the envelope of ledger sheets and handing them to Hoppy. "These apparently are the ledger sheets to the books of Carlos's operations. Andrea Christofides, who I think you know, tells me that one is the real set, and the little stack is the set Carlos showed the world."

Hoppy leafed through the big stack and then handed it to Damon, while she leafed through the small stack. "How did you find these?" Damon asked. "Christ, we've been searching high and low for these!"

I looked at Hoppy. "Remember the reference in Carlos's letter to me to read about my win in 2002?" Hoppy nodded, as I stood up and opened the scrapbook, turned to the page with the 2002 clipping, and pointed to the writing on the picture.

Hoppy and Damon leaned down to read it. "A storage room?" Damon said.

"The storage room Carlos used to stage his cigarette bootlegging operation," I said. "The only thing in the room was this pack of cigarettes." I pulled the package from my shirt pocket and laid it on the table. "And a metal lockbox."

"A metal lockbox?" Hoppy said. "McPherson just asked me if we had a metal lockbox in the evidence pool."

"She's got the key to the lockbox," I said. "I think she got it from where Carlos kept it hidden."

"How do you know she has the key?" Damon asked.

Then I remembered my promise to Hank not to involve him. "I can't divulge that right now," I said. "But it was a good source."

"Have we ever really clarified what McPherson's involvement with Carlos was, and where she was the night of the murder?" Hoppy asked Damon.

Damon shrugged. "No, to both questions."

"Run a background on her, and get it to me as soon as possible," Hoppy said to Damon.

"I'll start that as soon as I leave here," Damon replied.

Suddenly, I returned to reality. "In those ledger sheets, there is an irregularity that Andrea told me looks like a possible embezzlement." I picked up the ledger sheets and leafed through them to the one with the erasure changing thirty thousand dollars to eighty thousand dollars. I handed that sheet to Hoppy. "Somebody doctored this entry to cover the disappearance of fifty thousand dollars. I wonder if that somebody is Tammy McPherson?"

Hoppy studied the erasure and then handed the sheet to Damon.

"You say Andrea Christofides said this looks bogus?"

"Yes."

"Do you mind if we talk to her about it?"

"Not at all."

"I'll take care of it," Damon said.

All right, Maxxon, I told myself, *time to spring the news.* "There's going to be a bail hearing for Rachael Mellon at one o'clock."

Hoppy swung to look directly at me. "Is that why the bailiff has left me voice mails?" Hoppy leaned forward and punched a button on the phone. "Three messages." She picked up the handset and punched another button. "This is Sergeant Hoppy, Pierre County Sheriff's office," she spoke into the phone. She listened. "One o'clock, okay. I'll be there." She cradled the handset.

"Are you behind this hearing?" she asked, looking at me.

"Yes," I said, "I don't like Rachael as the killer."

Hoppy lifted her left eyebrow and looked at me for a long time.

Damon said, "Do you know her?"

"She was my first love in high school," I said.

"Oh, Christ," he said.

I remained impassive.

"We've gathered an awful lot of incriminating evidence," Damon said, "DA likes the case so far." He looked at Hoppy, as if to reassure her that the evidence was sound.

"Who's today's judge?" Hoppy said.

"Hermosa said she thought it would be Crosbey," I said.

Hoppy looked at me. "You probably stand a chance with her."

Damon frowned. "What evidence have you got that trumps the DA's case?"

"I don't know for sure," I said, shaking my head, "with the illegal status, the gambling, the prostitution, and the apparent forgery, there's an awful lot of doubt in my mind. The Rachael I knew never had it in her to get angry enough or crazy enough to kill someone."

Damon frowned, "You mean this is just a gut—"

Hoppy interrupted Damon. "I wouldn't bet against Kurt Maxxon's hunches. He's giving us all he has. Let's do some legwork of our own. Do you have anything else besides this stuff, Kurt?"

"I don't have anything else," I said. "I am interested in how you plan to handle the part in Carlos's letter about Congressman Regnault Claymore." I fought down a smile for the intelligence that LeRoy Kitchens had given me about "ole Reggie."

Hoppy and Damon looked at each other and took deep breaths. *Bingo,* I thought.

"He's very popular with the voters," Hoppy said, looking warily at Damon. "He's kind of a rowdy old soul."

I sat silently.

Damon's eyes became animated.

"This doesn't leave this room," Hoppy said. Damon nodded and got up to close the door.

I said, "Agreed."

"He's in our logs several times. Drunk and disorderly, but we always got him home. Naked in the backseat of his convertible with an equally naked woman, a couple of times."

"He likes booze and women, and he's slow to learn," I said.

"Right," Hoppy said. "And money. I'll have to take the letter to Sheriff Morton. He's the one who'll decide what to do about it."

"That's what I would do," I said.

"It'll be interesting to see if he's still the source of illegal social security numbers," Hoppy said. She looked at Damon and said, "Detective Hertz, our jobs just became very complicated."

Damon nodded vigorously.

She turned to me. "You mentioned Hermosa. I assume that's Hermosa Anderson, and she is the attorney for Rachael Mellon?"

"Yes," I said.

"Makes sense," she said as she stood and moved toward the door. "I need to visit the little girl's room. Then, I'll walk with you to the courthouse."

Damon excused himself, saying, "Let me go get a judge to approve these. I'll be in my office if you need anything."

I sat in Hoppy's office, hoping I hadn't ignited a wildfire that would burn us all severely.

*   *   *

When Hoppy and I walked into the courtroom, Rachael was sitting at the defendant's table talking to Hermosa. Deputy sheriffs stood guard at the door into the room. A county marshal stood by the judge's bench.

Polished, hand-sawn red oak covered everything in the room. The judge's bench was an ornately decorated oak square, raised from the floor about two feet. The witness stand, to the left of the bench, was about one foot above the floor and carried on the ornate carving.

Directly in front of the bench were two conference-sized tables, with four chairs facing the bench. To the left of the bench, along the wall adjoining the witness stand was a beautifully carved jury box, with twelve ornate chairs cushioned in a rich blue fabric. A railing stretched behind the conference tables, from the jury box to the opposite wall. Every six inches there was an exquisitely turned post, and at the center was a swinging gate.

A court stenographer sat to the right of the bench, poised to start her recording duties. There was no one else present.

Hoppy went through the gate to the defense table. She shook hands with Hermosa and said something to her. Then she moved to the prosecutor's table and sat down. I sat down outside the railing in a regular seat. I knew it would be better if I didn't make an effort to talk to Rachael. Rachael acknowledged me with a wan smile.

In a rush of commotion, a young lady who looked ready to start college flew into the courtroom, her huge purse banging the railing. She moved to the prosecution table and threw the purse onto the table. With fumbling hands, she opened the purse and dug inside. Before she had located anything, the door behind the judge's bench opened, and the bailiff yelled, "All rise, for the Honorable Judge Jamie Crosbey. This court is now in session."

A robust woman bustled through the door, her black robes ballooning about her. She climbed up to the bench, stood to arrange a couple of items on her desk, and then she sat down. She looked to be in her early fifties; her round face was framed with red hair, now sprinkled with gray, and emerald eyes were set above a pointed nose. She picked up a folder, examined it, surveyed the room, and hammered her gavel down.

"This is in the case of State versus Rachael Lynn Mellon. Is that correct?" She looked at Hermosa.

"That's correct, Your Honor," Hermosa said.

"Are you Rachael Lynn Mellon?" the judge asked.

Hermosa nudged Rachael, who replied, "Yes, ma'am, I am."

"You are asking bail be set?"

"Yes, ma'am."

"You pled not guilty last Monday at your arraignment. Why didn't your attorney ask for bonding at that time?"

Rachael swung her head to look at Hermosa. Hermosa said, "Your Honor, at her arraignment, the attorney representing her came from the county legal aid."

"Okay," the judge said. From there on, the judge directed the hearing, asking questions, wondering whether Rachael presented further danger to society, in general, and did she present a flight risk?

The young assistant DA had one line: "We believe, Your Honor, that, due to the seriousness of the charges against her, that Rachael Lynn Mellon should not be granted bail."

Hermosa argued that all the evidence against Rachael was circumstantial and that Rachael did not present a significant risk to society, nor was she a flight risk.

At one point, the judge looked at me. "Are you Kurt Maxxon?"

I stood and walked to the railing. "Yes, Your Honor."

"Please approach the bench, Colonel Maxxon."

I pushed through the gate and walked to the bench. "Your honor?" I said.

"The petition states you are prepared to guarantee that this defendant will appear for trial and will not flee the jurisdiction. Is that correct?"

"Yes, Your Honor."

"Okay," she said. "My order will be that bail be set at two hundred and fifty thousand dollars. The defendant shall not leave the jurisdiction of this court without permission from this court. The defendant shall appear before this court when summoned. Is that clear?"

I nodded. "Yes, Your Honor."

"Ms. Mellon, do you understand my order?"

I didn't hear Rachael's reply, but it apparently satisfied Judge Crosbey.

The judge banged her gavel, said, "This court is now adjourned," stood up, and disappeared into her chambers. The rest of us had barely gotten to our feet.

Hermosa gathered papers into her briefcase. She smiled at me.

Hoppy came to the table, arriving at the same time as one of the deputies who had been guarding the door. "Go ahead and start processing her out, Dale." She looked at me. "Do you have a bondsman lined up?"

"Mike Collins will be down at the desk as soon as we are ready," I said. "I'll call him."

"Good. It'll take about an hour to get the paperwork done. I'll move it along as fast as possible," Hoppy said. "You can wait in my office if you like, Kurt."

Something started nagging me about the evidence against Rachael.

I couldn't put my finger on it.

CHAPTER EIGHTEEN

Thursday, September 14

Kurt Maxxon, Afternoon

Mike Collins came through the door and stood looking for me. I stood up and met him about halfway. "I'm proud of you, guy. Hell, ain't too many people can get a murder-one suspect released on bail."

"Hermosa did all the heavy lifting," I said.

Mike led me to a small alcove with a desk and pulled paperwork out of his briefcase. He sat down and pointed for me to sit opposite him. "Of course, you know I trust you, but I have to have this paperwork signed for insurance purposes," he said. He slid three sheets of paper toward me. "This one says you will personally guarantee the $250,000 bond I put up for Rachael Mellon. This one gives me permission to attach everything you own, or ever hope to own, in case she don't show up for her court appearance. It also mentions $250,000. The third one is the receipt for the $25,000 you're going to give me today. Make the check out to Certified Bail Bond."

Mike led the way, and we went down a long hallway, through security, and into the jail area. Just inside that area, we encountered a desk, manned by a deputy sheriff who watched me approach and then looked at Mike. "Wow, Mike, you really do know some important people."

Mike grinned. "I've told you all along, Andy, I know some important people. I run with the fast crowd, in the fast lane."

The deputy stood and reached to shake my hand. "I'm very pleased to meet you, Colonel Maxxon. You ran a damn good race last Sunday. Fortunately, my driver won it."

"Jimmy's one of my favorites, too. Thank you."

Mike said, "We're here to bond out Rachael Mellon."

"Oh, yeah," the deputy said. "I heard she's on her way down now."

As if on cue, the elevator door slid open, and a female deputy sheriff led Rachael out. I noticed she was wearing her own clothes, and handcuffs, only they were in front of her.

Mike and I followed them to a glassed-off counter. Rachael and I stood off to the side while Mike dealt with the paperwork. Eventually, the deputy who had escorted Rachael down moved forward and unlocked the cuffs.

Mike led Rachael and me back out to the parking lot, showing the paperwork when needed to get Rachael out through the secured area. On the sidewalk outside, he shook both our hands, said "Good luck," and double-timed toward his car, which was parked in a No Parking zone, with the meter maid just four cars away.

I helped Rachael up into my truck. As I climbed in on my side, I remembered that it was over forty years since she and I had been in a vehicle together. That brought to mind the 1949 Hudson Hornet I had owned at that time, but memories of the car vanished when Rachael said, "Thank you, Kurt."

The overnight thunderstorms had cleared, and the sun was fighting its way out from behind high, thinning clouds. It would be hot and humid shortly. The sun and Rachael's successful bonding out made life feel a whole lot better.

After some uncomfortable and tense moments, Rachael and I relaxed, as we discussed the weather and a few other innocuous subjects. When we arrived at the Trattoria, I noticed Hermosa's car in her normal parking spot. She'd left immediately after the hearing to run errands. I had hoped she would be available to kind of chaperone Rachael and me as we reestablished our friendship.

This visit to the Trattoria seemed strange, as no one met us at the door to usher us to a table. I led Rachael to a quiet corner table. We had just gotten seated when Hermosa came striding into the room. She detoured to our table. "I had them prepare some food for you two," she said. "Let me go have them bring it out." She walked back to the kitchen area. A few minutes later, a waitress came to our table with a serving tray. She unloaded plates of finger sandwiches, fresh vegetables with a spicy dip, and a bowl of fresh fruit onto the table. She asked what we would like to drink.

"Iced tea," I said.

Rachael nodded. "The same," she said.

We both grabbed sandwiches and then put vegetables and fruit on our plates. The food hit the spot, even though it was spartan, compared to what I normally ate for lunch.

After we'd eaten several sandwiches, Rachael stopped, looked at me, and softly said, "I didn't kill Carlos. I'm sure I didn't." Her eyes took on a moist sheen, and she swallowed hard, making the muscles at the base of her neck stand out.

The waitress delivered our iced teas.

"I believe you," I said after the waitress had left. I looked at Rachael for several moments, as she tipped her glass to drink. She was only fifteen days younger than me, but she had aged far faster than a lot of our classmates, although I could still see traces of the movie-star attractiveness that she'd had as a teenager. Her red-auburn hair was now dull gray and frizzy from too many permanents. Her eyes were a lusterless gray that sat over puffy bags. Her cheeks were bloated, and her voice had a smoker's gruffness. She had put on several extra pounds in her abdomen.

I realized that Rachael was avoiding direct eye contact with me. I took a copy of Carlos's letter from my shirt pocket, opened it, and handed it to her. She read, stopped and reread parts, and eventually finished. She looked at me briefly, nodding her head.

"Everything in that letter … you pretty much knew about all of it," I said.

Rachael fidgeted and tugged at the V-necked sweater she was wearing, as if trying to provide room for her generous bosom. "I didn't know it was Reggie Claymore shaking down Carlos."

"Do you know Regnault?"

"Probably better than most people," she said, letting her gaze float over my head again. "Does the sheriff have Carlos's ledger sheets?" she said.

"Yes. I found them and turned them over to Hoppy this morning."

"Carlos has been different the last several months, maybe even over a year. It seemed like he was always short of money—paying bills late. So now I know what it was—who it was."

I nodded, encouraging her to keep talking.

"Carlos was a strange person," Rachael said. "He was very—cavalier, about cash. He left cash lying around everywhere—in his office back in the kitchen, in his office over on Magnolia Street, and, especially, in his condo."

"He had a checking account," I said. "He's given me checks in the past, several times."

"Oh, he had a checking account," she said. "He knew checks and credit card charges should be handled quickly. He deposited those in the bank religiously. And the bank account was all he ever looked at for liquidity. All the cash—there were times when he had two, three hundred thousand dollars lying around, and he couldn't pay bills because the checking account was empty. Hell, one time, he came to get me at the airport, and there was a bundle of cash lying on the floorboard of his car—probably fifty thousand dollars."

I shrugged and pursed my lips. I'd heard about Carlos's carelessness with cash a lot lately.

I remembered Hermosa's comment to me on the phone about her suspicion: *There's probably a huge amount of cash gone.*

"You're saying it could be hundreds of thousands of dollars in cash."

"That wouldn't surprise me a bit." Rachael tugged at her sweater again and sipped on her iced tea.

Another thought struck me. "Can you decipher the codes in the real books?"

"Probably."

"We need to call Hoppy and tell her that," I said. Then I had a thought. "Can you work with the sheriff's office to do that?"

"Anything I can do to help solve Carlos's murder, I will do."

The waitress arrived to refill our iced tea glasses. "Can I get you anything else, Colonel Maxxon?"

"We're just fine," I assured her, and she moved back to the kitchen.

"Tell me about the cigarette operation," I said.

Rachael tugged at her sweater again. "Two, three years ago, when the state raised the tax on cigarettes a buck a pack, Carlos saw the opportunity to bring in untaxed cigarettes from one of the Caribbean islands. I don't know which one. The return on investment was something like 400 percent. It got out of hand, though; the demand was way more than Carlos could supply."

"What did he do with that operation?"

"He gave the business to one of his relatives," Rachael said, seemingly in deep thought. "He got out of that business fairly quickly."

"Did he have a partner?"

"No. Carlos tried to run it by himself."

"You loaned Carlos money to start that operation?"

"Yes. I loaned him fifty thousand dollars, and he promised to pay me back sixty thousand in two years. When the note came due last December, he asked for another six months and promised to add extra interest. I agreed, and we talked about June 30. I need the money now."

"Why do you need the money now?" I asked, even though I sensed it was a stupid question before I finished it.

Rachael hesitated. "I want to check into a detox camp down near Ford Junction."

"So Carlos missed the June deadline."

"Yeah. He just kept putting me off. I want to get my life back, Kurt."

I bobbed my head. "I'll help you all I can to do that," I said.

Rachael's eyes softened, her gratefulness evident. "Thank you," she whispered. "I don't have a lot of friends in this town. It's kind of lonely."

"What did you know about the gambling at the Trattoria?"

"Not a lot to know about that. It was just a bunch of good ole boys who got together to play penny-ante poker. I think the cops knew about it and decided it wasn't worth their time."

"Was Carlos involved directly with that?"

"Not directly. Carlos stayed away from it. He did set up a cash bar and snacks that he made money from. Confidentially, Carlos did run a numbers game and an off-track betting thing out of another office over on Wabash Street. He gave the numbers game to a nephew as a wedding gift, and he gave the betting operation to another nephew as a graduation present."

"Is that the same person who was taking off-track bets on the auto races at the Trattoria?" I asked.

"I didn't know there was any betting on the auto races."

I paused to organize my thoughts, preparing for the sensitive subject. "Did you know about the prostitution associated with the Trattoria?"

Rachael brought her eyes to focus on mine for the first time. "I was Carlos's madam for many years."

"You what?" I'm sure the confusion in my mind showed on my face.

Rachael smiled and said, "You were always so naive, Kurt." She nodded her head slowly. "Hell, I've been a prostitute most of my adult life," Rachael said. "Before Tammy Lynn elbowed her way in, I was Carlos's madam. I ran the operation for Carlos."

I wondered if my leaving her to go to school had caused any of this activity. *Did I make this woman a whore?* "I—I had no idea," I sputtered.

"Life happens," Rachael said, shrugging.

"And, is that Tammy McPherson who pushed you out?"

"Yes. I was ready to quit, anyway. In fact, I had already scaled back a lot. However, I had planned to have another girl take over from me. I'd trained her. She was pretty close to being ready."

"Sergeant Hoppy told me they had an informant, and I saw Tammy leaving Hoppy's office this morning—"

"She's a lying, cheating, scheming *bitch!*" Rachael's voice was back to strong.

Dick Schaeffer had told me he saw Rachael at the restaurant, and then Hoppy told me she had evidence that Rachael had fought with Carlos. *No, wait, Hoppy said she and Carlos had "argued."*

"You were here, at the Trattoria, Thursday night."

"Yes, I was," she said, looking at me again. "For a few minutes."

"Did you and Carlos fight about something?"

"I didn't see Carlos," she said, with an edge to her voice. "He wasn't here," she said. "He told me he would be here, and we could talk. I wanted him to give me twelve thousand dollars, so I could sign into the rehab center. When I got here, they told me he'd left for the night. So I went into the meeting room, there, to get a drink at the gambler's cash bar. Then I went back into the kitchen and fixed myself an omelet. I like that sausage Carlos gets from Puerto Rico. I ate a little of the omelet, decided I wasn't hungry right then, put it in a carryout box, and took it home."

I sat looking at Rachael for a long time. *Was Rachael lying to me? Or had booze destroyed her memory?*

My memories of Rachael during our time as lovers was that she was very creative at covering herself when cornered or caught, even if she had to stretch or ignore the truth. *Was she being even more creative now?*

Rachael returned to her pensive look, staring over my head. "Why are you getting involved with this?"

"If you didn't kill Carlos, you need someone broadcasting that to the world. My sense of the whole matter is that the sheriff believes they have an open-and-shut-case against you. You're telling me they don't. I need all the information I can get from you to run this mess to ground. So, tell me what you know about Carlos. How well did you know him?"

"Not romantically, if that's what you mean," Rachael said. "Carlos organized and ran the prostitution operation and was involved up to his neck in everything except the screwing and collecting the money from the johns. However, I never considered him a pimp, like the movies show. Carlos always let me handle the girls. He never used any of them, he never even asked."

I sat looking at Rachael. Maybe I should have heeded Mike's advice. "I went off on the gambling angle early," I said. "Only recently did I realize that the gambling was minor, while the prostitution was a very big component of Carlos's operation."

"The prostitution was important to Carlos," she said. "The gambling wasn't."

"The sheriff mentioned that you had skimmed money from Carlos. Was that—"

"That's Tammy Lynn lying through her teeth, pure and simple."

I sat for several moments, thinking. "Carlos always impressed me as being a successful restaurateur. Nothing more."

"That's how just about everyone saw him." Rachael coughed, and I worried that years of smoking might be catching up with her. "And, for the most part, that's what he was. But he had some skeletons in his closet."

"To sum everything up, you were at the Trattoria Thursday night but didn't see Carlos. You cooked an omelet and took it home in a take-out box. Regnault Claymore was shaking Carlos down, and there's probably a significant amount of cash missing." I paused to organize my thoughts. "Carlos has been financially strapped for several months, now," I continued, "but no one knew what caused that until now."

Rachael bobbed her head at each major point. "Carlos mentioned back taxes last year. He had businesses down in Ford Junction and in Farmers' City. I doubt that could have hurt him so badly."

"Hermosa is trying to keep the Trattoria running," I said.

"She's a good girl," Rachael said. "I hope she isn't inheriting Carlos's problems."

My cell phone jangled, and I excused myself to go outside to answer it. Sergeant Hoppy was brief, but concise. She told me Tammy's rap sheet showed several pickups for solicitation, but no convictions. The only biggie was a conviction for embezzlement, in Nashville, Tennessee, six years ago, and she had served two years of a five-to-ten prison sentence.

"Embezzlement?" I said.

*　　*　　*

Tammy McPherson

During the cab ride home from Hoppy's office, Tammy tried to decide whether Hoppy had been truthful when she said they did not have a metal lockbox in the evidence pool. She'd replayed the conversation, bit by bit, trying to analyze some of the comments Hoppy had made. She'd signed the release form to let a vendor have some of the furniture from her condo.

Suddenly, Tammy remembered she had been remiss in watching to see if anyone was following the cab. As was her usual tactic, she'd asked the cabbie to drop her off at the Speedway Hotel. If anyone was following her, he or she would park the car and try to determine where she had gone in the hotel. Tammy would go in the front door and straight through the meeting areas and out the rear door.

She walked to her room at the Capri Motel and let herself in. Once inside, she peeked out the window to see if anyone suspicious was hanging around. Satisfied, she sat down in the easy chair. *If I have to leave town fast, which direction do I go?* Shirley lived in Saint Louis. But they had stopped exchanging "loving sisters" Christmas cards ten years ago. *I know several girls in New Orleans, a couple who work the quarter.*

Amtrak was the easiest way out, but it only ran north or south out of town. *What if you don't have time to catch the train?* "West is best," she remembered her daddy saying many times, before he left her mother alone with her and her sister, never to come back.

"Oklahoma City," Tammy said out loud. "I like Oklahoma City." *Why Oklahoma City? You've never been there.*

A vehicle pulled up outside. Tammy jumped up, walked to the window, and slowly slid the drape aside. A plumber's truck had parked two spaces down from her room, and a man was at the mounted side box getting out tools. He carried them into the room in front of the truck. Tammy waited for her breathing to calm. She wrung her hands a couple of strokes and then moved back to the chair.

She clicked on the TV set for white noise. The local station was going to break and Tammy tuned out the loud commercials. But her attention was jerked back to reality, when the promo for the five o'clock news said: "The woman accused in the murder of Carlos Guerrero has been released on bail. Stay tuned for details at five."

They'd never let Rachael out of jail unless they had doubts about being able to prove she did it. Now, what the hell is going on? What went wrong?

She tried hard to recall the entire conversation with Sergeant Hoppy. Hoppy had been working on another case when she arrived, and she'd seemed a little distracted while she dug out the file folder to find the release form Tammy needed to sign. *Was the distraction a ploy to get something out of me? What did she talk about? Did she ask me any questions? What did she say?*

Tammy was sure that Hoppy knew about her past record. But she'd paid her debt to society, served without problems, and gotten out early

256

for good behavior. Carlos had discovered that she had gone back to her old ways, but he said he couldn't afford to turn her in, "and have the cops snooping around." He simply warned her that he was going to be watching her a lot closer.

She'd been stupid to take the fifty thousand the way she did, but she'd needed it by Monday morning, and there'd been no other way to get it. Eventually, Carlos had confronted her about it. "You're the only one who could have done it," he'd yelled. "Why you do me that way?"

"Oklahoma City … that's where I'm going from here," she said. *Hell, I'd never been to Carpentier Falls before I came here.*

*   *   *

Kurt Maxxon

Hermosa appeared at our table and started to bus it. The waitress realized her faux pas and moved to take the dishes from Hermosa. I thought of talking to Hermosa about the sixty thousand dollars Carlos had asked me to take care of. But I decided to wait and talk to her when Rachael wasn't with me. I had no idea how Hermosa felt about Rachael, other than that she had been friendly enough during the bail hearing and afterward. She'd invited Rachael and me to come to the Trattoria to talk. But it might be better to discuss business at a different time. However, I did want to get a better handle on the loose cash factor.

"You mentioned you think there is some cash missing," I said. "Do you have any idea as to how much?"

Hermosa looked at me and then at Rachael. "I doubt we'll ever know. But Uncle Carlos was notorious for leaving cash lying around."

Rachael nodded agreement. "Carlos was absolutely cavalier about getting loose cash into the bank. However, if you want my opinion, I'd bet it could be a couple hundred thousand dollars. And, if it were me," Rachael said slowly, "I'd be watching Tammy Lynn McPherson."

"I'll second that," Hermosa said. "She must have left town. I haven't seen her for several days."

"She's still in town," I said. "And I might just do what you suggest." Mike had warned me to stay away from Rachael. Now I wondered what he would say about Tammy McPherson.

CHAPTER NINETEEN

Thursday, September 14

Kurt Maxxon, Late Afternoon

I drove Rachael to her house and awkwardly declined her invitation to come in. It was probably best that I not get *too* involved with her, and my "to-do" list had several items fighting for not only attention, but priority. I drove straight to the hotel, grabbed two cups of coffee in the lobby, went to my room, and sat down at the desk with my writing tablet. For several minutes, I studied the sheets, scribbling notes in the margins and between lines. I added several notes to the bottom about this morning's meeting with Hoppy, the bond hearing, and my talk with Rachael. I now had seven pages of notes, and, to make sense of them, I decided to create a summary sheet. I tore off the note sheets and laid them in numerical sequence on the desk. I scanned down each sheet, marking or circling key items. From the notes and my memory, it occurred to me that I had heard the name Tammy McPherson too many times recently. I scribbled a TM next to every entry where her name occurred. After a few minutes of experimenting with formats, I wadded the sheet up, chucked it toward the wastebasket, and started a new sheet, doodling what I call a flowchart.

The second attempt went awry, and I tore that sheet off, wadded it up, and tossed it toward the wastebasket, but it missed and rolled around on the floor. My third attempt was much better, and I started to see a credible roadmap for future thinking.

Patchy clouds to the east were the only aberrations to the sunny vista. The western sky was clear, with the hue of heavy humidity. That would probably produce a red sky at sunset—which brought to mind the old adage, *Red sky in the morning, sailor's warning; red sky at night, sailor's delight.* The fact that it wasn't raining was the best part of the weather.

I was sweating heavily, and I realized the cleaning person had turned the air-conditioning off, in accordance with hotel rules. I got up and reset the thermostat to seventy-two, in strict violation of the hotel rules, not to mention the federal government's decrees, and I listened as the air-conditioning kicked on. I sat back down and returned to analyzing my newly created flowchart. After a few minutes of looking at it, I had a better sense of all the references to Tammy McPherson. I decided to start looking for her by talking to the cab driver with whom I'd seen her leave the law center this morning. The cab company was located on the east side of town in a decaying building probably destined for demolition under urban renewal. There were seven taxis parked in a row waiting to be dispatched. The Number 0027 cab was fifth in line. I parked in the cab company's lot and walked to the cab. The driver was reading a paperback novel. He didn't look up until I said, "Excuse me."

He was a typical cabbie, with a perpetual smile and bright brown eyes. "What'ya need?" he said.

"This morning, you picked up a woman—"

He swung to look at me, and I saw recognition spread over his face. "You're Kurt Maxxon, aren't you?"

"Yes, I am," I said.

He swung the car door open and stood up, extending his hand. "Pleased ta meet ya, Colonel Maxxon."

Since I didn't know his name, I looked for a name tag, but there was nothing. "I'm glad to meet you, too, uh—"

"Kirk—Kirk Holly."

"Well, I'm glad to meet you, Kirk."

"I don't root for nobody in particular, but I watch the races whenever I can," he said.

"That's good," I said. "I always like to talk to race fans."

The first cab in the line drove off. Kirk glanced at it leaving the lot and watched the next three cabs move up in line. He didn't seem to worry about it.

"This morning, you picked up a woman at the law center—"

"Yeah. The one with the nice ass."

"Uh-huh," I nodded. "Do you remember where you took her?"

"Sure do," Kirk said, smiling, "'Cause it was kinda funny; she wanted dropped at the Speedway Hotel. So, after I dropped her, I drove over to Gus's Diner, over there on the corner of K Street and Dolphin, to have a sandwich. While I'm eating, I saw her walk by, swinging that nice ass from side to side, and go into a room in the Capri Motel, catty-corner from Gus's place."

"When she went into the room, did she knock and someone let her in?"

"No. No, she had a key. She let herself in. Like she lived there."

"Could you tell which room it was?"

"Well … I'm not sure, but it was on the first floor, toward the far end of the building … maybe halfway down. But I wasn't really paying that much attention."

"Did you see her leave?"

"No. She was still in that room when I had to leave and go back to work."

I walked back to my truck and added a line to my notes that Tammy had more than likely holed up at the Capri Motel at K Street and Dolphin. I drove across town on Roosevelt to the Speedway Hotel, turned north on Speedway Road to K Street, then west on K, and spotted the Capri Motel on the corner. I parked in the No Parking zone in front of Gus's Diner to survey the motel. The office faced Dolphin, and the two-story building faced K Street. Angled parking spaces were in front of the first-floor rooms. There looked to be twelve rooms on each floor, with a stairwell in the middle and stairways at each end.

I kept checking my rearview mirror to see if anyone was watching me, or if a cop was coming along to cite me for stopping in a No Parking zone. The traffic light controlling the intersection cycled several times. Suddenly Tammy was out her door and walking down the sidewalk toward the far end of the building. Once clear of the motel structure, she angled through an adjoining parking lot and disappeared behind a brick warehouse building. I waited for the light to turn green. *I might have to run the light in order to tail her.*

When I could move, I drove west on K Street, then turned south three blocks past Speedway, and edged up to the intersection at Roosevelt. I saw Tammy walking toward me along the south side of Roosevelt, so I sat waiting. Tammy went another block, and I sat watching her until she disappear into Dino's Sports Bar. Remembering what the cabbie had told me, I thought she might be pulling another diversion, so I drove west on Roosevelt and pulled into a paid parking lot midblock, where I found a space big enough to handle my truck. I double-time walked back to Dino's.

I walked through the door, knowing I'd have to let my eyes adjust once inside. As the darkness eased, I spotted Tammy sitting in a booth facing the door. I walked to her booth and stood looking at her. Tammy didn't acknowledge me; she was looking toward the door. After a long moment, she swung toward me. By the light of the candle on the table, I saw her eyes narrow to focus on me.

"Tammy McPherson?" I said.

"Yes." She looked back toward the front door; her eyes hardened and then eased. "What can I do for you, Mr. Maxxon?"

She knew who I was. That helped. A little. "I'd like to talk to you."

"What about?"

I slid into the booth across from her, uninvited. "Carlos Guerrero, the Trattoria, and several other things."

She stiffened but recovered quickly. "I don't know a lot about any of it," she said.

Tammy is tall and well proportioned, even though maybe five pounds over her ideal weight. She wears her medium-brown hair in a pageboy cut, which gives her oval face a youthful look, even though her makeup was covering up years of age. Her piggish nose and straight red lips complemented her steel blue eyes.

A waitress arrived to ask what we wanted to drink. Tammy ordered a whiskey sour, and I ordered a cup of coffee. The waitress frowned but didn't argue about it.

Tammy glanced around the room and said, "I only have a few minutes. I have an appointment."

I waited while the waitress brought Tammy's drink and then left to go to a back room for my coffee. "What kind of work do you do?" I asked.

Tammy hesitated, as if she were deciding whether to tell me straight out. "An escort service," she replied. Her eyes kept scanning the diner. *Who was she looking for?*

"I see."

Tammy appraised me with her eyes. "What else would you like to talk about?"

The waitress returned with my cup of coffee. I waited until she was out of earshot. "I was wondering what you could tell me about Carlos Guerrero and the Trattoria's operations."

Tammy's shoulders hunched slightly, as she studied me. She shook her head. "Not much to tell. The food was excellent and the clientele approved."

"Why is your name and phone number on the management list for the Trattoria?"

"I was Carlos's marketing manager. I planned events for Carlos," Tammy said, with a secret smile, as if she were pulling one over on me.

"Your escort service operated out of the Trattoria?"

"Hell, no," she spat. "I ran my service from another location."

"Was Carlos your partner?"

"How do you mean that, Mr. Maxxon? I already told you I was doing marketing for him."

"Was Carlos running a prostitution ring?"

"Not that I know of."

I decided against beating around the bush. "Who do you escort?"

"Oh, the usual—wealthy businessmen in town for meetings, who don't want to dine alone," she said, trailing off into a long pause that I assumed meant: "and the rest is none of your business."

I pushed. "I think I understand." I put on my best manager's persona. "Do you escort these wealthy men yourself, or do you have other women doing that as well?"

Tammy hesitated and fidgeted, eyeing the door she'd entered. "Both."

"And if the men don't want to sleep alone?" I asked.

"What are you after, Mr. Maxxon?" She glared at me, daring me to transgress her genteel façade.

"I'm not interested in you or your businesses. I know for a fact that a bookie was taking bets on car races at the Trattoria, along with other gambling. That's really my main involvement, since I'm president of the SRVSCRA. However, I'm also very interested in finding out who killed Carlos and why. The question that pops into my mind is: Was prostitution or gambling—either or both—the reason why Carlos died?"

Tammy's eyes blinked several times. "The only gambling I ever knew about was just penny-ante stuff on the weekends by a bunch of good ole boys."

I nodded. "And the prostitution?"

She leaned toward me. "Look, Mr. Maxxon. I know Rachael told you all this bullshit; she's the only one who would lie like that. But it's not true. Rachael's just trying to keep from getting hung for killing Carlos." Tammy paused for breath, sipped her drink, and then continued, "Rachael has been trying to destroy me for a couple of years now. If there ever was any pure raw prostitution going on at the Trattoria, it was because Rachael was promoting it without Carlos knowing about it."

"Rachael Mellon?"

"Yes. Rachael always was pimping girls, using underage girls all the time, since they were better attractions. Rachael stole money from Carlos. Rachael stole Carlos's books, since I can't find them. Then Rachael killed Carlos to keep him from turning her in to the law." Tammy took a long breath and picked up her drink.

"You sound convinced that Rachael killed Carlos," I said.

"You bet she did," Tammy spat. "I know Rachael just stole my most popular escort, Chaundra Dunkin, and has her whoring somewhere. I hope they hang that bitch with a new rope high up on the gallows—and fast."

"Rachael's been in jail. How could she do that?"

"She's got friends all over this town. She's the one. And now someone got her bailed out." Tammy clammed up and looked furtively around the bar.

I sat studying Tammy. For a fleeting moment I thought of telling Tammy that I had bailed Rachel out, just to see how she would react. But I quickly decided that would probably bring all contact to a crashing end. She'd clammed up when she realized she had lost control. After a brief rest, she might be amenable to further talk. *Tammy is obviously lying.* Carlos wrote in his letter to me that he didn't trust her anymore. *Did Carlos hide his books from Tammy? Why?*

I wondered what else I could hope to glean from Tammy. *Had Tammy killed Carlos? Did Tammy go to the Trattoria last Thursday night, see Rachael cooking in the kitchen, and then leave with a take-out box? Did Tammy then formulate a plan to kill Carlos and make it look as if Rachael had done it? Did Tammy kill Carlos with the same skillet Rachael had used to cook her omelet, knowing Rachael's fingerprints were all over it? Could I get Tammy to say something she shouldn't?*

"Carlos had a lockbox—"

Tammy swung to view me again. Her eyes narrowed. "Yeah, and Rachael probably has that, too."

"Do you have any idea what's in that lockbox?"

"I don't know everything in it. But I kept some of my personal papers in that lockbox, and I'd like to find it, so I can get my papers back."

"I have the lockbox, but no key."

Tammy's eyes flew open. "You've got the lockbox?" She blinked.

I bobbed my head.

Tammy wet her lips with her tongue. "That's great," she said. "You can just give me the lockbox, since you don't have the key. There's nothing in it of interest to you—or anyone else, for that matter."

"I'm thinking of giving it to the sheriff. It might be helpful in solving who killed Carlos."

"Oh, I wouldn't do that," Tammy said, a little too quickly. "They already know who killed Carlos."

"Do they?" I asked.

"Sure they do. Rachael killed Carlos," she said. "But, about the lockbox, I don't know what all is in it, but I don't want the sheriff looking at my personal papers."

"What would you do with it?"

"I have a key to it," Tammy said.

Suddenly I realized that this was a whole new path—Tammy had been out searching for the lockbox. She was probably the one who had taken the key from Carlos's garage door. It must be very important to her. *But why? What made the lockbox so important to her? Carlos had specifically made sure she couldn't find it—Carlos had gone to great lengths to secrete the lockbox.*

"How did you find the key?"

"Carlos gave it to me. Since we were partners, we shared everything."

"I think I'll give the lockbox to the sheriff, and then you can make arrangements to get your papers from them."

"Like I just told you, I don't want no *damn* sheriff reading my personal papers."

I leaned back against the booth, forcing my expression to remain neutral.

Tammy leaned toward me. "Why don't you meet me in my room in a few minutes, and I'll make it worth your while to just leave the lockbox with me."

"The lockbox is in my hotel room."

"Where are you staying?"

"At the Speedway Hotel," I said.

"That's just down the street from my motel. I'm in the Sleepy Hollow. So it won't take long to go get it and meet me."

Sirens and alarms went off in my head. I'd just seen her leave her room at the Capri Motel. What was this about the Sleepy Hollow?

Tammy scribbled her cell phone number on a napkin and slid it to me. "Here, call me when you're ready to come meet me."

I picked up the napkin and looked at the number. "I'll think about it," I said as I slid out of the booth and walked toward the door.

*   *   *

Tammy McPherson

Tammy discreetly followed Kurt and watched him climb into his truck, which was parked in a paid lot, and drive east on Roosevelt. Tammy walked east on Roosevelt, keeping Kurt's truck in view until he turned into the Speedway Hotel. Tammy walked to the Sleepy Hollow Motel and went into the office.

"Hi, Tabby," the matronly woman at the counter greeted her. "Need a room?"

"Yeah."

"How long?"

"Let me have it for all night."

"All night will be fifty bucks," the woman said.

"If I rent it four hours, that'd be forty bucks, right?"

The woman smiled and nodded. "Yep."

Tammy took the key and slipped it into her fanny pack. She hoped a paying customer wouldn't want her for the evening. She couldn't turn off her cell phone, in case Kurt Maxxon called. She left the Sleepy Hollow and walked north toward the Capri Motel.

Knowing the location of the lockbox made her feel better. She was ready to give this racecar jockey anything he wanted to get the box. She'd always wondered why Carlos made such a big deal over having Kurt Maxxon as a regular patron of his restaurant. She'd seen the scrapbook that Carlos kept for the Trattoria, and she knew there was a major section in it about Kurt Maxxon's racing career at the racetrack across the street. *Who is this Kurt Maxxon, anyway? Just how horny is Kurt Maxxon?*

* * *

Kurt Maxxon

I knew Tammy had followed me and knew what my truck looked like, so I made a loop and parked on the street one block west of Dolphin, then nearly ran to Roosevelt Boulevard. When I arrived, I could see Tammy entering the Sleepy Hollow Motel office. "This woman is playing a real game," I said to myself. I watched as Tammy left the Sleepy Hollow and walked north on Dolphin to the Capri Motel. On a hunch, I stayed put even after she had arrived at the Capri. Sure enough, in a few minutes, she came *back* to the Sleepy Hollow and entered a room on the second floor, toward the back. I walked back to my truck, drove to the Speedway Hotel, and went to my room. *You've put Tammy on ice for a while.*

In my room, I jotted notes about the encounter with Tammy, noting all the lies she had told me. *She's definitely a key player—but did she kill Carlos?* The motive might be in the ledger sheets.

As I scanned my notes, the name Chaundra Dunkin attracted my attention, and I tried to remember all the times I'd heard that name. Tammy had just mentioned her name again, but in a way that made me wonder why Tammy was so interested in her. I shuffled the note sheets and found the one:

LeRoy Kitchens said someone told him they'd seen Chaundra leave with another woman.

I couldn't remember what else LeRoy had said. *Did he say they left in a car? Or did they leave in a taxi? Was that woman Rachael? Did Rachael tell me the truth, the whole truth? Was that what Tammy was talking about when she said, Rachael "stole" Chaundra? But why?*

I was to meet Rachael for supper at the Trattoria in a little while. I'd just ask all the questions that were bothering me—no beating around the bush—and cut to the chase. Tammy had lied to me about just about everything we talked about: that some of her personal papers were in the lockbox—and everything involving Rachael. Rachael deserved a chance to respond.

My cell phone jangled. I put it on speakerphone.

"This is VI Rosh," the voice said.

"How you doing, VI?"

"Just fine, but not as good as you, from what I just saw."

VI Rosh is Vladmir Igoryok Roschov, a local talk-show host and investigative reporting stringer for several newspapers. When I first met him, he was an up-and-coming DJ at the most popular country-and-western radio station, who had dreams of being top dog in the radio market. He'd started doing interviews on his morning segment, and that had turned into a very popular all-talk segment each morning. I had done several PR tours, and the first radio talk-show host to interview me, on his Saturday Morning Talk, had been VI Rosh.

Since it was race weekend, I was a natural for his show. I've been on his show four times now. VI follows racing and roots for Oscar Danielson in the number 51 Chevy Lumina.

"Oh, yeah," I said. "I lost the race Sunday, so I'm not doing all that good."

"So you let the kid win Sunday. That didn't surprise me at all. What did surprise me is that you're into prostitutes. God, I would think a guy like you could score anytime, anywhere you wanted to. That lady friend of yours is a mighty good-looking woman."

"Exactly what are we talking about, VI?"

"I just saw you meet Tabby Christianson at Dino's. Is she there with you now?"

"No."

"You going to meet her later?"

"Noooo."

"You playing detective again?" VI asked.

"Yes."

"Aha. What are you up to, then?"

"I'm not sure," I said, being honest about it.

"Not sure, or not talking?"

"Believe me when I say 'not sure.'"

"Can I help you any?"

"Not at this point. How do you know, uh, Tabby?" I asked.

"I've ridden along with the bunko squad several times when they tailed prostitutes," VI said. "Tabby has been involved a few times."

"Are you on a project now?"

"Yeah, sort of," VI said slowly. "I'm working on a piece about predatory lending—you know, payday loans, legalized loan sharks, those things. I don't have anyone sponsoring it yet, but the *Centralia Post Courier* is thinking about it."

"Not on prostitution?"

"No. I finished that piece a couple of months back. It was in the *Post Courier*. Didn't you read it?"

"I missed it. I've never paid much attention to prostitution."

"Yeah, well, like I said, while I was researching for the prostitution piece, I saw Tabatha Christianson frequently."

"Did you dig up her connection to the Trattoria?"

"Yeah. As Tammy McPherson, she really didn't have much to do with the food there."

"What's her real name?" I asked. "Do you know?"

"I have no idea, and I doubt the cops do, either. I don't think she's ever been arrested. She's just always somewhere around the edges, usually ready to bail her girls out PDQ."

"Okay," I said. "I appreciate you tailing me, but—"

"Oh, I wasn't tailing you, or her. I use the phone just inside the door of Dino's all the time. That way anyone with caller ID doesn't know it's me calling. I was on the phone when she arrived, and then you came in and went to sit down with her. She was watching me. I don't think she knows who I am, but she senses I'm trouble. I guess I just jumped to conclusions. Sorry about that, old horse. But don't let her get her hooks in you. Take care of what you got."

The line went dead before I could say, "I will."

Even with the interruption, my mind went back to wondering who Chaundra Dunkin was and what part she played in this whole matter. I should have asked VI if he knew anything about her.

Major question: *How do I find her?*

CHAPTER TWENTY

Thursday, September 14

Kurt Maxxon, Evening

Ernesto Vasquez was back on station when I arrived at the Trattoria. He greeted me, led me to a corner table, and laid out two menus.

"Do you know a young girl named Chaundra Dunkin—or she might have gone by 'Candy'?" I asked Ernesto.

He looked around the room, and, satisfied no one was within earshot, leaned down and said, "She ... as Candy, came in frequently ... to meet men."

"Any idea where she lives? Where I can find her?"

"She was living in one of Carlos's plush condos," he said and then looked around again. "Her mother was here last Thursday night, talking to Carlos about her. I heard them arguing in the kitchen."

"Arguing?" I let that filter into my brain. "Did you see Carlos after that?"

Ernesto's eyes took on a blank look. "I think so." He glanced around the room, and his eyebrows knitted together. "Hmmm ... now that I think about it ... I'm not sure."

"What time was that?" I asked.

"Oh, let me see. The cooking and wait staff left about eleven thirty. I went to the office and did some work for half an hour or so. Then I went to the bar in the meeting room and got a Scotch and water, took it to the table over there, and made out an order for silverware and napkins we need in the dining room. That's when I heard them in the kitchen. Probably half past midnight."

"They were arguing?" I prodded.

"Well, she was yelling at Carlos about Chaundra being too young and needing to finish school. But Carlos was his normal cool and controlled self. I got the idea he didn't know what she was talking about."

"And you're not sure you saw Carlos after that?"

Ernesto paused, pursed his lips, and said. "I just don't remember."

"What did you say the woman's name was? Did you see her leave?"

"Her name is Michaelson, and I did not see her leave."

The name Michaelson bounced around in my head. "Is she married to Gordon Michaelson?"

"Yes, that's his name."

I knew how to find Gordon Michaelson, since I had his business card in my wallet. I was sure it had his office address and phone number, as well as his home address and phone number. "How does Rachael's visit fit into all this, time wise? We know she cooked an omelet and left with most of it in a take-out box."

Ernesto shrugged his head. "Rachael was here shortly after the kitchen staff left, probably eleven thirty or quarter to twelve. She actually had been in the meeting room having a couple of drinks for some time. Then she went into the kitchen and fixed the omelet. I was working in the office at the back of the kitchen and heard her cooking."

"Did Rachael do that often?"

"Well, she was a friend of Carlos's, and she did pretty much whatever she pleased. I think she was waiting to talk to Carlos, but he didn't come back while she was here."

273

"Did you see Rachael leave?" I asked.

"No," Ernesto said, "but I really wasn't paying close attention. I mean, I was busy wrapping up the day."

"I understand," I said.

"Damn," Ernesto said, screwing up his face in deep thought, "I might have messed up. Now that I think about it, Carlos and Rachael weren't the ones arguing like I told the sheriff. It was Candy's mom who was yelling at Carlos." He looked around, having reached the limit of his fear of getting caught spreading gossip. "I'd better call that sergeant and tell her about this," he said, and he walked smartly toward his station at the front door.

I watched Ernesto make a phone call and then seat four different couples before Rachael came in. Ernesto led her to my table and held her chair while she sat down. He looked at me. "Mrs. Mellon can tell you about Fran Michaelson, I believe."

Rachael watched Ernesto walk away. "What was that all about?"

"Do you know Fran Michaelson?"

"Yes. She was Fran Dunkin until she married Gordon Michaelson a couple of years ago. She's the office manager at the law firm where Hermosa's husband, Tim Anderson, is a partner."

"Do you know Chaundra Dunkin?"

"I did when she was a little girl. Since she's grown up, I haven't had any contact."

"Apparently, she was working in the prostitution ring that Carlos ran through Tammy."

Rachael seemed to shiver at that, and she recoiled. "Chaundra's not old enough to be doing that. She's only ..." Rachael stopped and ran years through her mind. "Well, maybe. If she's sixteen, she's just barely sixteen."

"Chaundra's turned up missing," I said. "Did you see Chaundra at the Trattoria last Thursday night, or Friday morning?"

Rachael swung her head to face me. "I probably wouldn't know Chaundra if I saw her. The last time I saw her she was maybe nine or ten years old."

"Do you own a car?"

"No. They jerked my driver's license after my DUI, so I started taking cabs. I sold my car a year ago."

"Apparently, Chaundra was here at the Trattoria just after midnight, to meet up with a man who had called for her. But she was seen leaving with a woman in a car before she and LeRoy hooked up. I don't know if there's a connection to Carlos's death. But it's interesting."

"That was LeRoy Kitchens?" Rachael asked.

"Yes. Do you know him?"

"Yes. He's just a normal guy who got a raw deal from his wife," Rachael said. "I doubt Chaundra could kill Carlos, even if she were here," Rachael said, shaking her head and pursing her lips.

"I have no idea," I said. "But, she's probably connected somehow." I paused as our waitress arrived to ask what we wanted to drink. I ordered iced tea and Rachael followed suit. "If there is a large amount of loose cash missing, would it have been easy to disappear with?"

"Carlos left it in his condo, his office, and his car. He had a safe in the office, but he only locked it when he was going out of town, or sometimes on the weekend, so the answer is yes."

"Who would have access to those places?"

"Tammy Lynn," Rachael shot back without thought. "She had a small office adjoining Carlos's office. Carlos could lock it so she couldn't get into his space. But, knowing Tammy as well as I do, I'd say she probably had a key made or simply figured out how to pick the lock."

I'd heard Tammy's name so much lately, she had moved up on my radar screen as someone who might have had a pretty good reason to kill Carlos. And I now knew for sure she had blatantly lied to me earlier. "I need to make a phone call," I told Rachael and excused myself to go out outside. Once I was sure I could talk privately, I dug out my cell phone and dialed Hoppy's number. She answered on the third ring, so she was still at her office.

Unfortunately, once Hoppy was on the other end, my mind went into hibernation. I should have planned this call beforehand, but I charged forward. "I have some real problems with Tammy McPherson," I said.

"Like what?" Hoppy said.

I went through the litany of things I'd thought of. I told her about the various references I'd picked up about Tammy. I told her about VI Rosh's call, even though I didn't identify him outright. I told her about the large amount of loose cash that was thought to be missing, which she told me she already knew about, and that Tammy was the only one who had easy access to Carlos's office.

"If she's the killer, why did she do it at the Trattoria?" Hoppy quizzed.

"Probably convenience. That was where Carlos was at the time."

"What was Tammy doing there?"

"Watching out for her girls? I don't know."

"I'll have to talk to Damon," Hoppy said. "Let me call him and see what he thinks about Tammy McPherson as the killer. I don't know if Damon has even talked to her yet."

"She's living at the Capri Motel on K Street and Dolphin Avenue," I said.

"She is? That's interesting," Hoppy said. "You know what room?"

"It's the third room west of the stairway on the ground floor. Probably one-oh-nine or so."

"Okay, good," Hoppy said, and I could hear her rustling paper. "Let me talk to Damon and see what he thinks. You're on your cell phone, right?"

"Yes."

"Later."

"What's Hoppy going to do?" Rachael asked after I returned to the table.

"How'd you know I called Hoppy?" I asked.

"You are so transparent, Kurt—you always have been. If you've ever made mistakes, they've been in the name of justice or mercy or humility. You haven't changed a bit from when we were kids in high school."

Damn. "She's going to talk to her lead investigator about it. See what he thinks."

"They probably won't do anything," Rachael said. "And Tammy will waltz out of town, never to be seen again—with all of Carlos's cash."

"I'd just about bet I know where Tammy is right now," I said, ruminating over my earlier meeting with her.

"Where?" Rachael asked.

"In a motel, waiting to seduce me."

Rachael's face took on a quizzical look.

"I already talked to Tammy once today. I wanted to see what information I could get from her."

Rachael relaxed into a satisfied smile.

*   *   *

Tammy McPherson

Tammy sat at the cheap chrome dining table watching the TV set, oblivious to what was on. She glanced occasionally at her cell phone lying on the table. She'd placed all the girls before she'd left for Dino's for supper. So the next call had to be from Kurt Maxxon.

The lockbox had to be where Carlos had kept the ledger sheets. The more she thought about it, the more convinced she became of it. *Bring me that lockbox, Kurt Maxxon. Let me open it and act surprised.* "Well, gee-whiz, none of my personal papers are in here after all," she practiced in a singsong voice.

"What are those?"

Oh, those are just the ledger sheets that Carlos and I used to keep our books.

Getting out of town will have to wait, now. Rachael had been released from jail, probably because they had someone else in mind. *If they're onto me, I might have to move fast. But I've got to get those ledger sheets.*

Even a high-school accounting major could tell from the ledgers that Carlos had very carefully recorded the cash coming in, even though he'd been lax about getting it to the bank. It wouldn't take an accountant long to see that there had to be a lot of cash missing. The cash she now had in the suitcase.

Her plans were to pack her bags, take a taxi to the airport, rent a car, and drive west to Oklahoma City. *Do I have time to go get the car now?*

She glanced at the alarm clock on the nightstand. Eight-fifteen. *Where the hell are you, Kurt Maxxon? Why aren't you here, letting me lull you into submission?*

The increase in volume on the TV brought her back to awareness, and she got up to pour another glass of Diet Pepsi, added some ice cubes from the container, and waited for the fizz to die down. She took a long sip. For an instant, she worried again about having the cash in the suitcase in her room. *Better than having it in that locker at the train station.*

When she'd gone to get the briefcase from the locker, she'd encountered the same security guard who'd approached her about the parked car. He watched her closer than she would have liked, which convinced her it would not be smart to go back to the train station. The guard could identify her—and identify her as carrying a briefcase. He didn't know it contained over $450,000 in cash, but he could connect her to the briefcase. After transferring the cash to the new suitcase, she'd thrown the empty briefcase in a dumpster several blocks away.

Tammy took a sip of her drink. *Where are you, Kurt Maxxon? What are you waiting for?*

"Oh, well, I've got this room until six tomorrow morning," she told herself. *Surely, he'll show up before then. I know where he's staying. I could go there and flush him out.*

"No," she murmured. "It's best if he comes to me."

Is there any way to get information about Oklahoma City beforehand?

Maybe AAA.

*   *   *

Kurt Maxxon

Rachael sipped her iced tea. I hoped she could stay on iced tea—and off the booze. We were waiting for the waitress to come to take our orders, when my cell phone jangled. From the caller ID, I saw it was Christina.

"Where are you?" Christina asked.

"I'm at the Trattoria, getting ready to order supper," I said.

"You with someone?"

"I'm with Rachael Mellon. We bonded her out of jail this afternoon, and I wanted to talk to her."

"Okay, I just dropped my friend off at her house. Our flight back got in early, so we got to Carpentier Falls earlier than expected. I'll drive over and be there in about ten minutes—unless you don't want me to join you."

"Come on over," I said.

"That was my good friend, Christina Zouhn," I said to Rachael. "We'd planned to meet for supper tonight, but she had a change of plans. Now she's on her way. You don't mind, I hope?"

Rachael wobbled her head. "Why should I mind? I would expect you to have a lady friend."

Rachael and I chatted about her life, at least the portions of it she wanted to share. I didn't notice Christina coming, until she was standing next to me. I stood up to hug her, as I usually do, and she stood on her tiptoes and kissed me. *Well. This is something new.* I gave Christina an approving look and smiled.

Christina held my hand as she moved to the chair next to me. I moved to hold the chair for her as she sat down and scooted under the table.

"Christina Zouhn, this is Rachael Mellon," I said, as my supercritical brain flashed through the proprieties of introductions. Deciding it was okay, I went on, "Rachael and I graduated high school together," I said to Christina, knowing she already knew of my relationship with Rachael. "Christina was my late wife, Vicki's, dearest friend," I said to Rachael. Both seemed to accept my efforts, and they spoke to each other in glowing friendliness.

I'd never talked much about Rachael, with Vicki or Christina, because there had never been a need to. My confession to Sergeant Hoppy on Monday, with Christina listening, worried me a little. *I hope Christina doesn't think I've been sneaking around while she's away.*

But why? Christina is just a good friend—a very close and dear friend. It's the first time she has ever kissed me, though.

"How was your trip?" I asked.

"Those seminars are always very enlightening," Christina said. "There are always new things to learn about animal shelters, preventing animal cruelty, and how to deal with the numerous pets abandoned each year. They presented some very interesting material."

"You work at an animal shelter?" Rachael asked.

"No. I volunteer with the Humane Society. The animal shelter is one part of it," Christina said.

"That's nice," Rachael said.

"Whenever they need to place a puppy," I said, grinning widely, "they just call me to help out, and I fall in love with the puppy and adopt it."

"We took in thirty-seven new puppies last week," Christina said. "I'll let them know Beau is interested, and the Maxxon family has room for more." She almost giggled.

Rachael gave me a puzzled look. "Beau?"

"He's my three-year-old puppy," I said.

The waitress arrived and asked what Christina would like to drink. Christina glanced around the table, surveyed the two iced-tea glasses, and said, "Iced tea, please."

I almost let out a sigh of relief. Christina at times likes a glass of white wine. Maybe she sensed this was a nonalcoholic group.

We ordered our dinners and ate in near silence.

I had finished my dinner and was thinking about dessert, when my cell phone jangled. It was Damon Hertz.

"I just want to confirm what Hoppy said you told her. It might be interesting."

"I'd say so," I said and proceeded to tell him the same thing I'd told Hoppy.

"It probably warrants looking into. I'll start the paperwork right away," Damon said.

CHAPTER TWENTY-ONE

Friday, September 15

Kurt Maxxon, Early Morning

I poured my first cup of coffee, walked to the desk, and sat down. I slid the writing tablet in front of me and scanned the loose note sheets and the flowchart. It was five-fifteen, and I figured it would probably be another hour before Christina called to tell me she was ready to go to breakfast downstairs at the buffet. As I scanned my notes, all the entries associated with Tammy McPherson stood out. So far, however, none of the evidence I'd gathered clearly showed that Tammy McPherson had been at the Trattoria last Thursday night or early Friday morning. But, if she was intent on killing Carlos, would she have let anyone *know* she was there? Had Tammy arrived at the Trattoria, seen Rachael cooking an omelet in the kitchen, and formulated a plan to kill Carlos and make it look like Rachael had done it? Had Tammy already stolen the loose cash lying around? What had Carlos written in his letter to me? Tammy was 'up to no good.'" Had Carlos learned that Tammy had stolen all his loose cash and confronted her about it?

I wondered what Hoppy and the sheriff's department intended to do about Tammy McPherson—if they were going to do anything.

* * *

Tammy McPherson

The banging on the door woke her up. She sat up on her elbows, listening, to determine if it was real. She'd stayed at the Sleepy Hollow Motel until midnight, waiting for Kurt Maxxon to come with the lockbox. Then she'd walked to her room here and had trouble getting to sleep, wondering why Maxxon hadn't showed up.

Maybe this was him. But how would he know where she really was staying? She swung out of bed, moved to the door, and looked through the peephole. Her eyes flew open. *A dozen cops stood looking at her door.*

"Yes?" Her voice quivered.

"Sheriff's Department," a voice said. "Open the door."

Tammy hesitated, trying to decide if she should dress first. The door locks clicked. Only the security chain remained. The door opened, a gloved hand took control of it, and, in a practiced move, undid the chain. "I'm naked," Tammy screamed as she backed away. She hadn't made it to the bathroom, when the door swung open and two female deputies came through the door.

"Get dressed," one of them ordered.

The other had papers in her hand.

They moved to prevent Tammy from shutting the bathroom door.

"You are Tammy Lynn McPherson, also known by various other names listed here on the warrant?" one asked.

Tammy nodded her head.

"Please say 'yes' or 'no', Ms. McPherson—this conversation is being recorded. Thank you."

"Y—yes," Tammy said. She walked to the chair and shrugged on panties and a bra. She moved to the closet, struggled into a pair of jeans, and then put on a button-up shirt.

"Ms. McPherson," the second deputy said, "this is a Warrant to Arrest, issued by the Circuit Court of Pierre County, to take you into custody as a person of interest in the homicide investigation of Carlos Guerrero. This second document is a Warrant of Search and Seizure to impound any and all pertinent and/or relevant evidence found at this location. From this point on, you have a right to remain silent. If you say anything at all, it may and will be used against you in the future. You have the right to have a lawyer present in any and all discussions and questioning from now on. Do you understand what we just told you?"

Tammy's eyes fluttered toward the suitcases in the closet. *Dammit. I should have left last night. That damn Maxxon set me up.*

The rest of the incident was a blur. Tammy sat in the patrol car, watching the deputies' move in and out of the room. She saw the suitcase full of cash carried to another car and put into the backseat. Her eyes moistened, and she was glad she didn't have mascara on. *Dammit. Dammit all to hell.*

*   *   *

Kurt Maxxon and Christina Zouhn

Christina called, and I met her at the entrance to the restaurant. We both chose the buffet and worked our way along it. I filled my plate to overflowing and turned to see Christina sitting down at a table. When I arrived at the table, I noted that Christina's plate had a lot of empty space around the fruit and bowl of oatmeal she was eating.

"We need to go get Beau," Christina said, as she moved her empty plate to the side for the waitress. She took a sip of her coffee and continued, "If you want, you can call Buster, and I'll go up and get him."

"I'd like us to go get him together," I said.

"I'll be going home this evening or early tomorrow morning," Christina announced. "I *have* to be in Albertstown Sunday morning."

I nodded acceptance.

"What do you have planned for today?" Christina asked.

"I want to track down a young girl," I said. "Her name is Chaundra Dunkin. Several people have mentioned her to me. She was a prostitute in Carlos's ring. She was at the Trattoria about the same time that Carlos was killed. I want to know if she saw anything or anyone out of the ordinary that night. Plus, I doubt she has been interviewed by the sheriffs. I think I know how to find her."

Christina pursed her lips and lifted her left eyebrow. "You figure she'll talk to you?"

"I don't see why not," I said. "I'm not a threat to her."

Christina shrugged. "It's worth a try, Maxxon."

Christina wanted to do some work in her room, and I wanted to pore over my notes one more time. We jokingly synchronized our watches and agreed to be ready for action at nine o'clock. We agreed it was a decent hour to call a residence that I didn't know. I fished Gordon Michaelson's business card out of my wallet and laid it on the desk next to the phone.

At five minutes to nine, Christina called to tell me she was ready. I told her to come to my room and we'd call Chaundra Dunkin using the room's speakerphone. That way, if Chaundra had any reservations about the call, Christina would be there to assuage any fears.

Chaundra answered the phone on the fourth ring. I told her who I was and that I'd like to talk to her about last Thursday night or early Friday morning at the Trattoria.

"I don't remember too much," Chaundra said. "Except that my mother showed up, and then we came home to talk."

"What time was that?" I asked.

"Oh, probably ... about one o'clock. That's about when the poker games end."

"Can we meet and chat about it?"

"I'm just about to leave for an orientation meeting at the community college," Chaundra said. "I'll be out of there about eleven. We can meet at the coffee shop on the corner there across from the campus."

"Do you know its name?"

"No. But it's the only coffee shop for miles around. It's on the corner of Harrison and the street into the school, just west of the bridge over the Swift River."

I had a pretty good idea of where she was talking about. "Okay, we'll meet you there just after eleven o'clock."

"How will I know you?" she asked.

"I'll be driving a big white Ford four-door pickup, with KurtMaxxonRacing.com in red letters across the bottom of the doors."

Christina leaned forward and spoke into the phone, "Chaundra, my name is Christina Zouhn, and I'll be with Kurt, so you won't be meeting with him alone."

"Oh, hi. Are you the Mrs. Zouhn with the Albertstown Schools?"

"Yes," Christina seemed to perk up.

"I met you the year before last, at the cheerleaders' state finals competition in Centralia. You talked to us about keeping our grades up. I remember that talk, and I really thought you were great giving it."

"Well, thank you," Christina glowed in the praise.

"That's good," I said. "I'm glad you already know one of us."

After we hung up, Christina said, "We should take my car when we're running around here. I get almost twenty-five miles to the gallon. That would be cheaper than pouring gas through that gas-guzzling truck of yours."

Christina had never attacked my truck before. Was this a new openness I'd have to tolerate? I gazed at her for a long minute. "We told Chaundra we'd be in a big white pickup," I said gruffly. "Too late to change that now."

"Okay, Maxxon, I'll give you this one. But, next time, let's think about it."

* * *

Christina and I drove to the community college and spotted the coffee shop—the River Inn—on the corner of Harrison Street and Buchanan Avenue. Across the street was the community college, occupying nearly one hundred acres along the west bank of the Swift

River. The campus included modern glass and steel buildings along with a few older brick-frame buildings that had originally made up the sole high school in Carpentier Falls. Now the school district has grown large enough to fill four high schools, the latest one a half mile southeast of the racetrack.

Behind the River Inn was ample parking, including several spaces big enough to accommodate my truck. Christina and I decided to get out and sit on a bus-stop bench to wait for Chaundra. We were more than fifteen minutes early, and the fresh air was inviting.

We watched for the bus, because we didn't want to make the driver stop for us. We quietly watched the pedestrian traffic flowing across the street both ways. At one point, I suddenly remembered that we were not in my big white truck. "Do you know Chaundra Dunkin?" I asked Christina.

"No. There were three hundred and forty girls at that program when I spoke."

"Hopefully, she'll let us know it's her," I said.

"You're just mad because, for once, someone knows me and not you," Christina said, and I could hear the laughter in her voice.

"What are you talking about?" I said. "There are hundreds of people in Albertstown who know you but don't know me from Adam. Remember how surprised I was you knew Terry Grossman?"

"That's true," Christina said and broke into a giggle.

Our levity almost made us miss the girl waving to us, before she crossed the street at the crosswalk. Chaundra walked toward us, but, before she could reach us, a young man in tattered jeans and shirt, and unruly hair, rushed up to Chaundra and gripped her elbow in a steering hold. The boy started to force Chaundra toward the rear parking lot, but Chaundra stopped against his force, ducked down to concentrate her muscles, and then spun out of the boy's grip. The boy was knocked off balance, but he recovered and moved to grab Chaundra again.

Chaundra yelled, "Quigley, leave me alone."

"You have to go with me," the boy said. He moved toward Chaundra again, caught hold of her shirt just below her breasts, and started tugging her toward the back parking lot. Chaundra fought him off again. "Quigley, damn you, leave me alone. You and I are history. Get away from me."

I decided that Chaundra could probably take care of herself, especially since the boy looked to be about as coordinated as a slinky spring on a stairway. He would probably be more of a nuisance than anything else. However, Chaundra didn't seem to want the boy's attention, and I *did* want to talk to her. So I walked over to intercede and make my presence known. I said, "Quigley, Chaundra doesn't want you bothering her."

Quigley tried to focus on me, but his eyes weren't tracking in sync. "Who the hell are you?" he sputtered.

"I'm a friend of Chaundra's," I said. "I came here to meet and talk to her."

"Bullshit," Quigley spat. "She's going with me. We have some things we have to do, now."

"Forget it, Quigley," Chaundra said. She took on a defensive posture. "As I told you the other day, you and I are done. It's over."

"You fucking him, too?" Quigley said, pointing his chin toward me.

"Even though that's none of your business, Quigley," Chaundra scolded, "the answer is no. Now good-bye."

Christina invited herself to the party, as she took up a stance in front of Quigley that blocked his access to Chaundra, while I faced down Quigley.

After a few brief moments, Quigley straightened up to full height and said, "She's going with me." Then he turned back toward Chaundra. When he realized Christina was blocking him, he yelled, "She owes me, goddammit. She owes me."

I wondered if the boy was going to start crying. But then he made a quick move to go around Christina, and I blocked his path to Chaundra. I said, "Son, why don't you just leave her alone. Go on home, now."

That Quigley stuffed his hand into his pocket didn't bother me—but when his hand came out of his pocket with an eight-inch switchblade knife, I moved so I was between Quigley and both the women. Christina had Chaundra by the arm and was moving her away from Quigley. In a wild gesture, Quigley flashed the blade out of the knife and took up a posture he'd obviously seen on TV. I stood still for a moment, studying Quigley. His eyes were still not tracking in sync. He was on something—drugs or alcohol, I didn't know which—but I hoped he couldn't hurt any of us. A small crowd was forming to watch the action.

When Quigley lunged at me, the crowd gasped, and I moved to avoid the attack. I grabbed his wrist, and in a move drilled into me—faster than he could say "ex-marine, huh?"—I twisted his arm and threw Quigley over my shoulder. He did a somersault in the air and landed flat on his back, which knocked the wind out of him and sent the knife skidding off toward Christina and Chaundra.

I was breathing hard, probably more from adrenalin rush than exertion, but I walked and stood over Quigley, who was gasping for air. I checked to make sure he hadn't swallowed his tongue, and then I grabbed his pants at the waistline and lifted his midsection up to help the diaphragm get back in rhythm.

"I'm calling the police," Chaundra said, pulling her cell phone out of her backpack.

I thought about dissuading her, but then someone in the crowd said, "They're on their way."

I decided the police were a good idea, especially if Quigley had been bothering her a long time. I looked back down at Quigley. His eyes looked stranger than I'd seen before. They were like vacant orbs floating in white oil. His breathing was back to near normal. A couple of days in detox would probably help him.

Quigley regained some of his senses and looked at me. "What the fuck you doing, man? Why'd you do that to me?"

"Because I don't want you bothering Chaundra again. Do you understand she doesn't want anything to do with you?"

Quigley sat up. He looked in the direction of Chaundra. "She didn't say that. You made her say that. She doesn't feel that way. "

A police squad car skidded to a stop at the curb. Two officers got out, carrying batons, and walked toward us. The crowd had gotten larger. I figured every one of them would give a different version of what had just happened. Chaundra talked to one of the officers, while the other talked to Quigley. I knew Quigley didn't stand a chance of leaving the scene except in handcuffs. For a minute I felt sorry for him. He was so young and had so much to look forward to. Hopefully he would learn his lesson. A person can't make a good life living on booze or drugs or anything else not natural to a body.

It really didn't take too long before the cops cuffed Quigley, loaded him into a drunk wagon, and left. At one point, I turned to ask Chaundra if she was okay and saw that Christina was already taking care of her, guiding her into the coffee shop. I followed them into the River Inn—and then out the side door to the outdoor dining area under a giant canopy.

So much for my involvement. I smiled, glad Christina was doing this interview.

As the adrenalin evaporated from my bloodstream, I realized I was parched.

*   *   *

Christina and Chaundra took to each other like long-lost cousins. They talked about the speech Christina had given to the cheerleaders and how impressed Chaundra had been with Christina's ideas and delivery. They talked about other things. Then Chaundra told us about getting back into school; she was just starting her GED classes. She told us of her plans to get an accounting degree. Christina is always naturally encouraging when she talks to young people, which comes from her years as administrator in the Albertstown Consolidated School District.

As Chaundra became more comfortable with Christina, she told us some of the problems that had led to her dropping out of school and going into prostitution. The main factor seemed to be her mother divorcing her father. "Daddy worked hard to make a living; he worked six nights a week, from 8:00 PM until 4:30 AM, as a pressman at the Carpentier Falls newspaper. Mother started going to a lot of civic group meetings in the evenings. That's where she met Gordon Michaelson."

When she mentioned Gordon Michaelson, she didn't seem to have a great affection for the man. She referred to him as "Mother's husband," or "my stepfather" in very cold ways. I was sure Christina observed this as well.

When Chaundra got on the subject of believing she was the reason for her parents' divorce, Christina moved quickly to dispel it. She made soothing comments designed to help Chaundra understand she was not the cause, had nothing whatsoever to do with the cause, and should put those thoughts out of her mind. "Your parents had other problems that they obviously hid from you," Christina counseled, "but it was those problems that brought on their divorce. You were not the cause."

"Yeah," Chaundra agreed, bobbing her head, "I've grown up a lot this last year. I understand love and marriage much better after talking to men about their lives with women of all stripes."

Then Chaundra wandered into her teenage problems, which Christina assured her were normal to coming-of-age persons. There was the peer pressure and social pressure to succeed and get good grades; the hoping to get scholarships for college; plus, she had been dating Quigley, the boy Kurt had just decked, and he wanted sex morning, noon, and night. With all the problems, Chaundra related how she had gotten behind in her classes and struggled to catch up, but saw her grades going steadily down. At one point, in total frustration—and with no help or support from her mother, who was gaga over her new lover—she decided to take the easy way out. After the principal said she was going to talk to her mother about her falling grades, she had panicked. She had dropped out of school and met Tammy McPherson, who had offered her an opportunity to make big money the easy way.

"You were at the Trattoria last Friday morning, early," I said, glancing toward Christina.

Christina took the cue. "When you arrived at the Trattoria, did you see anything or anyone out of the ordinary?"

"Not really," Chaundra said. "I arrived by cab, who dropped me at the edge of the building. The john who called for me was playing poker, so I usually sat and waited for him in the vestibule. He's called for me the last three or four Thursday nights, so we've kind of gotten to know each other."

"The same man asked for you every Thursday night?" Christina asked.

"Oh, sure. Some guys find a girl they like, and they ask for her over and over."

Christina nodded to keep Chaundra talking.

"Mom was there. She came up and asked if we could talk. She was different than before. She wasn't ordering me around. She was talking to me like an adult. So I thought about it. Being a whore just didn't do that much for me. The money was great. But the work … well, it's not exactly the best job in the world." Chaundra looked at Christina for understanding, and found it.

"You'd already convinced yourself it wasn't what you wanted to do the rest of your life," Christina murmured.

"Right. Mom and I went home and talked until two in the morning, drinking wine. She asked if I was happy doing what I was doing. I told her no woman could be happy being a whore. She told me that if I came home she and Gordon would help me get through college."

"Was that the first time your mother offered to help you?" Christina asked.

Chaundra hesitated for a beat. "Yeah, it really was. And it made me really think about what Mom was saying. The more we talked, the more I was glad Mom had come to the Trattoria to get me. I hated Tammy McPherson—like most of the girls. Tammy always was belittling you,

you know, about everything. Some of the girls felt Tammy was jealous of their good looks, attractive bodies, and everything else that Tammy didn't have anymore."

Christina paused for a short time, formulating a question about something we both suspected. "Chaundra," she asked, "how old were you when Tammy recruited you?"

Chaundra sat quietly for a few moments and then shrugged her shoulders and said, "I was actually fifteen. I'd dropped out of school, but I wasn't sixteen yet. That's why I went so far underground, you know, in case the school people came looking for me. I didn't want them finding me. I'm still not sure how my mother found me."

"You said your mother was at the Trattoria about one o'clock Friday morning?" I said.

"Yeah, she was there," Chaundra confirmed. "She said she talked to Carlos about me."

"Your mother talked to Carlos about you?" I said.

"Yeah, in fact Mom told me she and Carlos had an argument about me."

I knew about the argument, from Ernesto. Now something nagged at me. I sat back in deep thought, wondering what all this meant. Ernesto had heard the argument between Fran and Carlos. But Ernesto had originally thought it had been Rachael arguing with Carlos. He'd thought he'd seen Carlos after that argument, which might well be the reason he hadn't deemed it to be important and hadn't conveyed that information to the sheriff. But now Ernesto was not sure he had seen Carlos after the argument. Had that argument culminated in Carlos's death?

Christina recognized my mental deliberations and engaged Chaundra in innocuous talk, while I wrangled my way through the questions bouncing around in my mind. "Chaundra, has the sheriff's office talked to you or your mother about Friday morning?"

"They haven't talked to me," Chaundra said. "I'm pretty sure they've never talked to Mom about it, either."

So that meant the sheriff's investigators had never been given this information.

"I'd like to talk to your mother," I said. "Kind of off-the-record. Maybe she saw something or someone that might be out of the ordinary."

"I don't think Mom had been to the Trattoria before last Friday morning. So I don't know if she would know whether anything was different or not."

"In most murder cases, its people noting little, not-suspicious things, or people seeing things that don't fit the ordinary. I'd just like to see if she saw or heard anything that might bear on the case."

"I'll call Mom and see where she's going for lunch, although she just about always goes across the street to Klatch's. If she does, we can meet her there."

Chaundra speed-dialed a number and sat looking off into space while she waited. Then she greeted her mother. They exchanged small talk, and then Chaundra asked where her mother was going for lunch. "Across the street to Klatch's Café," Chaundra repeated. "I'm talking to Kurt Maxxon right now," she said, "and he wants to talk to you."

"About what?" her mother apparently asked.

"About last Friday morning at the Trattoria," Chaundra told her. "I'll come along with them to meet you at Klatch's," Chaundra said.

They exchanged other chitchat, and Chaundra disconnected.

"She'll talk to us?" I asked.

"She says she doesn't remember a lot about what happened last Friday morning at the Trattoria, other than going home and talking with me, but she'll discuss it with you. She says she already knows who you are, Mr. Maxxon, but she said I could come along anyhow." Chaundra beamed a wide grin.

CHAPTER TWENTY-TWO

Friday, September 15

<u>*Kurt Maxxon and Christina Zouhn, Lunchtime*</u>

I parked my truck in a paid lot a block and a half away. The rain had let up to sprinkles, so Christina stayed dry under her tiny, purse-sized umbrella. She'd offered to protect me, but since she couldn't hold the umbrella high enough to keep me from walking hunched over, I demurred, saying, "A little rain never hurt me." We walked to Klatch's Café and saw Chaundra getting out of her silver and black Mustang a few spaces down from the front door. She waited for us under the awning across the front of the building.

Inside, some businessmen occupied a few tables, while most were occupied by couples. I didn't know what Fran Michaelson looked like, but she would have been watching the front door for Chaundra, so, if she were here, she would make herself known. When no one jumped up and waved, I followed the women to a large table away from the main crowd.

A waitress materialized and took our orders. I wanted plain-Jane, regular coffee, which is extremely difficult to order today among the multitude of coffees, lattes, and cappuccinos—not to mention a dozen flavored creams and six different sweeteners. Christina and Chaundra chose flavored lattes. The waitress had just delivered our coffees when a woman walked through the door, and Chaundra stood to wave. The woman came directly to our table.

She was an attractive lady, of medium height, with a healthy looking body, auburn hair, and fierce brown eyes that sparkled in the fluorescent lighting. A forced smile had created deep wrinkles on either side of her mouth. She wore more lipstick than needed, but it seemed to blend in to her overall appearance.

Chaundra stood, hugged her mother and said, "I can't stay, Mom. I just wanted to make sure you people got together." Chaundra was nearly a perfect copy of Fran, just two inches taller. They had the same oval face framed by auburn hair, although I could tell that Fran's hair underwent a monthly rinse, whereas Chaundra's was lighter and more natural. Fran wore her hair in a short, easy-to-manage cut, whereas Chaundra's was long and flowing over her shoulders. They had the same nose and chin shapes, although Fran's mouth appeared larger, which I realized was due to the lipstick versus Chaundra's bare lips.

"So, you all have fun, and I'll be at home," Chaundra said as she walked to the door.

We introduced ourselves in freestyle fashion and sat down.

"Not very often a famous race driver wants to talk to me," Fran said with a smile. The waitress arrived, and Fran ordered pastrami on rye, potato chips, and a latte of some kind.

"Unfortunately, it's about a fairly serious subject," I said, glancing at Christina to make sure she had all her antennae up. I worried about having used Chaundra as a decoy.

"How serious?" Fran asked.

"We talked to Chaundra," I said, nodding my chin toward the door Chaundra had exited, "and she told us you were at the Trattoria last Thursday night … actually, very early Friday morning. She told us she arrived there about one o'clock, and you met her in the parking lot." I looked at Christina to see if I was doing it right and got an approving nod. "Why were you at the Trattoria?"

Fran paused, looked around the room, and then shrugged and pursed her lips. "I was at a party last Thursday evening, and someone told me that Chaundra was whoring around and that she usually went to the Trattoria to meet with her tricks, or johns, or whatever they call them. So I went to the Trattoria from the party to check it out."

"Did you see Carlos Guerrero?" I asked.

"Yes, I did," Fran said.

"Did you know Carlos?"

"I'd met him a couple of times, and I *thought* he was a reasonable man. I never would have guessed he was running a prostitution ring—"

"We're pretty sure Tammy McPherson operated the prostitution business from another location, not at the Trattoria," I said. "Carlos was probably involved, but not front line. You talked to Carlos," I prompted.

"I *tried* to talk to him," Fran said, "but he kept ignoring me, telling me he didn't have anything to do with prostitution, and he didn't know who my daughter was. But I didn't believe him. He wasn't convincing enough. He wouldn't look at me. He kept fussing with stuff in the dining room, and then he went into the kitchen." The waitress delivered Fran's latte.

"I followed him into the kitchen, and the first thing he noticed was that someone had left a bag of trash on the counter. Carlos went ballistic, cursing the kitchen staff for leaving it. I tried to talk about Chaundra again, but all he could talk about was that damn bag of garbage—like my daughter's life was less important than that bag of garbage. He grabbed it and went out the back door. I followed him. On the way, I picked up a skillet from the stove. I was so mad. He walked toward the dumpster back in the corner of the lot. I tried to talk to him, but there was so much noise coming out of the meeting room: a lot of people talking, and a radio was playing, too, I think. He didn't hear me. I was so mad at him. He stopped several feet from the dumpster and tossed the bag from there. I walked up behind him. I whacked him a good one. He went down to his hands and knees, and he started cursing at me." Fran paused for a breath.

I frowned. "Carlos was cursing at you?"

"Well, he said something like, 'Goddamn, lady, why you do that?' and I yelled, 'I want my daughter back!'" Fran sipped on her latte. "And Carlos just kept cursing me, 'Goddamn, lady, you see her here?' he said to me; 'Goddamn lady, you crazy woman.' I walked back around front to my car."

"And … Carlos was still talking to you?"

"Yelling and cursing is more like it," she said.

"And you got in your car and left?"

"No. I'd just opened my car door, when a taxi pulled up, and Chaundra got out. She was walking toward the restaurant. I ran over to her and caught her by the arm. That startled her, but when she realized it was me, she calmed down pretty fast. I asked her how she'd been. She told me she was okay, but I could tell from her voice, she was—what? Scared?—no that's not it; she seemed confused." Fran fought down the emotion.

Christina reached out to take Fran's hand and bond with her as only Christina knew how to do.

"I asked Chaundra to talk to me. Right then. We could go to an all-night coffeehouse or come home. She said, 'I've got an appointment in a few minutes.' And I said, 'Just talk to me, baby—let's go somewhere and talk about it.' She looked toward the restaurant and then said, 'To hell with it,' and she walked to my car and got in. When I asked her where she wanted to go, she said, *'Home.'* I was happier than I've been in months."

I knew the skillet was the murder weapon. The question was, had Fran Michaelson delivered the fatal blow, or had someone else come along afterward and done the deed? Had Tammy McPherson observed the confrontation between Fran and Carlos and then finished Carlos off? I glanced at Christina and realized she was staring at me, probably wondering what I was thinking about. I came back to the present. "Fran," I said, "Carlos was killed by a blow to the base of the skull, by the skillet they found near the body. When you hit him, what part of the skillet hit him, the flat bottom or the edge?"

Fran's eyes widened. "You surely don't think—" and the light went on in her eyes. "Oh, my God," she said, swinging her head from side to side. "I don't know what part of the skillet hit him. But he was talking to me, yelling at me, cursing me, as I walked around front."

"What time was this; what time did you hit him?"

I noticed Fran's hand tremble as she reached for Christina's. "Probably a little after one o'clock, maybe later; I don't know for sure."

I excused myself and walked outside to stand under the awning. The rain had stopped but was still dripping off the edge. I dug my cell phone out of my pocket and dialed Hoppy's number. When she answered, I asked if she had the medical examiner's file handy. She said, "It's somewhere here on my desk." When she confirmed she had it, I asked her to read me the part about Carlos living after the blow. I couldn't remember what it said, but something was bothering me. I heard Hoppy shuffling papers.

"Here's what it says," Hoppy said. "'Victim lived at least several minutes, perhaps as long as two hours after the blow was delivered.'"

"Could Carlos have talked after the blow?" I asked.

"There's nothing in here to tell either way," she said. "I can call the ME. I just talked to her about another case, so she's on her cell phone. Why? What are you up to, Maxxon?"

"Could you do that and call me with the answer?"

"You have to tell me why it's important," she persisted.

"I'm working through one of my hunches," I said. "That's all I can tell you."

"You can't or *won't* tell me all," Hoppy said and then sighed. "Oh, well. I'll get back to you."

I hadn't made it back to the table before my phone jangled, and, since I had it in my hand, I looked to see who was calling. It was Hoppy. I stopped and walked back out onto the porch.

Hoppy told me the ME had said it was quite possible Carlos could have talked normally for several minutes, but his ambulatory functions would have deteriorated quite rapidly as swelling in and around the brainstem disrupted its functioning.

I let the information filter into my thinking apparatus. *Carlos could talk but not walk.* Then another question popped into my mind. "Hoppy," I said. "How come Rachael's fingerprints weren't on the handle of the skillet?"

"Rachael told us she always used a potholder with those cast-iron skillets."

"Did the cops find the potholder?" I asked, and I heard Hoppy leafing through more paper.

"It doesn't look like we were able to find one," Hoppy finally said.

I thanked Hoppy for her help and fended off another round of "why?" I walked back to the table.

Christina and Fran both stared at me as I returned and sat down. I realized that both women were fidgeting apprehensively. I took a sip from my coffee cup and said, "Fran, was there a potholder on the skillet you hit Carlos with?"

Fran let her gaze wander above my head. She sat for several beats. A frown formed on her forehead. Small worry lines appeared between her eyes. "Yes … yes, there was," she said. She sat thinking. "I'm pretty sure I had it in my hand when I opened my car door."

"What did you do with it?" I asked.

"Chaundra arrived at that same time. So I probably threw it in the backseat of my car. I ran over to catch Chaundra. I wanted to talk to her."

I sat for several minutes, mulling over what Fran had just told me. Then I decided there was no reason to beat around the bush. I glanced at Christina, who sensed I was about to deliver the coup de grace. I looked at Fran and said, "I'm sorry to have to tell you this, but you probably delivered the fatal blow to Carlos."

Fran gasped and jerked back against the chair. Christina stood, walked to Fran's side, and embraced her. Fran's eyes were huge and unblinking. Tears began flowing down her cheeks, as the enormity of what she might have done sunk in.

I sat in silence for a long time. My thoughts were with Fran, who was facing a terrible ordeal. I reasoned that Christina's thoughts were running along the same lines as mine, and I knew Christina would be the one to comfort Fran.

I watched Fran's hands tremble, as she reached for her latte. She took a long swig. Then she dug a cell phone out of her purse, opened it, punched speed-dial buttons, and hit Send. "Maggie, I need to speak with Eldon, please," she said softly. "Yes, immediately. It's urgent." She waited. Then, with her voice trembling, "Eldon, I'm across the street at Klatch's. Could you come down and talk to me? Yes, yes, it is very important." She closed the phone.

Christina continued to comfort Fran. A few minutes later, Eldon Williamson came through the door, looked around, and made his way through the crowd to our table. He was a tall, athletic person with silver-gray hair and dark blue eyes. He was wearing a dark blue pinstriped three-piece suit with a red and blue striped tie.

I stood to shake his hand. "Colonel," he said, "I missed the race last Sunday. Had to go over to Nashville on business."

I introduced Christina to Eldon and sat back down. Christina continued standing next to Fran.

Eldon stood looking at Fran, and a worried frown spread across his forehead. "What do you need, Fran?"

"I … I probably killed Carlos Guerrero," Fran said in a weak voice. Her head went down, as if her neck could no longer support it. She buried her face in her hands and wept.

"What?" Eldon gasped, and the air seemed to rush out of the room.

I looked at Christina, who was giving as much succor as she could. Fran's violent heaving slowly subsided to an occasional sob. Christina strengthened her embrace. No one said a word. We waited for Fran to lead the discussion.

"I fought with him …" Fran said, her voice gaining some strength. "I hit him—I hit him with a skillet."

Eldon sat down and studied Fran's face. "You were at the Trattoria last Thursday night?"

Fran bobbed her head. "I hit him with that damn skillet."

"Don't say anything else right now, Fran," Eldon said to her. He looked at me, and I knew what he was thinking.

"Just because she hit him doesn't mean she was the one who delivered the fatal blow," I said. "Someone else could have come along after and finished the job."

"I like your reasoning, Colonel Maxxon," Eldon said. "Can I ask you to keep this to yourself until you absolutely have to divulge it?"

"You got it," I said as I stood and reached my hand to shake his. I gave Fran a supporting pat on the shoulder and led Christina to the door. I probably should have called Hoppy, but I was sure that Fran, with Eldon at her side, would turn herself in, very quickly, potholder in hand. And I had given Eldon my word that I wouldn't grandstand this terrible situation.

*   *   *

I called Buster, told him I needed to pick up Beau, and was heading his way even as we spoke.

"I doubt he's missed you," Buster said, and I knew he was smiling. "Hell, he's been having so much fun he might not even want to go home with you."

"Well, we'll have to try to entertain him like you guys do."

"You can't," Buster said. "He's been running with Aphrodite and Hercules, as they chase the girls all over the place on their horses. You got room for a couple of horses on your place there in Albertstown?"

"You got me there," I said. "I'll just have to try to keep Beau happy."

"Come on up, partner," Buster said. "I'll be up there when you get there."

Suddenly, the grumbling in my stomach reminded me that we hadn't had anything to eat since breakfast. We'd met Chaundra a little too early for sandwiches, and then our meeting with Fran had not lent itself to ordering sandwiches. I knew Christina would never countenance us stopping to eat on the way to get Beau, so I tried to ignore the grumbling and wait until after we'd picked up Beau. I would scout a place to eat on the way up to Buster's, and we could stop there on the way back to town.

As we drove along the river toward Buster's place, the clouds thinned, and the sun made off-and-on appearances. By the time we arrived, the sky was almost cloudless, and the sun was bright and hot. As Christina and I climbed down out of my truck, Beau and the two border collies came running toward us, Beau hardly able to keep up, with his shorter legs. Beau welcomed us with his normal wagging tail—which shook his whole body—and wanted to be picked up to give us welcome kisses. But, after the greeting, he wanted down and went back to cavorting with Aphrodite and Hercules. He probably thought we should move in with Buster and family, so he could continue to play.

Roxanne came out of the kitchen to greet us. I introduced Christina to her and watched them bond.

"Buster is on his way," Roxanne said. "He'll be here in a few minutes. He had to stop at the cleaners to pick up a couple of suits he left there six month ago. They called this morning and told him they were going to donate them to charity if he didn't come pick them up."

"That sounds like Buster," I said and ignored Christina's grimace.

"Are you hungry?" Roxanne asked, and I worried my face might betray my true feelings. I shrugged. Christina gave me a "be-a-good-boy" look.

"Buster's coming home for lunch, so I heated some baked ham for sandwiches," Roxanne said. "And there's potato salad, macaroni salad, and fresh tomatoes."

It was probably the "fresh tomatoes" that forced my capitulation. "Maybe a bite or two," I said.

"Buster would be unhappy if you didn't stop for a chat over lunch," Roxanne said.

Buster had a lot of good qualities—and the fact that he also liked to eat was one of the best.

"Let's go in, so I can watch the ham," Roxanne said, and she led us toward the kitchen door. We hadn't reached it when Buster's pickup truck came around the bend in the driveway, roaring toward the farmstead. The women went inside, while I walked toward the driveway to greet Buster. Beau and the border collies came running, and the collies greeted Buster, while Beau hung back. But when he was invited, he moved to let Buster scratch his ears. That done, Beau came wandering over to me. I picked him up and scratched his ears.

Buster watched Beau and me, then chuckled, and said, "I'll be damned—he was telling me he didn't care if you ever came to get him. Oh, well. I still got those two ruffians," he said. We shook hands and walked to the house. When we walked into the kitchen, the smell of food—a lot of home-cooked food—overwhelmed my senses. The table was covered with bowls and plates, and the ham was still in the oven. Besides the gigantic bowls of potato salad and macaroni salad, there were bowls of homemade dill pickles and pickled beets, fresh green onions from the garden, tomatoes from the garden, and fresh lettuce from the garden. I stopped counting.

Buster went down the hall; he returned as Roxanne took the ham out of the oven and set it on the stove to carve. He sat down at his place and looked at my plate. "You not eating?" he asked.

"We were waiting for you," I said.

"Is that what Emily Post says to do?" Buster said.

"You know it is, Buster," Roxanne intervened. "So shut your face and show these guests how to eat heartily."

Buster smiled. "Okay, my love. Now, Colonel Maxxon, this is what you do. You take your fork in your right hand—you are right-handed, aren't you?"

"*Buster,*" Roxanne said.

"Help yourself," Buster said, and he waved to all the food on the table.

Christina was smiling a strange smile I'd never seen before. But she and I filled our plates. I made a Dagwood-sized sandwich with ham, cheese, lettuce, tomatoes, and sliced pickles. As I ate, I remembered that we had agreed to meet Rachael at the Trattoria for supper. It was two o'clock now. Maybe we could hold off eating until eight or so.

"How's the Guerrero murder case coming?" Buster asked after he had filled his plate and made a sandwich to rival mine.

"It's solved," I said.

"It is?" Buster said with a frown. "How come I haven't heard about it on the nightly news?"

"It just happened this morning," I said. "In fact, it's probably wrapping up about right now." I envisioned Fran Michaelson, flanked by Eldon Williamson, turning herself in to Sergeant Hoppy. I wondered what Tammy McPherson was doing at the moment.

"Who murdered him?" Buster asked.

"Well, I don't think it was a murder. It'll probably be more like involuntary manslaughter. I hope the news people do it right; you should be hearing the details on the news. The woman who probably did it is Fran Michaelson."

"Gordon Michaelson's wife?" Roxanne asked.

"Yes. Do you know her?"

"Not well. We've met. Since she married Gordon," Roxanne said.

"I don't think I know who she is," Buster said.

"She's the office manager at that law firm downtown where Michelle's friend's brother is a paralegal."

"Oh, her," Buster said. He looked at me. "Okay. Did you track her down?"

"I helped," I said.

CHAPTER TWENTY-THREE

Friday, September 15

<u>*Kurt Maxxon and Christina Zouhn, Evening*</u>

For the drive back to Carpentier Falls, Beau curled up on the backseat and ignored Christina and me. I wondered whether running around Buster's place had completely exhausted him or extracting him from all that fun had made him mad. He didn't seem overly affectionate, as we carried him up to Christina's room.

Once inside her room, Beau jumped up on the bed and curled up in the middle of it. He seemed indifferent to what was happening, so Christina and I decided to let him work it out on his own.

We left him and went about our business; I wanted to check in with Edwin Jamison, the manager of my auto parts store. Surprisingly, Edwin hadn't called me all week, and I was getting a little worried that he might be running things too efficiently. Christina said she had some phone calls to make. "What time should we go to dinner?" I asked.

Christina wrinkled her face. "I probably won't be hungry until tomorrow morning," she said, and she shrugged. "We'll have to do something, however, since we promised Rachael and Hermosa we'd be there tonight."

I bobbed my head. While I would probably be able to eat again tonight, it would be a few hours before I really wanted to. "It's four o'clock," I said. "How about you call me about six thirty and we go from there?"

"Sounds like a plan," Christina said.

I left and walked to my room.

I brewed a pot of decaf coffee, filled a cup, and sat down at the desk. My writing tablet and pile of notes were lying there. I picked them up and went through them again. Fran Michaelson's name did not appear anywhere in them. However, Chaundra Dunkin was the key ingredient there.

My cell phone jangled; I dug it out and answered on speakerphone. It was Hermosa.

"Sergeant Hoppy just called me and said I could come in and get the copies of the ledger sheets and Uncle Carlos's scrapbook. They only want to keep the last batch of sheets you found in the scrapbook, and the ones which include the apparent embezzlement."

"That's good," I said.

"Hoppy said that since you'd solved the case, they didn't need that stuff anymore."

"She told you *I'd solved* the case?"

"Yes. Apparently Fran Michaelson has been charged with manslaughter three and will be out on bail later this evening."

"That's good," I said again.

"I agree with you. If what Hoppy told me is true, she probably didn't mean to kill Uncle Carlos. That doesn't bring him back, but at least it wasn't a malicious act. You understand, don't you?"

"Yes, I do. Fran will suffer enough. I don't think the law could inflict any worse retribution than what she'll do to herself."

"You're probably right. I'm glad you got Rachael out of jail."

"What's going to happen now with Rachael's case?" I asked.

"Hoppy already is working on that. I'll work with her and the court to get Rachael cleared. And, hell, get you off the hook, too, huh? You guaranteed her bail."

"I need to call Mike Collins and tell him what's going on."

"He probably already knows," Hermosa said. "News travels pretty fast in the bail-bond sector."

"Can we get the scrapbook back yet today?" I asked. "I'll go get it, so I can leave town tomorrow morning."

"Already done," Hermosa said. "I asked Ernesto to send his son to the law center to pick the stuff up. You can get the scrapbook this evening when you come for dinner."

After I hung up from talking to Hermosa, I dug out Mike Collins' business card from my wallet and dialed his number. He came on the phone and said, "You're good, Maxxon."

I suppressed a chuckle. "What happens now with Rachael and her bond and everything?"

"We'll try to get it all done tonight. First, the court will have to dismiss the charges against her, but with Hoppy pushing it, any Pierre County circuit judge can sign the papers. It shouldn't take more than an hour or so. If we can't get it down this afternoon, then it'll have to be Monday morning. Since she's out on bail anyway, they probably won't give it a high priority."

"Does Rachael have to go into court?"

"Yeah. If we get the papers signed this afternoon, what I'd like to do is have you and Rachael meet me at the clerk's office, and we can unravel the deal. I'll give you your check back."

"Give me my check back?"

"Yeah. Hell, I haven't deposited it yet. I've paid a couple hundred bucks in fees. You can pay me that, and I'll call it even. "

When I hung up from Mike, I went to get a cup of coffee. My phone jangled again, and I answered it on speakerphone. It was Rachael.

"They just called me and told me the charges against me were dropped and I should come in to sign all the paperwork. What's going on? Do you know?"

"Yes, I do."

"Mind explaining it to me?"

"I'll do that. But let me and Christina get you and bring you there. I just talked to Mike Collins, and he's ready."

Rachael agreed, and then I called Christina.

"Do you want to go with me to unravel Rachael's arrest?"

"Let me ask Beau if he wants to ride along," Christina said, and I heard her mumbling over her hand clamped on the phone. "He wants to stay here."

"You don't want to go?"

She quietly said, "Beau still seems lethargic, and I don't want to leave him here alone."

"Okay," I said. "Let me go get this matter over with. I'll call you about supper."

*   *   *

It took nearly an hour to get all the papers signed. But, eventually, Rachael was no longer a charged felon, and I was off the hook for her bail. When I told Mike that I'd write him a check for the two hundred dollars I owed him, Rachael immediately said, "I'll cover that," and dug her wallet out of her purse. She handed Mike two crisp hundred-dollar bills.

Mike pulled a receipt book from his briefcase and wrote Rachael a receipt.

After we finished, Mike scurried off to avoid getting a parking ticket. Rachael and I started to walk toward my truck, but Hoppy intercepted us and asked if she could talk to me alone. She and I went off a little ways and stood on the sidewalk along the parking lot.

"I wanted to thank you for your help on this case," Hoppy said. "We obviously went off on the wrong track and might not have got it right, although I like to think Rachael wouldn't have been convicted even if we had taken her to trial. Turning us onto Tammy McPherson makes me feel Pierre County is a little safer. At least our underage girls are safer."

"I couldn't help thinking about the case," I confessed to Hoppy. "I kept talking to people, but the dots just didn't line up to make any kind of a picture, as they normally do."

"Well, I just found out about the Irene Wallace case. Terry Grossman called me this morning to tell me he's coming over here next Wednesday to do some investigating. He was surprised you hadn't solved the case before today." She spread a wide grin. "You've got quite a reputation among law enforcement agencies."

"I always worry about Brad Langley," I said.

"Why?"

"He and I have been good buddies for thirty years. But he doesn't like me playing detective."

"For good reason, Maxxon. Remember Masonville?"

"Uh ... what's the latest on Tammy McPherson?" I asked, changing the subject and hoping Hoppy wasn't going to rat me out to Brad.

"Well, she had a suitcase with over $430,000 cash when we took her into custody. She claims it all belongs to her, from her escort service, i.e., prostitution ring. Hermosa Anderson tells me it's probably Carlos's, since he was very lax about cash. I called Andrea Christofides, and she tells me she can probably show it all was Carlos's from the ledger sheets that I kept as evidence in the McPherson case. If we can show the money was Carlos's, then we can charge her with plain old grand larceny. I talked to the DA's office. They'll work with us to have Andrea and another CPA audit the books."

"That's good," I said, realizing I'd been saying that a lot today. The bright sun made it an even better day. I motioned Hoppy to follow and walked toward Rachael.

"Rachael, the codes in Carlos's books were difficult to understand, and Hoppy might need help. You said you could probably do that, right?"

Rachael blinked at me for a few beats and said, "Yes, I probably can decipher them."

"That's going to be very helpful, Mrs. Mellon," Hoppy said. "That may help us prosecute Ms. McPherson."

I glanced at Rachael and saw a satisfied look of relief. Hoppy excused herself and walked back toward the building. I helped Rachael up into my truck. She seemed more relaxed than before, as I drove her home. She thanked me, got out of my truck, and went into her house. I drove back to the hotel and went to my room. The clock said it was six o'clock. I called Christina to let her know I was back and to see if she still wanted to leave for supper at six thirty. She did. So I called Edwin Jamison.

Edwin answered and told me there had been no problems, so he hadn't bothered me. Maurey Kennedy was at the store and wanted to talk to me.

"I checked the gearbox," Maurey said. "You might be right about not being in third gear coming out of the turn. The shift ring bearing was loose, and so, while you might have put it in third, it really was still in fourth gear."

I swung my gaze heavenward. *Thank you, Big Guy.* "I thought something was wrong," I said to Maurey.

"Yeah, well, I fixed the damn thing," Maurey said. "So you won't be able to use that excuse again."

"Okay," I said.

"How're Joshua and Jacob doing?" Maurey asked, and I suddenly knew why Maurey wanted to talk to me.

"They're doing fine," I said and chastised myself for not having called them. "I'm going to Kings Rapids Monday to see them. I think Christina said she will be able to go. Do you want to ride along?"

"Let me see if Hazel wants to go see our daughters down there," Maurey said. "That way we can take the boys out to dinner."

"That'll work," I said. We hung up after I told him that we'd solved Carlos's death and that I would be home Saturday afternoon.

I called Christina and asked if she wanted to join me in calling Kings Rapids.

"What time do the boys get home from school?" she asked.

"They stay at the day care in the law center until Marguerite goes home, I believe."

"I'll come over, and we can try," she said and hung up.

After Christina arrived, we talked about the trip to Kings Rapids on Monday.

"That's a good idea," Christina said.

I dialed the number from the room's speakerphone. Terry Grossman answered. "I was wondering what time the boys get home from school," I said.

"They're here now," Terry said. "You want to talk to them?"

"Yes," I said. "Christina and I are planning to drive down to your place next Monday. Stay a day or two. Are you and Marguerite and the boys free for dinner Monday night?"

"If we aren't right now, we will be by then," Terry said and laughed. "Something tells me you know I'm going to Carpentier Falls Wednesday."

"It's good you all will be available," I said, "and, yes, I did know you will be coming to Carpentier Falls next Wednesday."

Christina said, "Hello, Terry. How are you?"

"We're all just fine, Mrs. Zouhn. Those two boys have changed our lives so much for the good—you can't believe how much."

"Oh, I think we can come close," Christina said. I had to agree with her about that.

I talked to Jacob first, since Joshua was in the bathroom. "Have you found any good diners there in Kings Rapids?" I asked him.

"Happy Face Pizza is great," Jacob said. "They have the best pizza I've ever had."

A ringing endorsement like that doesn't come every day. "Pretty good pizza, huh?"

"So much cheese, it's piled on high, and lots of pepperoni. That's what I like."

Christina asked, "How's school going, Jacob?"

"Real good," he said. "I like science. We're studying the solar system right now. You know, the planets, like Mercury, Earth, Mars … uh, I left one out, didn't I?"

"Venus," I said and watched Christina give me a congratulatory smile.

"That's the one," Jacob said. "I can never remember all of them."

"Just remember the saying: 'My Very Elegant Mother Just Served Us New Potatoes,'" I said.

"What does that mean?" Jacob asked.

"'My Very Elegant Mother Just Served Us New Potatoes' is a way to remember the order of the planets: Mercury, Venus, Earth, Mars, Jupiter, Saturn, Uranus, Neptune and Pluto."

"I gotta write that down," Jacob said, excited. "Let me get my tablet. Here, talk to Josh, while I get a pencil."

I thought Christina was going to burst out laughing.

"Hi, Mr. Kurt," Joshua said.

Christina said, "Hello, Joshua; I'm here, too."

I asked Joshua, "How's school going?"

"I'm learning math," he said. "So I can learn to fly an airplane. The teacher says he's a pilot, too, and he'll show me how to plot flight paths on the charts."

"Amazing," I said, truly impressed with how well he and Jacob were adjusting to their new life.

"I like science, too," Joshua said, just as Jacob returned. "Jake wants to talk to you."

Jacob came back on the line and said, "Give me that saying thing again."

I went through the way to remember planets again. I heard Jacob say, "What?" and then they were on speakerphone. Terry said "You there, Maxxon?"

"Yes. Sure am."

"I put it on speakerphone, so they both can talk to you."

"Good," I said. "Okay, guys, Christina and I are coming down there next Monday. We'll be there when you get home from school. You want to go out for supper?"

"Yeah," they said in unison.

"Is there a place here like that Mr. Carlos's place over there?" Joshua asked. "I really liked those things we had over there. What were they called?"

"Pappas rellenas."

"Yeah, them."

"There's a Cuban restaurant there, but I don't think it's as good as the Trattoria. How about Happy Face Pizza?" I asked.

"That's only good for birthday parties," Joshua lamented. "It's good for that, but not so good for a big supper."

"You guys both got birthdays coming up the end of next week," I said.

"We do?" they said in unison.

"If I remember right, Joshua, your birthday is Saturday and Jacob's is Thursday," I said. Christina gave me an "atta-boy" smile.

"How old am I?" Jacob asked.

"You're going to be ten, and Joshua is going to be twelve."

"You stole our thunder, Maxxon," Terry said. "Marguerite and I were planning a surprise party for them at the Happy Face."

"You can do that next weekend. How about we go to the Mule Sale Barn Restaurant Monday night?" I asked.

I heard one of the boys ask, "Where's that?" and Terry said, "That place on the way to Happy Face Pizza I showed you, where Mrs. Marguerite buys all the old furniture we got."

"We've been by it, but not in it," Joshua offered.

"That okay with you, Terry?" I said.

"As good as any around here," Terry said.

Christina bobbed her head, and I remembered her trips with Vicki to the Mule Sale Barn antique complex in their quest for Raggedy Ann and Andy dolls. *You just scored some points on that decision, Maxxon.* We ended the call to Kings Rapids and sat quietly at the desk.

After several minutes, Christina cradled her chin in her hand and looked at me. "Why are you and I sleeping in separate rooms?" she said casually. "Living in separate houses?"

I really hadn't thought about it.

After a quick fly through all the possible answers, I decided there probably wasn't a good one. I shrugged my shoulders.

*   *   *

We took Christina's Lincoln, and I drove to Rachael's house. The western sky promised a bright red sunset, forecasting a rainless night. Rachael was waiting for us; she came out as soon as I pulled into the driveway. I got out and opened the rear car door for her. Beau had ridden on Christina's lap from the hotel, but now he wanted to be introduced to Rachael, so he hopped by way of the console between the seats into the backseat. He welcomed Rachael, and then he hopped back into the front and onto Christina's lap.

We arrived at the Trattoria and were ushered to a large corner table in the larger of the meeting rooms, which was set up for dining. I thought about Friday nights past, when the tables would be dining tables until the witching hour of eleven, when they would magically became poker tables. I knew Hermosa had put a stop to the gambling.

Ernesto laid menus in front of us and told us that our server would be Juanita; then he went back to seat the next group of waiting people. Juanita materialized and asked what we would like to drink. We all ordered iced tea again. Rachael seemed to be riding the wagon pretty well. Rachael and Christina chatted about her ordeal, and I sat silently mulling how I was going to catch up on all the work I'd let slide while I stayed in Carpentier Falls this last week. I wished I'd brought my writing tablet, so I could start a new "to-do" list.

Hermosa came to our table and sat down. "Would four hundred thousand dollars be too much for Uncle Carlos to have left lying around?" she asked Rachael.

"No. What might've happened," Rachael said, and then paused to think about her words, "in my experience with Carlos, is he might have gotten worried about something—he'd seen a strange face hanging around, or something—and he might have told Tammy to keep the

315

funds she normally would've turned over to him in her desk at the office—plus, if she vacuumed up the loose cash lying around, four fifty is about right, I'd say."

Hermosa looked at me, a stunned expression on her face. "I never would have guessed that much," she said. "When they arrested Tammy this morning, she had $430,000 cash in a suitcase?"

I nodded. "Sergeant Hoppy told me about it this afternoon."

Hermosa rested her chin on her right hand. "Hoppy thinks it's all Carlos's, but she said it might take some time to prove it."

I said, "I don't think it'll be much of a problem. She's going to have Andrea Christofides and another CPA go over the books. Rachael, here, will be helping them decipher the accounts system; they'll find out who did what to whom."

Hermosa looked at Rachael. "I'm going to give you the sixty thousand owed to you, to pay off the note Uncle Carlos gave you."

Rachael nodded. "Thank you."

"There's some money in an account at the Carpentier Bank," I said. "I have no idea how much. Maybe you two can go get it and then figure out what to do with it."

"I'll go with you," Hermosa said to Rachael, "to get the money, just in case there is any question about it. But you can have all that, too."

"Thank you," Rachael said again.

My cell phone jangled, and I answered it. Chaundra Dunkin said, "Is Mrs. Zouhn with you?"

"Yes, you want to talk to her?" I said, and then I regained my manners. "Have you eaten supper yet?"

"No. I've been so upset about Mom." Chaundra didn't sound too good.

"We're at the Trattoria Restaurant," I told her. "Come on over and eat while you talk to Christina."

"I'll be there in about twenty minutes."

"Here's Christina," I said and handed my cell phone over to her.

They chatted for a few minutes; then Christina hung up. "She's on her way."

Hermosa went back to managing the restaurant, which had filled to near capacity. So many Friday nights in the past I'd seen the place with a waiting list right up until the ten o'clock cutoff.

When Chaundra arrived, it was Hermosa who led her to our table. I introduced Rachael to Chaundra and let Christina lead Chaundra to the ladies' room for consultation. When they returned, Juanita had arrived to take our supper orders. The three women ordered small dinners. I ordered a big dinner.

"I feel—I feel responsible for Carlos's death," Chaundra said.

Christina's face eased, and she said, "You were the subject of a dispute between your mother and Carlos that led to an unfortunate and tragic end. But you in no way directly caused your mother to act the way she did. And you shouldn't beat yourself up about it."

"And remember, Chaundra," I said, hoping to augment Christina's soothing words, "your mother did not premeditate or in any way plan what happened. She acted in the heat of passion. That you were the subject of that passion does not make you responsible. Nor does it make her less of a mother. She was worried about you."

Chaundra broke down in tears, and Christina wrapped her arms around the girl and snuggled her close. "Chaundra," Christina said, "there is something you can do to lessen the pain and help you feel better. Carlos didn't recruit you, did he?"

"No. Tammy McPherson did."

"And you were underage at the time."

"By just a few months."

"A few months don't count," I said hastily—then I wished I'd let Christina handle it.

A kitchen helper summoned Hermosa, and she fled to the safety of the kitchen.

Rachael looked at Chaundra. "You should go talk to Sergeant Hoppy," she said. "Tell her all that happened, how it happened, etcetera, and if she wants further help from you, then you could help save other girls from getting tangled up in prostitution."

Chaundra's tears had subsided, and she was into the sporadic sob stage. But she had listened to Rachael's advice. "I'll go in and talk to Hoppy Monday morning," she said. "And I want to do it on my own."

Christina and Rachael nodded agreement. "If you need anything," Rachael said, "just call me."

"That goes for me, too," Christina said, "and for Kurt."

Chaundra's cell phone chirped. She answered it. "You're home. Good. Gordon got you out. Great. I'll be home in a little while."

Our food arrived before she hung up. Chaundra closed her phone and said, "That was Mom; she's out on bail, at home."

Everyone around the table was glad to hear that.

Chaundra ate pretty heartily. Then she begged off, and left.

"She'll be okay," Christina declared.

Rachael nodded, "Yes, she will. I'm gonna make sure of it. It's just the thing I need to help me stay off the booze, until I can get into that detox hospital I told you about." Christina looked at me, and I knew she would want to know the whole story.

Christina and I dropped Rachael off at her house and drove to the hotel—and into a whole new environment.

I'm sure Beau wondered what was going on. *Mom and Dad in my bed?*

CHAPTER TWENTY-FOUR

Saturday, September 16

<u>*Kurt Maxxon and Christina Zouhn, Morning*</u>

Christina and I sat up talking into the wee hours of the morning, long after Beau had sauntered over to the bed and gone to sleep.

We discussed our schedules for the next few weeks. "I'll be running at Jamesboro next weekend," I said. "That's the last scheduled race for the season, but I'll probably get an invitation to the Centralia Shootout the second week in October."

"I have one more conference to go to, up in Chicago, the first week of November. Then that's it for traveling," Christina said. "However, when I get back from that, the shelter goes into high gear for the holidays. They're usually pretty successful in placing animals during the Christmas season."

We discussed how we could merge our two households. "Your house is a little smaller," Christina said. "But you have a bigger backyard than I do, and Beau prefers the big backyard."

"I've got a double-car garage," I said. "Yours is only a single-car."

"That's true," Christina said. "I think I'd prefer keeping your house and selling mine. Besides, I like your kitchen better than mine."

We discussed what we should tell the kids. We both came up with a multitude of things. Some made sense, but most didn't. "Why not just tell them that we love each other and decided to share our lives?"

"That'll work," I said.

Our discussion even wandered to Chaundra Dunkin. "It's going to be difficult for her for a while," Christina told me. "Obviously, her mother's situation is the major hurdle, but on top of all her other problems, she is now coming out of the closet."

"Coming out of the closet?"

"Yes. She's openly admitting she's lesbian."

"If she's lesbian, how could she be a prostitute?" I asked.

"Many prostitutes are lesbians," Christina reported. "They just sell their bodies for money."

And thus I was introduced to one of the modern mysteries of the universe, dealing with human sexuality.

When I'd woken up this morning, I'd thrown the covers off me, as I normally do, only to hear a "hummph" from someone under the pile. I'd scrambled to get her free and apologized. When all was calm, Christina dressed enough to take Beau out to do his business, while I made a pot of coffee, and we sat at the table sipping coffee and planning the day. "Beau can ride with you," I conceded. Beau's ears lifted, and he wagged his tail. "We're going home, Big Guy," I said, "home to Beau's house."

"I'll have to start calling him 'Big Guy', too," Christina promised. "We don't want to traumatize him in any way."

"Good," I said.

"We'll drive to your place and unload the luggage," Christina said. "Then I'll run over to my place to check it out."

"We need to make a list of what we want to wind up with after the merger," I said, hoping I didn't sound like the CEO of merging companies. "I definitely would prefer your sofa to mine. But my recliner is in better shape than yours."

"Where are we going for breakfast?" Christina asked.

My original inclination leaned toward the hotel's breakfast buffet, but this was a special morning. "Have you ever been to Sam's Diner?"

"No," Christina said. "Where's it at?"

"On the east side of town."

"Is it good?"

"It was the boys' favorite place."

"In that case, I'd better try it, so I can say I've eaten at Sam's Diner, right? Especially around the boys."

"That's a good idea," I said and smiled so broadly my cheeks burned.

I showered, shaved, and dressed, only a little awkward at having Christina present. I was amazed when Christina showered and dressed unfazed by me sitting at the table. The coming together had been swift, seamless, and easy.

On the way to Sam's, Christina asked if Marguerite had told me more about the boys' background. I told her that Marguerite and Terry had talked to the boys and found out that their father had been extremely abusive to them and their mother. So Irene had packed the boys and a small suitcase and had a cousin drive her to an aunt's house east of Carpentier Falls. Then she and the boys had moved to Carpentier Falls, when she got the job at Arnold's Toolboxes. She'd trained the boys to use the false name, and they actually nearly forgot their real name. She'd also trained the boys to avoid strangers, so the boys hadn't talked to anyone—even after she failed to come home. Apparently, the boys had taken up with a gang of other homeless kids living around, stealing food and other things. But the police had picked up all those kids one night, while the boys were at Auntie Jean's for supper. So the boys moved to another bridge, but they had learned how to survive on their own, to a certain extent. They told Marguerite they had been tired of taking care of themselves by the time I caught them in the kitchen. They felt comfortable with me, because their mother had showed them the picture of me with their grandfather—Mickey Lawlor. That's why they'd stayed with me.

As we walked toward the door of Sam's Diner, I wondered if Sam would be here. Did the woman work seven days a week? As we pushed through the squeaking door, Sam was delivering plates to a couple in the same booth the boys and I had used.

I led Christina to a booth closer to the door. Sam watched us slide into the seats and abandoned what she was doing to walk to our booth.

"How're Joshua and Jacob doing?" Sam asked me.

"They're doing just fine," I said. "We talked to them last night."

"That's good," Sam said. "I'll be back in a little while." She walked to the kitchen and disappeared.

I realized I hadn't introduced Christina to her, and I felt bad about that. But Christina apparently didn't feel left out. The older waitress I'd seen before was working the booths. She came to our booth and asked if we'd like coffee.

"Please," Christina said.

The waitress left to get our coffee. At Sam's, the menus are always on the table, stuck into the rack that holds napkins and the variety of sweeteners. I reached for one and gave it to Christina. I took a second one and laid it open on the table. The waitress delivered our coffee mugs and went to the kitchen. She returned with a large tray of plates, which she delivered to another booth occupied by four teenagers.

"Is the food good here?" Christina asked.

"Everything I've had has been very good."

Sam came back out of the kitchen and walked to our booth. "What are you going to have?" she asked Christina.

"I'll have the Belgian waffle with a side of bacon," Christina said.

"You," Sam said, looking at me.

"Do you remember what I had the last time?"

"You want that again?"

"Yes."

Sam returned to the kitchen.

"What's the connection between Sam and the boys?" Christina asked.

"Did I tell you about Auntie Jean?"

Christina shook her head. "I don't think so."

I hadn't finished telling her about my talk with Auntie Jean when Sam arrived with plates for Christina. She went back to the kitchen and brought my plates. "You need anything else?"

"I'd like you to meet Christina Zouhn," I said, hoping Christina would accept that Sam was the elder.

"Your wife?" Sam asked.

Christina nodded acceptance. "We're going to Kings Rapids Monday to visit the boys," she said.

Then I remembered that Sam might not know the entire story. "If you've got a minute, I'd like to tell you what has happened with the boys and their mother."

Sam waved to the waitress and sat down next to Christina. The waitress arrived, and Sam said, "I'm busy for a few minutes; please handle it."

The waitress nodded and left.

I let Sam settle in and then looked at her. "The woman they found stabbed ..." I started slowly, "was Irene Wallace." I paused to let Sam digest the news.

Sam wiped her face with her left hand. She said, "Lord Almighty," and used both hands to wipe away tears streaming down her cheeks. Then she leaned down and stroked her forehead with her left hand. She looked at me and said, "Have they caught the killer?"

"Yes, they have. Since they had no ID, her murder went unsolved until we got information about the family's past. Then the cops found out the boys' father was from Marysville, and that set off another sweep. They found him in a local motel, with the murder weapon lying on the backseat of his car. He told the cops he found Irene here in Carpentier Falls and took her to Marysville, where he stabbed her to death."

"Do the boys know about this?"

"I don't really know what Marguerite and Terry have told the boys. But they are going to adopt the boys. The boys are going to be taken care of."

Sam relaxed noticeably. "That's good," she said. "Those boys deserve to have a good home."

"They'll have that with Marguerite and Terry Grossman," I said.

"The boys are happy with them?" Sam asked.

"As far as I know," I said.

"We'll know for sure next Monday," Christina said, "when we see them. Would you like me to call you after we see them?"

"Would you?" Sam said, her eyes pleading for agreement.

"Sure," Christina said. "I'll call you, or I might even drive over here to talk to you in person, have lunch one day."

"I worry about those boys," Sam said. "But you can just call me." She got up and walked to the front of the diner, searched the cash register area, and then returned to give Christina a business card. "I appreciate your keeping me up-to-date. Are you going to tell Auntie Jean about this?"

I hadn't thought about Aunt Jean. "Yes, we can stop there on our way back to the hotel," I said.

Christina excused herself and went to the rest room. My cell phone jangled. It was Kenny Arnold. He told me he had talked to the lawyers and CPAs, and all had agreed it would be appropriate to send Irene's two final checks to the boys. He asked if I had an address for them. I told him I didn't have it with me; it was at my house, and I would call him back with it later. I mentioned we were going to see them Monday. Kenny suggested that if I was still in Carpentier Falls, and I wanted to, I could run by his office and get the checks. He always worked Saturday mornings and would be there until noon. I told him I could be there in half an hour or so.

I told Christina about the call, as we walked to my truck. "We can go there first," I said. "Then we can go meet Auntie Jean."

Kenny Arnold tried again to sell me a toolbox for my truck, and I told him I was on my way to the track to load my cab-over camper onto it. He gave me an envelope with Irene's checks, and I promised to deliver it faster than the post office.

We drove to the apartment complex where Aunt Jean lived. I parked in the lot and locked the truck. Christina and I walked up the steps, and I led the way to Aunt Jean's apartment. I knocked on her door and watched Christina's face as the dead bolts and chains clinked, and the door opened. Aunt Jean stood hunched over in her walker, staring at me. "How're dem boys?" she asked.

"They're fine," I said. Aunt Jean stepped back and motioned us to come in.

"You know 'bout der mama yet?" she asked.

"Yes," I said. Christina moved, so she was beside Aunt Jean. "Irene is dead."

"Oh, Lawd," she said with a grimace. "What doz boys goin'ta do now?"

"The Grossmans are going to adopt them," I said. "Do you know who Marguerite Vinssant Grossman is?"

"I don' tink so."

"She's the chief of police in Kings Rapids."

"Mebbe I seed her on TV. Sounds familiar," Aunt Jean said. "Why de boys wid her?"

"They're friends of ours," I said. "They fell in love with the boys last weekend. They took them to Kings Rapids last Monday. The boys are back in school, and they are settling in just fine."

"Dey be good boys," Aunt Jean said. She looked at Christina. "You be 'is wife?" she said, pointing her chin toward me.

Christina gave Aunt Jean a smile I would like to have a portrait of. "Yes," she said.

"You be lucky man," Aunt Jean said, thumping close to me in her walker to make sure I knew she was serious. I smiled broadly, because I agreed with her wholeheartedly.

"You need anything?" I asked her.

"No. I still got de groc'ry you git me when you was here. An' my med'cin is still 'kay. But dey done fixed de elevator. De repairman say sumbuddy speak ta de mayor, told de mayor a good friend lib' heah. I wonda who dat man was?"

I smiled. "We've got to go," I said. Christina and I made our way to the door. Aunt Jean limped along with us. I pulled the door open, and, as we went out, Aunt Jean said, "T'ank ye fo' gittin' de elevator ta workin'."

I turned to look at her and said, "Aunt Jean, everyone in this world loves you," and I leaned down to give her a peck on the cheek. Her eyes sparkled with life in a way I had not seen before.

As I helped Christina climb into my truck, she said, "How does it feel to be ten foot tall and bulletproof?"

"Not bad," I said.

We drove back to the hotel in relative silence. Beau was the only one who made any noise; while we were stopped at a red light, he spotted a white poodle in the car next to us, and he wanted to draw her attention to him. But the light turned green before any lasting romance could bud.

We'd finished packing and had loaded the luggage into the backseat of my truck, since we were going to the same place, and we were ready to leave. My cell phone rang, and I answered it. It was Sergeant Hoppy.

"Question," Hoppy said. "Do you have any other evidence about Regnault Claymore's involvement with Carlos?"

"You mean about his blackmailing Carlos?"

"Yes. Anything beyond the letter Carlos left for you?"

"No."

"Carlos never discussed it with you?"

"No."

"Did you know about it before Carlos's letter to you?"

"No."

"Does anyone else know about this?"

"I shared the letter with Hermosa Anderson and Rachael Mellon," I said. "But, other than that, I doubt Carlos talked to anyone about it while he was alive."

"Do you know of anyone he might have talked to about it?"

"No."

"You know where this is going, don't you?" Hoppy said.

"I think I do," I said. "The sheriff isn't about to take on Congressman Claymore."

"That's it," Hoppy said. "He's a very conservative person. He doesn't want to make waves, if there aren't too many people who know about it and precious little evidence to prove it."

"In today's political world, I probably don't blame him," I said.

"The sheriff wants us to investigate, so we can say we followed up. Don't hold your breath, however, that we'll be able to find any independent verification."

"I understand," I said. Hoppy told me to say hello to Christina and hung up.

Christina and Beau followed me to the track, and they supervised as I made the two-step process of loading the camper onto my truck. "I'll follow you and Beau," I said.

Christina and Beau led me out of the track and to the highway. The drive from Carpentier Falls to Albertstown is very easy. There are only three turns. You don't have to think real hard about the trip, and following Christina meant I could think about anything I wanted to.

My mind flashed back to Sunday night's celebration party—and Alisa Sharpe. Alisa was a very brave young woman. I was sure everything would work out for her. Christina and I would have to visit her and Mutt while we were in Kings Rapids next week.

As I passed through Farmers' City, I remembered my pledge to talk to Pearce Four about getting his life in order. After I got back from Kings Rapids, I would call the youth training center and see what I had to do to see one of the people in their facility. Then I'd call Pearce Two and tell him.

Suddenly, I realized that getting home Saturday afternoon, traveling to Kings Rapids on Monday, going back home on Wednesday morning, and then traveling to Jamesboro Thursday evening meant that I was going to be logging a lot of miles in the next few days. Then I was going to drive a 150-mile race on Sunday.

Is this getting old? A voice in my head asked. *Or are you just getting too old for it?*

It was something to think about for the rest of the drive home.

THE END